The TETHERED MAGE

The Falconer extended his hand toward the girl, to keep her attention.

"By law, you belonged to Raverra the moment you were born with the mage mark. I don't know how you managed to hide for so long, but it's over now. Come with me."

The balefire roared at him in a blue-white wave.

"Plague take you!" The girl raised her fist in defiance. "If Raverra wants my fire, she can have it. Let the city burn!"

The TETHERED MAGE

Book 1 of the
Swords and Fire trilogy

MELISSA CARUSO

www.orbitbooks.net

ORBIT

First published in Great Britain in 2017 by Orbit

1 3 5 7 9 10 8 6 4 2

A CIP catalogue record for this book
is available from the British Library.

ISBN 978-0-356-51061-3

Typeset in Bembo
Printed and bound in Great Britain by Clays Ltd, St Ives plc

Papers used by Orbit are from well-managed forests
and other responsible sources.

Orbit
An imprint of
Little, Brown Book Group
Carmelite House
50 Victoria Embankment
London EC4Y 0DZ

An Hachette UK Company
www.hachette.co.uk

www.orbitbooks.net

To Dad,
for always believing I could do it,
and to Mom,
for showing me how to get it done.

The Winter Ocean

The Sunset Ocean

A Current and
Accurate Map of
ERUVIA

VASKANDAR

Markova
Vilskafat
Alevar
Morgrain
Kosemia
Roskoth
Kar
Gemed
Atruin
Eyrie Lake
Ordun
Asral
The Witchwood
Lethe
Kazerath
Tira
Elowan
Urshul
Sevaeth
Highpass
Durantain
The Witch
The Fellnells

Chapter One

Here, my lady? Are you sure?"

As the narrow prow of my boat nudged the stone steps at the canal's edge, I wished I'd walked, or at least hired a craft rather than using my own. The oarsman was bound to report to La Contessa that her daughter had disembarked at a grimy little quay in a dubious corner of the Tallows, the poorest district of the city of Raverra.

By the time my mother heard anything, however, I'd already have the book.

"Yes, thank you. Right here."

The oarsman made no comment as he steadied his craft, but his eyebrows conveyed deep skepticism.

I'd worn a country gentleman's coat and breeches, to avoid standing out from my seedy surroundings. I was glad not to risk skirts trailing in the murky water as I clambered out of the boat. Trash bobbed in the canal, and the tang in the air was not exclusively salt.

"Shall I wait for you here, my lady?"

"No, that's all right." The less my mother knew of my errand, the better.

She had not precisely forbidden me to visit the pawnbroker who claimed to have a copy of Muscati's *Principles of Artifice*, but she'd made her opinion of such excursions clear. And no one casually disobeyed La Contessa Lissandra Cornaro. Her word resonated with power in every walled garden and forgotten plaza in Raverra.

Still, there was nothing casual about a Muscati. Only twelve known copies of his books existed. If this was real, it would be the thirteenth.

As I strolled alongside the canal, my mother's warnings seemed ridiculous. Sun-warmed facades flanked the green water, and workers unloaded produce from the mainland off boats moored at the canal's edge. A bright, peaceful afternoon like this surely could hold no dangers.

But when my route veered away from the canal, plunging into a shadowy tunnel that burrowed straight through a building, I hesitated. It was far easier to imagine assassins or kidnappers lurking beyond that dim archway. It wouldn't be the first time I'd faced either in my eighteen years as my mother's heir.

The book, I reminded myself. Think of the book.

I passed through the throat of the tunnel, emerging into a street too narrow to ever see direct sunlight. Broken shutters and scarred brickwork closed around me. The few people I passed gave me startled, assessing glances.

I found the pawnbroker's shop with relief, and hurried into a dim wilderness of dusty treasures. Jewelry and blown glass glittered on the shelves; furniture cluttered the floor, and paintings leaned against the walls. The proprietor bent over a conch shell wrapped with copper wire, a frown further creasing his already lined face. A few wisps of white over his ears were the last legacy of his hair.

I approached, glancing at the shell. "It's broken."

He scowled. "Is it? I should have known. He asked too little for a working one."

"Half the beads are missing." I pointed to a few orbs of colored glass still threaded on the wire. "You'd need an artificer to fix it if you wanted it to play music again."

The pawnbroker looked up at me, and his eyes widened. "Lady Amalia Cornaro." He bowed as best he could in the cramped shop.

I glanced around, but we were alone. "Please, no need for formality."

"Forgive me. I didn't recognize you in, ah, such attire." He peered dubiously at my breeches. "Though I suppose that's the fashion for young ladies these days."

Breeches weren't remotely in fashion for young ladies, but I didn't bother correcting him. I was just grateful they were acceptable enough in my generation that I didn't have to worry about causing a scandal or being mistaken for a courtesan.

"Do you have the book?" I reminded him. "Muscati's *Principles of Artifice*, your note said."

"Of course. I'd heard you were looking for it." A certain gleam entered his eye with which I was all too familiar: Cornaro gold reflected back at me. "Wait a moment, and I'll get it."

He shuffled through a doorway to the rear of the shop.

I examined the shell. I knew enough from my studies of artifice to trace the patterns of wire and understand the spell that had captured the sound of a musical performance inside the shell's rune-carved whorls. I could have fixed a broken wire, perhaps, but without the inborn talent of an artificer to infuse new beads with magical energy, the shell would stay silent.

The pawnbroker returned with a large leather-bound book. He laid it on the table beside the conch shell. "There you are, my lady."

I flipped through the pages until I came to a diagram. Muscati's combination of finicky precision in the wirework schematics and thick, blunt strokes for the runes was unmistakable. I let out a trembling breath. This was the real thing.

The pawnbroker's long, delicate fingers covered the page. "Is all in order, then?"

"Yes, quite. Thank you." I laid a gold ducat on the table. It vanished so quickly I almost doubted I'd put it there.

"Always a pleasure," he murmured.

I tucked the book into my satchel and hurried out of the musty shop, almost skipping with excitement. I couldn't wait to get home, retreat to my bedroom with a glass of wine, and dive into Muscati's timeworn pages. My friend Domenic from the University of Ardence said that to read Muscati was to open a window on a new view of the universe as a mathematical equation to be solved.

Of course, he'd only read excerpts. The university library didn't have an actual Muscati. I'd have to get Domenic here to visit so I could show him. Maybe I'd give the book to the university when I was done with it.

It was hard to make myself focus on picking turns in the maze-like streets rather than dreaming about runic alphabets, geometric diagrams, and coiling wirework. At least I was headed in the right general direction. One more bridge to cross, and then I'd be in polite, patrician territory, safe and sound; and no lecture of my mother's could change the fact that I'd completed my errand without incident.

But a tense group of figures stood in the tiny plaza before the bridge, frozen in a standoff, every line of their bodies promising each other violence.

Like so many things in Raverra, this had become complicated.

Three broad-shouldered men formed a menacing arc around a scrawny young woman with sprawling dark curls. The girl stood rigidly defiant, like a stick thrust in the mud. I slowed to a halt, clutching my satchel tight against my side, Muscati's edge digging into my ribs.

"One last chance." A burly man in shirtsleeves advanced on

the girl, fists like cannonballs ready at his sides. "Come nice and quiet to your master, or we'll break your legs and drag you to him in a sack."

"I'm my own master," the girl retorted, her voice blunt as a boat hook. "And you can tell Orthys to take his indenture contract and stuff it up his bunghole."

They hadn't noticed me yet. I could work my way around to the next bridge, and get my book safely home. I took a step back, glancing around for someone to put a stop to this: an officer of the watch, a soldier, anyone but me.

There was no one. The street lay deserted. Everyone else in the Tallows knew enough to make themselves scarce.

"Have it your way," the man growled. The ruffians closed in on their prey.

This was exactly the sort of situation in which a young lady of the august and noble house of Cornaro should not involve herself, and in which a person of any moral fortitude must.

Maybe I could startle them, like stray dogs. "You there! Stop!"

They turned to face me, their stares cold and flat. The air went dry in my throat.

"This is none of your business," one in a scuffed leather doublet warned. A scar pulled at the corner of his mouth. I doubted it came from a cooking accident.

I had no protection besides the dagger in my belt. The name Cornaro might hold weight with these scoundrels, but they'd never believe I bore it. Not dressed like this.

My name meant nothing. The idea sent a wild thrill into my lungs, as if the air were alive.

The girl didn't wait to see what I would do. She tried to bolt between two of the men. A tree branch of an arm caught her at the waist, scooping her up as if she were a child. Her feet swung in the air.

My satchel pulled at my shoulder, but I couldn't run off and leave her now, Muscati or no Muscati. Drawing my dagger seemed a poor idea. The men were all armed, one with a flint-lock pistol.

"Help!" I called.

The brutes seemed unimpressed. They kept their attention on the struggling girl as they wrenched her arms behind her.

"That's it!" Rage swelled her voice. "This is your last warning!"

Last warning? What an odd thing to say. Unless...

Ice slid into my bone marrow.

The men laughed, but she glowered furiously at them. She wasn't afraid. I could think of only one reason she wouldn't be.

I flattened myself against a wall just before everything caught fire.

Her eyes kindled first, a hungry blue spark flaring in her pupils. Then flames ran down her arms in delicate lines, leaping into the pale, lovely petals of a deadly flower.

The men lurched back from her, swearing, but it was too late. Smoke already rose from their clothing. Before they finished sucking in their first terrified breaths, blue flames sprang up in sudden, bold glory over every inch of them, burying every scar and blemish in light. For one moment, they were beautiful.

Then they let out the screams they had gathered. I cringed, covering my own mouth. The pain in them was inhuman. The terrible, oily reek of burning human meat hit me, and I gagged.

The men staggered for the canal, writhing in the embrace of the flames. I threw up my arm to ward my face from the heat, blocking the sight. Heavy splashes swallowed their screams.

In the sudden silence, I lowered my arm.

Fire leaped up past the girl's shoulders now. A pure, cold anger graced her features. It wasn't the look of a woman who was done.

Oh, Hells.

She raised her arms exultantly, and flames sprang up from the canal itself, bitter and wicked. They spread across the water as if on a layer of oil, licking at the belly of the bridge. On the far side of the canal, bystanders drawn by the commotion cried out in alarm.

"Enough!" My voice tore out of my throat higher than usual. "You've won! For mercy's sake, put it out!"

But the girl's eyes were fire, and flames ran down her hair. If she understood me, she made no sign of it. The blue fire gnawed at the stones around her feet. Hunger unsatisfied, it expanded as if the flagstones were grass.

I recognized it at last: balefire. I'd read of it in Orsenne's *Fall of Celantis*.

Grace of Mercy preserve us all. That stuff would burn anything—water, metal, stone. It could light up the city like a dry corncrib. I hugged my book to my chest.

"You have to stop this!" I pleaded.

"She can't," a strained voice said. "She's lost control."

I turned to find a tall, lean young man at my shoulder, staring at the burning girl with understandable apprehension. His wavy black hair brushed the collar of the uniform I wanted to see most in the world at the moment: the scarlet-and-gold doublet of the Falconers. The very company that existed to control magic so things like this wouldn't happen.

"Thank the Graces you're here! Can you stop her?"

"No." He drew in a deep, unsteady breath. "But you can, if you have the courage."

"What?" It was more madness, piled on top of the horror of the balefire. "But I'm not a Falconer!"

"That's why you can do it." Something delicate gleamed in his offering hand. "Do you think you can slip this onto her wrist?"

It was a complex weave of gold wire and scarlet beads, designed to tighten with a tug. I recognized the pattern from a woodcut in one of my books: a Falconer's jess. Named after the tethers used in falconry, it could place a seal on magic.

"She's *on fire*," I objected.

"I know. I won't deny it's dangerous." His intent green eyes clouded. "I can't do it myself; I'm already linked to another. I wouldn't ask if it weren't an emergency. The more lives the balefire consumes, the more it spreads. It could swallow all of Raverra."

I hesitated. The jess sagged in his hand. "Never mind. I shouldn't have—"

"I'll do it." I snatched the bracelet from him before I could think twice.

"Thank you." He flashed me an oddly wistful smile. "I'll distract her while you get close. Wits and courage. You can do it."

The Falconer sprinted toward the spreading flames, leaving the jess dangling from my hand like an unanswered question.

He circled to the canal's edge, calling to get the girl's attention. "You! Warlock!"

She turned toward him. Flame trailed behind her like a queen's mantua. The spreading edges crawled up the brick walls of the nearest house in blazing tendrils.

The Falconer's voice rang out above the clamor of the growing crowd across the canal. "In the name of His Serenity the Doge, I claim you for the Falcons of Raverra!"

That certainly got her attention. The flames bent in his direction as if in a strong wind.

"I don't belong to *you*, either!" Her voice was wild as a hissing bonfire. "You can't claim me. I'll see you burn first!"

Now she was going to kill him, too. Unless I stopped her.

My heart fluttering like an anxious dowager's handkerchief, I struggled to calm down and think. Maybe she wouldn't attack if

I didn't rush at her. I tucked my precious satchel under my coat and hustled toward the bridge as if I hoped to scurry past her and escape. It wasn't hard to pretend. Some in the crowd on the far side beckoned me to safety.

My legs trembled with the urge to heed them and dash across. I couldn't bear the thought of Muscati's pages withering to ashes.

I tightened my grip on the jess.

The Falconer extended his hand toward the girl to keep her attention. "By law, you belonged to Raverra the moment you were born with the mage mark. I don't know how you managed to hide for so long, but it's over now. Come with me."

The balefire roared at him in a blue-white wave.

"Plague take you!" The girl raised her fist in defiance. "If Raverra wants my fire, she can have it. Let the city burn!"

I lunged across the remaining distance between us, leaping over snaking lines of flame. Eyes squeezed half shut against the heat, I flung out an arm and looped the jess over her upraised fist.

The effect was immediate. The flames flickered out as if a cold blast of wind had snuffed them. The Falconer still recoiled, his arms upraised to protect his face, his fine uniform doublet smoking.

The girl swayed, the fire flickering out in her eyes. The golden jess settled around her bone-thin wrist.

She collapsed to the flagstones.

Pain seared my hand. I hissed through my teeth as I snatched it to my chest. That brief moment of contact had burned my skin and scorched my boots and coat. My satchel, thank the Graces, seemed fine.

Across the bridge, the gathering of onlookers cheered, then began to break up. The show was over, and nobody wanted to go near a fire warlock, even an unconscious one.

I couldn't blame them. No sign remained of ruffians in the canal, though the burned smell lingered horribly in the air.

Charred black scars streaked the sides of the buildings flanking me.

The Falconer approached, grinning with relief. "Well done! I'm impressed. Are you all right?"

It hit me in a giddy rush that it was over. I had saved—if not all of Raverra, at least a block or two of it—by myself, with my own hands. Not with my mother's name, or with my mother's wealth, but on my own.

Too dangerous to go to a pawnbroker's shop? Ha! I'd taken out a fire warlock. I smiled at him, tucking my burned hand into my sleeve. "I'm fine. I'm glad I could help."

"Lieutenant Marcello Verdi, at your service." He bowed. "What is your name, brave young lady?"

"Amalia Cornaro."

"Well, welcome to the doge's Falconers, Miss…" He stopped. The smile fell off his face, and the color drained from his bronze skin. "Cornaro." He swallowed. "Not…you aren't related to La Contessa Lissandra Cornaro, surely?"

My elation curdled in my stomach. "She's my mother."

"Hells," the lieutenant whispered. "What have I done?"

Chapter Two

My mother wasn't even here, and still she dominated the conversation. I bent over the unconscious girl, both out of concern and to hide my frustration.

"Will she be all right?" I asked.

"She's fine, my lady. Warlocks often collapse from exhaustion after loosing their power." The new stiffness in Verdi's voice smarted like salt on my burns. I shouldn't have told him my name.

He knelt, reaching for the girl's wrist. At first I thought he meant to check her pulse, but his fingers instead traced the delicate weave of the bracelet.

The jess was the most complex wirework artifice I'd ever seen. The intricate braid of the wire and position of the blood-red beads formed a language dictating the terms of the spell. It was too elaborate for me to follow.

Some of the golden wires had blurred and melted at the knot that bound the strands together. That shouldn't have been possible; jesses were supposed to be nearly impervious to physical harm. But balefire was a powerful magical force.

"It's fused," Verdi breathed. "I don't think it will come off."

I lifted my eyes and found his green ones. The worry in them was frank and unguarded, in a way I never saw in the drawing-room circles of the Raverran elite.

"Why would you want it to come off?" I asked.

"Because, my lady, *you* are the one who put it on her."

"Please, call me Amalia."

"I'm sorry, Lady Amalia. I should never have involved you in this." He shook his head. "We're trained to recruit civilian volunteers to put on the jesses in unexpected emergencies like this, but I've never heard of anyone accidentally enlisting a noble before."

"You didn't involve me. I chose to help. I did it myself." Crouching in the street with my face inches from his suddenly felt awkward. I straightened, cradling my burned hand. The growing pain of it intruded into everything, like an unwelcome guest.

"And you were magnificent. I'm the one who bungled things." Verdi rose, too, rubbing his head. "I'm not sure what happens now. I need to get our new Falcon to the Mews before she wakes up. The law says she can't be out in the city without her Falconer, but..." He let out a nervous laugh. "*You* are her Falconer."

"But I can't be." Now I understood his alarm. "None of the great families of the Assembly can be Falconers. My mother—"

"I know; believe me, my lady." Verdi grimaced. "I'm not sure who will have my head first: La Contessa, my commanding officer, or the doge himself. But you put the jess on her, so you're the only one who can bind and release her power. With the jess damaged, nothing can change that now."

A bracelet couldn't have made such a huge decision for me. Not even the doge dictated the fate of a Cornaro. The only one who could do that was...I swallowed. "Someone's going to have to tell my mother."

Verdi saluted me.

"Oh, no," I protested. "I can't."

"Better she hear it from you than from the doge." His brows

drew together. "Normally I'd take you both straight to the Mews with me, but I don't dare interfere with La Contessa."

"I'm afraid we already have." Though I wasn't displeased to have acted outside the scope of her approval. I was more concerned about breaking Falconer regulations and Raverran law.

"I'm sorry, my lady." Verdi bowed. "This is all my fault. And I don't want to make it worse by leaving you now. But if I don't get our new recruit to the Mews before she wakes up, even the Grace of Luck won't be able to save this mess."

He hesitated over the unconscious Falcon a moment, then scooped her up, settling her on his back with a wince at his singed shoulders. One skinny arm hung limply in the air.

Disquiet filled me at the sight. I'd meant to help her, not capture her. But the Falcons were kept in luxury. It must be an improvement over whatever lot in life had left her dressed in rags and running from scoundrels.

"Are you certain she'll be all right?"

"We'll take good care of her," Verdi said. "She's not a prisoner."

The jess gleamed on her wrist, and I wasn't so sure.

"My apologies, my lady." Verdi attempted another bow, then curtailed it as the girl started to slide off his back. "I must go. I'll report to your palace once I get her settled, to speak further about this. Or at least, someone will, and I hope it's me. Because if not, that probably means I'm in a great deal of trouble."

A great deal of trouble. The words lingered like the scent of smoke on my coat as I climbed the marble stairs to my mother's study. My hand throbbed on the cool banister. Dark oil portraits of great Cornaros of the past watched me from the walls, with my mother's shrewd eyes.

I tucked my book behind a silver urn in the hallway, to give myself a better chance of glossing over exactly where I'd been. I considered going to my room to change, but La Contessa placed more value on timely information than on appropriate dress. I had no excuse to put this conversation off.

Still, I stood for a few minutes outside her study door. I stared at the gilt-carved doorframe, picking out the same familiar shapes I'd found as a child, while I practiced my opening line under my breath.

Finally, I knocked.

"Enter," she commanded from within.

I opened the door. Warm sunlight caught on the baroque moldings and bright frescoes of my mother's study. A huge map of the Serene Empire of Raverra hung on one wall, and a bookcase ran up the full fifteen feet to the ceiling on another.

My mother sat at her writing desk, her back to me, quill moving as she worked. I loved that writing desk. It was full of secret drawers and cubbies, and my mother had asked me to help her test it when I was a child, offering me sweets for each hidden compartment I could find. Her auburn hair cascaded artfully over rich emerald-velvet shoulders. When the doge himself might call for her at any time, or the Council of Nine convene for an emergency meeting, La Contessa believed in always looking her best.

I cleared my throat. "I saved Raverra from burning today."

"That would explain why you smell like an unswept chimney." She kept writing, without a glance in my direction.

"Yes." I shuffled my soot-stained boots. "There was an out-of-control fire warlock, and I . . . I helped. A Falconer gave me a jess, and I got it on her."

The scratching of the quill stopped. My mother turned, slowly. She wore her business face, beautiful and unreadable, with penetrating eyes.

"You put a jess on a rogue warlock." Her voice was flat as a slab of marble.

"Yes." My mouth stretched, from sheer nerves. I shouldn't smile; I twisted it to a grimace instead. "It, ah, seems it won't come off."

The moment lengthened. My mother didn't move. Finally, the pen in her hand twitched, the feather quivering, as if she stuck a decisive period at the end of her thoughts.

"I knew you'd gone shopping in the Tallows," she said. "I didn't realize you brought me back a Falcon."

She already knew where I'd been. Of course.

I twisted my good hand in the strap of my satchel, but said nothing. My mother once told me that when you didn't know where you stood, you should keep your mouth shut and listen.

"Amalia, do you know why I let you run around Raverra without an escort?"

I hesitated, then shook my head.

"Why I let you study magical science in Ardence, or allow you to go out dressed like a country squire's seventh daughter, or pretend I don't notice when you visit pawnshops in unsavory areas?"

"No, Mamma."

"To see what you do, given freedom to make your own choices." Her words cut the air like a thrown knife. "And to see what you learn. Because I hoped this independence indicated a spark of intelligence or ambition that might serve our family well, and that you might prove yourself worthy to be my heir."

I had thought, perhaps, it was because she wanted me to be happy. "I did learn things."

"Hmm." La Contessa tapped her quill against the edge of her desk. "You have certainly taken bold action. For that, I must commend you."

"Thank you, Mamma." She was probably being ironic, but better to be safe.

"The question is what will happen now. The law is clear:

you cannot be a Falconer. Yet you are. Do you realize what this means?"

I swallowed. "I'm causing headaches for everyone?"

"You miss the crucial point, child. It means we are the only family in the Assembly to have control of a Falcon."

I blinked. I hadn't considered that angle at all. The hundreds of patrician families that made up the Assembly, the great legislative council of Raverra, constantly maneuvered for advantage against each other. Strong magic was a privilege reserved for the state, an edge that could disrupt the delicate balance of Raverran power. "I can't imagine the doge would allow—"

"You are my heir," La Contessa cut in. "The doge does not control you. I do."

My eyebrow shot up in annoyance. "With all respect, if that were entirely true, we wouldn't be having this discussion."

My mother laughed. She had a lovely, warm laugh, which still set the hearts of courtiers and kings aflutter. "Very well then, child. You are a Cornaro. No one controls you. But be careful; the doge will not appreciate that fact. Especially with things as they are now in Ardence."

That didn't sound good. "Is something wrong in Ardence?" Domenic and my other Ardentine friends hadn't mentioned any trouble in their last letters, though I hadn't heard anything from them within the past few weeks. Nor had my mother's cousin, the doge's envoy to Ardence, said anything at our family dinner a month ago. But La Contessa was on the Council of Nine, and personally oversaw Raverran intelligence; she'd know about trouble before its perpetrators did.

"Nothing serious yet. The young duke is testing his limits. You should pay more attention to the world around you, Amalia."

Her gaze traveled over my clothes, and my empty satchel, before arresting at my hand.

"What happened to you?" she demanded, rising from her desk.

I tucked my hand into my coat. "She was on fire, Mamma."

She crossed the room and lifted my hand out of hiding, tenderly. I tried not to wince.

"I'm fine."

"You will be," my mother agreed. "But that must hurt. We'll have it seen to."

She brushed loose hair from my face, bringing locks up as if to style it. By the look in her eyes, it was a hopeless effort. She let my hair drop, smiling at me almost sadly.

"Remember, Amalia. You are my heir. That comes before any other responsibilities life may thrust upon you, including those of a Falconer. Stick to that, above all else, no matter what he tries to get you to agree to."

"He?"

"The doge, of course."

The doge. Of course. Sometimes my mother and I seemed to be having two unrelated conversations.

She gave my singed clothes another glance, frowning. "Go get dressed, girl. And don't forget your elixir."

"I never forget my elixir."

"Evidently, given you're still alive." My mother leaned forward and planted a quick kiss on my forehead. The scent of her perfume, as delicate and complex as one of her intrigues, enfolded me. "I'd like to keep you that way. Be careful, child."

"Of course, Mamma."

"Now, go change. It's going to be a long day."

When my mother told me to get dressed, I knew she meant in attire more suitable for the heir to one of the Council of Nine—the secretive body that, together with the doge, wielded the true power in Raverra. The Assembly made the laws, certainly; but the Council controlled the military, intelligence, and diplomatic services, and had final say in all matters of justice, foreign policy, and the security of the Empire. All nine members had once been elected from the Assembly, but over the centuries, the Empire's most powerful families had permanently claimed four of the seats, making them hereditary. I'd been confirmed as my mother's successor before I was born.

Why governing the Serene Empire should preclude comfortable trousers, however, I couldn't say. I dutifully pulled a gown from my wardrobe and laid it across the bed; but the corset laced up the back, and I was the only one in the room. So I wound up sprawled on my stomach next to it, reading my new book.

Muscati made artifice seem so simple. Use runes to dictate a new property for an object, or bind it to new rules with wirework, and conduct magical energy through the pattern to empower it. Studying his breathtakingly intricate schematics, I hovered each time on the edge of epiphany not just about the particular magic they invoked but about the natural laws they employed or circumvented.

As I read, the sky outside darkened. The luminaries in their wall sconces came on, glowing with a soft echo of the light captured by the solar artifice circle on the roof. The new Falcon must be awake by now—this stranger who could never again leave the cloistered Mews without me at her side.

I cradled my aching hand. She had to be a fire warlock, of all things, the rarest and deadliest of mages. Fire warlocks left charred and smoking holes in the pages of history: cities laid in ruin, battlefields of ash and bone.

But nothing had disturbed the serenity of the Empire in fifty years, since the Three Years' War. Under the Serene Accords, its client states governed themselves peacefully enough. They gave Raverra trade privileges and Falcons in return for military protection, as well as infrastructure such as good roads, aqueducts, the Imperial Post, and the courier-lamp network. Raverra mostly left its tributaries alone, its Serene Envoys murmuring an occasional well-heeded word in the ears of their leaders, be they kings, dukes, or consuls. No foreign power had had the strength or will to threaten the Empire since it defeated the mad Witch Lords of Vaskandar in the Three Years' War, in the time of my grandparents. Without an enemy, there was no need to unleash the power of a warlock. My Falcon might stay hooded for the rest of her life.

Hooded, and trapped in the Mews, her life bounded by a line as stark as one of Muscati's circles.

A familiar, peremptory double rap on my door warned me in time to stuff *Principles of Artifice* under my pillow before my mother swept into the room. Her attendant, Ciardha, paced behind her, holding a small chest. Ciardha was no mere servant, but a scion of a prominent Ostan merchant family with a discerning eye and a sharp mind, to whom my mother entrusted her most important tasks.

"Good Graces, you haven't even started yet." La Contessa's eyes swept the bed. I forced myself not to glance at my pillow, hoping my book didn't show. "Were you reading again?"

"I was thinking about fire warlocks." It wasn't a lie.

Ciardha, without fuss, took up my burned hand and started smoothing salve on it. I stood at stiff attention.

My mother gave the gown I'd laid out an appalled look. "You can't receive the doge in *that*, child. What were you thinking? You could wear that dress to the market, perhaps. Ciardha, when you're done with her hand, help Amalia get ready."

"Of course, Contessa," Ciardha murmured.

My mouth went dry. "I'm seeing the doge? Today?"

"Didn't I tell you as much? Did you think I was joking? His

message came through the courier lamps while you were in here failing to get dressed. He commanded your presence at the Imperial Palace." She flung open my wardrobe and scanned my gowns. "I managed to buy us some time by pleading your burns, and he's agreed to come here instead. So, Ciardha, make sure that hand looks dreadfully serious."

"Of course, Contessa." Ciardha took a roll of bandages out of her chest and went to work, her nimble fingers moving skillfully.

A powerful urge possessed me to snatch my hand back, run out of the room, and find somewhere to hide. "The doge is coming *here*? When?"

"Calm down, child. It's not as if he hasn't been here before. I've bought us an hour or two. Forty people will try to talk to him on his way out of the palace; they always do. I have a servant on the roof with a spyglass watching the Imperial Canal for his boat, so we'll have a few minutes' warning before he arrives. The peacock-blue silk, I should think, Ciardha. Make sure she puts on appropriate jewels, and do something about her hair, too."

"Of course, Contessa." Ciardha spun a gauzy cocoon around my hand.

"I can't move my fingers."

"Of course, Lady." There was a smile in Ciardha's voice, though her face stayed serious. "You are far too grievously injured to do any such thing."

La Contessa squeezed my shoulders. "Listen, Amalia. I'll stay with you if I can, but the doge will ask to speak with you alone. You have to hold your own against him. Do you understand?"

"Yes, Mamma—" I stopped myself. "Wait. No, Mamma. What does he want? Why is he coming to talk to me?"

"Your little adventure today has put high stakes on the table. The control of the Serene Empire's only fire warlock. The unchallenged authority of the doge over the Falcons. The disposition of the heir to one of the most powerful families in Raverra. Of course he wants to talk to you."

All Muscati's words I'd drunk in ignorant bliss while I was supposed to be preparing sat uneasy in my stomach. "Is it really that important, what happened today?"

"You will be on the Council of Nine someday, Amalia. You had best get used to the idea that everything you do is important."

"What should I say to the doge?" Pain shot through my hand as I tried to clench it. Ciardha *tsked* at me.

"Get me the Falcon, if you can," my mother said. "But most importantly, do not let him establish dominion over you. You are no mere Falconer under his command. If you allow him to control you now, when you take my seat in the Council of Nine, you will be his tool."

"What do you want a fire warlock for, anyway?"

"I don't want a fire warlock. I want it to be known we have one." She brushed a stray wisp of hair from my brow. "The doge understands. You will, too."

"Done," Ciardha announced. I regarded my bandaged hand in despair. I had to receive the doge like *this*?

My mother patted my arm, giving me the smile that won the country of Callamorne for the Raverran Empire. "You'll do fine, child. Just remember who you are."

Who I was, or who she wished me to be? My throat tightened. "I'm not good at these games. Not like you are, Mamma."

"Then don't play. Figure out what you *are* good at, and make that the game."

And she swept out, with all the majesty of a swan taking off, leaving Ciardha's capable hands to get me into the peacock-blue gown. I hardly had to do a thing, save turn when told, or brace myself while Ciardha put a knee in my back to tighten my corset.

"I wish you could talk to the doge for me, Ciardha," I said when I could breathe again. "You're good at everything."

"You will do fine, Lady," Ciardha assured me with utmost confidence, her fingers now moving adeptly through my hair.

"How can you be sure?"

"Because La Contessa said you would. La Contessa is never wrong."

A cry rose up in the household, one servant calling to another. *He's coming!*

They had spotted the doge's gull-winged boat on the Imperial Canal. I had best hope Ciardha was right.

Chapter Three

The most powerful man in the world stood barely taller than I did, not counting the ducal crown. Niro da Morante was young for a doge; it was a lifetime post, and the Assembly rarely elected anyone with an undue allowance of lifetime remaining. His hair still showed dark between broad streaks of gray. But his deep-set eyes gleamed with a relentless intelligence, and he had a presence about him that had nothing to do with the richness of his robes—or even the fact that he commanded an empire spanning most of the continent of Eruvia.

As I curtsied to him, those dark eyes drank in every piece of knowledge he could glean from my appearance. It was hard to forget, even here in the grand salon of my own house, that here was a man whose word held the power of war and peace, prosperity and ruin, life and death.

This must be how other people felt talking to my mother.

My petticoats swept the marble floor as I finished the curtsy. My mother uttered words of greeting, and I made appropriate noises. Servants swirled around like dancers, offering him wine and refreshments, which he waved away. The hall stretched too large around us, built to host masquerade balls and the occasional state ceremony. I spent little time in this room, with its frescoes showing the accomplishments of Cornaro doges and its gilded molding overwrought almost to the point of hysteria. It was meant to impress guests, not to live in.

When the doge settled into the chair we offered him, it was with an air of dissatisfaction—not with our hospitality, or even with me, but with the entire situation.

"I wish to speak to my new Falconer alone," he said.

The servants discreetly withdrew from the room. My mother smiled, all grace and poise. "Surely there is nothing you would say to my daughter I could not hear as well."

I couldn't help but notice the emphasis they both placed on *my*.

The doge raised an eyebrow. "Is she a child, to hide behind her mother's skirts?"

Stung, I opened my mouth, but a sharp jab at my shoulder stopped me. My mother's hand lay there, casual and relaxed; but she'd reversed a ring so the stone pressed into my skin in warning.

"Amalia is fully capable of standing on her own," she said, with more confidence than the collected history of our prior conversations would suggest. "But what could you have to discuss that must be kept private from her mother, and your old friend?"

The corner of the doge's mouth quirked. "Nothing. But you know as well as I, Lissandra, that if you are in the room, it will be a conversation between you and me, not with your estimable daughter."

There was a silence. The ring still dug into my shoulder.

La Contessa laughed, and dropped the doge an ironic curtsy. "Very well, Niro. I can't deny you're right. I'll leave you two unchaperoned, then."

My mother's velvet skirts swished. The salon doors opened and closed. I was alone with the doge.

He gestured me to sit, his eyes lingering on my overbandaged hand.

I settled onto the edge of a chair, as best as I could in my corset; between the plunging waist and stiff stays, it seemed designed for ladies who never sat down. Layers of gathered silk and petticoats rustled and bunched beneath me. This was why I preferred a jacket and breeches.

The doge raised his brows. "Well, Lady Amalia. You have chosen an...untraditional method to become one of my Falconers."

Every word he chose staked a careful position on a playing board I couldn't see, counting points I couldn't reckon. My gauze-wrapped palm grew damp.

"Your Serenity, I assure you I had no intention of doing any such thing. My only aim was to protect Raverra from balefire."

"Regardless. You and your Falcon pose quite a pretty problem." He spread an empty hand as if to show me. "Normally, we bring Falcons into the Mews as children. And Falconers live in the Mews as well, undergoing several years of training before they link to a carefully chosen Falcon, at which point they forgo all other responsibilities, oaths, and titles. If they are of a patrician family, they lose the right to sit in the Assembly."

My mother would never stand for that. "But of course, that is impossible in this case." I kept my tone light but unwavering. "As I am the Cornaro heir."

The doge gazed at me thoughtfully. Across the room, a clock ticked. Dozens of painted dignitaries watched me from the frescoed ceiling.

"Do you know," he said at last, "why the ruling families of Raverra are forbidden to be Falconers?"

"To avoid giving one family too much power."

"Yes. But that's not the only reason." He leaned forward. Deep in his dark eyes came a gleam, like sunken gold. "Do you understand, Amalia Cornaro, the paradox of force?"

I hesitated. "I'm not certain to what you're referring, Your Serenity."

"The naval and magical power of Raverra is unparalleled. None doubt it is the foundation of the Empire, along with our great wealth. And yet we haven't needed to use force to secure our position in decades. It is precisely because all know we are capable of exercising unstoppable military power that we do not need to do so. It is by the implicit threat of war we secure the peace of Eruvia."

"True power wields a light touch, because a light touch suffices," I quoted my mother.

"Usually." His eyes narrowed. "But what happens, Lady Amalia, when someone attempts to call our bluff?"

"But...the power of the Serene Empire isn't a bluff."

"No. No, it is not." Satisfaction in his voice, he leaned back in his chair. "As Celantis learned, three hundred years ago. You know the story, I presume?"

"Of course." It was a story Eruvia had found hard to forget, as the Serene Empire of Raverra continued to grow from the few coastal cities of its cradle. "Raverra and the island of Celantis were at war. When the doge moved the fleet and the Falcons into position to attack Celantis, he offered them one last chance for peace, but the king of Celantis sent back the emissary's head as his reply. So the doge shot one more message over the city walls on an arrow: *You may think your kingdom powerful, that it can destroy one man. But with one man, I will destroy your kingdom.* And he"—I swallowed—"he unleashed his fire warlock."

"That's right." There was no humor in Niro da Morante's smile. "The balefire swept the city, in three days and nights of terror. For each victim the flames claimed, they grew stronger, feeding on the lives of the fallen. After a hundred deaths, and a thousand, nothing could stop the blaze, not even the warlock himself. Only the word of the Falconer could end it."

I nodded mutely, my lips pressed tight.

"But by the doge's order, the Falconer withheld that word,

until the king of Celantis was dead at the hands of his own people and the generals came out to surrender and beg for mercy."

That Falconer had watched Celantis burn, knowing he could stop it at any time with one word. But he chose not to speak that word, out of loyalty to his doge. Did that silence cause him pain? Did he wake from nightmares every day for the rest of his life, hearing the screams, smelling the burning flesh?

"Since then, few indeed have dared refuse Raverra, the Serene City." The doge steepled his fingers. "Thus, we have not needed to burn any more kingdoms. So you see the role a fire warlock plays in maintaining the serenity of the Empire."

"Yes." He'd circled back to my Falcon. He must be closing a trap. My heart beat twice for every tick of the clock. "Knowing we have a fire warlock makes it far less likely anyone will start hostilities with us in the first place."

"And you also see why I cannot afford any doubt that if I call for you to unleash your Falcon's fire, you will do as I command without hesitation."

There it was. I stared, caught. A cynical smile pulled at the corner of his mouth. *You see?* it said. *It's not so easy.*

"Your Serenity," I said slowly, "should the security of Raverra require me to unleash my Falcon, I will do so."

"No matter what the target?"

"I will defend Raverra if it is threatened."

"Hmm." His eyes flicked across my face as if he were reading a page. "You agree, then, to follow my orders?"

I clenched my bandaged hand until pain flared in it like a red sunrise. I couldn't say yes, but I couldn't say no. I hoped he didn't see on my face how I wished my mother were in the room to answer for me.

"I cannot imagine, Your Serenity," I said at last, "you would ever ask me to release my Falcon save for the security of Raverra."

The doge laughed, thin lines fanning beside his eyes. "Well said." He stood; I followed suit. "Very well, then. I suppose that will have to do for now."

It seemed the game was over. But I had no idea if I'd won or lost.

"You will require at least some training," he said. "We can't have you accidentally saying the release word and burning down the Mews."

Release word? Now I was afraid to say anything at all. The doge saw it, and laughed again.

"Report to the Mews at your convenience tomorrow morning, and we will make sure that doesn't happen."

"Your Serenity, with due respect, I cannot move into the Mews."

"Perhaps you cannot. But you can pay a brief visit there, to receive some simple training."

That seemed reasonable enough. "Yes, Your Serenity."

"Until we meet again, Amalia Cornaro."

I stood alone in the grand salon as they escorted the doge to his boat with proper honor and pleasantries. My legs trembled as if I'd ridden twenty miles.

Before he'd been gone long enough for me to consider sitting down, my mother glided into the room.

"That will do," she told me without preamble. "You didn't lose us any ground, and that's what matters."

"You were listening? You eavesdropped on our conversation!"

"My dear child, of course I listened. Your great-grandfather didn't go to all the trouble of building secret spying chambers into this palace so his heirs could respect the privacy of others. Now, we need to determine our next move."

Our next move. My mother had never included me in her

machinations. I wasn't sure whether to be proud or afraid. Probably afraid.

"Mamma . . . What about the Falcon?"

"It shouldn't compromise our control over the Falcon for you to take some lessons at the Mews. Just don't let them order you about or give you a military rank."

"That's not what I meant." I struggled to put into words a worry that had been growing in my mind like a gnawing caterpillar. "No matter what happens, this girl and I are linked for the rest of our lives. She can't leave the Mews without me."

"True," my mother agreed. "It's an awkward situation."

"If she doesn't like me, it could be *very* awkward."

"Then," she said, "make her like you."

Make her like you. For my mother, no doubt it was that easy. But I was not, as I had proven on numerous occasions, my mother.

To be sure, most people I knew *acted* as if they liked me. The Cornaro name drew throngs of admirers at each genteel party my mother pulled me from my books to attend. But even with my scholar friends from the Imperial Library or the University of Raverra, there was a certain unctuous note to their smiles as we bent over books together, an oil of flattery and fear lubricating their words. I'd had to travel to Ardence, where not everyone realized I was *that* Amalia Cornaro, before anyone would point out flaws in my artifice designs or argue with me over the causes of the Three Years' War.

I didn't know how to *tell* if someone liked me, let alone encourage them to do so if they were not already thus inclined.

La Contessa often brought a gift the first time she paid someone a visit. I'd lay a wager the ragged, starving-thin girl from the Tallows hadn't gotten many presents in her life. So on my way to the Mews, my valiant oarsman battled the morning market traffic to secure me a spot to disembark and visit a jewelry booth. I bought the first trinket that caught my attention, a pretty amber necklace. A bespectacled woman wrapped it in silk for me with careful fingers.

Back in my golden-prowed boat, I wondered what she was like, this woman I was bound to for the rest of my life. Spirited, certainly. Clever, perhaps, to have hidden the mage mark for so long. The sort of person I'd want as a friend, if I hadn't destroyed all chance of that the minute I slid the jess onto her wrist.

The sort of friend my mother would never approve, if she weren't a Falcon.

My boat escaped the exuberantly congested Imperial Canal and navigated the short distance across the green waters of the lagoon to Raptor's Isle, nudging up against the visitors' dock between rows of sleek military cutters. The gray walls of the Mews loomed above, forbidding despite delicate stonework and pointed arches. Protective artifice runes ringed every door and window, sealing them against assassins and arrows. Armed guards with muskets and sabers watched me. No one came forward to hand me out of the boat. Thank goodness I'd worn boots and breeches again today, though the embroidered brocade bore as little resemblance to what I'd worn in the Tallows as a peacock's plumage did to a sparrow's.

Just as I started to become uncomfortable under the assessing stare of the guards, the bronze doors flew open. Lieutenant Verdi strode out to meet me, a relieved smile on his face.

I stared. A black eye shone gloriously purple from beneath his wavy bangs.

"Lady Amalia Cornaro." He bowed. The guards, hearing my name, stood straighter. "I'm so glad you came."

He did sound glad. *Too* glad, with an edge of desperation. "Is something amiss?"

Verdi grimaced. "Come in, my lady, and I'll explain."

I had never been inside the Mews before, though I'd seen its fortresslike walls and irregular scattering of towers across the water all my life. I'd always imagined it to be a moody, brooding place full of mad sorcerers, and was disappointed when Verdi led me through the outer fortifications into a lovely garden.

Flowering trees and shrubs created nooks and private spaces. A young man sprawled under a tree reading a book; on an open, grassy lawn, a handful of shrieking children kicked a ball around. Golden bracelets glinted on their wrists. Only a pair of uniformed officers, pistols at their hips, reminded me that this was a military stronghold; they crossed the garden briskly, heading for the gate.

I drew closer to Verdi as my guide in this forbidden place. I caught a soldierly whiff of leather, gunpowder, and steel from him. It was nothing like the wine-and-rosewater miasma that wafted off the dandies at court.

"How is she?" I asked, pulling my mind firmly back to the matter at hand. "My Falcon?"

Verdi touched the edge of the bruise around his eye. "She's... not transitioning well."

"I can't say I'm surprised."

The corner of his mouth quirked in acknowledgment. It was a little thing, but the informality sprouted a seedling of hope in my chest.

We passed a pair of girls who sat chattering by a fountain. One wore a jess, and one didn't—Falcon and Falconer, I supposed. Lieutenant Verdi nodded to them, and they waved back. After he passed, they burst into stifled giggles, but he didn't notice. I wished I could linger behind and find out whether it was because of the bruise, or if they thought he was handsome. But I'd always been terrible at that sort of conversation.

"We've treated her with respect, and set her up in comfort in her own room." Verdi gestured to one of the many-windowed brick buildings surrounding the rambling garden. "But it doesn't matter. You were there yesterday; you can guess how it is."

"She hates being shut in here."

I'd heard of peasants trying to fake the mage mark in their children so the whole family could move into the Mews. But I supposed one would feel a bit differently about it if one were knocked out and dragged here.

"She considers us enemies." Verdi sighed. "Especially me. I'm hoping you may have more luck with her."

"Me? I'm the one who caught her."

"But you stood up for her first. That must count for something."

I remembered the gleam of the jess on her limp arm. "I doubt it."

Verdi stopped and turned to me, his brows drawn together. "My lady, please. I know you owe me nothing. But Colonel Vasante, the commander of the Falcons, has charged me with salvaging this mess I've created. I'm doing my best, but Falcon and Falconer are a pair. A team. I need your help."

"It's not your fault. You didn't put the jess on her." Quenching the warlock's fire and unintentionally claiming her for the Falcons was a rare thing I'd done on my own, as Amalia, not as the Cornaro heir. I couldn't turn away from it and let the consequences fall on Verdi and my Falcon alone. "I'll do what I can."

"Thank you, my lady." He put his hand over his heart and bowed; I glimpsed the hollow of his throat down the collar of his doublet. "I'll pray to the Graces it's enough."

The autumn air seemed warmer as we continued past rosebushes and an herb garden to one of the brick dormitories. Verdi led me through the unlocked door and up an oak-paneled staircase.

"One way or another, we have to introduce you two," Verdi said as we reached the second floor. "If she seems too, ah, aggressive, we can cut it short."

I clutched my silk-wrapped package. "Is there anything I need to know before I meet her?"

"I wish I could tell you anything about her, but she won't talk about herself or her past. We don't even know enough to contact her friends and family to let them know what happened to her."

I had a bleak suspicion there might not be anyone to tell. "That's unfortunate."

"One important note. Whatever you do, don't say 'Exsolvo.'"

"Ex—"

He whirled. I caught a white flash of eyes, and his hand clamped over my mouth. I teetered on the edge of the topmost stair, tasting the salt on his palm, the word caught on my tongue.

He steadied me, his strong hand warm against my back. Then he quickly released me. His face was chalk pale.

"I'm sorry, my lady. But you must not say that word, not even out here. Not halfway across the world. That's the release word."

I laid a bracing hand on the wall, my heart stumbling. The taste of his skin lingered on my tongue. It took a moment to sift through mingled indignation and embarrassment to grasp the meaning of his words.

"Oh!" I remembered the doge's grim joke about burning down the Mews. Two syllables more, and it would have lost its humor. "So, if I say that, she gets her magic back?"

"Yes. And in her current mood, she wouldn't hesitate to use it."

I swallowed. "What's the word to seal it again?"

"Revincio," he replied. "That one you can say all you want."

"Revincio," I repeated.

"You've got it. Don't forget that one." He winced. "And I apologize again for being so familiar, my lady."

I waved his words off. "Don't. I'd far rather get grabbed than set the castle on fire or fall down the stairs."

"A lady of sense. Still, I'd appreciate if you didn't mention it to the colonel."

"I've already forgotten it."

It was a flat-out lie. The print of his touch still warmed my back.

As he led me down a long hallway, he didn't seem quite sure what to do with his hands, and his eyes kept drifting sideways to catch glimpses of me. If I'd noticed him glancing at me, I must be looking at him, too. I peeled my gaze off the clean lines of his face and stared resolutely at the portraits of long-dead Falcons on the walls.

He stopped at last at a sturdy oak door. "Here we are." He eyed the handle as if it might transform into a viper at any second. "Are you ready?"

I took a deep breath. "Probably not. But I'm willing to try."

"Brave lady." He flashed me a grin, showing dimples I hadn't noticed before. "But I already knew that."

I warmed inexplicably at the words.

Verdi squared his shoulders and knocked on the door.

"Go away," a rough voice called in response. "I warned you, if you come in here again, I'll give you a matching pair."

He gave me a *you see how she is* shrug. "Perhaps another time, my lady," he said.

"It's all right." If I didn't do this now, I'd lose my courage. "Excuse me," I called out. "I'm Amalia Cornaro, your new Falconer. I was hoping to meet you."

There was a pause. Then she replied, "Come in, then. I suppose I'd better see your face, so I can hate it better."

"My lady, you don't have to do this," Verdi murmured. "If I send you home with a black eye, I'll never forgive myself."

"I don't bruise easily," I assured him.

I opened the door.

Chapter Four

The room would have been quite pleasant if it didn't look as if animals had been nesting in it. The wardrobe stood open, with everything from petticoats to corsets strewn across the furniture and floor. Plates streaked with sauce and half-full glasses stood on tables, chairs, and windowsills, and lay spilled and broken on the rug. Warlocks needed to eat a lot to fuel their magic, but I still didn't see how one skinny girl could have consumed so much in less than a full day. To complete the disaster, every drawer and chest had been flung open and dumped on the bed. Ink and cosmetics stained the fine coverlet.

In the center of the chaos stood the girl from yesterday, a wild cascade of unbrushed curls tumbling down her back. She wore a midnight-blue gown that must have been the finest of the dresses they gave her; it seemed shockingly out of place in the filthy room. She'd been admiring herself in an oval mirror. As I hesitated in the doorway, she glanced over her shoulder.

"So, you're my jailer," she sneered. "Lady Amalia Cornaro."

I stepped into the room, placing my foot between a spilled wineglass and a tangled heap of stockings. "I fear you have me at a disadvantage. We were never properly introduced."

The girl snorted, turning to face me. "'I fear you have me at a disadvantage,'" she repeated. "Well, that's nice. You can't have *all* the advantages."

Ignoring a stab of annoyance, I tried again. "So . . . what's your name?"

"Zaira."

I waited a moment for a surname before I realized none was coming.

"Well, Zaira, I'm hoping we can get along, since we have to work together for the rest of our lives." I extended my silk-wrapped package. "I brought you a gift."

Zaira lifted a contemptuous eyebrow. Without a word, she crossed the room, stepping on clothes and plates, and snatched the parcel out of my hand. This close, I could see the mage mark in her eyes: an extra ring around the pupil. Hers was black, and her irises were so dark it was easy to miss. So that was how she'd managed to hide it.

She tore away the yellow silk, casting it onto the floor, and barely glanced at the amber necklace before tossing it onto the bed.

"This wasn't enough?" She shook the golden bracelet on her wrist. "You had to get me a collar, too?"

I caught a retort between my teeth and forced a polite smile instead, as if she'd said thank you.

"My lady," Verdi broke in from behind me. "Perhaps it would be best to try another time."

I'd forgotten he was there. I turned to find him hovering in the hallway. "Actually, could you give us a few moments alone, Lieutenant?"

"Are you sure?" He didn't need to say a word of warning; his black eye spoke for him.

"Quite sure."

"All right," he agreed dubiously. As he closed the door behind me, he added, "Call if you need me. I'll wait out here."

The door clicked shut, leaving me alone with my Falcon.

Before Zaira could speak, I blurted, "I'm sorry."

"You're sorry?" Zaira's brows lifted.

"I only meant to help you. Against those men."

"Well, if you were trying to help me escape, you did a stinking-awful job."

"This wasn't what I wanted. I didn't know I'd bind you to me. But I couldn't let you burn down the city."

"So now you've trapped me here for the rest of my life." Zaira tugged at the jess. "Don't expect me to thank you."

"I don't. But we're both stuck with this situation, and I'd like to make the best of it."

"That's very well for you to say. You're not the one locked up in here."

I refrained from pointing out I hadn't seen a single locked door inside the Mews. "Is it so bad? They've given you every luxury. The people I saw on the way in looked happy."

"Of course they're happy. They were raised here. They don't know any better. And," Zaira added, glaring, "they can leave."

"You can, too. Just not alone."

Zaira snorted. "I'm sure you'll be happy to take me out with you anytime I want. You'll drop everything and head right over to the Mews whenever I call. Three times a day if I like."

I didn't need my mother to tell me that could never happen. "Well..."

Zaira adopted a prancing, limp-wristed stance. "You'll come get me for all your fancy parties. We'll have tea with the doge each Thursday. And when your mamma retires and you're on the Council of Nine, you'll gladly spend hours with me every day, following me around while I do my shopping."

"That's not realistic, and you know it!" I snapped.

"No," Zaira agreed, dropping the foppish act. "What's realistic is maybe once a day you'll pause and wonder how I'm doing, and a couple times a month you'll take me out for a horrible, awkward afternoon in town. And I'll have to act like I love it. Because when you're starving, you'll eat shit like it was a feast."

"I...I hope not." I yearned to make promises. To tell her I would come every day, and we could go wherever she wished. But I could feel my mother watching me, from all the way across the lagoon. *Never make promises,* La Contessa always said, *unless you are certain you can keep them. And even then, if you can, make the promise in your mind only, to yourself.* "I would like to do better by you than that."

"Good intentions don't buy bread."

"Well, what do you want to do so badly that you're desperate to get out of here?" I asked. "Forgive me, but you didn't seem very happy where you were."

Zaira looked away, anger in the line of her shoulders. Her gaze fell on the room's single window—and through it, across the lagoon to the city.

"There's an old man," she muttered, grudgingly.

"Who? Your grandfather?"

"Hells, no." Zaira brushed the idea off like dust. "If I have any family, they don't care enough to let me know it, so they can rot. No, just an old ragpicker. I owe him."

"You want to see him?" I tried to imagine visiting a ragpicker. And explaining to my mother afterward.

"No, idiot." Zaira shook her head. "I told you, I owe him. I want to pay him back."

"Well"—I struggled to force out the words—"I suppose, if that's what you truly wish, then when Lieutenant Verdi gives his permission..."

Zaira made a gagging noise. "Stop, before you make yourself a liar." She looked me up and down, as if assessing how little a cheap vase was worth. "You did try to stand up to Orthys's lot for me. I don't owe you anything, but in return for your good intentions, I'll tell you mine."

Zaira stepped in close, her voice dropping to a hiss. "Here's what I intend, Lady Jailer: the minute you release me, the very second you drop this stupid binding, I am going to burn my way out of here. And if anyone gets in my way, I'll burn down the whole cursed Mews if I have to. Do you understand?"

"You make yourself quite clear, yes."

"Good." Zaira smiled. "Then call your watchdog. I think we're through."

Verdi sighed. "I suppose it was too much to hope she'd warm to you."

"It's hard to imagine her warming to anyone, unless you count setting them on fire."

I sat on a bench in the Mews garden. Lieutenant Verdi perched on the head of a stone lion, a rueful smile on his lips. Honey-fruit bushes surrounded us, teasing the air with their delicious scent. The muffled calls of a formation drill in another courtyard belied the peace of the scene.

"I'm sorry for wasting your time, my lady."

"She didn't give me a chance." I ripped a leaf from an inoffensive bush. "The worst part is, she has a point. Zaira's going to be trapped here most of the time in a way other Falcons aren't, whose Falconers have no duties but to follow them around and keep them safe. And it'll get worse when I ascend to the Council of Nine."

Verdi spread his palm and examined it, as if he might read instructions there. After a moment he said, with exquisite care, "You could try living in the Mews. For a few days a week, at least. We really aren't such terrible company."

I shook my head. "It's not possible. The quality of the company isn't the issue, I assure you. I can't do anything that places me under your colonel's command, even symbolically. Which includes living in the Mews."

His hands flexed on his knees. "So you're telling me you can't do anything to so much as *imply* you take your duty as a Falconer as seriously as your duty as your mother's heir."

"Yes."

"I see." His shoulders tightened with frustration. For a moment I thought he would shout at me. But then he let out a long sigh, anger descending into disappointment. "That makes matters difficult, my lady."

I'd rather he'd shouted. The taste of guilt soured my mouth. "I'm sorry."

"If a Falconer can't live in the Mews and accompany their Falcon, the whole system falls apart. The serenity of the Empire depends on the loyalty of the Falcons, and we can't win their loyalty without giving them freedom." He lifted rueful eyes to my own. "I may have already gotten an earful from Colonel Vasante about what an impossible situation it is militarily that you're across the lagoon from your Falcon. For Zaira personally, it's a prison sentence."

"I don't want to do that to her." I started shredding my leaf. "If the jess binds Zaira's magic, she's not a threat, is she? Those with magic too weak to bear the mage mark don't have to stay in the Mews. They can live their lives however they want. With the jess on, Zaira has less power than they do. Couldn't you set her free, Lieutenant?"

"Please, my lady, call me Marcello."

"Marcello, then." My face warmed. It was the legacy of my barely remembered Callamornish father; I blushed far more easily than a pure Raverran would, with their darker, olive-bronze skin.

"And I wish we *could* just let her go, but it's not that easy." His tone became somber. "What do you think would happen if she wandered the city alone, without you there to unbind her power if she needed to defend herself?"

"I'm guessing the answer you're fishing for isn't 'She could live a normal life, happily ever after.'"

"She's a warlock," he said. "Even artificers and alchemists have to guard against kidnapping. There are murder attempts on our two storm warlocks every year. If we let Zaira go, she'd be dead or captured within the week. And if someone found a way to get the jess off, they might turn her fires on Raverra."

"I thought the whole point of jesses was that you *couldn't* get them off. At least, not without the Falconer's permission and the Master Artificer's help." It was the key to the Serene Empire's power. Hundreds of years ago, when all the other nations and city-states of Eruvia either hunted down the mage-marked or fell under their rule, Raverra's invention of jesses offered an alternative. A way to hold the mage-marked accountable to the rule of law and keep them from being used against their own country by the unscrupulous, at the cost of their independence. The slim golden bracelets had remained one of the Empire's most closely guarded assets ever since.

"No magic is absolute, as you saw when Zaira's fires fused her jess shut. They're supposed to be indestructible—I've never heard of jesses being so much as scratched before." Marcello shook his head. "We can't take the chance someone could find a way to remove or circumvent them. Not with a fire warlock."

I twirled the mangled leaf stem between my sap-sticky fingers. All that remained was a ragged spray of veins. "It still seems wrong, to keep her against her will."

"Maybe. Maybe it's the lesser evil to keep the Falcons protected here, and not the good I wish it was." He surged restlessly to his feet and began to pace. "You've hit on the core of every argument I have with the colonel. I believe the primary duty of the Falconers is to protect and care for the mage-marked. Or at least, that's how I *want* it to be. But nothing I do, no amount of compassion I can bring to my work here, changes the fact that this is a military corps. These are soldiers." A shriek of laughter rose up from elsewhere in the garden, and he winced. "Even the children."

"And they have no choice." That was the part that bothered me, like a splinter under my fingernail. "From the moment they're born."

"The mage-marked don't have much chance to make choices, even if the Falconers never find them."

Some heavy knowledge burdened his voice. I'd heard tales of all manner of tragedies happening to mages: murdered by superstitious folk, forced to use their powers in unsavory ways, or cast out in fear by their own families. Those without the mage mark could at least hide their abilities; and some did quite well in the open, starting magic shops or finding wealthy patrons. But the weaker magic of those without the mage mark was far less of a temptation or a threat. Perhaps one in a hundred people could manipulate magical energy at all; but without the mage mark, their capacity was limited and they lacked precise control. There was only so much they could do.

The mage-marked were a hundred times again more rare, and could channel far more power, handling it as easily as breathing, thanks to the additional magical dexterity and perception that came with the telltale ring in their eyes. They were human beings, people who loved and dreamed and feared the same as I did, with families and lives of their own. But their power was also a priceless resource, and some saw only that. I could only imagine the sort of awful stories Marcello had seen unfold in his years as a Falconer.

"Marcello." I hesitated, rolling the question around in my mind to find a way to put it. "Have you ever unleashed your Falcon to . . . to do harm?"

"No," he said quietly. "My Falcon is an artificer; she just

makes things. So, no. I haven't had to face that. But after five years in the Falconers, I've seen what magic can do. I gave the order to release a vivomancer, who bespelled a lion to kill three brigands in Osta. That was…messy. And I ordered a storm warlock to sink a pirate ship with all hands on deck." He shook his head. "Magic doesn't kill cleanly."

I crumpled the mangled leaf. "I suppose it's no different from when the Council of Nine passes a judgment of death. I should get used to the idea."

"Maybe not. Maybe you should never get used to it." He smiled sheepishly, as if I'd caught him doing something foolish. "The colonel thinks I'm soft. She says I'll have to toughen up if I want to take over the Falcons someday."

"And is that what you want?" I tried to picture him commanding the Empire's most important military unit. I sat in on military councils a couple times a month, out of my mother's hope I'd learn something; they were full of hard-eyed old men and women, jaded and cold. Marcello had too much warmth and expression in his clean, young face.

But he nodded, with firm resolve. "Yes. There's no better place from which to champion the Falcons than the top. I'm already second in command of the Mews itself—which sounds like a more important job than it is; I'm mostly in charge of training, since the Mews has never seen combat. But I could do more if I were the colonel." He smiled, and something moved in my chest at the pain in it. "Besides, for as long as I can remember my father and brother always insisted I'd be a disappointment. I can think of no better way to prove them wrong."

"Really? Your own family?" The idea seemed foreign and threatening. "I disappoint my mother all the time, but because she expects more of me than I deliver, not less."

He sank back down onto his lion head. Some old, bitter ache ghosted his eyes. "My brother is the golden child, the heir, born of the first, beloved wife, who died too young. My little sister and I are the unwanted afterthoughts born of the inconvenient second wife who ran off to join the theater and left us behind."

"That's cruel. To abandon her children like that."

Marcello shrugged. "I don't blame her. Much. My father can be a hard man to live with. There's a reason I became a Falconer at fourteen. Well, more than one, but getting out of his house was part of it."

I stared at him. A wistful gravity had drawn his brows down and sobered the lines of his face. Some quality about him had been nagging in the back of my mind since we met, like a piece of a song I'd forgotten. Something I never saw in my mother's world of carefully chosen words and courtly glamour. I recognized it at last: vulnerability.

For a moment, I couldn't think of any words that weren't stupid, and busied myself fiddling with a loose thread on my jacket.

"Marcello," I asked at last, "what will we do about Zaira?"

He let out a long breath. "We try again tomorrow. It's the only thing we can do."

La Contessa pulled me aside in the foyer of our palace, less than a minute after I'd stepped out of my boat on returning home from the Mews.

"It didn't go well, did it?" she said after one glance at my face.

"She's not happy with me, Mamma."

"I want to hear everything. But right now I have a few of the Council here, to discuss intelligence updates. Wait for me in the library; I'm sure you can amuse yourself there."

"An intelligence meeting?" I frowned. It wasn't the usual day, which meant something had happened to trigger one. "Does it have to do with my Falcon?"

"Perhaps. I hope not. Now, go to the library, and I'll join you there afterward."

"Yes, Mamma."

She slipped back into the drawing room from which she'd emerged, as if swept once more into the center of intrigue by a powerful current. I turned dutifully toward the library, though after my ill-fated meeting with Zaira and my mother's ominous pronouncement, I was more in a state of mind to brood than to read.

My mother's voice floated after me, through the drawing room door: "Back to the matter of Ardence."

I froze in midstep, as if she'd said my name. Ardence again. And a matter she hoped wouldn't involve my Falcon.

It couldn't be good for the city I'd called home for a year to draw such interest from the Council of Nine, whose attention was rarely healthy even when there was no chance of fire-warlock involvement. But before I could hear more, Anzo, one of our older servants, breezed through with a wine tray, casting me a sideways glance as I hesitated in the foyer. I had no legitimate reason to linger; if I was still here when he emerged from the drawing room, he'd shoo me gently but firmly off.

There was a listening post in the library, though. I hurried on my way.

The leather-and-old-pages smell of the library drained the tension out of my shoulders, and my favorite fainting couch beckoned me to sprawl with a good book and order a glass of sweet dessert wine and some biscuits. But instead of succumbing to the pull of my usual shelves of history, science, and magical theory, I made straight for a certain narrow bookcase in the wall the library shared with the drawing room. I hooked my fingers behind a carved vine in the decorative molding and eased open the secret door, careful not to yank too vigorously and spill the books as I'd done once as a child.

The narrow room between the walls held nothing more than a bench with a red velvet cushion, barely wide enough for my hips, and an artifice circle drawn on the wall. The runes and pattern of concentric circles amplified sound coming into the listening post, and reduced it going out.

I settled myself in and shut the door, plunging myself into darkness. The doge's voice immediately surrounded me.

"—new duke has gone too far. Fractious nobles daydreaming about Ardentine independence is one thing, but if Duke Astor Bergandon himself has levied a tax on Raverran merchants, that's in direct violation of the Serene Accords. I will not countenance such a brazen challenge to the agreement that forms the foundation of the Empire."

I gripped the edge of my bench. That didn't sound good. What was the duke of Ardence thinking? Raverra gave its vassal states almost complete liberty to govern themselves; but the Serene Accords, the pact that defined the fundamental relationship between Raverra and the tributary cities and countries of the Empire, were inviolate.

"This only proves what I've been saying. We allow city-states like Ardence far too much license." That was a new voice, a nasal male tenor: Baron Leodra, who fancied himself my mother's rival. "The Serene City should take direct command, to put a stop to such nonsense before it can occur."

"Duke Astor has been granted no more license than his father, or all his Bergandon ancestors before him, who abided by the Serene Accords peacefully for two hundred years." La Contessa's tone dismissed Leodra's suggestion. "The issue isn't that Ardence rules itself. It's that this particular duke is an ass."

"And yet the Serene Envoy to Ardence, your own cousin, requested weeks ago we empower him to overrule Duke Astor." Leodra's voice rose in pitch and volume. "I say we take it a step further and remove the duke of Ardence from power entirely."

"Do you *want* all our tributary states to rebel?" my mother asked acidly. "Because that's what will happen if you forcibly remove a sovereign ruler for so little reason. I worked too hard to bring the entire nation of Callamorne into the Empire to lose it over a minor disagreement with a single city. And as for my cousin…" Silk rustled. "Ignazio had a fine rapport with the old duke, and has maintained warm relations with Ardence as Serene Envoy for ten years. However, it seems this new duke is too brash to respond well to Ignazio's subtle guidance, and fails to understand how severely he has provoked the Serene City. We need a heavier hand at the tiller until Astor Bergandon settles down."

"You would remove your own cousin from such a coveted post?" The doge's dry surprise mirrored my own shock. Ignazio—Uncle Ignazio, as I called him—had hosted me during my year in Ardence, and was the one who brewed my elixir. He'd indulged me with gifts of alchemy and history books, and hours of intelligent conversation. I couldn't imagine he'd be happy to lose his position as the imperial power behind the ducal throne of Ardence.

"Call him home to give him some other honorable title." I could hear the shrug in my mother's voice. "Make him the Chancellor of the Exchequer. He's quite good with numbers."

"We must respond to Ardence's treason with decisive punishment, not a new nursemaid," Baron Leodra objected. "Besides, we already have a Chancellor of the Exchequer. I appointed her last spring."

"And she's a dull creature, without flair or imagination, who makes mistakes." The clink of a glass. "She can be removed."

"Very well." The doge's voice cut across Baron Leodra's indrawn breath. "We can discuss Ignazio's replacement as Serene Envoy at tonight's general meeting of the Council. Do we have any other new information pertinent to the Ardentine situation?"

"One more thing." La Contessa's voice dropped, and her tone went grim. "Something that could cause us far more trouble than breaking the Serene Accords, if we don't counter it soon."

I strained to listen.

Light fell across me, illuminating the artifice circle on the wall, and the voices went silent. I whirled to find Ciardha standing in the open door, one eyebrow raised in elegant disapproval.

Chapter Five

"I can explain!" I sprang to my feet, banging my head on the low ceiling of the listening post. "I was just—"

Ciardha lifted a finger to her lips. "A Cornaro does not need to explain, Lady. But your mother would be disappointed."

Shame scalded my neck. "I shouldn't have eavesdropped."

"No, Lady. Eavesdropping is a fine tradition of the Raverran elite. You shouldn't have gotten caught." She stepped aside and gestured me out of the secret room. "You need to be more aware of your surroundings, Lady. For your own safety."

"Ah." My voice came out thick with embarrassment. "I'll work on that."

"Still, La Contessa will be pleased you are taking an interest in politics at last." Ciardha's cocked head suggested a silent question mark.

I sank into a chair by the library fireplace. "I'm not so much interested in politics as worried about Ardence."

Ciardha nodded. "You have friends there."

"Yes. All my friends from the university." I laced my fingers and squeezed them together. "My old study partner, Venasha, has a baby. She and her family are at risk from this foolishness."

Venasha had a theory that new surroundings sparked the mind, so I'd spent hours poring over books with her in all manner of unlikely places: an amulet shop, a boat moored in the River Arden, the university roof. We'd found lacy undergarments up there once, and Venasha had somehow become convinced they belonged to her philosophy professor; I hadn't been able to look the professor in the eye since.

"Plus Domenic is the duke's cousin," I added, "so he may take some of the blame. And Uncle Ignazio, of course." My shoulders hunched under the memory of my mother casually proposing to strip him of his office. "The doge as much as told me he intends to use my Falcon to threaten anyone who goes against the Serene Empire. So it's not political. It's personal."

Ciardha smiled faintly. "All politics are personal, Lady."

"I don't like the idea of being used against my friends."

"Then, Lady, I have one piece of advice." Ciardha caught my eyes with her dark ones. "Don't let them use you."

"The Grace of Wisdom must hate me, to stick me with such a bunch of idiots." Zaira faced Marcello and me, arms crossed, in a bare-walled classroom. A half circle of wooden chairs embraced a low, broad stage at one end of the room. Marcello and I had taken seats with one empty chair between us, but Zaira remained standing.

"If you will deign to talk to us nonetheless," Marcello said wearily, "we can finish the interview regulations require us to conduct with new Falcons, and move on to the training for which Lady Amalia has come to the Mews. I only have an hour before I need to take a boat to the mainland to investigate an accusation of cattle cursing."

Zaira snorted. "Good to know I rank below cows for you."

Oh dear. I supposed I shouldn't be surprised we were off to a bad start, but he'd stumbled straight into that one.

Marcello looked as if he might argue, but sighed and let it pass. "So. Zaira, welcome to the Falcons. Our first priority after assuring your safety is taking care of your family. Is there anyone who might be worried about you?"

"You asked me this before." Her face was a locked gate, hard and blank.

"And you didn't answer. So I'm asking again."

Zaira's shoulders moved in the barest shrug. "I don't have family."

She said the word as if it were a particularly filthy social disease with which she disavowed all connection.

Marcello's voice softened. "Even family whom you don't care for, or whom you think don't care for you?"

"No one." Zaira clipped the words off with utter finality.

"Friends?" Marcello pressed. "Business associates? It's important for us to know about your connections. Not only do we want to do right by you but we want to make sure Raverra's enemies can't use them against you."

Zaira made a show of peering at Marcello's face. "Your black eye is fading. If you keep asking me the same question over and over, I can refresh it for you."

Marcello winced. "All right. How about enemies?"

"Orthys," she said immediately. "May the Demon of Corruption rot his poxy bowels."

"His men who attacked you said something about an indenture contract," I remembered.

"The old bilge rat claims he has a piece of paper that means my mother sold me to him, and I have to work for him." She showed her teeth. "But I don't have a mother. And I can't read. And paper burns."

"Ah." I digested this compelling legal argument. "Well, I'm glad he didn't get his hands on you."

Zaira shot me a contemptuous glare. "Don't fool yourself into thinking you saved me from anything. A jess is worse than any damned indenture contract."

Marcello passed a hand across his eyes. But he didn't rise to her bait. "So you were serving out this indenture contract to Orthys, and you ran away?"

"He never had me in the first place. I was free as the seagulls who crap on the Imperial Palace until you jailers found me." She spat on the floor. Marcello winced at the practiced smack of it striking the polished boards. I looked away. "I never heard of this contract until five or six years ago. My dear mother didn't stick around after I was born to tell me about it. Orthys comes through town every few months, so I have to dodge his scum when his ship is in port."

"He's a smuggler?" I guessed.

"I'm sure he's a fine, upstanding, tax-paying citizen of the Empire like everyone else around here who tries to drag a girl off against her will."

Marcello ignored that. "So who raised you, if you have no family and didn't grow up working for Orthys?"

Zaira flung herself down in a chair at last, as far from us as possible, with an attitude of exhaustion. "No one. It doesn't matter. Grace of Mercy's tits, can we skip my life story? Once there was a girl named Zaira, who lived just fine in the Tallows until some stuck-up morons shut her up in the Mews and bored her to death. The end."

"All right." Marcello sighed. "There are more questions I'm supposed to ask you, but we can move on to training instead."

Zaira straightened, her eyes glittering. "Oh? You'll have to loose my fire, if you want me to practice using it."

I glanced at Marcello. That sounded like a terrible idea, especially when she said it so eagerly.

He leaned on his elbows, meeting Zaira's gaze. "Before we

get to any practical training, we have to first build a partnership between you and your Falconer."

"Partnership," she said flatly. "Is that what you call it?"

"An equal partnership," Marcello affirmed. "Your Falconer can't give you orders. Only your superior officers can do that. Some of whom, I will point out, are Falcons."

"Oh, so I suppose they can just order their Falconers to come with them whenever they want to leave the Mews?" Zaira raised a skeptical eyebrow.

"They don't need to order anyone. They can just leave when they want, and their Falconers accompany them. Because they trust each other." Marcello put his hand over his heart, straining forward as if he could *will* Zaira to relent and believe him. "The first thing a Falcon and Falconer must learn—the first and most important—is trust. That is the foundation on which any partnership stands. Without it, we can't move on."

Zaira's lip curled. "I suppose now you'll expect me to sit here and listen to a lecture on how you can't count on a Tallows brat like me."

Marcello's brows dug a groove between them, and for a moment I thought he'd argue with her. But he shook his head. "No. I'm saying I can't expect *you* to trust someone who brought you here by force. Not yet. We have to earn *your* trust. By the time we've done that, we'll already know we can rely on you as well."

"Well, you're out of luck, then. Because I don't trust anyone." Zaira stood and turned her back on us, staring out the window at the sea.

"You could learn," I said.

"This lesson is over." Her voice was flat and hard as a dagger blade. "If you want trust, go buy it in the market with your mountain of gold, rich brat. Mine isn't for sale."

Out in the hall, Marcello slumped against the wall like a sail when the wind dies. "She's impossible. I don't know what to do."

"You must have had this problem before." I hesitated a moment, then leaned my back against the fine oak paneling beside him. "Surely not every Falcon comes eagerly to the Mews."

"No, they come as children. It's very different. Our challenge is getting the parents convinced this is best for their child, and settling whether the family will move into the Mews too, or if they'll just visit each other." A shadow passed through his eyes. "Or sometimes the child has no family, but if that's the case, usually we're rescuing them from a situation bad enough they're thrilled to be here. I've never had to deal with a new, uncooperative adult Falcon."

"Never, in five years?"

"The mage mark is usually fully formed by four years old. It's too hard to hide, and we find them, if someone else doesn't first. But you've seen her eyes—her mage mark is black, and you can barely make it out. She must have hidden it all these years."

I let out a long breath. "That's why she doesn't have anyone close to her. No friends, no partners, no lovers. Because they would meet her eyes."

"Grace of Mercy." He brought a hand to his face. "That's awful."

"It sounds like a terrible way to live," I agreed.

"I don't know how we overcome that to build a bond between you." He gave me a rueful half smile. One dimple formed a comma on his cheek, and suddenly the space between us seemed too narrow and too warm. "Especially with you only here for an hour or two at a time."

I wanted to protest, but it was the truth. I drummed my fingers against the wall, turning the problem over in my mind.

"I should take her out of the Mews with me." It was a daunting notion.

He ran his fingers through his hair, a worried gesture. "Yes. Graces help us, I think you should."

Exsolvo was not a word that came up in casual conversation. But I found myself nonetheless terrified it would somehow slip out.

It didn't help my peace of mind that Zaira kept glaring around the market in a manner suggesting frustrated disappointment that nothing was bursting into flame. With canopied wooden stalls overflowing with fruit and vegetables and thick crowds moving between them, there were a disturbing number of flammable objects about. I supposed I wouldn't have to worry about unleashing Zaira to burn Ardence if she burned Raverra first.

"This is stupid," Zaira grumbled, fingering a cluster of honeyfruit. The merchant glanced nervously at her scarlet uniform as he haggled with another customer. "I don't want to shop for moldy vegetables. I want to go talk to the ragpicker in the Tallows."

The vegetables were far from moldy. I didn't come to the produce market often myself—my interactions with food tended to begin when it arrived prepared at my table—but the lush greens and vibrant reds of the bounty around me shone bright as precious jewels. Scents of peach and fig teased me, and the calls of the merchants made a lively music. The Temple of Bounty loomed benevolently over the square, its columns carved with fruit and flowers; shrinekeepers passed out the merchants' leftover grain and bruised fruit to the poor on its steps.

I had to make this work, no matter how grumpy Zaira was. I had no doubt my mother and the doge would both receive reports of this outing.

"I did ask the lieutenant if we could go find this ragpicker of yours." I glanced at Marcello, who hovered a few paces away. His eyes shifted from me to Zaira. He'd been watching us closely all morning. "He felt we should start with something simpler."

Zaira snorted. "You mean he thinks that if we go to the Tallows, I'll knife you both and dump you in a canal."

"Well, perhaps."

"I notice you didn't have any trouble overruling him when he asked you to wear a uniform." The black ring around her pupils made Zaira's stare even more pointed.

I glanced down at the golden falcon's-head brooch pinned to my shoulder, the only concession I'd allowed poor Marcello. "On that question, my mother was his invisible opponent. In the matter of the ragpicker, she was his invisible ally."

Zaira lifted a skeptical eyebrow. "Your mother can turn invisible, now?"

"Of course not! I meant—"

"I know what you meant. You meant you've got jelly for a spine and always do what your mamma says." She jerked her head at Marcello. "And Lieutenant Black Eye over there isn't any better."

"That's not true!" I almost added, *If you met my mother, you'd understand*. But she might take it as an invitation, and I wasn't sure I could survive those two in the same room.

Zaira turned away from the fruit stand, boredom in the slouch of her shoulders. "Of course it's true. Or we'd be in the Tallows right now, talking to the ragpicker. Come on, I see someone selling meat on a stick."

Forcing my annoyed frown smooth, I stepped up beside her so I wasn't left trailing behind like a servant. Marcello moved in to walk at her other side. When Zaira picked out three hot skewers of chicken and mushrooms, Marcello paid for them from a purse embroidered with the winged horse of Raverra.

An Ardentine accent in the crowd jolted my memory, spilling other images of Ardence from the cauldron of worry that had simmered in the back of my mind since I overheard the intelligence briefing. The old men fishing off the Sunset Bridge, who told Venasha and me grisly stories of the Battle of the Arden, when the imperial infantry had lured Vaskandar into a deadly trap during the Three Years' War. The heartbreakingly perfect taste and cloud-light texture of the half-penny summernut pastry from the corner bakery across from the university library. Throwing coins in the Wishing Fountain outside the Temple of the Grace of Luck—Venasha had wished for her baby to be a girl, and I had wished for Domenic to notice me. Neither of us had gotten what we wished for, but were happy enough with the results anyway.

My sunny bedroom at the Serene Envoy's Palace, with its window overlooking the garden. Ignazio would be moving out now, to make room for the new envoy. One with a *heavier hand at the tiller,* whatever that meant.

Nothing good, I suspected, for the people and places I loved.

"Be careful," Marcello murmured, pulling me back to Raverra and the bustling market, his breath tickling my ear. "There may be pickpockets in the crowd."

Willing myself not to flush never worked. "Of course."

"Our charge possibly among them."

I looked more sharply at Zaira. Even in the crowded market, most people left an uneasy space around her bright Falcon's uniform. A brocaded patrician couple eyed me as well, from a distance; the woman whispered to the man behind her hand, no doubt spreading gossip about the Cornaro Falcon. My mother would like that. Or they could be commenting on my breeches, which my mother would like less, but at least my coat was impeccably fashionable this time, covered in baroque gold embroidery over rich green velvet.

Not everyone gave Zaira a wide berth, however. She brushed by a shawled gentlewoman whose dreamy attention stayed locked on the mounds of golden apricots she was perusing.

A moment later, I noticed a dark lump tucked into Zaira's hand.

Marcello lunged for her arm, turning it to reveal a small leather purse.

"Give it back," he hissed.

Zaira yanked her arm free. She threw the stolen purse into Marcello's chest. "Do it yourself."

No one in the crowd had noticed anything yet, but from the stubborn lines of Marcello's shoulders and Zaira's jaw, this could explode into a full-blown scene any minute. The last thing I needed was rumors flying around that the Cornaro Falcon was a thief.

"I'll do it." I scooped the purse out of Marcello's hands before anyone could object.

I hurried to the lady Zaira had jostled, who now contemplated purple-tipped tartgrass, and tapped her shoulder.

"Excuse me. I think you dropped this."

The woman gasped in recognition, and she heaped such profuse thanks on me I had trouble disentangling myself. By the time I made it back to Zaira and Marcello, they were deep in argument.

"Maybe you should have thought about whether you wanted someone like me in this uniform before you forced me to wear it," Zaira snapped.

Marcello turned to me, grimacing. "My apologies, Lady Cornaro. The last thing I intended was to embarrass or endanger you. We should return to the Mews."

Zaira's dark eyes flickered, and she tensed. I had the impression she was ready to bolt off into the crowd.

Marcello must have thought the same, because he lifted his hand, and all at once four large men surrounded Zaira. A moment ago, they had been part of the crowd: farmers and workmen. They made no move to threaten her. One pretended to point out the spires of the Temple of Bounty to another, while two compared purchased fruit. But they stood between her and any possible escape, poised and ready on the balls of their feet.

Zaira laughed. "So, I'm not a prisoner, am I?"

"Apparently you should be, given your behavior," Marcello retorted.

"I did it to draw them out." Zaira surveyed the four disguised soldiers, hands on her hips. "And it worked. Though I'd spotted three out of four. Might want to work on that."

I'd had no idea about any of them. I turned to Marcello, biting back anger. "Lieutenant Verdi, I thought we were here to build trust. Was this necessary?"

He winced. "For your safety, my lady, yes."

My hands curled tight at my sides. I didn't trust myself to speak.

Zaira had no such compunctions. She rolled her eyes. "Yes, because I'm so terrifying, especially with your stupid jewelry keeping my fires out."

"I'm sorry it came to this." I fought to keep my tone level. "Perhaps we can try again soon, with more honesty on all sides."

"I've got something better than honesty now," Zaira said. "Truth. Now I know how to value all your talk about trust and partnership."

"And I have your measure as well," Marcello replied through his teeth. "Now I know how you survived in the Tallows."

He didn't say the word, but it hung silent in the air between them. *Thief.*

We took two boats back to the Mews. Marcello and I rode in one, and Zaira and the disguised guards in the other. Marcello must be worried she'd try to heave us out into the lagoon if we sat with her. By the glower on her face, I couldn't blame him.

He remained silent at first, as the uniformed oarsman guided us down the Imperial Canal, always keeping Zaira's boat at our side. Other craft gave the red-and-gold boats space, passengers and oarsmen casting dubious glances at Zaira's uniform. No one wanted to tangle oars with a Falcon.

After today, I didn't much fancy her company myself. Why couldn't I have put the jess on a nice, willing artificer or alchemist, who could collaborate with me on magical research? But here I was, tethered for life to a surly pickpocket of a fire warlock, with whom the only thing I shared in common was that someday we might bring disaster upon a city I cared for.

"I didn't handle that well, did I," Marcello said at last, his brows drawn down in worry.

"No. You didn't." I wasn't sure what angered me more: that I hadn't known about the guards or that they'd been necessary.

He sighed. "I shouldn't have kept the guards a secret from either of you. I'm sorry. I hoped Zaira wouldn't notice, and feel less like a prisoner, but it backfired."

"What were you so afraid of, anyway? Did you know Zaira was a thief?"

"No." Marcello glanced down into his lap. His rapier hilt and the butt of a flintlock pistol flanked his hips. It must have taken a fair amount of practice to master boarding a boat with the former. "The soldiers weren't to keep her in line. They were there to protect you."

I stared. "Me?"

"Both of you."

"Marcello, I go out in the city without escort all the time. It's insulting to pretend I need four guards—four *secret* guards—in a public market in broad daylight."

"I know, my lady. It's excessive." He rubbed the back of his head. "But your safety is my first priority. If anything happened to you..." He trailed off, glancing away at the canal.

"Yes?" The end of that sentence mattered. I willed him to finish it.

"Well, for one thing, I'd probably lose my position." He laughed, but it was a stiff sound, not his usual free and easy one. "I can only imagine what they'd do to me if I allowed harm to come to the Cornaro heir. And Zaira's security is critical to the Empire. The doge is after the colonel already, asking if our new fire warlock is safe and sound and ready for duty. And the colonel's on *me* to let me know it's my head if she isn't. If anything happened to either of you, at best I'd be heading back home to tell my father and brother they were right, and I failed."

My lips tightened against his words as if they were sour wine. "I see."

For a moment, silence lay between us. It was an uncomfortable thing, heavy and rough, like a wet wool blanket.

Finally, he met my eyes. "Also, my lady, I consider you a friend. If it isn't too presumptuous."

Something eased in my shoulders. "Not at all."

This time, the quiet that fell on our boat was softer, punctuated by the working of the oar and the rush of the prow through the deep green waters of the lagoon.

"Well," he said at last, "at least you and Zaira can agree on one thing."

"What?"

His mouth quirked. "That a certain lieutenant is an infuriating fool."

"Only sometimes." I smiled, so he wouldn't take it too much to heart. "Most of the time, I think we'd still disagree about you most vehemently."

The last of my anger slipped away as the Imperial Canal fell behind us and our oarsman rowed us toward Raptor's Isle. But something else crept in after it, growing with the inexorable chill of the shadows that swallowed the canals each day at sunset.

The doge is after the colonel already, asking if our new fire warlock is safe and sound and ready for duty, he'd said.

Ready for duty.

For Marcello, that word meant following his colonel's orders and keeping his Falcons safe. For me, it meant fulfilling my social obligations and learning to govern the Empire. But for Zaira, *duty* meant destruction and death.

She was such a skinny thing, hunched grumpily in her boat, glaring across the water at the Mews. It seemed impossible she could contain so much fire.

All I wanted on returning home from our disastrous outing in the market was to skulk off to my room and bury myself under the covers with my Muscati spread across my knees, consoling myself with artifice theory and perhaps a rosemary biscuit. But Old Anzo waited for me in the foyer, and diverted me from my path to the stairs with a discreet cough.

"La Contessa wants you in the drawing room, Lady Amalia."

Foreboding lodged in my throat like an olive pit. The drawing room door was closed. That meant Council business.

"Should I change first, Anzo?"

He shook his head, sympathy softening the motion. "I believe she wants you now, my lady."

Perhaps she merely wanted to ask me how my day had been, and the drawing room door was closed because she had a headache. I straightened my lace cuffs and took a deep breath.

"All right. I'm ready."

Chapter Six

I wasn't ready. And if my mother had a headache, it had no bearing on the status of the drawing room door.

The handful of people gathered in the oak-paneled room had the power to order executions, mobilize armies of spies, or start wars. I'd often heard their voices murmuring downstairs late into the night when I was a child, as golden light filtered in through my bedroom window from the drawing room below. Sometimes, when the voices kept me awake, I'd crept to the long balcony at the top of the stairs to listen, pressing my cheek against the cool marble balustrade. I'd only caught occasional words: snippets of espionage and assassination, machinations and stratagems, negotiations and judgments. To my young ears, those words that governed and shaped the Empire had sounded so impenetrably dull they'd soothed me into sleepiness, like a lullaby.

One of my few memories of my father was of him finding me there, half asleep on the balcony floor, and laughing as he scooped me up to carry me back to my room. *That talk is not for you and me, little one,* he'd said. *Leave it to your mother.*

But now my mother beckoned me in among them. Jaded old eyes assessed me, some glancing to compare me to La Contessa, as if wondering how we could possibly be related.

The doge himself occupied my favorite chair. Beside my mother sat the marquise of Palova, a white-haired woman who'd once ordered the bloodiest assault of the Three Years' War, and who was well into her sixth five-year term in one of the elected seats on the Council of Nine. She swirled the wine in her glass, little finger extended to trace her thoughts in the air. Baron Leodra greeted me with a sniff of disdain.

"I suppose she'll do," the marquise said.

That was not a reassuring start to the conversation. I swallowed a sudden dryness.

"Do you know Prince Ruven of Vaskandar?" the doge asked.

Whatever I was expecting, it wasn't that. "Ah…" Was Ruven the general who'd led the Vaskandran invasion of Loreice during the Three Years' War? No, that was Halven. I tried to remember the names of the seventeen Witch Lords who ruled Vaskandar, but with half the Council staring at me, I could only recall six of them. "No, Your Serenity. Should I?"

My mother's fingers flicked up from her lap, a creamy envelope tucked between them. "The Vaskandran ambassador has invited you to meet the prince, who is his guest, in an informal gathering at his town house."

A tired flare of anger warmed my chest. "I was unaware of the invitation." *Because you intercepted my mail.*

"I've sent your acceptance." If my mother noticed any edge in my words, she declined to acknowledge it. "We have some concerns about Ruven's purpose in Raverra. His visit is unusual; our peace with Vaskandar remains an uneasy one, even fifty years after the war, and Ruven's father is hardly the most cordial of the Witch Lords. This invitation may provide a chance to find out what he's up to."

None of this made any sense. My mother knew full well I was no spy. "I don't understand. You want me to ask him the reason for his visit?"

The marquise of Palova laughed. "He's already given one. It makes you uniquely suited to speak to him."

My mother's mouth quirked. "He claims to be seeking a bride."

"Oh, no." I shook my head, stepping back. "You can't possibly want me to—"

"To attend a harmless social gathering with him?" My mother's eyes gleamed. "You don't have to court him, Amalia. Just let him talk, and listen to what he says, and perhaps nudge the conversation in a useful direction."

"Isn't there someone else? I have no idea why he invited me. I don't know the man, and I've barely been introduced to the ambassador." Not to mention everything I knew about Vaskandar came from reading bloody histories of its ruthless expansion across northern Eruvia. Its princes hardly seemed the types to make genteel drawing room conversation.

The doge fixed his glittering eyes on me. "Prince Ruven is the heir of one of the Witch Lords of Vaskandar. They have a rather inflated regard for their own bloodlines, and will only consider marriages with the best families—and those with some history of magical power." His brows bunched, as if breeding magical potential into royal lines were some annoying and messy habit, like shelling summernuts in bed. "Your father's line carries the blood of artificers and vivomancers, and your mother's cousin Ignazio is a minor alchemist. Your pedigree is golden, rich with doges and royalty, and you will inherit your mother's place on the Council of Nine. There are few in Eruvia he would consider so desirable a match."

"Which means you have something he wants," the marquise concluded. "And thus a far better chance of getting useful information out of him."

Baron Leodra grunted. "I still say Ruven isn't worth our attention. He's just a spoiled princeling indulging himself abroad. Surely if he had a more sinister purpose, our intelligence services would already have some hint of it. Or are they not worthy of the faith we place in them?" He stared significantly at La Contessa.

"We have someone in the Vaskandran ambassador's household." My mother shook her head. "So far, he's learned nothing of Prince Ruven's true purpose in Raverra. But he did discover that Ruven stopped in Ardence on his way here, shortly before the tax trouble began. Apparently he spent some time there, gaining influence with the local nobility, and there is now an entire faction in the Ardentine court pushing for closer relations with Vaskandar."

"That borders on treason," the marquise of Palova observed.

The doge steepled his fingers. "Many things Ardence does these days border on treason."

So this princeling had been stirring up trouble in my second-favorite city. All right, then. Maybe I wanted to know what he was up to after all.

"Fine," I said. "I'll go and talk to him. When is this little soiree?"

"Afternoon tea. A Vaskandran tradition." My mother passed me the invitation. "Next Tuesday."

"I was going to train with Zaira at the Mews that afternoon."

"Zaira?" Baron Leodra asked sharply.

"My Falcon," I said, without thinking.

Baron Leodra scowled his disapproval. "The *Empire's* Falcon."

"Regardless," the doge cut that line of conversation short, "she can wait."

Lovely. Now I had to cancel my training, disappoint Marcello, and confirm everything Zaira thought about me, all for the privilege of awkward flirting with a mad tyrant's son.

My mother looked pleased as a cat licking cream off its whiskers.

Prince Ruven did not appear, at first glance, to be mad.

I had never met a Witch Lord's son before, but Vaskandar's

rulers had a certain reputation. The Witch Lords had begun as a handful of powerful and universally feared mages in the far north, long before the birth of the Empire. Every thirty or forty years they'd engulfed a new domain in bloody conquest, raising a new Witch Lord to rule over it, until they ran up against the Witchwall Mountains over a hundred years ago.

They'd tried to take Loreice twice, where the mountains gentled to hills on its northern border. The first time, it had still been an independent country, and the king of Loreice had begged Raverra for aid; his country wound up safe, but a client state of the Serene Empire. The second invasion launched the Three Years' War, fifty years ago. The Witch Lords had left a scarlet-edged impression on my grandparents' generation with their ruthless cruelty in that war, and even the Vaskandran diplomats and merchants I'd met spoke of them in hushed tones, making the old peasant sign to ward against demons.

I'd heard them called mad often enough that I'd steeled myself for tea with a lunatic.

Prince Ruven, however, greeted his guests with perfect manners, a vision of civility. He cut a genteel figure in his impeccable blond ponytail and high-collared coat of soft black leather. The angular designs of its violet embroidery set off the matching ring of the mage mark in his storm-gray eyes.

The Vaskandran ambassador danced attendance on him like a fawning servant. Perhaps two dozen guests, split between young Raverrans of patrician birth and visiting nobility from other cities of the Empire, milled around the ambassador's great hall. The architecture was far more austere than the town houses of Raverran nobility, with dark beams and a high, vaulted ceiling. Candles flickered on little round tables set with silver and draped with violet brocade.

I didn't want to be here. False laughter floated up to the rafters, and the stuttering candles and weak sunlight streaming through the high windows did nothing to appease the gloom of the hall. The place might look nothing like the Raverran drawing rooms I knew, but it was yet another party my mother was making me attend, full of near strangers with whom I had nothing in common.

For this, I'd called off my training at the Mews. I'd gone out to Raptor's Isle in the morning to try to make up for it, but Marcello was with the colonel and a handful of other senior officers in a meeting, and Zaira refused to see me.

"Lady Amalia Cornaro." It was the prince himself, his Raverran accented but flawless. "It's time to sit for tea. Won't you join me at my table?" He laid his fingertips against my elbow, in diffident guidance.

Time to be charming. What did charming people do? I tried a smile. "I'd be delighted."

The tables were set for four, but no one else sat at ours. A Raverran lordling veered in our direction, eyeing an empty seat; the Vaskandran ambassador himself graciously directed him elsewhere.

Glancing from this interception to the avid glitter in Ruven's mage-marked eyes, I had the sudden, gut-tightening feeling this was a trap.

"So." Ruven laced his fingers together and set his chin on them, staring at me. "You are the unexpected Falconer I've heard so much about these past few days. The rule breaker."

I shifted uncomfortably. My corset stays dug into my lap. "I never intended to become one, I assure you."

"Ha!" He flashed his teeth in a vulpine smile. "You and I, we are beyond the reach of rules. They are beneath us. Don't you agree?"

I doubted the doge would. "There are those who would argue law is the foundation on which the Serene Empire stands."

Ruven chuckled. "Laws. Laws are an armor of words in which

fools gird themselves. They provide no more protection than the wind spent to speak them." A Vaskandran servant arrived with a bone china teapot and began filling our cups. The prince didn't lean back to give him room. "In Vaskandar, the merest whim of a Witch Lord is greater than law. A Witch Lord wears his domain like a glove; the land itself bows to his will. It is why your Empire has never conquered us."

His gesturing hand glanced off the servant's elbow, and a few drops of tea spilled on the tablecloth. A soft gasp sucked between the servant's teeth.

Quick as a striking viper, Ruven seized the man's wrist. The teapot crashed to the floor, shattering into leaf-patterned pieces. The servant paled.

"Your Highness," he whispered, "Forgive me. Please."

The conversation in the hall paused a brief moment, then resumed. Ruven did not let go of the man's wrist.

"For instance," he continued conversationally, his eyes with their violet mage mark still turned on me, "My father is a Fur-witch. They call him the Wolf Lord of Kazerath. If this fool spilled at *his* table, the wolf pack that guards our hall would rip him apart."

The servant's hand spasmed as if in pain, and a wild grimace stretched his features, but he made no sound. I half rose from my chair.

Ruven still didn't release him. "My aunt is a Greenwitch, so she might prefer to impale him with thorns. I, on the other hand, am a Skinwitch. You would call all three of us vivomancers, but in Vaskandar we consider the distinction important. Humans, not animals or plants, are my specialty. So I could melt the bones in his arm, or rot his flesh, or stop his heart—"

I couldn't bear the naked terror on the servant's face any longer. I cut my words across Ruven's like a knife. "But you aren't in your father's hall. You are in Raverra."

A delighted smile lit Ruven's face. "But you see, it doesn't matter. Power is power. I am a Skinwitch, and I wear no silly golden bracelet like your tame Falcons do. No one here could stop me from doing whatever I wish. And I am a prince of Vaskandar, beyond the authority of your Council or your doge. They would not dare attempt to seize me over such a trifle as a servant's life."

The servant's lips moved, mouthing *please, please, please,* over and over again. But no sound came out. Ruven's grip seemed loose enough, but a trickle of blood ran down the man's wrist.

I forced myself to ease back into my chair, as if I didn't care what happened to him. "The graveyards of Eruvia are full of powerful men who thought they could predict what the doge and the Council would or wouldn't dare." I shrugged my stiff shoulders. "But that's irrelevant. You won't do any of that, because it would be uncouth. A gentleman does not make a scene and ruin a party thrown in his own honor."

"Ah." Ruven nodded thoughtfully. "You make a fine point, Lady Amalia."

He released the servant at last. I glimpsed a red handprint on the man's wrist before he pulled it into his sleeve. He bowed to the prince and bent to clean up the teapot, as if the threat of death were a normal part of his workday.

Perhaps it was. I resolved never to move to Vaskandar, even if Raverra sank into the sea and the rest of the Empire were on fire.

"So," I said brightly—anything to draw his attention away from the servant until he could get out of here—"My reading suggests most vivomancers can only affect plants and animals, and even those whose powers work on humans do so only weakly. But you specialize in them?"

"Indeed." Ruven stretched his spine straight, like a satisfied cat. "What you call vivomancy originated in Vaskandar. We have few other types of mages—perhaps a handful of alchemists and artificers, and no warlocks. But in the magic of life itself, we are stronger than any other land in Eruvia, and we deepen our power with a specialty. Furwitches and Greenwitches feel a connection to lesser forms of life, and often claim that bending their skill upon humans is uncomfortable, or even revolting. But I find working human flesh has certain...advantages."

Was that a leer? I fought the urge to scoot my chair back a few inches. "So your focus on humans is a choice, or perhaps a calling, rather than an inborn trait like being a storm or fire warlock."

"Ah, yes, fire warlocks." Ruven's eyes narrowed. "I do believe yours is the only one currently alive in Eruvia, you know. Such a lucky catch."

I didn't feel lucky. "The Serene Empire is fortunate to have her."

"Not so fortunate for her, though." He produced a sigh. "If only she'd been born in my country. We are not so backward as your Empire. Our mage-marked are not slaves. In Vaskandar, we rule."

"Falcons aren't slaves. Unless you consider soldiers to be slaves. Raverra gives them orders no differently than it does to the rest of the military. Their Falconers don't own them, or even outrank them. They stay with their Falcons to protect them."

Ruven smirked knowingly. "Except you."

I thought of Zaira, stuck in the Mews because I was here instead of with her. Guilt pinched my middle. I nodded in reluctant acknowledgment. "To the consternation of virtually everyone involved, yes. Except me."

He ran a finger along the rim of his untouched teacup. "I'm sure you realize this makes you quite a delicious catch yourself."

I laughed nervously. Another servant placed a tiered tray of cakes on the table, buying me time to swallow my bile and think of a response.

"A Cornaro is no fish to be caught," I said at last, bringing my cup to my lips to steady my hands. "We are the masters of the fleet."

The spark in Ruven's eyes sharpened to a hard gleam. "There is nothing more attractive than power." His reach for a cake strayed in my direction.

Thud. A heavy, leather-bound book thumped down on the table next to me. "Amalia! What good fortune! I never dreamed I'd meet you here."

I spun in my seat, choking on my tea. "Domenic?"

There he was, like a miracle: Domenic Bergandon, resplendent in a slashed-sleeve doublet and a dashing swagger, throwing himself into an empty chair at our table with the ease of a man always sure of his welcome. The frizzy coils of his hair and the deep-brown skin he'd inherited from his mother, an Ostan princess, presented a polar opposite to Ruven's sleek paleness.

"My abject apologies for being late." Domenic placed his hand over his heart and bowed to Ruven from his seat. "My carriage lost a wheel on the road from Ardence, and I only arrived in Raverra this morning. I almost missed your invitation entirely."

Ruven glared across the hall at the Vaskandran ambassador, who was caught in conversation with another late guest and hadn't noticed Domenic's trespass at the prince's table. "That would have been a terrible shame," he said.

"I didn't know you were visiting Raverra." I tried to pour all my gratitude into my smile. "This is such a pleasant surprise."

"I do like to make a well-timed dramatic entrance." Domenic's near eyelid twitched half a wink at me. So he'd noticed what was happening, and rescued me on purpose. "But in truth, I didn't know I was coming either, until the morning I left. The squabbling on the Council of Lords got to be too much for me, and I needed to get away from the pompous old scoundrels."

"I see you know each other." Prince Ruven showed his teeth. "I had no idea. I made the viscount's acquaintance during my visit to his charming city on my way here from Vaskandar."

Domenic nodded. "We met in the Ducal Library. Did you know Prince Ruven is a scholar?"

"Truly?" I grasped at the subject, eager to talk about anything besides my own eligibility or the various ways one might murder one's servants. "Have you studied at a university?"

Ruven waved a depreciative hand. "My expertise and interests are limited to practical applications of magic. We do not have universities in Vaskandar. It is a wild land, a beautiful land, where we learn the rough lessons the forests and the mountains teach us. But it does mean I must travel to the Empire to sate my craving for books and learning."

"Well, we do have one thing in common," I said. "I am quite fond of books as well, with a particular interest in the magical sciences."

"You would love our family library in Kazerath, then." Ruven held my eyes. "I have assembled the finest collection of books on magic in Vaskandar. You must come and visit."

"Speaking of books Amalia would love..." Domenic drummed his fingers on the volume he'd dropped on our table, grinning. "You'll never believe what I found in a bookshop in Palova."

"Oh?" I raised an eyebrow. I wanted to tell him about the Muscati, but Ruven's presence would spoil the revelation. Better to wait until I had it in hand to show him.

"Volume one of *Interactions of Magic!*" He spread his hands wide, as if inviting applause.

I frowned, trying to remember. "Didn't they have volume two in the Ducal Library in Ardence?"

"Indeed! But it kept referring back to volume one, so it didn't make much sense. Which was a pity, because it laid out some interesting ways to combine seemingly incompatible types of magic, like alchemists and vivomancers working together, but we couldn't figure it out without all the pieces."

Ruven leaned forward. "I am interested in this book as well. I have heard of it."

"But now you have the first volume!" I eyed the book with more appetite than I'd had for the cakes. "Have you had a chance to read it yet?"

"I've only perused it a bit. I'm hoping to read it along with the second volume when I eventually return to Ardence."

"Perhaps I can join you in the Ducal Library on my return trip, then." Ruven eyed the book. Relief washed over me to have his attention directed elsewhere. "Ardence is a fine city, and merits more of my attention on my way back to my beloved Vaskandar."

From there, the conversation turned to the merits of the university library versus the Ducal Library. Ruven remained a perfect gentleman, showing no signs of his earlier viciousness. I relaxed enough to nibble a couple of apple cakes and a miniature summernut tart, though I still felt any social occasion that didn't serve wine was an aberration against the Grace of Bounty.

I managed to avoid Prince Ruven's attempt to kiss my hand when it was time to leave, giving him a cheery wave instead as I offered my thanks to him and our host.

"It was a pleasure to make your acquaintance at last, my lady." Ruven placed a hand over his heart, in lieu of a bow. "And I am quite certain we'll meet again."

What did he mean, *at last?* I couldn't manage more than a perfunctory smile in return.

I felt his violet-ringed eyes on my back as Domenic and I made our way through the milling guests, all the way across the hall.

Chapter Seven

Domenic and I paused to say our good-byes on the floating town house dock, where our boats awaited us. The lowering sun caught glints of gold and rose in the water on one side of the canal, draping the other in advancing shadows.

"Thank you," I murmured to Domenic. I couldn't help admiring the way the light caught his cheekbones and gilded his broad shoulders. I'd given up on him years ago, but he still cut a fine figure; my old admiration provided a comfortable warmth, like the bright, small flame of a reading lamp.

He laughed. "I thought you might need some company. I wouldn't want to be alone with Prince Ruven myself. He's a nasty one."

"What was he doing in Ardence?"

"Causing trouble." Domenic grimaced. "A certain segment of the Ardentine court finds him impressive—my younger brother, Gabril, sadly, among them. They've started a fight in the Council of Lords over whether we should cozy up to Vaskandar in place of Raverra, and it's gotten to the verge of rude names and hair pulling. That's why I left; I refuse to get involved. But Ruven's friends on the Council of Lords seem to think Vaskandar is the magical answer to all the city's financial woes, ever since that viper talked to them."

I thought of the red print Ruven's hand had left on the servant's wrist. "I wouldn't want to owe anything to Vaskandar."

"That's because you're no fool, Amalia Cornaro." Domenic shook out his arms, as if casting off dust that had settled on him. "Bah! Let's not talk about it. Politics! I'm not cut out to be on the Council of Lords."

"But you have so many good ideas." I nudged him with my elbow. "I remember you holding forth at a party, somewhat drunk, about how the River Arden is the city's lifeblood and... something fine-sounding about reducing docking fees."

"I wasn't drunk! Not more than a little, anyway." He sighed fondly. "I remember that party. I filched a bottle of heirloom reserve Loreician white from the River Palace wine cellars to celebrate the birth of Venasha's baby."

"It was a good party." I tilted my head. "I thought that when you reached your majority and took your father's empty Council seat, you'd surely change the world."

"I thought that, too, in my few and fleeting moments of embracing responsibility. But the lords of the Council don't want to change the world, Amalia. They're selfish and cynical, and they only want more status and money for themselves. They're running the city into the ground and ignoring its problems, to the point of disaster." He kicked at a mooring post. "Thank the Graces my father abdicated before the ducal throne fell to him, or it'd be my rock full of stingroaches to deal with instead of Astor's."

I stared at him. "I didn't realize your father was in the direct line of succession. You would have been the ducal heir?"

"Yes." Domenic's cocky smile returned. "But that bullet missed, thanks to my departed father's foresight in passing up the throne in favor of his younger brother. Now I have the freedom to run off and visit my friends when the company of my peers starts chafing like a saddle rash."

I forced a laugh. But I couldn't help but think if Domenic were duke, Ardence wouldn't be stirring up so much trouble.

"You must come visit me soon, and bring your new book," I said. "I have one to show you, as well."

"It will be my greatest delight." Domenic flourished a bow. "I can't wait to look at *Interactions of Magic* with you. Some of it is brilliant, and some of it is...ambitious?"

"Oh? Like the time you tried to design an artifice device to do your artifice homework for you?"

"Perhaps not *that* ambitious." He grinned. "The author has some grandiose ideas. He has wild dreams of using a combination of vivomancy and artifice to harness forces normally beyond the control of either. He babbles about inscribing gargantuan circles around entire forests or mountains." He snorted. "As if you could maintain any kind of precision at that scale. It'd be more unstable than a drunk Loreician's periwig. Have you ever heard such madness?"

Madness. I caught his eyes. "Domenic...All the same, don't show this book to Prince Ruven."

"I can't imagine this technique would work. And Ruven did say he was interested in the book." A frown pinched a divot between Domenic's brows. "But you have a point. I don't think I will."

I didn't remember until I was on my way home, with the canal waters lapping at the prow of my boat and the sun stooping to touch the roofs of the town houses, that I was supposed to find out why Prince Ruven had come to Raverra. So I felt a fool, no matter what Domenic said, when my mother came home from the Imperial Palace and called me to the drawing room to ask what I had learned.

I told her everything Ruven had said and done. She pried more details from my memory with fine-edged questions as Ciardha brought her a glass of wine and a silver tray with paper and writing tools. La Contessa dashed off a note and passed it to Ciardha while I spoke.

Ciardha glanced at the paper and nodded. "It will be done, Contessa."

It could be anything, from getting a nice piece of toast to assassinating the king of Osta. Ciardha's efficient glide as she left would remain the same.

"I had hoped you would learn more," my mother sighed when I was done at last.

Shame heated my cheeks. "I did my best, Mamma."

"No matter." She tapped her pen against the tray. "He is far too interested in you. You and your fire warlock. And I'm sure he's not the only one. I want you armed and wearing a flare locket at all times."

"I don't have a flare locket."

"You will by morning. If you ever need to open it, remember to close your eyes, and move quickly: the light will only blind your opponents for a few seconds." She frowned. "I'll have Ciardha give you further instruction in the dagger, as well. Daily lessons, every morning."

I wanted to tell her this was silly, and no one would attack me. But the elixir I took twice a day to neutralize an old poison suggested otherwise, as did the faint scar on the back of my right wrist from an assassin's knife at a garden party in Palova three years ago. My mother was untouchable, sure in the power that surrounded her like Zaira's nimbus of fire. Her enemies considered me more vulnerable.

So I bowed my head. "Yes, Mamma."

She came and laid her hand on my hair, like a benediction, wineglass still in her other hand. "Be unafraid, Amalia. If you are without fear, they will assume there is a reason, and hesitate. And the Grace of Victory will favor you."

I would rather the Grace of Luck favored me, and kept me

out of dangerous situations altogether. But she hadn't shown me much affection of late.

"You should go change into something suitable for entertaining family. Your Uncle Ignazio is coming in two hours."

I glanced, without meaning to, at the wall that hid the library listening post. "He's...no longer in Ardence?"

La Contessa followed my gaze, then raised an eyebrow. "You don't need to be coy about it, child. I sent you to this library that day for a reason; I wanted you to know. Yes, he's returned to take up his new post as Chancellor of the Exchequer."

"It..." I swallowed. "It doesn't seem right, Mamma."

"Right has nothing to do with it. We can't risk rebellion in a city three days' ride from Raverra over my cousin's feelings. The fact that Astor Bergandon instituted those illegal taxes at all shows Ignazio wasn't the right man for the job anymore."

Rebellion. My breath snagged on its way in. When I'd been in Ardence, sometimes the young nobles' sons lamented their proud city owing fealty to Raverra, with typical Ardentine passion. But in restless Ardence, that was mere drawing room conversation, with no spark of true rebellion behind it. Something must have changed.

La Contessa's voice dropped to a murmur. "So far as Ignazio is concerned, the decision to replace him was the doge's alone. We can spare him that much."

I didn't like the idea of helping my mother mislead Ignazio, even to spare his feelings. But I nodded. "He's coming here?"

"Yes. I invited him for a glass of wine, to welcome him back to Raverra. Don't mention Ardence unless he does first. Follow his lead, and mine."

Since Ignazio was family, my mother received him in the parlor. Its wide windows opened on the fairyland of water-mirrored light that was the Imperial Canal in the evening. Lush pastoral paintings adorned the inner walls, and a harpsichord stood in the corner.

Ignazio rose when we entered, a glass of wine in his hand. He wore his customary sober gray, with a white lace collar spreading across his shoulders. His pale, thin face lacked my mother's vivacious beauty, but his eyes held the spark of the Cornaro drive and intelligence.

"Amalia," he greeted me, in his dry voice. "A pleasure to see you."

Ignazio wasn't the sort of man you hugged, and I wasn't wearing skirts to curtsy, so I bowed. "And you as well, Uncle Ignazio."

"You seem well. How is your stock of the elixir? Do you need me to make any more?"

"It's fine," I began, embarrassed. But my mother didn't wait for me to finish.

"We could use a few more bottles." She bestowed one of her smiles upon him. "I think she's down to four. Thank you so much, Ignazio. I don't know what we would do without you."

I was fairly certain my mother had the resources to find someone else with the glimmer of alchemy necessary to brew the elixir that kept me alive, should it come down to it. But Ignazio gave her a satisfied smile as if he took his cousin at her word. So I said, "Yes, thank you," even though I had five and a half bottles left, not four.

We settled down and talked about the weather and other inconsequential matters as the servants passed around lemon tarts. The unspoken subject of Ardence stiffened Ignazio's shoulders and clipped off every word. The tension coming off him seemed to settle in my own spine, until I had to stuff a lemon tart in my mouth to keep from asking what had gone so wrong with the city I loved.

"I hope you had no trouble hiring a carriage," my mother said, watching Ignazio's face. "I've heard the duke of Ardence is making even simple matters difficult for Raverrans, with his recent rashness."

Ardence at last. I straightened, listening.

Ignazio sighed. "Duke Astor Bergandon has the ambition of his great ancestors, but he lacks temperance. His father listened to my advice, but Astor and his court seem bent on driving the city to ruin." He took a draft of his wine. "If the doge had given me the powers I asked for, this ugly situation with the illegal taxes would never have happened."

"Mmm," La Contessa said. I knew she clashed often with Baron Leodra over issues of sovereignty. I wouldn't be surprised if asking for those additional powers was what sealed Ignazio's removal from his post.

Ignazio eyed his empty glass morosely. "Even without the authority to simply overrule Astor, I was doing well enough. I had agreements in place with some of the duke's more competent people, and I was flattering him to our side. If I'd had another two weeks, I could have had things back under control."

"Of course," my mother murmured, signaling the servants to refill Ignazio's cup. "But you know the doge. He wanted immediate results."

"He'll get them," Ignazio said darkly. "He sent Lady Terringer. She's a retired general, not a diplomat. She'll be the spark to Bergandon's tinder. Appointing Terringer is courting war."

My tart went dry in my mouth. I swallowed, with difficulty. "Surely it won't come to that."

"I hope not."

But my mother chuckled. "Don't be dramatic, Ignazio. You're scaring the girl." If she noticed me stiffen, it didn't give her pause. "They're a long road from taking up arms against the Empire."

"Not if the Shadow Gentry get their way."

"The Shadow Gentry?" I'd never heard the name before. "What's that, an assassin's guild?"

"Not at all." He chuckled. "Though it does sound rather dramatic, doesn't it? They're a secret society of Ardentine aristocrats who keep posting public declarations against Raverra and calling for a return to the old days of Ardence's independence and glory." He shook his head. "I'm fairly sure it was their urging that prompted the duke to instigate the taxes on Raverran merchants in the first place."

"One wonders how such a rebellious faction managed to gain enough influence with the duke to convince him to break the Serene Accords." I knew my mother well enough to hear the silent corollary: *And why you didn't see it in time to stop it.*

Ignazio, however, seemed deaf to any implicit criticism. "They were harmless enough when they just muttered against Raverra in dark corners, wearing their gray domino masks to look mysterious. But they're bolder and more dangerous now that Ardence is facing serious economic troubles, and the duke is reaching for any solution he can get. We're lucky he hasn't taken out massive loans from Vaskandar, like some of his nobles have." He sighed. "Besides, he's easily swayed. I fear the young duke's passions are all too simple to inflame."

"Then let us hope they will prove as easy to cool," my mother said.

"I could have done it, if the cursed doge hadn't called me back." Ignazio shook his head. "Sending a military relic like Terringer won't help calm him down. It introduces the idea of violence first, before Ardence could come close to broaching it."

"I believe the doge is well aware of the message he's sending." My mother swirled the wine in her glass.

The paradox of force. Securing the peace by the implicit threat of war. I put my glass down, my fingers numb. "They have to back down," I said. "The duke surely isn't foolish enough to risk his city over something as trivial as taxing merchants...is he, Uncle Ignazio?"

Ignazio considered the question, turning his glass to catch the lamplight. "No," he said at last. "Even with the Shadow Gentry pushing him. If nothing else happens to stir up the Ardentine court against Raverra, he'll likely back down rather than risk war."

A grim heaviness in his tone carried the burden of terrible possibility hanging on that *if*.

The next day, I returned home from training with an uncooperative Zaira at the Mews and a too-brief stop at the Imperial Library to find Ciardha waiting for me in the foyer. She held herself with her usual perfect poise, my finest emerald velvet coat draped over her arm and a bottle of my elixir in her hand.

"Welcome home, Lady." She bowed. "But I regret I must ask you to postpone your rest. La Contessa requires your presence at the Imperial Palace, to audit a strategy session."

My borrowed books sagged in my arms. Of course she did. Never mind that dusk had fallen across the city, the luminaries kindling awake like evening stars. Never mind that I'd hoped to spend an evening relaxing with good books at last, for the first time since putting the jess on Zaira.

"Now?" I asked.

Ciardha nodded, handing me the elixir bottle. "I'm afraid so, Lady."

"I wish she'd ask me if I had plans before making these pronouncements." I took a deep swallow of elixir; the piercing taste of anise traced a path down my throat. "She doesn't need me at that meeting. I could watch and learn some other time."

Ciardha took the bottle and my books from me and set them on a table, then held out my coat. "Perhaps La Contessa doesn't need you there, Lady. But others might."

I paused halfway into the first sleeve. "What do you mean?"

"This is a military-strategy discussion, Lady, regarding how to deploy the Falcons against potential threats to the Empire. I believe Lieutenant Verdi will be there."

Cold settled in my belly. If my mother wanted me there, they might be talking about deploying *my* Falcon. "What potential threats?"

Ciardha's eyes gleamed in the lamplight. "It isn't my place to say, Lady. But I think you know."

The Map Room in the Imperial Palace was aptly named: painted murals of the Serene City and the Empire covered the walls, and even the floor was an inlaid map done in varying shades of marble and precious metals. But the map unrolled on the great table in the center of the room was one of all Eruvia, with colored stones scattered on it for markers. Gathered around the table, casting their shadows across the world from the lamps hanging above, were the doge, the full Council of Nine, a handful of generals and other high military officers, Colonel Vasante of the Falcons, and a very nervous-looking Marcello.

I slipped in beside him, half a step back from his iron-haired colonel, who leaned on the table with both hands. Marcello shot me the look of a drowning swimmer who sees a friend reaching out with an oar to grab.

No one else paid me any attention. Even my mother didn't lift her narrowed eyes from the map.

"We have the troops to quietly reinforce all the forts in the mountain passes along the Vaskandran border," the doge was saying. "And we can pull ships from Osta to better position our navy in the north, to attack the Vaskandran coast on both flanks should they be so foolish as to try anything. But we don't have enough available Falcons to cover the entire border plus Ardence. We need to make some choices."

Startled, I looked more closely at the map. The Empire's northern reach ended in the Witchwall Mountains, a long range that marked the Vaskandran border. Beyond it lay the wild, dark tangles of the Vaskandran forests and the fog-shrouded folds of its hills and moors, a vast country under the Witch Lords' complete dominion. Stones marked the fortresses in the passes, forest green for Vaskandran castles and ocean blue for Raverran forts. But a cluster of green stones gathered at one of the passes, a clump as telling as a swarm of ants on a dead beetle.

"Is Vaskandar invading again?" I whispered to Marcello, alarmed.

He shook his head. "No, thank the Graces. But they've moved troops to the border."

"They'd be mad to attack us, after we defeated them so soundly in the Three Years' War." The Witch Lords held near-absolute power in their own domains, but outside their realms they lacked the military might to mount a serious offensive into an Empire protected by the Falcons, and they had no navy to speak of.

"Well," Marcello murmured, "they do have a certain reputation."

"I don't think we can ignore Ardence." My mother tapped the city with an elegant nail. "Though by all reports Lady Terringer is making good progress bringing the duke around. The unrest there still makes it a weak spot for the Empire, and the River Arden has its source in the Witchwall Mountains, not far from where the Vaskandran forces are gathering. It's a road for invasion they've used before, in the Three Years' War. And we know Prince Ruven has been meddling with Ardentine politics. Whatever gambit Vaskandar is trying, Ardence is part of their strategy."

Baron Leodra sniffed. "Don't try to shield Ardence from the consequences of its actions by shifting blame to Vaskandar. If their unrest weakens us, let us respond with strength. If we occupy Ardence, we can oust the would-be rebels there and be well positioned to defend if Vaskandar invades."

La Contessa shook her head. "You're showing your inexperience, Leodra."

He twisted a flinch into a scowl. This was Baron Leodra's first elected term on the Council of Nine, a fact my mother rarely let him forget. "How so? It's common sense to keep a strong hold on such a key position."

"They're trying to draw us out." My mother cast a jaded glance at the map. "That force on the border is so obvious, it has to be a distraction or a provocation. It's Loreice they've been after the last two times they went to war, not Ardence; we can't assume this isn't a trap. They haven't made a true move yet. We need to keep our cards hidden, but be ready to act swiftly when the moment comes."

Colonel Vasante straightened. The lamplight caught harsh lines beside her mouth. "I agree. Which is why I think it's too early to move more than a handful of Falcons into position in the field."

"We're discussing an entire city-state that has broken the Serene Accords." Baron Leodra's voice sharpened. "Every vassal city in the Empire is watching what we do. If we don't decisively answer such an open challenge, others will try to see what *they* can get away with. If Ardence doesn't bend the knee swiftly, we need to be ready to respond with overwhelming force."

"I am aware of the gravity of the situation." Vasante's jaw

flexed as if she ground Leodra's objections between her teeth. "My statement stands. A few Falcons will suffice."

"What can a mere handful of Falcons do?" Baron Leodra scoffed.

"If it's the right Falcons?" The colonel's finger fell on an island off the coast of Osta, marked on the map with scorched stone ruins. *Celantis.* "Just about anything."

Everyone turned and stared at me.

I wanted, very badly, to duck behind Marcello. But I froze instead, hoping I looked impassive rather than nervous.

"Well?" The doge's sharp eyes moved between me and Marcello. "Can I count on our fire warlock, if we face a threat to the serenity of the Empire?"

No. If I released Zaira now, I'd count her far more likely to burn a path of ashes across Raverra in a grand resignation from the Falcons than to follow the doge's orders. But if I said that, it would humiliate Marcello in front of the entire Council of Nine, and jeopardize my own precarious position as an independent Falconer as well. There was no safe answer to his question.

I couldn't help myself. I looked to my mother.

She wore her Council face, cool and regal. It was a closed door. She couldn't help me here, not with everyone watching.

Marcello cleared his throat. "Your Serenity." He bowed, then clasped his hands behind his back. Only I could see his fingers trembling. "Zaira has just begun to settle into the Mews. It's a delicate time of transition. I don't recommend deploying any Falcon until they've adjusted and completed training."

The doge's brows lifted. "Colonel? This is not what you told me."

Colonel Vasante's back faced me, stiff as a bayonet. "Warlocks don't need much training, Your Serenity. They use their power instinctively. Lieutenant Verdi is correct that it's our normal peacetime procedure to allow Falcons time to settle in, but if war breaks out, her balefire is yours to command."

"Do you agree, Lieutenant Verdi?" The doge's tone was mild, but his gaze could have cut stone.

Marcello's knuckles whitened behind his back. Seconds stretched endlessly by. The colonel rocked back on her heels, adjusting her stance to bring her weight down on Marcello's toe.

Marcello jumped, then bowed. "Of course, Your Serenity."

I clamped my lips shut on a noise of surprise or protest. The idea of Zaira following anyone's commands right now was ludicrous.

"And you, Lady Amalia?" The doge's attention turned to me, and I tried not to flinch. "Are you prepared to take the field and unleash your Falcon if necessary?"

I could feel my mother's eyes boring into me. Here in front of the Council, one wrong word, whether of submission or of rebellion, could reroute the rest of my life.

"Your Serenity," I said carefully, "forgive me, but I'm not clear on where you are suggesting we deploy my fire warlock."

Someone let out a breath of surprise or relief. I couldn't tell who.

The marquise of Palova frowned. "Yes, it's a bit early to be throwing a fire warlock into the fray, isn't it? We're not at war." She waved at the cluster of green stones. "This troop movement could be a show of force by one Witch Lord to impress another, or an attempt to intimidate the Empire—a baring of the teeth. Vaskandar does things like this every few years, and it usually comes to nothing."

My mother leaned in, her fists on the table. "I suggest we hold the Falcons in reserve for now. Give our new Serene Envoy a chance to bring Ardence into line, and wait for better intelligence on Vaskandar's true intentions. They are our strongest weapon, and best kept up our sleeve."

A rumble of assent rose up from the generals and half the Council. The doge nodded. "Very well. We'll wait before deploying any Falcons. But I want them ready to move at a moment's notice."

Colonel Vasante saluted. "Of course, Your Serenity."

The tension fell from Marcello's shoulders, and he swayed as if it had been the only thing holding him up. Without thinking, I grabbed his elbow, steadying him.

His startled eyes flicked to mine, and I released him at once, flushing. But he smiled.

"Thank you," he whispered.

It took me a moment to realize he wasn't talking about my overly familiar hand. I smiled back, but only faintly. I'd bought us time, perhaps. Nothing more.

If the duke of Ardence didn't prove himself amenable to reason soon, Zaira's balefire might become the doge's next tool of persuasion.

Chapter Eight

You can't hide in those books forever, Amalia."

My pen jumped, leaving a trail of ink across my carefully drawn diagram. I turned to face my mother, struggling to hold in a bitter outburst.

"Hello, Mamma. I didn't realize you were in my room."

She lifted an eyebrow. "Then you need to work on your awareness, girl. Even with the wards and Ciardha protecting it, our palace is not assassin-proof."

"I'm not hiding." It was mostly true, though I was eager for some time alone after last night's alarming strategy session. "I'm designing a more efficient way to pass the sun's energy through a wire coil to light a luminary crystal."

My mother did not appear impressed. She glanced at a letter in her hand, then at me. "Can you dance a minuet?"

I groaned. "You're going to make me go to some awful party with detestable people again, aren't you?"

"Not I." She tossed the invitation onto my desk, on top of my drying design. The winged horse of Raverra reared up at me in the seal. "The doge requests your presence at a reception for the new diplomatic contingent from Ardence."

"Not another tedious—" I stopped. "Wait. From Ardence?"

"Yes."

"The doge requests *my* presence, specifically?"

"*Requires* might be a more accurate word," La Contessa said. "You and your Falcon both."

"He wants *Zaira* there?" The pen fell from my hand as I sagged in my chair. "He *is* trying to start a fight, isn't he?"

"No, but someone else may be." My mother settled down on the stool of my little-used vanity to look me in the eyes. "The doge is raising the stakes to flush out the troublemakers, and see how deep this goes. Do you understand?"

I understood the cold fear in my gut. "No. I don't see what Raverra could possibly gain by flouting a fire warlock in Ardence's face at a time like this."

"The most obvious reason for Ardence to defy Raverra is a simple testing of boundaries, to see if the Serene City has grown weak enough to relax its hold on the Empire. This is common with ambitious young rulers, and nothing to worry about." She made a brushing movement, as if Duke Astor Bergandon were an annoying insect. "If that is the case, a warm welcome of the new Ardentine ambassador makes it clear we are still willing to embrace Ardence, while having a fire warlock in pointed attendance sends a message about the potential consequences of rejecting the Serene Accords."

"And you think the duke will back down."

She shrugged. "If he's not a fool, he will. But if this is more than a mere testing of limits, we can learn a great deal from the duke's response—and that of others who may be influencing him."

"You mean Vaskandar."

"Perhaps. That's the most obvious possibility. They'd stand a better chance of seizing territory in Loreice if the Empire were distracted with another war. But it's too early to make assumptions."

I stared in disbelief. "Who else could it be? The Empire is at peace. How many enemies do you think we have?"

La Contessa regarded me through narrowed eyes. "Power always has enemies."

I stared at the scar on the back of my wrist. "I suppose it does."

"Speaking of which, watch out for Baron Leodra at the reception. He may try to draw you into his schemes. He's pushing hard to come down on Ardence with punitive force, which would destroy all our hopes for peace."

"Why would he want that?" It seemed both cruel and foolish.

"As a gambit to gain him greater influence." She exhaled her contempt for such tactics. "Right now, the doge listens to me. Leodra sees Ardence as a point of weakness for me, since my intelligence services and your Uncle Ignazio didn't warn of Duke Bergandon's rebellion or prevent it. Leodra has always been a proponent of greater imperial control, and he's pushing the doge and the Council to adopt *his* methods instead of mine."

My fingertips raked my ruined diagram, crumpling the paper. "That would be terrible for Ardence."

"Don't worry too much about it." La Contessa's lips spread in a feline smile. "Baron Leodra will learn his own limits shortly. Everyone has secrets, and I've found out his: he has a bastard son he wants to keep hidden. He'll do what I tell him after we have a little talk at this ball."

I couldn't summon any enthusiasm at her triumph. "Lovely."

She came and laid a hand on my shoulder. "Be careful at the reception. Your actions may become moves on the board. I'd rather you were a player than a piece." Her voice and touch were surprisingly gentle. "As I said, you can't hide in those books forever."

She left in a swish of silk, shutting my door behind her as noiselessly as she'd opened it. I stared down at my marred design, unease spreading like spilled ink.

I couldn't even keep Zaira from committing petty theft in the marketplace. Now I'd be responsible for her behavior at a ball with the doge himself in attendance, where one wrong move could trigger a war.

"I'm invited to a ball at the Imperial Palace?" Zaira snorted. "That's a good one. Whose idea was that?"

"The doge's, actually."

Zaira didn't so much as glance up from her seat on a third-floor balcony overlooking the lagoon. She plucked a summernut from a bowl at her side and hurled it at a gull coming in to land on the Mews pier. The bird veered off, and Zaira laughed.

"I'm not joking," I said, vexed.

"I know that. You don't have the sense of humor the Graces gave a fish." She tossed another nut into the deep green water and watched the splash. "I'm sure the old bastard's up to something. But if the food's good, I don't care."

I considered whether to tell her she was being used to implicitly threaten Ardence. But no doubt that would just open me up for more ridicule. I tried another tack. "It's a delicate situation. It's going to be very important not to offend anyone."

She turned a look on me of disbelieving contempt. "How stupid do you think I am?"

"I know you're not stupid."

"What do you think I'm going to do? Piss in the doge's wine? I'm not an idiot."

"Well..." I tried to think how to put it. "In our interactions so far, you've sometimes been a little...rough around the edges..."

She shrugged. "That's because I don't give a damn about you."

"Well, I'm glad we have that clarified," I snapped.

"I'd have thought it was clear already."

I pressed my lips together to keep any more hasty words from leaping out. *Friends,* I reminded myself. I wanted to be friends.

I tried again. "Do you have anything appropriate to wear?"

"How should I know? I've been to so many ducal parties."

I'd seen most of her wardrobe strewn across her floor, and I doubted she had a suitable gown. Raverra provided well for its Falcons, but most of them would never need court dress.

"I could loan you something," I suggested. She was a good deal shorter and thinner than me; but the servants could take up the hem, and we could lace the corset as tight as it would go. "I have a crimson dress that would be spectacular on you."

The mocking indifference in her eyes flickered. I remembered catching her in the act of trying on the blue gown. She probably hadn't had much chance in her life to dress up.

I had thought to send over a servant with the gown. But...

"Would you like to come to my palace beforehand, to get ready with me?" I hurried the words out, before I could change my mind. "I have a maid who's very good with hair, and you'll need help getting into your corset."

Emotions passed over her face like the shifting shadows of leaves on a windy day. Finally, she tossed her head. "Oh, very well. If you're so concerned I'll embarrass you if I get ready on my own."

I harbored a suspicion she was bent on embarrassing me regardless. "I look forward to it."

I didn't tell her I'd far rather she pissed in the doge's wine than started a war with Ardence. She might take that as an invitation.

"Ridiculous," Zaira declared. "This whole place is absurd."

I turned from my wide window overlooking the Imperial Canal, where I'd gone to draw the drapes, to find Zaira staring around my room with an expression of mingled wonderment and disgust.

"Yes, well, welcome to my home," I said.

It hadn't occurred to me what my palace would look like to a girl who'd spent her life in the Tallows. The gilding that felt bright, warm, and homelike to me must convey unfathomable excess. The fine paintings and lush fabrics, the luminaries and protective wards—everything she saw must seem the extreme pinnacle of decadence.

She probably thought I'd invited her here to flaunt my wealth. A flush burned my neck and crept up my cheeks.

Zaira shook her head. "I could steal enough trinkets to feed half the Tallows for a year, and you'd never notice they were gone."

My maid, Rica, saved me from the alarming prospect of finding an answer to that by arriving with Zaira's crimson gown. She laid out all the layers of petticoats, corsetry, skirts, underskirts, and hose, eyeing Zaira all the while as if calculating how to make everything fit on her smaller frame. Zaira regarded the formidable array with trepidation.

"When will she leave so I can get dressed?" she whispered, jerking her chin at Rica.

I coughed. "She won't. She's here to help us."

"I don't need anyone's *help* getting dressed."

"Forgive me," I said, "but with this gown, you do. It's impossible to get into on your own."

She stared at me in disbelief. "You're serious, aren't you. Good Graces. What *is* this idiocy? The Empire is literally run by a bunch of imbeciles who can't even get *dressed* by themselves?"

"There's a reason I prefer breeches." I looked with some foreboding at the second gown Rica now laid out for me, an extravagant affair in shades of champagne and bronze.

"Solid-gold breeches, no doubt. Grace of Mercy. No wonder

you're so useless." The contempt in Zaira's voice seared the air between us. "You don't know what the world is like. You've never even *seen* it."

"Fair enough," I said wearily. "Do you want to wear the gown, or not?"

She stared at the rich piles of silk and velvet, and a bitter longing touched her dark eyes. "I might as well wear it. Even prisoners need a bit of fun now and then."

Rica helped me with my gown first, all business, then turned to fuss over Zaira with obvious relish; she clearly planned to enjoy this transformation. Zaira suffered through being dressed, though she kept trying to do things herself, getting in Rica's way. I settled in a great cloud of champagne skirts on the edge of my bed to watch.

"Do I get a dagger?" Zaira asked. "*She* has a dagger." She pointed at the jeweled sheath at my hip.

Rica glanced at me. "My lady?"

I blinked. "I don't know. Do you usually carry a dagger?"

Zaira snorted. "Every Tallows brat carries a knife if they want to live to see Sunday. Your lieutenant wouldn't give me one, though."

"Why not? Are there regulations against Falcons going armed?" That didn't seem right; they were soldiers. I knew I'd seen Falcons carrying weapons at the Mews.

Zaira shrugged. "Something about a fist to the eye being bad enough without a dagger in it."

I bit my lip. If Marcello hadn't armed her, it seemed impolitic and perhaps unwise to contradict his decision. But Zaira stared a challenge at me. This was a test.

"Well, so long as you don't plan to stab any party guests in the eye—or anywhere else, for that matter—I see no harm in it," I said lightly. There would be a full complement of imperial guards at the reception, after all, in plain sight and watching for assassins.

"Huh." Zaira tilted her head back in apparent surprise; Rica gently corrected her position to begin styling her hair. "You trust me with a weapon?"

"I trust you not to make stupid mistakes."

Zaira laughed, full and raucous. "Fair enough."

Rica found a small ornamental dagger for her; Zaira eyed it with disdain, but took it anyway. The slim golden sheath provided a dashing accent against the vibrant silk of her gown. The blade itself would likely snap off if she actually stabbed anyone with it; still, Zaira seemed more content to sit through the application of subtle color on her lips and cheeks now that she had it. Her hand dropped to touch the dagger once or twice, as if for reassurance.

"There," Rica said proudly when she was done. "Come look in the mirror. You're a vision of the Grace of Beauty."

She was hardly exaggerating. With jeweled pins in her hair and acres of red silk setting off her shining dark hair and olive-bronze skin, Zaira was nothing short of gorgeous.

Rica wheeled out a tall mirror from its corner, and Zaira stared at her reflection with an expression of shock. She touched an artful tendril of hair cascading down from the great elegant pile on her head, then her own face, as if wondering whether they might belong to someone else. Then she spun, watching her skirts swirl out like a little girl, and laughed.

"You're going to turn heads at the ball." I gave Rica an approving smile. She grinned back, pleased at her handiwork.

"Damned right I will," Zaira crowed. Then her face sobered. "What poor bastards am I threatening?"

"What?"

"By attending this party." She turned from the mirror to face me. The lamplight caught her eyes, bringing out the sharp black ring of the mage mark against their murky brown.

I raised an eyebrow. "I thought you didn't care."

"I don't care if the doge's grand plan is to take over the world or to bugger a goat. But if he's using *my* fire to make some sorry wretch wet himself, I want to know who."

Rica withdrew discreetly from the room, with a bow and a sympathetic grimace. I sighed. "Ardence."

"What, the entire city?" Her brows lifted toward her elegantly coiffed hair.

"Of course. If he wanted to send a warning to an individual, he'd have an assassin attend the party, not a fire warlock." I rose from my bed, a restless unease chafing at me. "I know it's an unpleasant reason to be invited. But we don't either of us have a choice about going. We may as well try to enjoy ourselves."

"Oh, I'll enjoy myself." Zaira smoothed the front of her dress, glancing back at the mirror. "Me, attending a ball at the Imperial Palace? This is too good a joke not to laugh. We'll see by the end of the night who's the butt of it."

She smiled a narrow smile that didn't reassure me at all.

We were an hour into the ball, and Zaira hadn't stabbed anyone yet.

Raverrans and Ardentines mingled, drinks in hand, tension in their shoulders. I stood behind a statue and watched the ballroom, trying to get a feel for the situation before plunging myself into it.

Zaira appeared to be having a grand time. She looked spectacular in the crimson gown and knew it, with jewels sparkling at her throat and the corset flattering her figure. Young courtiers clustered around her. Her teasing laughter rang through the crowd, more delicate than usual, and every motion of her wrists as she talked or sipped her wine carried an extra twirl. I suspected she knew very well the men and women surrounding her found her fascinating largely as a curiosity; but I doubted *they* knew she was mocking them with her courtly flourishes. Ignazio lingered nearby, thank the Graces, keeping an eye on her.

The doge himself presided at the head of the room, with attendants and advisers dancing a screen around him to manage everyone seeking a moment of his time. My mother glided through the crowd with the ease of a shark, equal parts fascinating and dangerous. The Ardentines gathered in knots and dispersed again, like a murder of crows. I scanned the faces of the diplomats for anyone I might know from my days in Ardence, when I attended functions with Ignazio while he was Serene Envoy.

I spotted Domenic, impossible to miss even across the ballroom with his bold laugh and slashed sleeves. He was looking fine tonight. His doublet tapered smartly to show his strong shoulders and narrow waist to full advantage, and he moved with the grace and confidence that had caught more eyes than mine in the Ardentine court. I hurried across the ballroom, snatching a glass of wine from a servant's tray in passing.

"Domenic!" I called as I approached. "I didn't know you'd be here."

He turned, and a smile sparked his warm brown eyes. "Amalia. There may be some hope for this party, after all."

"I'm surprised to see you at a stodgy old diplomatic reception." I grinned. "Don't tell me you came just for the food."

"I only wish. Though they do have those tiny pauldronfish in lemon butter no one in Ardence can get quite right." He sighed, and a shadow passed over his lively face, stilling it to more somber lines. "I'm here because of last night's crisis with the Falconers."

I fingered my falcon's-head brooch. "Crisis?"

"You haven't heard? I don't know the full details; the news came in over the courier lamps just before the ball." He glanced over to where the ambassador spoke animatedly with the doge. "Best not to mention it here, perhaps. But we should talk later. In the meantime, give me something to be cheerful about! We never got to talk about your projects. Are you working on anything new? I'd love to hear—" he broke off, straightening, as he stared past my shoulder.

"Who's your friend?" Zaira demanded, bumping me to the side with her copious skirts. I suspected the glass of wine in her hand wasn't her first.

Uh-oh. I set my teeth in a smile. "Zaira, this is Viscount Domenic Bergandon, cousin to Duke Astor Bergandon. Domenic, this is—"

"Ah! You must be the Lady Zaira." He swept into an extravagant flourish of a bow.

"You've heard of her?" I couldn't imagine that was a good thing.

Zaira lifted her glass to him, in lieu of a curtsy. "Of course he has. I'm famous throughout Eruvia. But I won't tell you for what."

Domenic laughed. "I must confess the ambassador only told me of you this morning, my lady. But in addition to leaving me ignorant of your no doubt richly deserved fame—and I would be delighted to guess the cause for it later—he also neglected to mention your wit and beauty."

A rosy glow touched Zaira's cheeks. "Well, don't you have a pretty mouth? I like a man with a nimble tongue. But if your ambassador forgot all the best parts of me, what did he tell you?"

I took a deep sip of wine to hide my flush. I'd never actually had a nightmare about Zaira crashing into a conversation with Domenic and making salacious comments, but only because my sleeping mind lacked a sufficiently cruel imagination.

"Well..." Domenic's expression slid from gleeful appreciation to something graver. He glanced at me, offering an awkward shrug. "To be honest, my lady, I've heard you were taken against your will to become a Falcon. But I also heard my friend Amalia here is your Falconer, which seems impossible. I confess I'm having trouble making the pieces fit. Might you enlighten me as to the truth?"

Zaira waved her glass in my direction, the wine sloshing to the rim. The jess gleamed on her wrist. "Ask her."

Domenic turned to me, gesturing an invitation. "Amalia? You've been holding back quite the story, it seems. What happened?"

"I, ah, yes." Heat climbed up my neck. Graces only knew what rumors he'd heard. "I'm afraid I met Zaira when she was in some duress, and had unleashed her powers. In the interest of protecting Raverra from balefire, given that she couldn't stop it on her own"—never mind that she hadn't seemed to have any intent of stopping regardless—"I was, ah, enlisted to put a jess on her."

Domenic's eyes widened. "So it's true? You captured her for the Falcons?"

"I didn't have any choice," I said. "Believe me, I didn't want to become a Falconer any more than she wanted to be a Falcon. I had to do it to save Raverra from burning." Although no one seemed to appreciate that part.

Domenic turned to Zaira, one brow lifting. "Would you have burned down the city?"

Zaira shrugged airily. "I believe that was my intent at the time. But I don't remember very well."

Domenic put a hand to his temple, shaking his head. "Well, I suppose we all want to burn down Raverra sometimes." He cast me a sympathetic look. "I'm sorry you got drawn into this, Amalia. Apparently they're conscripting Falconers now, too."

"I think our case was highly unusual," I said.

"But given what's happened in Ardence..." A light came

into his eyes I'd seen before. It was the same fierce gleam that had sparked there when a passing merchant had kicked a beggar woman in the Plaza of Six Fountains. He'd called the man out and left him with two black eyes. "I can't ignore this, Amalia. Maybe my brother, Gabril, and his friends have it right after all. There has to be a better way."

My skin prickled at the implication of rebellion.

Zaira snorted. "Better for me? Absolutely. I think it's worked out pretty well for Raverra, though. Having all the powerful magic tame to the doge's call."

"And that's the problem." Domenic nodded. "You have the courage to state it plainly, Zaira. I admire that." He glanced again across the room, toward the doge. "But this conversation is perhaps best continued in another place and time. Maybe tomorrow?"

"We'd be delighted," I said reflexively. Only after the words left my mouth did it occur to me they might be treason.

A soberly dressed Ardentine woman with tiny gold spectacles on a chain around her neck appeared at Domenic's elbow. "A moment of your time, Viscount," she murmured.

"Of course, Lady Savony." He bowed to us. "Excuse me."

Zaira watched him go. "Now, that's a fine view. He must be a swordsman, to have such a firm—"

"Zaira," I interrupted, almost spilling my drink, "I hardly think it's appropriate for you to be ogling a viscount."

"I was going to say 'stride.'" She smirked. "Besides, why not? You were."

"I was not!"

"Truly." She sighed dramatically. "What would the poor lieutenant say?"

My entire face burned as if I'd leaned too close to a blazing hearth. "I don't know what you mean."

"Hmmmmm?" Zaira lifted both eyebrows.

"That is, Lieutenant Verdi hasn't—I don't know if he—"
I swallowed the words stumbling out of my mouth and drew
myself up with great dignity. "At any rate, Domenic and I are
old friends, and I don't feel that way about him anymore, and...
and...it can't hurt to look."

"Ha!" Zaira's grin declared victory. "Well, there's plenty to
look at here. Have you seen the girl in the yellow dress?" She
gestured eloquently at her own chest. "Prettier peaches than in
the city market, and as much on display. I should go to fancy
parties more often."

"Graces preserve us, Zaira, that's the doge's niece," I groaned.

"Someone in the family had to be pretty, I suppose," Zaira
cackled.

Ignazio appeared then, like the Grace of Mercy, offering
Zaira a little dish of cheese and olives. "I see you were talking
to the young viscount," he observed. "Have you met any of the
other Ardentines?"

"No." Zaira popped an olive in her mouth with relish. "If
they're all built like that, though, I'm eager for introductions."

"I couldn't speak to that," he said with unruffled calm. "But
I'll bet you a ducat you'll never guess which one has half a dozen
mistresses."

"I don't have a ducat, but I accept your challenge!" Zaira slid
her arm through his.

He whisked her away to her next group of admirers, acknowl-
edging my grateful look with a wink. Her laugh at some comment of his floated behind them as they vanished into the crowd.
Thank the Graces *they* got along, at least.

I scanned the partygoers for more people I knew. My mother
stood in a corner with Baron Leodra. By the satisfaction in her
smile and the look of hopeless, crushing realization descending
across his face, she was breaking the news to him that she knew
about his secret bastard and explaining how things would be if

he preferred the rest of Raverran society did not share this revelation. I also spotted a poet whose company I generally enjoyed,
but she already had a crowd around her, laughing at her latest
witticism.

As for crowds...I had stayed still for too long. A swarm of
unmarried dandies descended on me, their eyes gleaming with
avarice for the Cornaro fortune.

I smiled and nodded my way through twenty minutes of
competitive bragging, trying to seem interested in how fast this
one's horse was or how opulent that one's personal pleasure boat
was. It would have been easier if any of them had given the barest deference to context, or asked me to express an opinion other
than agreement.

"Lady Amalia, your family is famous for its generous patron-
age of music. Well, I'm a fair hand at the harpsichord myself..."

"Harpsichords! The lady doesn't want to hear about harpsichords; she could buy all the harpsichords in Eruvia. But you
can't buy good breeding, you know. Did I mention I have the
blood of kings in my veins?"

I remembered when I asked my mother how she dealt with
fortune hunters, as the wealthiest widow in Raverra. *Just think
about how you could have them all executed*, she'd said. *They see it in
your eyes, and they leave you alone.*

"Lady Amalia."

I turned to face the new one, my fixed smile stretching toward
bloodthirsty, only to find Marcello there in full dress uniform.

"Oh! Lieutenant." My cheeks flushed as I remembered Zaira's
words. Next time, I was bringing a fan.

He bowed, formal in this public place. "May I have a word,
my lady?"

I made my insincere apologies to the gold hunters and stepped
aside with Marcello. "Thank you for rescuing me," I murmured.

"It's actually a matter of security." His tone was serious. "Do you know why that woman is watching you?"

His eyes flicked sideways. I tried to follow his gaze without staring. The prim lady who'd called Domenic away spoke to Ignazio now, consulting a leather-bound notebook through her golden glasses. She didn't seem to be paying me any attention, but I had the skin-prickly feeling her eyes had just left me.

"Is she?"

"I'm here expressly to see to your safety and Zaira's this evening. I've been watching you both all night. So has she."

I shrugged wearily. "Marcello, people stare at me at parties all the time, because of who my mother is. It's why I don't like them."

His mouth quirked. "Parties, or people?"

"I like *some* people." I smiled, in case he had any doubt he was one of them.

"But can you think of any reason she'd be watching you?"

I shook my head. "I don't even know who she is."

"Lady Colanthe Savony. Technically, she's Duke Bergandon's steward, but in terms of day-to-day matters, she essentially runs the city of Ardence."

"I have no idea why she would be interested in me," I said. "Unless she's attempting to get a sense of whether Zaira and I are about to set Ardence on fire, in which case she'll be reassured we are a very silly pair of girls who are no threat to her city whatsoever."

"It's not clear why she's here at all." Marcello rubbed his temple. He could be warding off a headache or signaling to his people hidden in the room. After the incident in the market, I wasn't leaping to any conclusions. "She's the voice and hands of the duke. She can't possibly be on the ambassadorial staff."

"Maybe the duke wants her personal report on Raverra's reaction to the unrest in Ardence."

"Or maybe she's helping make plans to attempt to neutralize Raverra's fire warlock." Marcello leaned closer and dropped his voice. "Be careful, Lady Amalia. Please don't go anywhere alone tonight."

The thin inches of air between us hummed, live as a luminary wire.

I could have counted the amber flecks in his intent green eyes. As my suddenly clumsy tongue fumbled after a reply, a court functionary approached us with a bow.

"Excuse me, Lieutenant Verdi, Lady Amalia. His Serenity would like to speak with you."

Surprised, I glanced over to where the doge presided in his informal court.

He was staring right at us, and he did not look happy.

Chapter Nine

"Lieutenant Verdi." The doge's voice was soft as an adder's hiss. "Has there been some incident with the Falconers in Ardence of which I should be aware?"

The heavy gold embroidery in his robes glinted in the lamp-light, and a storm brewed behind his eyes. His attendants had cleared a space around us for private conversation. Somehow I doubted it was Marcello's pride they were protecting, which worried me. Being part of something the doge wished to hide could be dangerous.

Marcello bowed stiffly. "No, Your Serenity. Not that I'm aware of. We have a handful of Falconers and Falcons there, but at last report everything seemed in order. The colonel would know better than I."

The doge brought his fingertips together under his chin. "The colonel is not here. And the Ardentine ambassador would disagree with you, it seems. Vehemently."

"Your Serenity, I am at a loss." Marcello bowed again, nervously. I could have told him that wouldn't help. A man like the doge would pounce on weakness like a cat on a fluttering feather. "I am not aware of any incident involving the Falconers in Ardence."

"Neither am I," the doge said. "And there, you see, is the problem." His voice sharpened until I winced. "All I have is a report from Lady Terringer that shortly before dawn half the noble court of Ardence stormed up to her gates making incoherent demands. And now this. When an ambassador comes to my court and starts complaining about an incident of which I am ignorant, Lieutenant, I must either bluff my way through the conversation or admit my intelligence services have failed me. Either way, it puts me at a disadvantage." He leaned back into his chair. "As to how fond I am of being at a disadvantage, I will allow you to exercise your imagination."

Marcello's throat jumped. "I am most distressed that I know nothing of this myself, Your Serenity."

"Then find out." The doge clipped each word off neat as a beheading. "And soon, Lieutenant. I await your report most eagerly."

Marcello bowed a third time. "Yes, Your Serenity."

The doge turned to me. I braced myself, but his tone modulated seamlessly to one of courtesy, cold and graceful as a swept-hilt rapier. "Lady Amalia. You are enjoying your evening, I hope?"

"Ah, yes, Your Serenity?"

"Do you have any reason to believe your Falcon may have a previous Ardentine connection? Does she know anyone here tonight?"

"No, Your Serenity. I've seen no signs of that."

"Hmph. Then her conscription into the Falcons couldn't be the incident to which the ambassador was referring." He flicked his fingers, as if casting the idea off. Then he leaned forward, his eyes piercing as an owl's. "I know you have Ardentine friends. Do try to do a better job this time."

"Your Serenity?"

"At getting information from them. Though I don't hold much hope, after your abysmal lack of results with the Vaskandran princeling."

I drew a sharp breath, stung. He'd never dare speak that way to my mother.

But I wasn't my mother. I nodded curtly, not trusting my words.

The doge waved his dismissal. "Enjoy the rest of the reception."

As we walked away, to clear the bitter taste in my mouth, I asked Marcello, "So you truly have no idea what he's talking about?"

"None." He spread his hands. "But I'd best find out quickly, if I hope to keep my position."

Domenic had mentioned a crisis with the Falconers. But I couldn't tell Marcello about our conversation without revealing Domenic had hinted at things that could skirt the edges of treason.

"If there were an incident involving the Falconers in Ardence, would you know about it?" I asked instead.

"Yes," he said. "Colonel Vasante keeps the officers updated on such things as soon as word comes in over the courier lamps so that we can be aware of potential threats. I don't understand."

I didn't need my mother's nose for intrigue to smell rot. "This isn't just miscommunication. The Ardentines know all about this supposed incident, but we don't. Someone's hiding something, or lying, or worse."

"Ah, Lady Amalia!" a foppish voice interrupted from behind me.

I turned, realizing with dawning horror I'd wandered too close to the dance floor. A courtier done up in full Loreician style, dripping with lace and sporting a bejeweled codpiece, extended a flourishing hand. "They're striking up a minuet, I believe. May I have this dance?"

Beyond him, another half dozen like him lurked in waiting. Panicked, I grabbed Marcello's hand.

"Alas, I'm afraid I already promised this dance to Lieutenant Verdi." I bestowed upon the courtier my most brilliant false smile. Marcello's hand spasmed in mine, but he didn't protest. I spun to face him and mouthed, *Help me.*

Without missing a beat, he bowed graceful assent, gesturing to the dance floor. "Shall we, my lady?"

As we moved into position, I whispered to him desperately, "Thank you. But I should warn you, I'm a terrible dancer."

"It's all right," he said. "I know my way around a minuet."

The first delicate strains of music filled the ballroom. Marcello's hand was warm around mine. His easy grin showed those charming dimples. At least he didn't seem annoyed with me.

I circled and dipped, watching the other dancers out of the corners of my eyes, feeling a bit like a pigeon with all the bobbing up and down. At least my skirts hid my feet; so long as I didn't bump into anyone, it didn't matter if my steps weren't quite right. Marcello's eyes laughed at me, and I grinned back.

"I've noticed you've spent half your time escaping the attentions of young men tonight," Marcello observed when we came together again. His sword calluses were hard against my palm, but otherwise his hand felt smooth and sure. He guided me with a gentle pressure from it, circling me in the right direction. "Is this a common problem for you?"

"It seems a popular belief that the heiress to a large fortune must be eager to marry at the earliest possible opportunity," I replied.

"Ah." He seemed about to say more; but the dance parted us again, and we bobbed around separately for a time. It was harder not to get lost among the other dancers without Marcello nudging me, but he caught my eyes and nodded in the right direction once or twice.

When we joined hands again, he drew me smoothly into position, making me look good through his own grace. He *was* a good dancer.

"They're fools," Marcello said. It took me a moment to remember he was talking about my erstwhile suitors.

"Well, yes. But was there a reason in particular you meant?"

"Because your fortune is the least of your good qualities, Amalia." It was the first time he'd called me by my name alone. A warm glow blossomed under my ribs.

"Oh, yes," I said. "I'm also an eccentric half Callamorne, who often dresses in breeches, and I fiddle about with artifice despite having no magical talent of my own. I'm sure I'd have no difficulty finding suitors if I weren't fabulously wealthy."

"I think you're brave, brilliant, and beautiful."

He wasn't smiling. His expression had gone wistful. I nearly tripped over my own heels. "How alliterative."

It was time to part again, circling around through the other dancers. I kept my eyes locked on Marcello, and nearly went the wrong way twice. I had a close call with a grand lady's swooshing skirts. My heart pounded against my corset stays.

He'd meant it. He thought I was beautiful. And brilliant, and the rest of it. He was too honest to flatter with a lie.

A twinge of confusion snarled the warmth unfurling in me. Marcello might have a bright future in the Falconers, but he was still no aristocrat. When I'd sighed over Domenic, I used to worry my mother would consider a viscount too far beneath me to approve a courtship. But questions of rank and station seemed distant and irrelevant when Marcello was here, now, gazing into my eyes across the sea of dancers.

The music brought us back together.

"Amalia," Marcello began. But he broke off, uncertainty vexing his brow.

"Yes?" I tried to keep any turbulence from my voice.

Marcello shook his head. "It's a fine evening. I wish it were pleasure that brought us here, and not duty."

For the rest of the dance, a shadow clouded his eyes.

I would have felt less uneasy about our meeting with Domenic the next morning if he had selected a different venue. The low ceiling of the coffeehouse gathered shadows and whispers under its wings, and there may as well have been a sign outside saying, "Welcome, Plotters of Sedition." It had been hard to convince the guards Marcello sent with us that we wanted a quiet moment for private conversation and they should wait outside.

Zaira seemed unconcerned, and peered around the dim interior with interest as we maneuvered between tables full of the disaffected younger sons of wealthy merchants and minor nobles to join Domenic in the far corner. At least she didn't seem ready to run off this time.

Domenic rose to greet us in a sudden surge of nervous energy, his attention on Zaira.

"Lady Amalia, Zaira. Have you tried coffee before?" He gestured to the steaming cups already awaiting us on the table.

Zaira shook her head.

I eyed the murky liquid dubiously. "Once. I will confess it was not to my taste."

"Well, that's a powerful recommendation." Zaira snatched up her cup and knocked back a swallow. A variety of expressions crossed her face, ending with her eyebrows lost in her hair. "Hot," she said. "But good!" She slurped more.

I nudged my cup. "I've heard it can be medicinal."

Domenic laughed. "It's all right, Amalia. They also serve wine." He called a server over and ordered me a glass, then turned to Zaira. "What did you think of the reception last night?"

She shrugged. "The food was good."

"And the company?" His eyes gleamed as if he expected something interesting.

"Very pretty." She took another draft of coffee, smirking at Domenic over the cup. "Very impressed with themselves."

"That sums up most of the noble courts of Eruvia," I said.

Domenic laughed, but his eyes never left Zaira. "You sound as if you weren't so impressed."

"It takes a lot to impress me. I'd be the same if the doge had rode in naked on the back of an elephant." She tipped her chair, enjoying Domenic's attention. "As a Tallows girl in a room full of half the Assembly, being unimpressed is my first weapon."

"Must it always be a battle?" I asked.

"Most of us don't get to choose, rich girl. I've been at war every day of my life."

Domenic put his chin in his hands, staring at Zaira in fascination. "I never know what you're going to say next. But it's always the raw truth."

"Sometimes a little too raw," I muttered.

My wine arrived, and I took a sip, grateful for the distraction. When the server left, Domenic leaned across the table, extending a hand to Zaira as if in supplication. "As Amalia could tell you, I'm often a fool."

"At least you admit it." Zaira let him take her hand, a smirk tugging at her mouth.

"Still, I've rarely felt as great a fool as I do now. I didn't realize until yesterday that not all Falcons went to the Mews willingly." He grimaced at his own ignorance. "I'm appalled that happened to you."

I hid my discomfort behind a sip of wine.

Zaira raised her brows. "You didn't know the mage-marked have no choice? I'm a Tallows brat who's never seen the inside of a school, and I know it's in the Serene Accords."

"I know the law, but I didn't know any Falcons, so I thought it was always like the stories." Domenic shrugged ruefully. "You know, the little orphan girl driven out of her village with stones, then discovered at last and whisked off to live like a princess in the Mews."

"I'll bet my front teeth mage-marked didn't write those stories," Zaira said.

"No bet." Domenic put a hand over his mouth. "I like my teeth where they are. But yes, I'm a selfish fool not to have wondered until yesterday what happens to the mage-marked who don't *want* to join the Falcons. And I'm sorry for that."

"Better late than never." Zaira fixed him with an assessing stare. "So what are you going to do about it?"

"First, talk to my brother. He has friends who've had some success standing up to the Empire. Maybe we can start by protecting the mage-marked in Ardence, then work on getting Raverra to alter the Serene Accords."

Zaira and I both stared at him in shock. By her expression, she hadn't expected a serious answer; as for me, I couldn't believe he was going to plan treason right here in front of me.

"Altering the law is a worthy long-term goal," I said carefully. "But what do you mean, *protecting the mage-marked in Ardence*? If you simply mean keeping them safe from misguided or malicious attacks, the Falconers do that."

"I thought they did." Domenic's brows lowered. "But after what happened in Ardence the other night, I'm not so sure."

Dread caught its claws in my heart. *Here it comes.* "What happened? I still don't know."

"The Falconers seized Ardentine nobles' children from their homes without warning." Domenic took a heartfelt swallow of coffee, as if he could wash the awful taste of the words from his mouth. "The Empire is holding them against Ardence's good behavior."

"That's impossible." The dismissal burst instinctively from my lips.

Zaira let out a harsh bark of a laugh. "That the Falconers would abduct someone? Oh, yes, completely impossible."

"Far from it. It's happened before, almost exactly like this." Domenic traced a pattern through the wet ring his mug had left on the table, as if writing history there. "When Raverra defeated Ardence and brought it into the Empire, two hundred years ago, there were nobles who refused to accept Raverran rule. The Empire took their firstborn hostage and kept them in the Mews with the Falcons until all murmurs of rebellion died down. I'm sure it's a historical footnote for you, but no one in Ardence has forgotten."

"I'm not saying the Empire would never do something like that." I smoothed out my voice, trying to make it reasonable. "I'm saying they didn't. The doge and the Falconers don't know anything about this."

"They must know." Domenic shook his head. "The whole Ardentine Embassy is on fire with the news. The courier lamps are flashing nonstop with it. I've now heard over the lamps from several people with firsthand knowledge of the incident, including my brother, and a friend whose child was taken."

"A friend! Not Venasha?"

"No, no." He lifted his palms, warding off the idea. "Venasha's baby is fine. A family friend; no one you know. But the point is, this is no rumor. It really happened."

I couldn't reconcile Domenic's earnest expression with the doge's fury at not knowing of the incident. I pressed my fingers to my forehead. "*What* really happened, exactly?"

Domenic sucked in a long breath. "During a grand state ball, when most of the high nobles of Ardence were out carousing late into the night, groups of Falconers and imperial soldiers stormed into the homes of over a dozen of the most powerful lords in Ardence and seized their children. Even though they weren't mage-marked. The Falconers had an imperial writ and seal they showed the governesses and nursemaids brave enough to challenge their authority."

I stared at him. He sounded so sure. "There must have been some mistake."

"There was no mistake. The Falconers left letters in place of the children they took, under the seal of the Serene Empire, declaring Raverra had taken the children to ensure their parents' cooperation. When the parents stormed up to the embassy demanding to see their children, the Serene Envoy refused."

"That doesn't sound right. What did she say?"

Domenic spread his palms. "I don't know exactly. She dismissed them out of hand. Some of them wanted to gather their household guard and search the envoy's palace by force, but Duke Astor arrived around dawn and pulled them into council to discuss Ardence's official response before anyone could do anything too rash."

Lady Terringer's message to the doge had mentioned incoherent demands. If she knew nothing of the incident and had been roused from her bed before dawn to find raging parents flinging accusations at her door, she might not have made much sense of what they were saying.

"This doesn't add up." I tapped the table. "This wasn't done with the doge's knowledge, and I can't believe the Falconers at the imperial garrison in Ardence would dare take such steps on their own. Even if they did, they wouldn't have access to the imperial seal."

Zaira frowned. "Curse my tongue for speaking well of those bastards, but I have to admit I never saw any brats at the Mews who weren't mage-marked."

"Even so, it happened. I know some of the children who were taken." Domenic's fingers tightened on his cup. "I know their families. Maybe Gabril and the Shadow Gentry are right after all, if the doge is stealing children. I've heard they're getting ready to do something about this. I'm half tempted to join them."

The Shadow Gentry—the gray-masked secret society Ignazio had mentioned, which wanted Ardentine independence. Hell of Discord. If Domenic's brother was a member, that wasn't good. And if they were taking action on their own, that was worse.

"Domenic, be careful," I warned. "Don't go stumbling into treason. We don't know what the truth is here. There's got to be some deception at work."

"The truth is the children are gone, and their parents are

grieving and angry." He shrugged, a defeated motion. "If it wasn't the Empire, I don't know who could do such a thing."

Zaira patted his shoulder. "The Empire isn't the only demon in the Nine Hells, believe me. It's just the biggest and ugliest."

That startled a smile out of him. He squeezed her hand. "Thanks. That's a great consolation."

"I'll help you find out what happened to the children." I caught myself before adding *I swear*. "My mother may have more—"

His chair scraped the floor. "You can't tell La Contessa what we talked about. For Graces' sake. I'd be dead by morning."

"She wouldn't do that."

"She's on the Council of Nine," he said. "She executes a dozen traitors before breakfast."

"Never before *breakfast*," I objected. "And she doesn't execute them. She just condemns them to . . . Oh, never mind. I won't tell her. But I won't be able to accomplish as much without her help."

"I'll take that trade." He relaxed. "Thank you. Even if you can't find out anything, I'm glad you're willing to listen. A lot of Raverrans would have just shouted at me about the Empire and never admitted the Falconer system might have problems."

Zaira crossed her arms. "Anyone who can't see it's got problems isn't looking too cursed hard. By the Demon of Madness's pimply buttocks, you're arguing about whether they stole *these particular* brats, not whether they're child stealers."

"They don't steal children," I objected.

"No, you're right. They conscript them into the army. That's *so* much better." Zaira gave me a challenging stare over the rim of her mug as she sucked down the rest of her coffee.

"Not much better, perhaps," I admitted, "but the Falconers are at least an improvement over the alternatives Eruvia has come up with thus far. Loreice burned the mage-marked at the stake before Raverra brought it into the Empire. In Vaskandar, the mage-marked have raised themselves as bloody conquerors, abusing the people as their whims dictate. Every place and time in history there have been no laws to protect or regulate the mage-marked, they've become either victims or tyrants."

"Less terrible is still bad. And I'll tell you an alternative: leave us alone," Zaira snapped. "I wasn't bothering anybody before the Falconers found me."

"You killed three men and were about to set the city on fire," I protested. "If you weren't in the Falcons right now, you'd probably be executed for murder."

She glared at me. "They had it coming, and you know it."

Domenic stared back and forth between us. "It sounds as if your induction into the Falcons was more dramatic than the incident in Ardence," he said. "And *that* involved angry aristo-crats storming the Serene Envoy's Palace."

"Damned right. I don't do things by halves." Zaira frowned. "Though, come to think of it, neither does the Empire. Maybe you're right about the Falconers not taking those rich brats after all."

"Oh?" I asked.

"I've never heard of Raverra being shy about admitting when they have someone by the bollocks. If they did something like this, they'd brag about it, not deny it."

Domenic put his forehead in his hands. "I don't know whether to hope you're right or wrong. If the Falconers have started grabbing political hostages, Gabril and the Shadow Gen-try may have the right idea; but I'd trust the Serene Empire to at least not harm the children. If this is some sick deception, there's no guarantee they're even alive."

I hadn't thought of that. "Graces protect them. We'd better pray Duke Astor and the doge listen to each other, and combine their efforts to find them quickly."

Domenic grimaced. "We may have to pray fairly hard. I know my cousin, and I regret to say he doesn't even listen to his own advisers."

Zaira grunted. "So long as he has the common sense to make sure he knows what really happened before he throws shit in the doge's eye and it's too late to say sorry."

I winced at the metaphor, but had to agree with the sentiment. Of all the blessings of the Nine Graces, Niro da Morante held Mercy in the least measure.

"Well, that was more interesting than when you took me to the market," Zaira said as we crossed the wide expanse of a public plaza on our way back to my boat.

If I ignored the guards walking a few paces away, pretending to be laborers who happened to be heading in the same direction, I could imagine the two of us were friends out for an innocent stroll. The sun struck warm and bright on the buildings ringing the great square, and scents of wine and herbs battled for dominance with the ever-present salty tang of the lagoon.

It was too beautiful a day to feel so cold and queasy. "I don't know what to do, Zaira."

"I'll tell you what to do. Take me for coffee with your friend again, but pick a less depressing subject of conversation next time."

I shook my head. "I mean about what we just learned. I need to pass on the information on the abduction of the Ardentine heirs. The doge must know more by now, but I doubt he has the full Ardentine perspective. But if the Council of Nine finds out Domenic has a connection to the Shadow Gentry, he could face serious difficulties."

"You're not allowed to get him in trouble. I like him." A savory smile curved her lips. "And he has quite a fine set of shoulders, that man. No turning him in as a traitor."

"He's my friend! I would never do that. Besides, he's not a traitor." I dropped my voice. "But his brother may be."

Zaira cast a glance at me sideways, her dark eyes sober. "The one who's mixed up with the group with the overly dramatic name?"

"The Shadow Gentry." I tucked my lip between my teeth. "From what Ignazio said, they sound flat-out treasonous, and they may have ties to Vaskandar. If Domenic gets drawn in, or gets blamed for his brother's actions... Well, I can't let that happen."

"No," Zaira agreed. "We can't."

The space between us seemed to warm with our agreement to protect Domenic. Finally, we had something in common.

Zaira and I were due back at the Mews for a special training session Marcello had arranged. We caught him as he emerged from a drill in a crowd of other Falconers, a long flintlock rifle resting on his shoulder. We walked with him as he returned the rifle to the armory, talking with our heads together, voices low.

"We learned what Ardence thinks happened in that supposed Falconer incident." I filled him in on the basics, without mentioning Domenic's name.

Marcello sucked a breath through his teeth. "That explains some things. We have some new reports in through the courier lamps, but they weren't making sense."

"What new reports?"

He glanced around as we entered the armory. A few other Falconers who'd attended the drill deposited their rifles in the racks along the wall and left, one teasing the other about spilling his powder. Marcello waited until they were gone.

"Reports that several nobles of the Ardentine court claim Falconers took their children in the dead of night, like you said. And that Duke Astor Bergandon is demanding we return them at once, in rather forceful terms."

"But we don't actually have them?" I tried to sound certain, but my voice rose to shape a question despite myself.

"We most certainly don't." Marcello shoved his gun back into its place with unnecessary force. "That's not how it works. It's impossible so many children would appear with the mage mark in the same place and time, and we don't just barge in and grab them in the night. We talk to the parents and give them time to think about it—days, usually, or even weeks, unless there's an immediate threat to the safety of innocents."

He flicked his eyes to Zaira, who gave him a mocking salute. "Threatening the safety of innocents, that's me. My favorite pastime."

"Would you know if they'd taken the children as political hostages? Normal children, without the mage mark?"

Marcello stiffened. "That would never happen. And besides, we've checked with the Falconers stationed in Ardence. They didn't do anything of the sort."

"Then someone set this up." The cold certainty of it settled in my stomach. "Someone staged the incident, with kidnappers dressed as Falconers, and a stolen or forged imperial seal."

Marcello frowned. "Or the Ardentines are lying."

"I've met plenty of liars," Zaira said. "Our Ardentine isn't one of them."

"So you think Ardence is deceived?" Marcello started pacing a tight arc between the weapon racks. "But why would anyone kidnap nobles' heirs and blame it on the Falconers?"

I could think of only one reason. "To cause trouble between Ardence and Raverra."

"Trouble?"

I didn't want to speak the dread certainty that had been growing in me, for fear of making it real. But I forced the words out.

"To start a war."

"Grace of Mercy." Marcello's gaze traveled around the racks of guns and swords that surrounded us, lined up neat and ready. "Vaskandar. Just like your mother said in the Map Room. They're trying to distract and weaken us so they can invade Loreice again."

"Maybe." I bit my lip, thinking. "What's Lady Terringer doing in response to the duke's demands?"

"Telling them we didn't do it, I presume." Marcello shrugged helplessly. "I mostly know the Falconer end, not the diplomatic one."

"She'd better convince them." I dropped my voice almost to a whisper. "And not just so we can get the children back quickly. I don't like what the Council said, about deploying Falcons to Ardence if needed."

"What's this about deploying Falcons?" Zaira asked sharply.

We both turned to look at her, like children caught with their hands in the sugar jar.

Zaira glared. "They were talking about me, weren't they? I'm not *deploying* anywhere, except back to the Tallows."

"No, of course not." Marcello forced a smile. "No one's seriously thinking of moving Falcons against Ardence, at this point anyway. This is a job for diplomats, not soldiers. And besides, we don't put untrained Falcons into battle." His eyes widened. "Hells. Training!"

"What?" I asked.

"Demons curse me, we're late." Marcello slapped his own forehead. "And he hates waiting."

Zaira frowned suspiciously. "Who?"

Marcello turned toward the armory door, a spark of something like anticipation lighting his eyes. "Come and find out."

"Here again?" Zaira glared at the familiar classroom door in the wood-paneled hall. It was the same room in which Marcello had tried to interview her. "Haven't you learned not to try to teach me?"

"I'm not going to try," Marcello said, a grin banishing the

lingering clouds of worry in his face as if he expected something good. "*They* are."

He flung the door open. The same classroom greeted us, with its bare walls, half circle of chairs, and low wooden stage. But the stage was no longer empty.

A pair of men about my mother's age waited on it, both in scarlet-and-gold uniforms. One, lean and wiry with spiky tufts of pale hair, stood with arms crossed on his chest, an impatient gleam in his eyes. A jess shone on his wrist. The other, heavy with muscle, had his hair cut so close I could see his deep-brown scalp through it. He stood more at ease, hands clasped behind his back, rocking on his feet as if he were used to waiting and didn't mind it.

"Finally," the thin one said. "Let's do this."

The other saluted Marcello. "Lieutenant. Reporting for duty."

"Thank you, gentlemen." Marcello gestured to the pale one first, then his muscular partner. "May I introduce Ensign Jerith Antelles and his Falconer, Balos."

Jerith flicked his fingers in a wave. Balos bowed. "His Falconer for twenty years, husband for fifteen."

"Mind you, marrying your Falconer is against regulations," Jerith confided, "but I bullied him into it anyway. He's worth the demotion, most days."

Balos winced with embarrassment at the word *demotion,* but the affection between them seemed comfortable and well broken in, like a favorite pair of boots. I glanced at Zaira's sullen face, and despaired of ever attaining a shadow of such understanding.

Marcello cleared his throat. "And I have the honor to introduce the Lady Amalia Cornaro and her Falcon, Zaira."

Balos bowed again, deeper, on hearing my name. Jerith took in Zaira with a glance and chuckled. "You don't have to tell me which is which. I could have won *this* game of Spot the Warlock from across a crowded market."

"What's that supposed to mean?" Zaira demanded.

"You have a certain look about you." Jerith smiled innocently.

Zaira snorted. "I suppose you're here to tell me the Mews isn't so bad, and I'll get used to it and come to think of it as a home, and all that other bullshit I've been hearing for two weeks from the idiots so addled they *like* wearing jesses?"

Jerith cocked his head. "Oh, you're funny. Was I ever this annoying, Balos?"

"Worse," Balos said.

"You should have punched me in the mouth."

Zaira stepped forward, fists clenched. "Go ahead and try it. But I'm not cleaning up the floor when I'm done with you."

I tensed, ready to jump out of the way if Zaira commenced the distribution of more black eyes. But Jerith laughed. "Very nice. I like this one."

Balos eyed his partner. "I think she meant it, Jerith."

"I know. That's why I like her."

Marcello grinned as though he were watching a circus. "Ensign Antelles," he explained, "is one of our storm warlocks."

Zaira's eyes widened. She stared at Jerith for a moment, her fists relaxing. Glancing back and forth between them, I understood Jerith's comment about a certain look: they were both thin and keen as stiletto blades, their movements full of a terrible energy barely held in check.

Zaira flopped into a chair, crossing her arms. "So are you here to tell me how to be a good little mage?"

"No," Jerith said. "We're here to teach you how to be an effective one."

"The first and greatest problem for warlocks," Balos began, his voice deep and calm, "is control."

"But you knew that, didn't you, missy?" Jerith flashed his teeth at Zaira, who scowled in response.

Balos continued as if he were used to ignoring Jerith's interruptions. "The warlock's challenge is to keep your control. The Falconer's is to recognize when the warlock has lost it and to make a quick and calculated judgment as to when to seal their power."

Zaira dug deeper into her chair, uncharacteristically silent. As I settled down two seats away from her, Balos met my eyes with his deep-brown ones. "Warlocks often collapse if they've used more than a small portion of their power, since the energy comes from within them until it starts taking lives. But once the lightning—or the balefire, in your case—starts killing, it draws power from the slain, and gains a life of its own. And the more it kills, the greater it grows, until it surpasses its wielder's control and possesses them with a madness of destruction, the hunger of the fire itself." Sadness softened his face. "Sometimes you need to let your warlock go for a while, even when the killing madness has taken them. Sometimes more people die if you stop it too soon, before the threat is over. But if you wait a moment too late, your own life could be in danger. And if *you* fall, no one can stop them."

I shifted uncomfortably in my chair. But it would never happen, I reminded myself. This was all mere theory, so long as the Empire remained at peace.

So long as whoever had sent false Falconers after the heirs of Ardence failed to start a war.

"All very grim," Jerith said lightly, watching Zaira's face. "But the point is, timing is key. And having a Falconer means you can let loose sometimes without worrying about hurting the wrong people."

Zaira scowled. "I know how to handle my fire, thank you very much. I'm not a child. I've lived with this for eighteen years."

"Of course," Balos agreed, his tone patient. "But now you have a Falconer, and it's different. Even more so for a warlock than for, say, an alchemist or an artificer."

"Why more so for warlocks?" I asked.

"There are strict rules about when you can unseal a warlock." Balos glanced at Jerith, who shrugged his disinterest in explaining regulations. "Since a warlock's power is so lethal, we're only allowed to unleash them in emergencies, or if we judge the situation to be dangerous. If we have reason to believe a threat may be active in the area, for instance."

"Like an assassin." Jerith's mage mark stood out silver as he trained his gaze at Zaira. "Get used to assassins."

"Or, of course," Balos added, "we can release our warlocks if we have orders from above to do so."

Zaira glared at him. "You're saying I should let the Right Honorable Spoiled Heiress here and a bunch of jewel-encrusted old carcasses decide when to use my fire, like telling a dog when it can piss. I'd rather make my own damned decisions."

I winced at her language. "Believe me, I have no desire to make them for you."

Balos frowned. "The Falconer doesn't decide for the Falcon. They're both bound by the same rules, and they make the choice together." He spread his hands. "Most Falcons can simply ask to be released anytime, and some leave their powers unsealed by default, especially within the Mews. But because a warlock's power is almost always deadly, there are additional levels of precautions, for everyone's safety. You wouldn't expect to be allowed to fire off a cannon in the middle of the Imperial Square for no reason, would you?"

"Don't talk to me as if I were a child. It's not unleashing my balefire *without* orders I'm worried about." Zaira kicked at her chair leg. "Besides, you're not the warlock. I'm not going to listen to this idiot."

Anger sparked in Jerith's eyes, and he stepped in front of Balos, almost protectively. "Oh, you'll listen. You know why warlocks are so rare, and fire warlocks especially?"

"Shut up," Zaira said through her teeth.

"Because they don't have good control when they're children." The storm warlock wielded his words like knives, and Zaira flinched under them. "They slip, and kill someone. Maybe a lot of someones. And either some brave soul kills the young warlock before the carnage gets out of hand, because that's the only way to stop them without a Falconer..."

"Stop." Zaira's voice was thick with fury. "I get it."

Jerith continued ruthlessly. "Or no one stops them, and the poor kid is so devastated when he wakes up and sees what he's done that he kills himself."

Zaira stood, fists balled. For a moment, I thought she'd walk up and punch the storm warlock.

But she turned without another word and strode out of the room. The door slammed behind her.

Balos sighed and put an arm around Jerith's shoulders. "Don't you think that was a bit cruel?"

Jerith relaxed into Balos's chest, bringing a hand up to meet his. "Not as cruel as what she'll do if she won't listen. She's tough. She'll get over it."

That evening, I couldn't chase worries about Ardence and the missing children out of my head to focus on my luminary-coil design. I leaned over my desk, the Muscati book vying for space with loose pages of notes and my elixir bottle. The strains of a trio sonata issued from a symphonic shell on my shelf, similar to the one I'd seen at the pawnbroker's, but tonight the music failed to help me focus as it usually did. My formulae blurred like faulty courier-lamp glass.

I leaned back and rubbed my forehead. There was no sense in fretting. The whole incident was staged—a lie. Once Lady

Terringer explained the truth, surely the Ardentine nobles would calm down and see that cooperation with the Empire was the fastest way to find out who had really taken their children. And with my mother pressuring Baron Leodra to keep his mouth shut, there was no reason to expect anyone on the Raverran end to push for an unduly severe response to Ardence's misplaced demands. Someone had tried an audacious gambit to set Ardence against the Empire, but truth would prevail.

If Duke Astor listened to Lady Terringer. If the anxious parents were willing to take her word over the evidence of their own eyes and the supposed imperial seal. If the Shadow Gentry didn't do something foolish to cross a line the doge couldn't ignore.

Footsteps sounded in the hall, and a knock came at my door.

"Lady Amalia?" Old Anzo's voice called.

"Yes?"

"A Lieutenant Verdi is here to see you, my lady. He says it's quite urgent."

That couldn't be good. The facades of the town houses across the Imperial Canal lay in shadow; soon night would fall, and the luminaries would kindle. Whatever brought him here at this hour was likely an emergency.

I rose from my half-finished calculations. "Tell him I'll be right down."

Marcello paced in the foyer, which meant he must have refused Ciardha's relentless hospitality. The half cape of his uniform swished behind him, and his rapier and flintlock gleamed at his hips. If the hour were less urgent, I might have paused to admire the effect.

"Zaira's gone," he said before I could greet him.

My hand went to my falcon's-head brooch. "Gone? You mean she ran away? How?"

"It's my fault. She locked herself in her room after Jerith

pushed her so hard this morning. I hoped to earn her trust, so I called off the guards I had watching her." He punched his own thigh. "I should have known better. I thought the Mews walls and wards would be enough, but they're meant to keep enemies out, not to keep Falcons in."

"But the Mews is on an island," I protested.

"She swam out into the lagoon, knocked someone out of a boat, and stole it. We found out when we pulled the boatman out of the water."

I failed to smother a laugh. That sounded like Zaira, all right. But Marcello wasn't smiling. I remembered what he'd said, about how if we let her go, she'd be dead within the week.

"Do you think she's in danger?" I asked.

"I have to assume so," he said. "Especially given the escalating tension with Ardence. I hate to ask when it's my own mistake that caused this, but... Will you help me find her before someone unsavory does?"

"Of course. What can I do to help?"

"I knew you'd say that. Thank you, my lady." Warmth flickered in his eyes. It could have been pride, or affection. I wasn't sure what to do with either. "If you get close, you may be able to detect her presence, since you're linked. But it won't work from farther away, and I have no idea where to start looking."

"I do," I said.

"You do? Where?"

"We need to go to the Tallows, to find a ragpicker."

Chapter Ten

A chill crept into the early-autumn air, stealing into the narrow spaces between the buildings as shadows swallowed the Tallows. I was glad I'd thought to throw on a coat, though the fine plum velvet and the white lace at my throat and wrists marked me out of place in a district of wool and patches. Lieutenant Verdi, in his scarlet uniform, stood out even more. Moving among tired laborers heading home for the evening, we might as well have worn masquerade costumes.

It was no wonder no one would answer our questions.

As we paused on a bridge, a pair of soldiers reported their lack of findings to Marcello, saluted, and hurried off to continue their search. I didn't catch everything they said, but one of them mentioned a familiar name.

"Have you learned anything more about Orthys?" I asked Marcello.

He grimaced. "He smuggles dream poppies into the Empire from Vaskandar. I had people look into him after we picked up Zaira. Unsavory at best, with a rough crew backing him."

"Dream poppies! I'm surprised the Council hasn't had him arrested already."

Marcello eyed me sideways. "Well, rumor has it he's provided useful information to the Council, and they've turned a blind eye.

But he's been pushing his luck, being too brazen and committing other crimes. I suspect his days of escaping official notice are over." He gazed out over the bridge, scanning the water traffic. "That won't save Zaira tonight if he's out for vengeance, though."

I cursed whatever contrary impulse had driven her out into the twisting alleys of Raverra now, when everyone from dreampoppy smugglers to Ardentine patriots wanted her blood. I peered down the canal as far as I could, but as it angled, it vanished between buildings huddled close across the water. There was no sign of a bushy mane of hair in any of the boats below. Most of the oarsmen had lit lanterns by now, and their reflections glimmered upon the water. In this part of the city, no one could afford luminaries to spark awake at dusk.

I felt Marcello's eyes on me and turned. He wore a strange expression, reflected lamplight shimmering on his face.

"What?" I asked. "Is something wrong?"

"Not at all." He leaned on the stone railing beside me. "Not with you, at any rate, my lady. You're exemplary."

My pulse kicked up to a canter. But it was probably a mere empty compliment.

"I hardly think so," I said. "I'm not being much help in finding our lost Falcon, I'm afraid."

"I apologize for dragging you all over the Tallows." He smiled ruefully. "You haven't complained a bit."

"I just hope we can find her before anything happens to her."

"This disaster is my fault," he muttered, looking out at the lights on the water. "Maybe my father was right about me."

I reached out toward him, then hesitated as if he were a hot kettle.

But I'd touched a girl who was actually on fire. So I laid a hand on his shoulder. That was safe: something a friend might do. "Zaira can create disasters without any help from you. Don't be so hard on yourself. We'll find her."

He reached up and covered my hand with his own. *Friends,* I reminded myself. "You're right. We will."

He took his hand back, too quickly. I dropped mine, too, and we stood a moment in silence together, gazing out over the canal. Warmth flooded me, kindling brighter than any luminary, and I could have lingered on that bridge for a long while.

But staring at the water wouldn't find Zaira, so we continued over the bridge and down a narrow street, walking a little closer to each other than we had before. Around us, shopkeepers shuttered their windows for the night.

"Do you feel anything?" Marcello asked. Before I could get flustered, he added, "From the link?"

"What exactly am I supposed to be—" I broke off, staring at a display table in front of a shop. The round-faced proprietress was clearing away a variety of trinkets, including a very familiar amber necklace.

I all but lunged across the table to point at the necklace as she scooped it up.

"Excuse me. Where did you get that?"

The woman tucked it away in a bag, her face shuttering like the shops around us. "I came by it honestly."

"I'm sure you did," I agreed. "The girl who sold it to you— she was quite thin, about eighteen years old, with curling dark hair, no?"

Her eyes narrowed until they nearly disappeared behind her round cheeks. "If you know Zaira, why are you asking?"

"We're looking for her, to help her. Do you have any idea where she went?"

There was a soft *clink* as Marcello laid a coin at the edge of the display table. The shopkeeper's eyes drifted to it.

"Maybe I remember something," she said. "Maybe she asked me if I'd seen a certain person."

Clink. Another coin. "Try to remember," I encouraged her.

"She sold me the necklace about an hour ago. She was going to see old Gregor, the ragpicker," the shopkeeper said. "I do seem to recall."

"Is he a friend of hers?"

The shopkeeper laughed, harsh as a crow. "Zaira doesn't have any friends."

I swallowed a lump like a mooring knot. "Where does this ragpicker live?"

Marcello slid another coin onto the table as punctuation.

"Across Lost Ring Bridge, on the Street of the Ratcatchers. The blue door." The shopkeeper swept up the coins along with the rest of the trinkets on the table and bustled inside without another word.

The sky deepened to a rich purple, and the canal waters flowed black below Lost Ring Bridge. Someone had lit a candle at a tiny wooden shrine to the Grace of Luck tucked up against the bridge railing—perhaps in hope of finding something, such as the eponymous ring. Or a missing warlock.

"I hope she's all right," I said. "If I were up to no good, I would strike when it got dark."

"We need to find her soon." Marcello let out a nervous puff of air. "If it comes to it, and we have no other choice, be prepared to release her seal. So she can defend herself."

The night air went dry in my throat. "I understand."

"You remember the word to reseal her power, right? '*Revincio.*'"

"*Revincio,*" I repeated. "Yes."

"Only as a last resort," Marcello cautioned. "She can't control the balefire, and it could spread quickly enough to kill you before you reseal her. But if, say, twenty armed louts come after us and we're about to die..."

That didn't make me feel any better.

The Street of the Ratcatchers was so narrow I could touch the buildings on both sides at once. They loomed like disapproving fathers as we waited for the blue door to open to Marcello's militant knock.

After an uncomfortable wait and a second knock, an old man holding a candle opened the door. His lined face showed more wear than his surprisingly clean shirtsleeves. His eyes traveled from Marcello's uniform to my velvet coat.

"Yes?" he asked. "Can I help you?"

"We're looking for Zaira," I said before Marcello could bring his more authoritative voice to bear. "We're worried about her. Has she been to see you?"

The old man regarded us warily. "You're Falconers."

"Yes."

"Zaira didn't want to join the Falcons."

"We'd noticed." The old man's lips pursed at that, as if he were suppressing a smile. I pressed my advantage. "We don't want to hold her against her will. But now that her secret is out, she won't be safe anywhere else."

The old man sighed. "I told her, Lady. I told her she wouldn't last the night in the Tallows, with Orthys crying for her blood. But she's fixed on that dog. I might as well have been talking Vaskandran."

"Orthys?" Marcello asked.

But I held the old man's gaze and spoke right over him: "Dog? What dog?"

The old man shook his head. "She made me take money. Said something about balancing the scales. All I did, Lady, was this. When Orthys's ruffians came for her a couple weeks ago, they cornered her in the abandoned laundry she used to sleep in, and she had that scrawny mongrel with her. *She* could jump out the window into the canal and swim for it, but the dog couldn't, and she had it in her head that if she left him for Orthys's men, they'd hurt him. I was in there buying scraps from her, so I promised I'd get the dog out, just so she'd run."

A wave of pity so strong it bordered on nausea flooded my stomach. "So all this was to pay you back for saving her dog?"

"They do say the mage-marked are a bit daft, Lady."

"Do you know where she is now?"

"I expect she's looking for her dog," he replied with the weary tone of an elder who knows better. "I told her I didn't see where the mongrel went once I got him out of the building. I'd check the laundry first, since that was where she last saw him."

Marcello stepped forward into the light of the candle. "How long ago did you talk to her?"

"She couldn't be more than half an hour gone," the old man said. "Less, maybe."

I wanted to clasp his hand, but it was full of candle. "Thank you."

Marcello reached into his purse, but the old man waved him off. "Take care of that girl, sir. That's all I ask. No one has since the old woman died."

"Old woman?" I asked.

The ragpicker nodded. "Zaira never had any family, but an old street sweeper used to watch over her when she was small. She died in the awful tenement fire, what, eight years ago? Zaira's been alone since then, except for the dog." He peered at Marcello. "So you find her, Falconer, and you keep her safe."

"I will," Marcello promised.

The blue door closed. We stood in the Street of the Ratcatchers, forced close together by the narrow passage.

"The old woman burned." I took a breath sharp with horror. "Marcello, do you think she..."

"It's not uncommon." Worry furrowed his brow. "You heard Jerith. Once they succumb to their flames, warlocks have little to no control over whom they kill."

"And *she* heard Jerith, too." I gripped my falcon's-head brooch until the pin pricked my skin. "We have to find her. Come on. Let's check that abandoned laundry."

The back door to the laundry hung off its hinges, splintered wood showing fresh and white. I caught a rank whiff of mouse droppings wafting out. With boards covering the windows, the interior was black as a demon's soul.

Marcello took out a pocket luminary from his pouch and shook the glass globe vigorously until a pale glow kindled within.

"This will only give us a few minutes of light," he warned.

"I know." Holding my breath, I stepped past him through the door.

The faint glow cast hulking shadows behind empty laundry vats and struck a glitter off some broken glass. A messy bundle of blankets lay on the stone floor in one corner, next to a cracked pitcher and the stub end of a candle. A stingroach scuttled away from the light.

Unease hooked cold claws through my chest. "She's not here."

Marcello shone the luminary around, but the spark inside it was already fading. "You're right. Let's go."

Back outside, I stood closer to Marcello than was strictly necessary, for the reassurance of his unquestionable solidity and warm gunpowder-and-leather smell. "Why would she prefer *that* over the Mews?"

"It's not that this is better," he said. "It's that she didn't get to choose."

The chill night air cut straight through my stockings. I rubbed my ankles together to keep them warm. We'd been walking for hours, and a dull weariness spread through my limbs.

"Now what?" I asked.

"We keep searching. She's around here somewhere, looking for her lost dog, of all things. Can you pick up any sense of where she might be?"

I tried to focus. Water slapped against the walls of a nearby canal. Someone was singing not far off, in a voice lubricated with wine.

An itch nagged at the back of my mind—a feeling I'd forgotten something important.

"Maybe," I said.

Marcello nodded encouragingly. "Where? Which way?"

"I don't know." But if I had to pick a direction..."That way?" I pointed, unsure why it felt right, only knowing it did.

"All right." His voice deepened with grim purpose. "Let's find Zaira, before someone else does."

We hurried across Lost Ring Bridge. My intuition kept pricking me to turn here, then there, through narrow streets and pocket courtyards, into the maw of an alley, past windows that glowed with golden lamplight. My breath came quickly from our pace, but I didn't dare slow down and risk losing whatever delicate thread I'd picked up. After what I'd seen and heard, I was more desperate to find Zaira than ever.

Finally, raised voices rang out not far ahead, one with Zaira's unmistakable brashness. I exchanged glances with Marcello, and we broke into a run.

We burst into a small plaza in time to see a man broad as a tavern door knock Zaira to the ground. Five more stood by, their restless anger charging the air.

"Bloody demon," one shouted as Zaira slowly raised herself off the flagstones. "Orthys will dice you into pieces for what you did!"

Hells. This was not how I'd hoped to find her.

"Stop!" Marcello called, drawing a rapier in one hand

and a flintlock pistol in the other. "In the name of the doge's Falconers!"

For lack of a better idea, I drew my dagger and stepped up beside him, trying to look dangerous in my plum velvet jacket. The word *Exsolvo* tickled my throat, but I swallowed it for now.

The men did not appear impressed. They spread out, drawing their own daggers, and a couple of pistols as well. One round mouth pointed directly at me. I tried to hold my dagger like Ciardha had taught me, despite the queasy flutter in my belly, planning where and how to strike once they came close enough. My flare locket might give us cover to escape, but I couldn't use it until we had Zaira back.

"Well, Orthys was right," the biggest one said, laughing. He had an odd scar across his cheek, with prongs like fingers. "They went and hooded the harpy. She was lying, boys. She can't light a candle with her jess on."

Zaira bolted, but one of the men grabbed her. She cursed and spat as he twisted her arms behind her back.

That left four to face Marcello and me. They advanced across the square, menace strung between them like a net.

"Unseal me, you moron!" Zaira screamed at me, struggling with useless frenzy. "Say the word, and I'll burn them all down!"

"My lady, don't," Marcello hissed. "She can't control it. And we can't trust her."

"Do it!" Zaira urged. "I'll kill them all!"

The big one rounded on Zaira, his fists raised. "Shut up!"

Another in a leather cap shouted, "Don't let them release her! Shoot her Falconer!"

My breath crystallized to ice in my lungs in one white instant.

The flintlock pointed at me fired.

Chapter Eleven

Two loud cracks hit my ears, echoes ricocheting off the walls around the square.

Two showers of sparks flared in the dim air—one aimed at me and the other from Marcello. A shriek sounded from one of the second-story windows overlooking the plaza.

The man who'd fired at me staggered, red blooming on his chest, and sank to the ground. Smoke rose lazily from the barrel of Marcello's pistol. He took a step forward, angling to place himself half in front of me.

The pain I'd braced for never came. The scoundrel had missed. A wave of dizzy relief swept through me.

"Let the Falcon go, and get out of here while you can," Marcello warned.

They wavered, fear in their eyes. For a moment, they might have run.

But then the man with the scar shouted, "That's his one shot! Shoot the girl, and let's get the harpy to Orthys!"

"Now!" Zaira yelled. "Unleash me, you idiot!"

"Very well."

The voice that came from my chest rang cold and clear, with the sure calm of command. It could have been my mother's.

Believe without a doubt you are in control, she had told me, *and you will be.*

They reacted to it. Even Zaira and Marcello. For an instant, they paused, and I had their absolute attention.

"If you want to burn like the others did, so be it. But you've chosen a terrible way to die."

Orthys's hirelings exchanged faltering glances.

"It's a good thing," Marcello added, "I have two more pistols."

I raised my arm skyward and took a deep breath, uncertain whether I was going to shout the release word or escalate my bluff.

It was too much for the ruffian holding Zaira, who knew he'd be the first to burn. He swore and pushed her away. The man with the last remaining pistol tried to discharge it, and nothing happened. He broke and fled, cursing the damp air.

The others followed in a panicked rush, their footsteps thudding on the stones.

That left us facing Zaira, who stood wary as a cornered animal halfway across the plaza.

"Please, Zaira." I held out my hand. "If you run, they'll catch you again. And this time, they'll shoot us both on sight."

"If it weren't for you, I could defend myself fine," she snapped.

"I'm not sure I'd call burning down the Tallows 'fine,'" Marcello said. "Lady Amalia, are you well?"

"Yes. It seems the aim of poppy smugglers is not up to the standards of the doge's Falconers."

"Thank the Graces." His voice shook. But he held his rapier steady.

Zaira turned a suspicious frown on Marcello. "Do you really have two more pistols?"

"Let's discuss that at the Mews." That meant no. "Lady Amalia, I am ashamed to have put you in danger. No apology can suffice."

I shrugged, trying to look as if mortal danger was an old

friend. And it was, after a fashion. "No apology is needed. But I agree, let's get to the Mews."

Zaira's eyes shone in the moonlight. "I'm not done here."

"We don't have much time before they'll be back with reinforcements," Marcello said. "We have to leave now. This isn't safe."

"I won't pretend it is. But..." Zaira's voice dropped to a mumble. "I haven't found Scoundrel yet."

"Scoundrel?" It dawned on me, then. "You mean...your dog?"

Marcello threw his free hand into the air. "A dog! That's right. You almost got the Lady Amalia killed over a dog!"

Unshed tears gleamed in Zaira's eyes. She rubbed at them fiercely.

"All right." Some strong, bitter emotion lay under the surface of her voice. "Fine. You've caught me, for now. Back to the Mews. I could use a bite to eat."

I shivered as a soldier rowed us across to Raptor's Isle. The chill settled into my bones, making my limbs weak and clumsy; I'd stumbled getting into the boat, to my embarrassment. And the feeling I'd forgotten something important persisted, though Zaira was right there, huddled sulking in the middle of the boat.

I couldn't erase from my mind the image of her jumble of blankets in the corner of the mouse-infested laundry. My own canopied featherbed seemed obscene in contrast.

I wanted to reach out to her, somehow, but I didn't dare mention the laundry. And certainly not the old woman.

"This Orthys seems like an utter bastard." The word sat uncomfortably on my tongue, but I offered it up like an olive branch.

Zaira glared. "No worse than you lot."

She turned her back to me and settled into angry silence. I didn't try again.

The lights of the Mews blurred across the water, until I could no longer tell how far away they were. Weariness dragged at me far more heavily than I'd expect this side of midnight.

Hells. I knew what I'd forgotten.

My elixir. I could see the bottle, sitting on my desk next to my books, ready for my evening dose. But with the Zaira emergency, I hadn't remembered to take it, or to bring one of my three-hours'-grace vials, and I'd never expected to be out this long.

Now the last dose was wearing off, and slowly as a bud unfurling, the poison that almost killed me ten years ago was taking hold again.

My breath came in little gasps, as if I'd run a race wearing a corset. I tried to slow it down, but I couldn't. My vision swam at the edges, narrowing toward the center. No one had noticed—Marcello was talking to the soldier at the oar, while Zaira muttered to herself—but I couldn't hide the poison's effects forever.

I could do this. I'd been late with the elixir before. I had a few hours to get home before I lost the capability to do so unassisted. I'd simply need to make my excuses as soon as we landed and head home. My mother didn't need to know I'd forgotten.

The boat bumped against the dock. Marcello extended a hand to help me out. I stared at it, thinking through the process of standing up and stepping onto the dock as if it were a complex mathematical formula. Zaira had already scrambled out on her own.

Marcello frowned. "Lady Amalia? Are you well?"

"Fine," I said. "Just tired."

"Lady Amalia!" a new voice called. That couldn't possibly be . . .

It was. Ciardha, impeccable in her Cornaro livery, stood on the dock among the soldiers, an earthenware bottle in her hand.

"Your mother was concerned you were out so late in the

chill." Ciardha's lie was smooth and fine as Loreician silk. "She sent me here to meet you with some mulled wine." She proffered the bottle, locking eyes with me.

Marcello laughed. "Well, well! Rank has its privileges! I wish someone met me with mulled wine after a long night."

It wasn't mulled wine in that bottle. I should have known no error of mine would escape my mother's notice. I climbed out of the boat, my cheeks heating. She had to be the most interfering woman on earth.

"Thank you, Ciardha." I took the bottle and uncorked it; the familiar scent of anise wafted out. I gulped the elixir down, trying not to make a face at the bitter aftertaste.

"La Contessa says to do what you need to do here, then come home and rest, Lady," Ciardha murmured. I noticed she wore daggers sheathed at both hips, and I'd wager she had more in her sleeves and boots. She must already be aware of the trouble we'd had in the Tallows.

"I'll just make sure everything is settled first." And sit down until the elixir had a chance to work and my dizziness faded, but I didn't tell Ciardha that.

Zaira's voice cut across my thoughts like a serrated knife. "I don't give a damn," she told Marcello. "I'm starving. You may have dragged me back here, but you can't stop me from going to the kitchens to get something to eat."

Zaira turned on her heel before Marcello had a chance to reply, stalking off into the Mews. Marcello jerked his head at a couple of soldiers, who followed her. Clearly he wasn't taking chances with Zaira anymore.

Marcello sighed and turned to me. "My lady, might I have a few moments of your time? There's a matter I should discuss with you."

"Certainly. Perhaps we could go in and sit down for a moment?"

"Of course." The tightness Zaira had left in his face softened.

"I've had you on your feet all evening. I apologize." He dipped a bow, which I waved off, and led the way through the Mews gates.

Instead of proceeding to the garden as we had last time, we entered a grand hall. Portraits of famous Falcons and Falconers of history lined the walls. My vision was still too blurred to make out the ceiling fresco, but the rush of movement and light in the painting suggested a scene of one of the great battles the Falcons had won for Raverra.

We'd scarcely crossed the threshold when Colonel Vasante strode up to Marcello, iron-gray braid swinging behind her, boots reporting like musket fire on the marble floor. Her uniform doublet hung stiff and heavy with gold embroidery. Marcello saluted; her eyes narrowed in response.

"A word aside, Lieutenant, about tonight's escapades," she commanded, without so much as a glance my way.

Marcello gave me an apologetic grimace. "My lady, would you mind waiting a moment? I'm so sorry."

I sank onto a convenient bench. "I'll just sit here."

Marcello and the colonel withdrew into a side room. I took the opportunity to put my head down until the hall steadied and my breathing came under control. Weakness still dragged at my limbs, and probably would until tomorrow morning. If past experience held true, there was a headache in my future, too, and I shouldn't walk too close to a canal edge for the rest of the night on general principle. But I wasn't going to die.

Once I felt a little more human, I got up and went to the modest door Marcello and the colonel had gone through, intending to knock and find out whether I might head home at this point. But they'd left the door ajar, and Colonel Vasante's voice cut through the gap.

"—a *fire warlock*, for Graces' sake. The doge himself made it quite clear he considers her both extremely valuable and incredibly dangerous. And you *lost* her, Lieutenant."

Marcello muttered a reply. I hesitated, then remembered my great-grandfather and the privacy of others, and leaned against the wall in a position to hear better.

"I'm sure the doge would be impressed by your excuses," the colonel snorted. "You absolutely cannot let it happen again, Verdi. She doesn't have to love us, but we need her cooperative and loyal enough to follow orders if the doge wants to use her. Especially now. And we must be confident she's not going to burn down the city or defect to our enemies. If she's not playing nice within a month, the doge will decide she's too much of a risk. You know what happens then."

"I know." Marcello's tone trickled icewater down my back.

"On top of that, I hear you got the Cornaro heir shot at." The disbelief in Vasante's voice could have withered roses. "You do realize if La Contessa's only daughter gets killed in our care, she'll have us executed within the week."

Marcello's voice was strained. "I'm aware. Believe me."

Why did all my friends think my mother would kill them?

"You do what it takes to keep them both out of trouble, Lieutenant. Do you hear me?"

"Yes, Colonel."

That sounded final. I retreated to my bench and sat down, heavy with the impossibility of Zaira "playing nice" within a month and the implied mortal consequences should she fail to do so. Mere seconds later, Marcello opened the door and reemerged, alone.

"Is everything all right?" I asked him.

He mustered a smile. "Of course."

"You're a terrible liar."

He shivered as if the cold of the air had finally reached him. Then he slumped on the bench beside me, face in his hands. "I can feel everything I've worked for collapsing around me," he said softly. "I don't know how to fix it. I got you shot at. I let Zaira run away, but worse, I can't win her trust no matter what I do. I'm going to lose my position and go home in disgrace to my father's scorn. And fail to save Zaira from herself. And maybe get you killed, too."

I stared at him a moment in silence. The burden of his words lay heavy on me, dragging me down along with the poison and the long night and all my days of fearing fire.

But impatience licked up in me like a candle flame, a spark of scalding light. "Hmph. Well, if you think like *that*, of course you will."

Marcello lifted his head, a stunned look in his eyes.

"We've failed to make any progress with Zaira, yes. That just means we're doing this wrong. We need a new tactic."

Marcello spread his hands. "Like what?"

"I don't know yet. But we'll think of something." A group of soldiers passed through the hall, shucking off their uniform coats on their way to bed, grumbling good-naturedly about the chill in the Tallows. They must have been some of the ones helping us search for Zaira. "She's angry at being stored here like a weapon in the armory; I can't blame her for that. Especially after we brought her back here against her will again, when all she wanted was to find her dog." The faint glimmer of an idea started to form in the back of my mind. "If we want to be her friends, we have to start treating her like one."

Shadows still haunted Marcello's face. "Kindness may work wonders, over time. But even if there's hope for her, that doesn't change the fact that I endangered you."

"You most certainly did not. I take my own risks, Lieutenant. It wasn't your doing."

His eyebrows formed a dubious line. "I brought you into harm's way."

"Do you think I can't make my own decisions?" I demanded. "I knew it might be dangerous. I chose to go. If you shoulder all the blame for risks we took together, you also by implication claim all credit for our success. And to that, Lieutenant, I must take exception."

The ghost of a smile pulled at his mouth. "You are too much for me, my lady. I am routed again."

"Well, good." I had to turn him to another topic before he could trot out his *buts* and *howevers*. I asked the first question that sprang to mind. "What would have happened if they'd killed me? In terms of the magic of the jess?"

"Your death would have released her powers," Marcello answered, his mouth stretching uncomfortably over the word *death*. "But only temporarily. If she didn't return to the Mews within a few days to receive a new Falconer, she would die. The idea is to make it not worthwhile to kill Falconers. It neither neutralizes the Falcon's magic nor frees the Falcon to switch allegiance."

"That leaves the Falcon in a rather unpleasant position." I wondered if Zaira knew the Empire would rather see her dead than working for an enemy. "Though I suppose it does remove the motivation to target us."

"Unfortunately, those ruffians weren't well enough educated to know that. And you are a valuable political target in your own right. You can't take risks to protect Zaira; we need to protect *you*. That's what I wanted to talk to you about."

I didn't like where this was going. "Marcello, I assure you I'm quite accustomed to the dangers of being a piece on the board. You don't need to protect me."

His brows pushed together. "Putting aside my own personal concern for your safety, which is not inconsiderable, it's my duty to keep you from harm. If you would allow me to assign you a guard—"

"Absolutely not." I could imagine what my mother would say. She'd consider it an attempt by the doge to get a spy in our house, and she might not be wrong. "I do appreciate your concern. But I'm afraid it's out of the question."

He tried again. "At least until things become more stable with Ardence."

Unease settled in my belly. "The Ardentines wouldn't target me. I have friends there." I could imagine my mother's lifted eyebrow at that. *Are you really so naive, Amalia?* "Besides," I added, "the security of Raverra is my mother's duty. If I need a guard, she'll assign me one."

"I can't argue with that," Marcello sighed. "But I'd worry less if I was sure we were at peace."

"Myself as well," I admitted.

There was nothing I could do to make peace with Ardence right now. That lay in the hands of Lady Terringer and the doge. But by all the Graces, I could at least do my best to make peace with Zaira.

Zaira opened the door to her room with a scowl. "Oh, it's you."

I smiled. No rudeness from Zaira could sour my mood today. "I'm glad to see you looking well after our adventures a couple days ago."

Zaira raised a skeptical eyebrow. A bruise across her cheek had attained full splendor, presumably from her scuffle with Orthys's ruffians. She hadn't brushed her hair, and the redness around her eyes suggested either recent crying, an excess of wine the night before, or both.

"Yes, I'm chipper as a little bird. Are you here to tell me if I'm a very good girl, maybe someday you'll take me to the world's most boring fruit market again?"

"No." I couldn't contain the grin spreading across my face. Zaira must think I'd lost my mind. "But I have something for you in the courtyard."

Zaira sneered. "Another gift?"

"No. Not really. But you should come and see." I held out my hand, confident. Not much might impress Zaira, but I had yet to meet someone who could resist a mystery.

Zaira brushed past my extended hand and out into the hall-way. "Oh, very well. It's not as if I have anything better to do."

I let Zaira precede me down the dormitory stairs. I stepped up in time to hold the door for her, gesturing her grandly through. My cheeks were ready to split.

Giving me one last, dubious look, Zaira stepped out into the courtyard.

And then they saw each other.

Zaira let out a wild, wordless cry and dropped to her knees, her arms outstretched. Ciardha let go the leash she held, and the lean, brown hound flung himself across the grass and into Zaira's arms. His tail wagged so vigorously his entire back half became involved. He put his paws up on Zaira's shoulders and licked her chin with frantic joy.

Zaira flung her arms around him, laughing, tears shining on her bruised cheek. "Scoundrel! You're all right! I can't believe it!"

I exchanged satisfied glances with Ciardha as the two wrestled, Scoundrel sniffing Zaira all over. I pretended not to notice when Zaira dragged a sleeve across her cheek.

"How did you find him?" Zaira demanded at last, her arm locked tight around the hound's bony shoulders.

"I wandered all around the Tallows, calling his name."

Her face froze in an odd mix of skepticism and laughter, clearly not sure whether to believe me.

"I may also have bribed a large number of children to help," I added. "Children are surprisingly knowledgeable about local strays, and love being bribed. Beef bones may also have been employed."

For a brief moment, good humor crinkled the corners of her

eyes. But then suspicion fell over her features, like the shadow of a cloud. "You want something for this, don't you."

"I don't want anything," I replied, exasperated. "I'm trying to make friends, Zaira. Sometimes friends help each other out, and don't need anything in return."

Scoundrel interrupted by stabbing his nose into Zaira's eye. She sprawled on the grass, laughing, and he sniffed and licked her face until she sprang up and ruffled his shoulders and haunches, making him squirm with delight.

"Friends, eh?" The bright, pure smile she had for Scoundrel packed up into something more guarded as she cast her eyes at me. "That's an easy word to say when you're the one holding the prison keys."

"I know." I spread my hands, helpless. "I can't change what's happened. I don't have the power to set you free. But given you're stuck with me, yes. I truly do want to be your friend."

"Hmph." Scoundrel rubbed his head up under her chin, and Zaira's eyes softened—for him, not for me. "I don't know about *friends*. It's not that simple, rich girl. But I'll remember this."

I couldn't tell from her tone if that was a promise or a warning. But looking at the two of them together, I didn't care.

For the moment, Zaira was happy. I'd take that as a gift from the Graces, whether she liked me any better or not.

"Ardence is on the brink of rebellion, Vaskandar is knocking at the gate, and you use the fabled wealth and influence of house Cornaro to find a *dog?*" Amusement softened the edges of Marcello's incredulity as he leaned across the age-scarred table in the Mews dining hall so only I would catch his words.

"Look at her," I said, "and tell me it wasn't worth it."

He glanced across the hall, which was mostly empty at this

hour save for a few tables of soldiers grabbing a quick meal, to where Zaira and a couple of girls nearly her age clustered around Scoundrel. They rubbed his proffered belly, chatting and laughing as he gazed up at them adoringly. They'd been there for at least an hour, lavishing affection on the dog and talking animatedly with each other.

"You're right. She's interacting with someone without threatening or offending them," Marcello murmured. "I'm so proud."

I smothered a laugh. "Come on, now. They look like they've been friends for longer than this morning. This can't be the first time."

"She's made a few friends among the Falcons," Marcello admitted. "She and Terika also flirt outrageously with each other." He gestured toward one of Zaira's companions.

So Domenic had competition. I wasn't sure whom to cheer on, though the day Zaira took my romantic advice would be the day Celantis rose back from the ashes.

I noticed a small knife rode Zaira's hip now; Marcello must have decided, after the incident in the Tallows, it was best to give her a means to defend herself besides balefire. Jesses gleamed on her friends' wrists as they laughed at whatever story she was telling them. One girl covered her mouth.

Then I made out a few of the words drifting across the hall, and my cheeks heated. "What is she *telling* them?"

"Ah...perhaps I'm less proud than I thought." Marcello adjusted his uniform collar. "Sorry, my lady."

I cleared my throat to drown out the climax of Zaira's story. "If you don't mind me asking, Marcello, how come I never see *your* Falcon?"

"Istrella's not one for company, I'm afraid. Though I think she'd make an exception for you."

"Oh? Is she shy?"

"Not really. She just prefers books to people." He waved an

arm up toward a window tucked high under the vaulted ceiling. "She rarely comes down out of her tower. I keep telling her she should, but she's always puttering around with some project up there. She could change the world if she would finish more of them."

There was an exasperated warmth in his voice. An unexpected jealousy stirred in my chest. "It sounds as if you have a great fondness for her."

"Of course I do! She's my little sister."

"Ah!" I tried not to let relief color my voice.

"I told her about you, and how brave you were in the Tallows. She was more interested when I said you'd studied artifice." He laughed.

That's right, his Falcon was an artificer. "I'd like to meet her."

Marcello's face reddened unaccountably. "I'd be delighted to introduce you. I think you'd like each other." He gazed up at the window, as if he could see through stone walls to watch her. "She's why I became a Falconer, you know. When she went to the Mews, I went with her so she wouldn't be alone. But most of the time, I think she forgets I'm here."

"Do you regret joining, then?" I asked.

"No. I have plenty of regrets, but becoming a Falconer isn't one of them. I can do a lot of good here. I can help mage-marked children find safety and peace."

Zaira threw herself down in an empty chair at our table, snorting with disdain. "Peace? Is that what you call it?" The girls she'd been talking to had their heads together now, whispering and giggling. Zaira waved an arm at them. "The Falcons are part of the military. If a war breaks out, you'll be throwing us all into it. How about that, Mister Bringer of Peace?"

Marcello grunted. "Do you really think if Raverra didn't protect them, no one would make them fight?"

Zaira scowled, but said nothing.

"You know Terika?" Marcello nodded toward the older of the two girls Zaira had been talking to, who now was drawing something on a scrap of paper that had the other girl breathless with laughter. "Her gift is alchemy. She was born in a remote village in Callamorne. Before word of her reached the Falconers, an assassins' guild bought her from her father. As soon as she was old enough to stir the magic into potions without spilling, they put her to work making Demon's Tears. Have you heard of it?"

My breath stopped in my throat. "Yes," I whispered. But Marcello and Zaira didn't notice.

"It's a deadly poison," Marcello went on. "It takes several hours to kill, so if you're lucky enough to find an alchemist before it's too late, they can brew a draft to counteract the poison and keep the victim alive; but they have to take that elixir for the rest of their lives, because there is no true cure. If the poison runs its course, no one can survive it."

My fingernails dug into my palms. I tucked my hands under the table so the others wouldn't see.

"The poisons that girl made killed dozens of people before she was seven years old." Marcello's voice was fierce but quiet. "She doesn't know. We got her out and brought her here, where she makes potions that cure, not kill. So yes, I call it peace."

I stared at the alchemist across the hall. She laughed and swatted playfully at her friend, who must have said something outrageous, by the grin on her face. She could be the one who had made the poison that still flowed in my veins. The timing was about right. We'd never found out who had tried to kill me.

"So you helped one girl." Zaira's voice sounded less sure than usual, her brashness hollow. "I was doing fine without you."

"I could tell you more stories like that, I assure you," Marcello said. "But what about you? Was the day we found you the first time your balefire hurt anyone?"

Zaira's face paled, and her lips pressed together. I almost reached out to her, but stopped myself. I doubted she liked being touched.

"I know it's hard to control," she snapped. "That's why I don't loose it often. Believe me, if I used it on every wretch who deserved it, I'd have burned down the Tallows long ago."

"But it would only have been a matter of time," Marcello insisted. "You couldn't have gone your whole life without needing to defend yourself. Once your secret got out, countless people would seek to use you, or to murder you. You already had to kill Orthys's men. It would have gotten worse and worse, until you became like a fiery angel of death, bereft of humanity."

Zaira gave him a sharp-edged grin. "You say that as if it's a bad thing."

But Scoundrel whined and licked her hand. I didn't need his cue to see the pain buried in her eyes.

Marcello let that pass. "It's not fair, of course. And I wish we had a better way. But please do understand that no matter how it seems, we are trying to protect you."

Emotions passed over Zaira's face, a series of doors opened and shut into anger, grief, pain, and finally a deep and abiding cynicism. "Oh, certainly, all you want is for me to be safe," she said. "Safe, and willing to burn down any poor bastards who don't toe the imperial line."

Marcello grimaced. "That's not what *I* want."

"That's because you're the sort of credible fool I'd rob blind six times on a Sunday." Zaira rose. Scoundrel danced his eagerness to follow, staring at her with adoration. "You keep on lying to yourself, Lieutenant Jailer. Go ahead and believe the Empire snatches up all the mage-marked for our own good, and not for our power." She shook her head. "Your table is boring and depressing. I'm going back to Terika."

She crossed to the other young Falcons across the hall.

When Zaira was out of earshot, I captured Marcello's gaze and dropped my voice. "She's right, you know."

"That I'm a fool?"

"That you might have to send them to war." I thought of those green stones on the Council's map, and the Shadow Gentry plotting a "response" to the false Falconer incident. "I don't like the idea that we brought Zaira back to the Mews just to force her to kill people, Marcello. But it could happen anytime."

"I know," he said quietly. "Some of them, like Jerith and Balos, I could send into battle with a clear conscience. They're soldiers. But others, well, I've had nightmares." He pressed his lips together.

A young man in a Falconer uniform hurried across the hall toward us, his footsteps scattering echoes around him. He reached our table and saluted, clutching a paper to his chest.

"Lieutenant Verdi. I have the full report from the garrison at Ardence."

Ardence. My heart quickened.

Marcello rose. "Tell me."

"We've verified none of the Raverran military forces stationed at the garrison were involved in the incident, Falconers or otherwise. And no one knows where the supposed imperial writs and letters came from. Not the garrison, and not the Serene Envoy. We haven't been able to trace them."

My shoulders began to relax; I'd braced for worse news. But Marcello asked, "What else?"

The Falconer laid the paper he held on the table. Elegant, formal script stood out boldly from the creamy vellum, and the imperial seal weighed down the bottom with red wax, the winged horse of Raverra rearing in a circle of nine stars.

"This is one of the letters. The seal is genuine." The young

Falconer's voice quavered. "An artificer at the garrison in Ardence checked it, and we checked it again here at the Mews. It's the real thing."

I gripped the table as if I could steady the tilting world.

Marcello turned to me. "Who has access to the imperial seal?"

"The doge, the Council of Nine, and anyone to whom they directly and personally impart imperial authority," I said.

"No one else?"

"That's all." I closed my eyes. I could see my mother's imperial seal, heavy with gold and purpose, resting in an artifice-locked secret drawer in her desk. She loaned it to Ciardha on occasion, when she needed proof she was acting on La Contessa's authority. I had never touched it. "My mother told me when I was little that if I tried to take hers without permission, the protective wards on the seal would knock me out for a week and turn my hand green. I have no idea if that's true."

"I see." Marcello addressed the Falconer. "Have you told the colonel?"

"Yes. She said I should show you and the other senior officers, sir."

"Tell her I'll be there in ten minutes."

The young Falconer saluted, gathered up the letter, and left. Marcello braced himself against the back of his chair, as if he needed it to hold him up.

"What will the Falconers do?" I asked. My breath felt too thin to support the question.

Marcello shook his head. "This is beyond us now. We don't have the information or the authority to pursue it further. We have to trust the intelligence services and the Council of Nine to take care of it."

I dug a nail against the tabletop, as if I could bore a hole through the wood. It would be easy enough to plunge back into my books and forget. To leave it to my mother and the doge and their ilk to unravel this scheme and soothe Ardence into peace.

"We can't let this go," I said. "We have to do something."

"Us, personally?" Marcello spread his hands. "What can we do?"

"I don't know. But there has to be something. You say leave it to the Council, but I'll be *on* the Council someday. I have to learn how to do these things." I jabbed a finger at him. "And *you'll* be in charge of the Falconers, so you don't get to dodge this either."

"All right." He nodded gravely. "We'll figure it out. Though I don't have any idea how."

"Neither do I," I admitted. "Not yet."

But a glimmering started in the back of my mind. I could think of two entities that might benefit from starting a war between Raverra and Ardence: the Shadow Gentry, who wanted to break away from the Empire; and Vaskandar, which could take advantage of the Empire's moment of weakness to make another attempt at seizing Loreice.

Domenic might be able to find out more about the Shadow Gentry for me. As for Vaskandar...

It was time to gird myself in corsetry and go into battle once more.

It was late in the season for a garden party, but they were a rare enough pleasure in canal-crowded Raverra that Lady Hortensia's town house overflowed with guests. Her gardens were considered some of the best in Raverra: a hidden enclave of green enclosed behind high brick walls, with trees and bushes and statuary all carefully placed to create dozens of little nooks and garden rooms in which one could have an intimate conversation and feel quite alone. It was the sort of party where young couples paired up and disappeared awhile behind cunningly shaped hedges, and you might want to clear your throat before rounding a corner.

Most important, it was the party my mother's contacts had assured me Prince Ruven was attending that afternoon.

As I strolled the garden's winding paths alongside Ruven, the scar on my wrist itched, reminding me that garden parties were also a fine place for an assassination. He could be hiding a dozen weapons under that long, high-collared coat of his. And as a powerful Skinwitch, he needed none at all.

"So clever, the ways you Raverrans find to tuck pockets of green on your little stone islands." Ruven sighed. "I wish I could stay and enjoy your wonderful city longer, but alas, I must depart shortly. I hope you will come and visit me in Vaskandar, Lady Amalia. Then you could see the true beauty of an ancient forest, with trees older than your Empire."

"Leaving so soon!" I tried to sound disappointed rather than relieved. "Will you be stopping in Ardence on your way back?"

"Of course." A Vaskandran page in Ruven's livery showed us a tray of sweets, his offering hand marked by thick stripes of burn scar. Something about that scar pulled at my memory, but Ruven waved him away before I could identify it; the page scurried off, eyes wide. "I wish to visit the libraries one more time. Besides, I have friends there."

"I do hear you've made quite a few friends in Ardence," I waved a hand. "The Council of Lords, the Shadow Gentry..."

Ruven laughed. "Yes, well, it's easy enough to make friends with Ardentines. Do them one small favor, and they put their hands on their hearts and swear to be yours for life. Such sincere, passionate people."

A knot tightened to thrumming in my chest. He hadn't denied befriending the Shadow Gentry. And if half the court of Ardence was truly *his for life,* we had more problems than I'd realized.

I lifted my hand in the artful gesture of a lady shielding a good piece of gossip from public view. "I do hope none of your friends were involved in the incident?"

He raised the pale wisps of his brows. "Incident?"

I looked around and stepped aside into a flowery nook shielded by a grape trellis. It was miraculously empty. Prince Ruven followed with the eager confidence of a man who has never had cause to fear assassins.

"Unknown ruffians dressed as Falconers kidnapped the children of some Ardentine nobles a few days ago," I whispered. "It's dreadful, don't you think?"

For a brief moment, pure surprise flashed on Ruven's face—and something more I couldn't read. Then his eyes narrowed, the mage mark gleaming violet between his lids. "What nerve! In Vaskandar, no one dares pretend to the authority of the Witch Lords. They would be chained to the mountainside with their entrails exposed, for the vultures to eat them alive."

Such charming garden party conversation. "I assure you, the Council of Nine will not treat them gently when they're caught."

Ruven stroked his chin. "These children—they were mage-marked?"

"That's the odd thing," I said. "They weren't."

"Ah." Ruven's expression cleared, as if I'd lifted some worry or confusion. "Then it was a ruse to take them for ransom, no doubt." He shook his head. "A tactic of the weak. Disgusting. True power does not stoop to such cowardice, and is not persuaded by it."

"I feel the same way." I tried to smooth a frown from my brow. Both Ruven's surprise and his contempt seemed genuine. Either he was a very good actor or he hadn't personally been involved in the kidnapping. And Ruven didn't strike me as a man who bothered to practice deceit; he'd been open enough about the Shadow Gentry a moment ago.

"Of course you do. We are kindred spirits, you and I." He lifted a hand toward my face.

I turned away as if I hadn't seen it, plucking a twig of grapes from the trellis. I popped one in my mouth to buy time, the sweet juice flooding my tongue. Did I dare press him further?

This was my one chance to figure out what he was up to. I couldn't shy away now.

"It's such a shame," I sighed.

"What is?" He flexed the hand I'd avoided, as if testing a new glove.

"I've heard you came to the Serene City seeking a bride." I rolled another grape between my fingers. "But in that case I don't understand why Vaskandar would send troops to the Empire's border. Is it marriage you want, or war?"

"Ah." He chuckled. It was a hard sound, like spilled nails. "No, of course we don't want war. Not now."

I laughed, not sure what else to do. That *now* was not entirely reassuring.

"No, no." A smile curled his lips, as if my misconception were the most delightful thing he'd heard all day. "We aren't fools. The Witch Lords are mighty in our own lands, yes, but Vaskandar cannot project its greatest power beyond our borders at the moment. We have fought the Empire in the past, and no doubt we will again; but that time is not now."

"Oh, good." I swallowed my grape whole, out of sheer nerves. It made a painful path down my throat.

"Indeed, we have much to learn from you. I have great respect and admiration for Raverran power." Ruven tilted his head, questioning permission, and reached out for one of my grapes. Without thinking, I offered him the bunch I held.

His fingertips brushed mine. A shock flashed through my skin, up my arm, and into my chest, and suddenly I couldn't breathe. My lungs simply stopped, halfway through an inhalation.

Ruven smiled insolently. "Vaskandran power is, as you can see, very different."

I recoiled back a step, panic pulling at my frozen lungs. Instantly, I could breathe again.

My pulse drove at me, wild and furious, urging me to flee or strike or scream for help. But no. If I acknowledged him as a threat, he won. I understood that much.

I drew my dagger. "Give me one good reason," I said coldly, "I shouldn't have you killed."

"Oh, that was just a little joke! See? You're fine." He spread his hands, laughing. "No one was hurt. A small jest; it is the Vaskandran way."

I glared. "Your jest lacks humor."

"Perhaps, perhaps." His face sobered. "But now you know," he said, "I truly do not want war."

"How do I know that, exactly?"

"Because I could have killed you." He held out his hand, palm up, as if waiting to catch rain. "Because I still could kill you with a touch, anytime. That would start a war, for certain, would it not?"

I nodded, reluctantly. The Council of Nine had the power to declare war, and my mother held most of the Council under her sway.

"But I did not." Ruven smiled brilliantly, like a child sure of praise from his teacher. "You are alive. Thus, you know my desire for peace is genuine." His expression changed, and his extended hand reached in invitation. "As is my desire to court a lady with such noble heritage, and such magnificent political and magical prospects as yourself."

I drove my dagger home in its sheath, but my face felt no less hard than its steel. "You have much to learn," I said, "about courting Raverrans."

I turned on my heel without another word and left him there.

I didn't start trembling until I was safely in my boat.

Chapter Twelve

My thoughts ran crowded and chaotic as the traffic on the Imperial Canal as my oarsman guided me homeward from the garden party. Dusk was starting to fall over the Serene City, and his oar broke and scattered the reflections of kindling luminaries and bow lanterns into thousands of points of light. People called to each other, from boat to boat, and the strains of music drifted down from a palace window above the canal.

I could now almost draw a line through the points on my map of the trouble in Ardence: Prince Ruven's visit, and his possible connection to the Shadow Gentry; Duke Astor's defiance under the Shadow Gentry's influence; the illicit use of the imperial seal in the abduction of the children. Almost, but not quite. I was still missing some crucial connection.

We glided beneath the golden lights of the Ardentine Embassy, and I spied a familiar figure on a balcony, leaning pensively on the rail and gazing out over the water: Domenic, his springy mane and broad shoulders unmistakable against the glow of lamplight behind him.

"Pull up to the next quay," I directed my oarsman as I waved vigorously to Domenic. "I'm paying a visit."

An embassy servant conducted me to the balcony, where Domenic waved me over with a grin, hoisting a half-empty wine bottle in invitation. "Amalia! Come stand with me. I can see all the aristocrats' bald spots from here. It's lovely."

I stepped up beside him. "Just don't drip ink on them."

"Once! Once, I did that, and only to Professor Clopis, because he'd been so unfair to Venasha about the classes she missed due to morning sickness." He sighed. "But you have to admit, my aim was impeccable. Smack in the middle of his pink crown."

"It took weeks for the splotch to fade," I recalled. "Did you use alchemical permanent ink?"

"Of course. Only the best for Venasha." He poured me some wine, and we clinked our glasses together.

"What brings you to the embassy?" I asked.

"The courier lamps again," he sighed. "I told my brother what you said, that the Falconers who seized the children were impostors, despite the imperial seal."

"And?" The glum look on his face wasn't reassuring. "Was he convinced?"

"He said it didn't matter. The wave of outrage has lifted the Shadow Gentry to new prominence in court, and they're rushing forward on the crest of it."

I took a breath. "Domenic, the Shadow Gentry may have ties to Vaskandar. Prince Ruven seems to count them among his friends."

"I have no doubt of it." Domenic shook his head, refilling his wineglass with a certain resolution. "Gabril was thick with Ruven while he was in town. My understanding is that's how the Shadow Gentry think Ardence can separate from the Empire—they think Vaskandar will support them as a free city-state."

"Swallow and digest them, more likely."

"Yes, well, you and I know that. But they apparently all think Prince Ruven is a fine fellow with their best interests at heart, because he's made a few loans and done a few favors."

"Your brother would do well to distance himself from the

Shadow Gentry." I tried to keep my voice light and gentle, but my fingers tightened on my wineglass. "If they're advocating leaving the Empire and backed by Vaskandar, well, it's hard to see that as anything but treason."

"Distance himself? Not bloody likely, alas. He wears his gray mask with pride. But maybe we can find some way to temper them back to a healthier degree of dissent."

"Are you still thinking of joining them yourself?"

"Someone has to stand up to the Empire occasionally, to keep it from falling into tyranny. The Shadow Gentry could take that role." He downed a swallow of wine. "But threatening to leave the Empire and turning to Vaskandar for help is a stupid way to go about it."

"*Stupid* is one word for it."

Domenic gazed out over the canal. "Maybe I should head back to Ardence. To try to talk Gabril out of making a huge mistake. I'm not ready to leave Raverra yet, though. I haven't even had honeyfruit trifle."

"Come over to our palace, and our chef will make you some. Honeyfruit's out of season, but there are a few vivomancers growing it, and I think we have some." I nudged his elbow with mine on the balcony railing. "Don't go yet. I'd miss you."

"Oh, I'll stay a bit longer. Though Lady Savony is returning to Ardence already, along with some of the diplomats. I gather Lady Terringer has incensed as many members of the court as she's cowed. My cousin will need Savony to help smooth feathers. He'd never admit it, but he's lost without her." He shook his head. "What few accomplishments he's claimed credit for as duke so far have all been hers."

"I hope she succeeds," I said. "The idea of us winding up on different sides of a...of a conflict makes me ill."

Domenic laughed. "You and I? We'll never be on different

sides, Amalia. If we can't find a side we both like to stand on, we'll make our own."

I wished I shared Domenic's confidence. But my feet fell heavy on the carpeted embassy staircase as I descended toward the canal-side door and my waiting boat. It was difficult to imagine a way for our friendship to survive if I had to unleash Zaira to burn his home.

As I stepped down into the embassy's foyer, hurried footfalls rang on the mosaic-inlaid floors. Baron Leodra crossed to the quayside door ahead of me, a footman conducting him to his boat. By the scowl on his face, whatever business brought him here had not gone well.

I hesitated, watching the embassy door close on his brocaded back. He'd stopped pushing for more aggressive imperial control of Ardence since my mother threatened to expose his bastard at the ball, but he still seemed an unlikely choice to conduct diplomacy with Ardence at this point. What brought him here?

Lady Colanthe Savony entered the foyer from the same gilt-framed doorway Leodra had, her spectacles catching the lamplight as they dangled from their chain on her chest. She met my gaze and nodded, as if she'd hoped to find me here.

"Lady Amalia. Might I have a word?"

"Certainly." I couldn't keep the surprise from my voice. I hadn't forgotten that Marcello had spied her watching me at the ball, but I still had no idea what the duke of Ardence's steward might want with me.

She gestured me aside to a corner, beside a potted plant, and waited until a scurrying aide passed through the foyer before speaking.

"Are you aware of the latest development in relations between our cities?" she asked.

My heart dropped at the severity of her tone. "Not if it

occurred within the past few hours, no. Has there been some change?"

"Duke Astor has rejected the doge's assurances that Raverra had nothing to do with the abduction of Ardence's heirs, and refuses to cooperate with the Empire in any way or even receive the Serene Envoy at the River Palace until the children are returned."

"But we truly don't have them!"

"I know that. His Grace likely even knows that." Lady Savony shook her head. "It's a matter of principle, to show his nobles he's taking a stand."

"That's folly." The words burst out of me before I could choose more diplomatic ones. "To refuse to receive the Serene Envoy is another violation of the Serene Accords, and an insult the doge can't ignore."

"There's a reason I'm returning to Ardence posthaste," Lady Savony said dryly.

"Is there anything you can do?" I implored her.

"Perhaps. I am hoping, Lady Amalia, that you may also be able to accomplish something for Ardence." She regarded me closely. I wasn't used to having to look up at women; my Calla-mornish father had left me a height advantage few Raverrans of my gender seemed to surpass, but Lady Savony had an inch or two on me. "For years, your family has been a true friend to our city. What is your stance, if I may ask, on the current tensions between us?"

"I find them most distressing," I said immediately. "I am eager to return to cordial relations between Ardence and Raverra as soon as possible."

Lady Savony fingered the chain of her spectacles. "You must understand, I am absolutely dedicated to the welfare of Ardence."

"Of course."

"Of course? I wish it were a given, my lady. Few among the leaders of our city put the good of Ardence before their own, as my family has always done." She replaced the spectacles on her nose. The eyes that met mine through them were sharp as a hunting bird's. "If more of them did, we wouldn't be having this discussion. Do you know the true root cause of the difficulties in Ardence?"

I hesitated, then shook my head. I might have my own opinions, but I'd rather hear what she had to say.

"Three years ago, Mount Enthalus in the Witchwall Mountains erupted. Hardly anyone in Raverra noticed." She stared off through the embassy wall, as if she could see across space and time to watch it happen. "But the eruption choked the River Arden with rock and ash, reshaping it. New lakes and rapids formed. Some stretches of the river split, or grew shallower. It is no longer the perfect channel for trade between Vaskandar and the Raverran Empire."

"Ah." I began to see where she was going. "And Ardence depends on that trade."

"Our city was *built* on that trade, and thrived on it for hundreds of years. Now it is suddenly diminished, since larger ships can no longer navigate the river near the border. Ardence faces a very real danger of poverty and ruin." The skin around her eyes tightened, as if the admission pained her. "But the nobility of Ardence seems determined to spend as lavishly as ever, including our current duke. They are making matters exponentially worse with their excesses, and are making no plans to address the problem. When I bring up the issue to His Grace or the Council of Lords, I am laughed at."

Knowing the city teetered on the brink of bankruptcy helped everything else make much more sense: Ardence's willingness to take help from Vaskandar, the duke's desperate ploy in taxing

Raverran merchants, and even the rise of the Shadow Gentry. "So that's why the nobles pressured the duke to levy taxes on Raverran merchants and break the Serene Accords? To bring in more money?"

"Hmm. Everyone pressures the duke." Savony shook her head. "To stand up to the Empire, or to appease the doge's wrath. To find their missing children, and to punish whoever took them. To pay for their indulgences. To find someone to blame. To make Ardence what it was when they were young. All his court want the duke to be the great man who solves all of their problems for them." Her gaze met mine, assessing. "But he is not that man. And so it falls to me."

"That seems quite a task for a steward," I admitted.

"And that," she said, "is why I am hoping for help from Raverra, to whom the nobles of Ardence have no choice but to listen. And from the shrewd and wealthy house of Cornaro in particular. Your cousin and I had a plan to save the city, despite Duke Astor. But Ignazio was recalled to Raverra." By the disapproval in her voice, I guessed she preferred Ignazio as Serene Envoy over Lady Terringer.

"I hope, after the current difficulties are settled, your efforts with him will not be in vain."

A faint smile touched her severe mouth. "I hope so as well. I will do everything I can to restore peace and good relations between our cities, both for the sake of the present and in hope for the future. I ask you to bear in mind that no solution to the current crisis will work if it does not account for the fundamental problems causing unrest in Ardence: financial ruin and poor leadership. I look to Raverra for help in creating a remedy. I hope you will be part of that solution."

"I would certainly like to help Ardence thrive again," I said carefully, wary of stumbling blindly into a hidden agreement lying in her words like a trap.

She gave me a stiff bow. "Perhaps, then, you may be the one who can save my city, Lady Amalia. If you don't destroy it first."

The next morning, I cleared my schedule and had my oarsman take me to the Mews. I'd related my interactions with Ruven and Savony to my mother as she was on her way out the door to the Imperial Palace, but I was desperate to really *talk* to someone about Ruven's connection to the Shadow Gentry, Duke Astor's reckless rejection of the Serene Envoy, and what might be done to keep the situation from sliding farther down into the Hell of Madness.

I hurried past the guards at the gates and through the dim, lofty entry hall, pausing when I broke out into the garden and realized I had no idea where to find Marcello. A senior Falcon was giving lessons to a handful of vivomancers nearby, twisting the rosebushes into fanciful and menacing shapes; a pair of Falconers leaned against a tree together, cleaning their pistols and talking. A Falcon in uniform strode briskly past, his Falconer at his side, heading for the docks. By the tool bag he carried slung across his shoulder, emblazoned with the winged horse of Raverra, he was probably an artificer off to see to some project for the Empire.

"Amalia!" Marcello's voice rang out cheerfully across the garden.

I spotted him waving from the doorway to the officers' quarters, where he stood with a clerk who was making entries in some sort of ledger. Marcello made his excuses to the clerk and headed over to me, the sun gleaming on the dark waves of his hair and catching bright sparks from the golden threads in his uniform.

"Marcello," I greeted him. "Are you free this morning? I was hoping to talk to you."

"As it happens, I am." He grinned. "My morning was set aside to discuss a new match for a Falcon whose Falconer is retiring; but the Falcon had a request who seems ideal, so that conversation took all of ten minutes, and I'm unexpectedly free. I was actually just thinking how I wished you were here!"

"Yes, well, we have a lot to talk about." I dropped my voice, glancing around anxiously.

"Right! Like meeting my sister."

"Like..." I blinked. Marcello beamed at me. Dire portents died on my tongue. "Of course. Meeting your sister."

Marcello led me into a dormitory and up twisting stone tower steps to a landing cluttered with broken oddments: broom handles, pothooks, jewelry boxes, all piled in twin precarious heaps on either side of the door, with barely enough room left to open it.

"She collects this stuff," he apologized. "She keeps saying she's going to use it in her work, but I don't believe her."

Tacked to the door was a note in an elegant, spidery scrawl:

PLEASE KNOCK

Or I Cannot Be Held Responsible
For the Consequences

Thank You

Marcello reached for the handle.

I grabbed his wrist. "Aren't you going to knock?"

"Oh, right." He sighed. "I suppose I'd better, after last time."

"Last time?"

He grimaced and rapped on the door.

There was no answer. I could faintly hear humming from within, and the occasional clink. Marcello knocked again.

"This is why I don't bother," he explained.

"Should we try another time?"

"No, no. She'd love to meet you." He knocked a third time. "Istrella! It's me, Marcello!"

"Busy," a voice sang through the door.

"I can come back another time," I murmured. "Really, it's no bother."

Marcello grinned and held up a finger. "Istrella, Lady Amalia Cornaro is here with me."

The door flung open with such force it crashed into one of the piles flanking it and tipped a broken model ship onto the stairs. "Why didn't you say so? Come in! Mind the chandelier."

The first thing I noticed was her glasses: one lens tinted green and the other red, the round frames ringed in artifice runes, large enough to dominate her narrow, pointed face. She couldn't have been more than thirteen, if a tall and lanky thirteen, full of knees and elbows. Her long, delicate fingers never stopped moving.

The room she ushered us into was cluttered with half-finished wonders of beads and wire, gears and glass, gleaming with promise and unfulfilled purpose beneath varying layers of dust. A gutted clock spewed its innards across one chair, and a flintlock with rune-carved golden bands around the barrel lay snarled in a tangle of copper wire on another. Workbenches fought with shelves for wall space, covered indiscriminately with parts, books, and projects in progress. The chandelier she'd warned us of hung low enough to force Marcello to duck, dangling crystal in elegant cascades, but lumps of quartz wrapped in beaded wire sat on rune-carved disks in place of candles.

"Is that chandelier a *courier lamp*?" My voice rose to a pitch I hadn't known I could produce as I stared up in wonder.

"That's the idea." She waved at it dreamily. "They have me making courier-lamp pairs all the time, and I thought wouldn't it be lovely to make an entire linked chandelier set instead? It would be more compact than the receiving rooms you see now...but I got distracted by my vanishing crown and never finished it."

I blinked. "Vanishing crown?"

"Yes! Here, I'll show you." She bounced on her toes, then raced to a shelf and pulled down a somewhat squashed circlet of wire and beads, trailing loose ends in a scraggly tail. "Not much has been done with illusion, because it's so tricky to get it right. But I thought if I anchored the spell with wirework and then draped down a veil woven through with silver threads to carry the energy, and seeded more beads into the veil..."

"That could work." I peered at the crown; she held it out, and I turned it in my hands. The wirework was nearly as delicate and complex as that in jesses, but with a feverish, haphazard twist. "But if the person moved around, wouldn't it disrupt the pattern in the veil?"

"Well, they'd have to stay still. I was more worried about a power source."

"You could use volcanic glass," I suggested.

Istrella pushed her spectacles up onto her forehead, bunching her wild hair behind them. Her mage mark glittered gold around her pupils. "Oh! I could stagger pieces of obsidian through the veil, to distribute the energy evenly!" She broke into a dizzying smile, and her fingers started working, as if twisting invisible wire.

"That's brilliant! And I've done some research that might help with the design for the sending circle in your chandelier, as well. I've been reading Muscati, you know."

"You have a Muscati?! Oh, can I borrow it?"

"Of course!"

Marcello burst out laughing. We both turned to face him. Warmth crept up my neck.

"I forgot you were there," Istrella said.

"I could see that." He grinned widely enough to split his face. "Carry on, by all means."

"Do you want to sit?" Istrella looked hopelessly around the room. Every chair was covered.

Marcello waved her concern off and settled down cross-legged on the floor. "It's all right. I'll get comfortable. I can tell we'll be here a while."

Half an hour later, he interrupted us as we bent together over the vanishing crown, muttering about how best to weave in the volcanic glass. "You know, that would be incredibly useful to the military, even if you couldn't move around in it. I'd bet I could get full support for that project from the Empire."

My gulp of joy had an odd bitter aftertaste. I hadn't considered military uses. Did it always have to be war? But Istrella grabbed my hands with open glee. "That's wonderful! We can make it work, Amalia. I'd love to do this with you!"

My smile widened until my cheeks hurt. "I can think of no one I'd rather collaborate with."

By the time I managed to successfully say good-bye to Istrella, a process no less complicated than helping her disentangle the wires of two devices she'd heaped on each other, the sky out her tower windows was bright with noon sunlight. My stomach grumbled for lunch.

Istrella stood in her doorway as Marcello and I started down the tower stairs, waving. "Thank you for bringing Amalia by, Marcello!"

"It was fated." Marcello laughed. "I had to."

"Come again any time, Lady Amalia," Istrella called as the curving spiral of the steps brought us out of sight. "You and my brother make a good couple."

I threw an embarrassed glance over my shoulder at Marcello, on the stairs above me, who waved his hands in frantic disavowal. "I didn't . . . Amalia, please believe me. I have no idea how she got that impression!"

I lifted an eyebrow. "That we make a good couple?"

"No, that we *are* a couple. I didn't—I wouldn't—"

We were halfway down the stairs, in a patch of shadow too far below Istrella's landing and too far above the next window to catch much daylight. It was a between space, perfect for secrets, demanding daring to make it through to the light again.

I stopped and turned. The shadows brought out the fine, clean angles of his face. Something stirred in my chest. "You wouldn't?"

One step above me, Marcello swallowed, feelings moving across his face like storm clouds boiling into shape over the open sea.

"I'm not another one of those useless fortune hunters." His voice was a dry whisper.

"I know you're not."

No one was watching. This moment was between the two of us alone: Marcello and Amalia, not the lieutenant and the Cornaro heir. A heavy pressure hung in the air, like an impending storm. Or some divine word of the Graces, balanced on the cusp of speech.

I could laugh, and turn to head back down the steps, and nothing would come of it. Marcello wouldn't say anything. He couldn't, even if the ache in his eyes meant what I thought it might. The single step between us was an impassable ocean for him. If anyone was going to cross it, it would have to be me.

Graces preserve me. I couldn't let this chance pass. It might never come again.

I reached up and pulled him down onto my step. Only our hands touched, but we were close enough I could feel the warmth of him all up and down my body in the chilly stairwell. His green eyes flickered, and his face bent closer to mine. A wild bird fluttered madly behind my rib cage.

"Lieutenant Verdi?" a voice called from below.

I jumped down a stair with a squeak, and Marcello straightened. "Yes?"

The space between us was normal air again.

"The colonel wants you," the voice called. "Report just came in from the Tallows."

Marcello let out a long breath. "I'm sorry, my lady," he murmured.

The sweetness of the twilight turned bitter on my unkissed lips. "It's fine."

"I'll be right down," he called. And he gave me a short bow, closing the door of formality between us. "This could be important. You may want to stay at the Mews, to hear how it goes. I'll find you after."

That could mean anything, or nothing. "All right."

So close. Curse it. And what did that *I'm sorry* mean? Perhaps I'd misread him, and it was relief that shuttered his expression now.

Words gathered on my tongue, full of prickles and edges and a longing to bridge the one-step gap that separated us. But his eyes slid away from mine, and he started down the stairs alone.

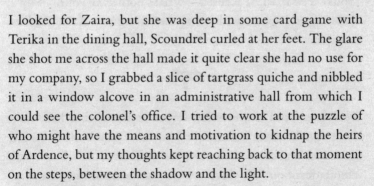

I looked for Zaira, but she was deep in some card game with Terika in the dining hall, Scoundrel curled at her feet. The glare she shot me across the hall made it quite clear she had no use for my company, so I grabbed a slice of tartgrass quiche and nibbled it in a window alcove in an administrative hall from which I could see the colonel's office. I tried to work at the puzzle of who might have the means and motivation to kidnap the heirs of Ardence, but my thoughts kept reaching back to that moment on the steps, between the shadow and the light.

I barely had time to finish my quiche and wonder if I should press my ear to the colonel's door when Marcello emerged, eyes downcast in apparent thought.

"Is everything all right?" I asked.

He rubbed the back of his head. "I suppose. Some new information to digest. Will you walk with me?"

"Of course."

I felt a certain fluttering in my stomach as I fell in beside him. As we proceeded down the hall, I cast glances his way, wondering if he would walk a little closer, or take my hand. Anything to show the moment in Istrella's stairwell had happened, and that things between us had changed.

But Marcello's eyes kept pulling away to things we passed in the Mews hallway—an old suit of armor, the door to a playroom for small children, a scrawled posting requesting the return of a missing wormwood jar to the alchemy lab. I wasn't sure he even knew he was walking next to someone at all, let alone a woman he'd maybe nearly kissed less than an hour ago.

I'd swear I hadn't dreamed it. How could he be so maddeningly oblivious?

"What did Colonel Vasante talk to you about?" I asked.

"Mmm," Marcello replied in the direction of his feet.

I stepped in front of him, startling him into meeting my eyes. "You're distracted," I accused. "What's bothering you?"

He sighed. "Come with me to the dining hall. Zaira needs to hear it first."

We found Zaira sitting with Terika in the dining hall, their heads together over half-finished bowls of pauldronfish bisque. Scoundrel waited at their feet, his eyes on Zaira's bowl with intense devotion. We wove our way to them through the thinning late-lunch crowd, passing between a table with half a dozen children throwing bread at each other on one side, and a group of uniformed soldiers struggling to ignore them on the other. As we approached, Terika threw back her head and laughed over something Zaira had told her.

When we got closer and Zaira saw Marcello's serious face, however, her wicked grin sobered. "Don't tell me you have more bad news about Ardence."

"So you do care what happens there?" I asked, trying not to make it a challenge.

Zaira shrugged. "I like Domenic. I don't want his geography rearranged."

Terika giggled, elbowing Zaira in the ribs. Zaira's return smile was strained.

"It's not about Ardence," Marcello said gravely. "It's about your indenture contract."

Zaira sank deeper into her chair. Her fingertips fell to Scoundrel's back, as if the touch of his fur gave her strength. He nosed her hand, though he kept his attention on the bowl.

Marcello eased himself into a seat opposite her. I followed suit, my spine stiff with tension.

"We did some investigation into Orthys, after your escapade in the Tallows. And into your contract in particular." Marcello took a deep breath. "It's fake."

Zaira bared her teeth. "That bastard."

"Yes." Marcello's voice thickened with anger. "Apparently he makes a practice of this. Forging indenture contracts for children without anyone to protect them, all over the Empire so no one notices he has too many. He smuggles his victims off and sells them in Vaskandar. They're his return cargo, after he unloads his dream poppies."

"Maggots take his eyes." Zaira brought her fists up onto the table. "I should have killed him when I had the chance."

A thought struck me, and I leaned forward. "You realize what this means."

"That burning's too good for him?" Zaira snorted. "Don't worry. I can make it slow."

"Your mother didn't sell you to him." I made my voice as gentle as I could. "Your family may not have abandoned you at all."

Zaira winced as if I'd struck her.

"We could find them." I offered. "Find out what really happened."

"No." Zaira's voice was so low I thought I'd misheard her.

"I know it's been a long time, but we could at least try. They could be alive and looking for you somewhere."

Terika tightened her arm around Zaira. "She said no! Can't you see she doesn't want to talk about it?"

Zaira shook her off, scowling. "I can fight my own battles."

"We may *have* to find them," Marcello said. "Falconer regulations state—"

"Stuff your Falconer regulations." Zaira half rose, looking ready to go after Marcello. "If you go poking your beak where it isn't wanted..."

Scoundrel whined, nudging her leg urgently. Zaira threw up her arms and dropped back in her seat. "All right, all right! Here it is!" She set her bowl on the floor, and the vigorous sound of his lapping drained some of the rage from her face.

"I don't understand," I said softly. "Why don't you want to know?"

"Because," Zaira said through her teeth, "there is no possible happy ending to your little fairy tale."

"But you could have been stolen from them, or lost, or—"

"Get your head out of your buttocks," she snapped. "The Tallows is full of parentless brats, picking pockets or begging or eating other people's trash to survive. None of us are lost princesses of Celantis." She shook her head as if she couldn't believe our naiveté. "Do you really think I'd feel better knowing my parents died of plague, or abandoned me at the Temple of Mercy because they couldn't feed me, or drowned in a storm?"

I felt a gulf between us as wide as the sea. *I'd* want to know. But *family* and *home* were foreign words to Zaira, with different meanings than the ones I knew.

"I'm sorry." I didn't know what else to say.

Zaira pushed her chair back with a resounding scrape and rose to her feet. "You don't know what *sorry* means." She said it without rancor, as a statement of fact.

Scoundrel danced around her ankles, hoping for play. Zaira sighed. "All right, all right, boy. Let's go to the gardens and get you a stick." The three of us watched her go, Scoundrel capering at her heels.

"You shouldn't push her," Terika said quietly.

I met her gaze. She was a pretty, plump girl, with honey-colored curls, freckles, and a mild Callamornish accent. I'd seen Zaira smile more at Terika than at the rest of the world rolled up together, but now her face was serious.

"You're right," I sighed. "Zaira doesn't like being pushed."

"It's not just that. Let her past stay dead."

Hearing those ominous words in Terika's sweet voice sent cold spider feet running up my spine. "What do you mean?"

Terika cocked her head at me, eyes grave. "All those years she lived in the Tallows, suffering and scraping to stay alive . . . I don't know what she went through, but I know it wasn't good." She tapped the edge of her empty bowl. "But at any time, she could have come here and immediately had all the food she could eat, a warm, soft bed, and anything else she could dream of. She knew it, but she stayed where she was."

I'd never thought of that. Marcello shook his head. "Why? That's what I don't understand. Why would she choose that life over the Mews?"

Terika's Falconer waved to her across the hall, beaming like an indulgent aunt. Terika waved back, her jess gleaming on her wrist.

"I'm mostly happy here," she said, her voice soft and thoughtful. "Though I wish I could go home and see my grandmother more often. It's a long way to Callamorne, and Lienne, my Falconer, doesn't travel well. I don't like to drag her there more than a couple of times a year, even though she says she doesn't mind. Zaira could be happy here, too. But imagine living all your life knowing you had a fire inside you that could kill thousands of people. Imagine knowing the castle that waited for you, with those soft beds and that warm food, was bait put out for you by people who wanted that fire, to use against their enemies."

"It's not—" Marcello began.

"It is," Terika interrupted him firmly. "I'm sorry, Lieutenant, but it is."

Marcello's lips tightened. He bowed his head. I wished I had words to comfort him that wouldn't have been lies.

"So here she is," Terika sighed. "A Falcon after all, comfortable and safe at last in the Mews. And all those sacrifices she made all those years—all the times she went to bed hungry or cold or did who knows what else, knowing there was a castle waiting for her—they were for nothing." She shrugged. "Of course she doesn't want to dig it all up again."

I stared at my hands, folded on the table. They were smooth and soft, bearing no calluses of hard work, unscarred save for the old mark of the assassin's dagger. I supposed if Zaira didn't want me to know what had unfolded in her life before the day I looped a golden bracelet over her wrist, well, I could afford her that privacy.

Lienne approached, two steaming mugs in hand. Terika gave us a knowing smile. "She tries so hard," she murmured. Then she rose to her feet, grinning. "Chocolate! Lienne, you're a wonder."

"Made like we do in Loreice, with milk and honey," Lienne said cheerfully. "Sorry, Lady Amalia, Lieutenant, but I only got enough for the two of us."

"That's all right." I stood, feeling as if I'd left some piece of myself on the chair behind me. "I was about to head home anyway."

Marcello rose as well. "I'll escort you to your boat."

This time, it was both of us who walked in distracted silence, not meeting each other's eyes. The Mews was Marcello's home, and the Falcons his family; I could only imagine what must be going through his mind after Terika's words.

As we passed through the gloomy grand hall, with its marble colonnades and dramatic paintings of Falconer history, we met Colonel Vasante coming in. She bore a sheaf of papers and an expression of relentless purpose. When she saw Marcello, she veered over to him, without slowing her brisk stride.

"Verdi!" she called. "We have orders from the doge."

Marcello stopped, his shoulders tensing. "What kind of orders?"

"Deployment orders. We're moving Falcons to the Vaskandran border." The colonel's lips thinned with distaste. "And to Ardence."

The colonel gave me an assessing glance when I followed Marcello into the same small side room she'd pulled him into before, but she didn't stop me—whether because I was my mother's daughter or because she wanted me to hear the orders too, I couldn't guess. No ornament graced the room's white-plastered walls, and its only furniture included a scattering of wooden chairs and a stained oak table. It was the sort of place guards might wait while on reserve gate duty.

Colonel Vasante closed the door, then slapped her papers down on the table. "Nothing drastic, Lieutenant; you can stop bracing like I'm going to punch you. A Falcon or two to each of the major border forts, as a precaution, and a couple more to move into the garrison outside Ardence. The full details are in there."

Marcello spread the papers out and started skimming over them. I caught Vasante's eyes. "Why Ardence?"

She snorted. "Why do you think? Duke Astor Bergandon is refusing to see the Serene Envoy. That's a slap in the face the Empire can't ignore. If they keep defying imperial authority, the doge wants to end this war before it starts. We don't have time to humor Ardence's tantrums when Vaskandar is knocking at our border, my lady."

I gripped the edge of the table as if the floor might buck me off, and leaned in over the papers next to Marcello. I knew too well which Falcon could end a war most quickly. "Who's on the list?"

"Not you. I don't give you orders." The colonel's clipped voice severed a line of tension in my back. I sighed with relief. At least things hadn't gotten so bad the doge was ready to use balefire.

But Marcello's palm struck the table, startling me with a loud *bang*.

"Istrella's on this list." His voice strained as if it stretched over rough stones.

I glanced at the page, alarmed.

Sure enough, the second name was Istrella Verdi.

Chapter Thirteen

Colonel Vasante barely glanced down at Istrella's name.

"Yes. Relax, Verdi. You'll be back here soon. I told him I needed you." The colonel pulled another set of papers out from under the deployment orders. "The doge wants her to pay a brief visit to Ardence to build a few of these. When she's done, you can both come home."

Marcello sighed with relief. But I stared down at the schematics Vasante had revealed, tracing the lines of wire that coiled around metal rings, the connections for a vast power supply, and the clever focal lenses.

"This is meant to enhance a cannon." My words fell on the table, cold and heavy as lead. "To make it many times more destructive. You want her to build weapons."

Marcello's eyes widened. He rounded on the colonel. "You can't have her creating tools to kill people. She's just a child!"

"She's a soldier." Vasante's tone brooked no argument. "And she's one of maybe a dozen artificers in the Falcons with the necessary skill and power. The others are all either getting sent to the Vaskandran border to make more of them there, too old or infirm to travel, or even younger than your sister. Would you rather I sent her to the Witchwall Mountains?"

Marcello snatched up the list and took a closer look, the paper bending from the force of his grip. "It's not just my sister. You're sending Halmur to the border—he's barely older than Istrella. Combat could break out there at any moment!"

"He's a powerful vivomancer," Vasante snapped. "We need a way to counteract the Witch Lords if they take the field."

Marcello stood stiff as a pike. "I object, Colonel. Sending adult Falcons into potential war is one thing. But we can't countenance sending children."

Vasante narrowed her eyes. "This is an order from the doge of Raverra and the Council of Nine." Her voice could have cut steel. "You don't have to like it. But you do have to obey it."

Marcello stood trembling, his fists clenched. The colonel's face softened, just a little, but her tone didn't. "You and I don't get to decide. We get our orders and we follow them. Is that clear?"

Marcello threw the list down on the table. But he said nothing. I caught myself from reaching out to him; anything I did now would make things worse.

Vasante frowned. "I said, is that *clear,* Lieutenant Verdi?"

"Yes, Colonel." He grated it out between his teeth.

"Good. Now go make preparations for moving those Falcons. You have three days to get them ready."

Marcello saluted, moving like rusty clockwork. Then he turned and strode from the room without another word.

I followed him into the great, dusky hall with its dramatic paintings, my bones aching with sympathy. He went straight to a marble column and punched it, then bent over his hand in pain.

"Ow. Damnation, why did I do that?"

"Because you're upset," I said gently.

He leaned his forehead against the column and closed his eyes. "I should have stood up to her. I should have said no."

"You wouldn't have changed anything."

"I could at least have tried harder to convince her." He turned to face me, pain drawing deep lines in his face. "I don't want Istrella to have to create something that kills people."

"Then we'll make sure it doesn't kill people," I said. "If the conflict with Ardence is resolved peacefully, she won't have to build it."

No spark of hope kindled in his expression. "I don't have that kind of influence, Amalia. Maybe you do, but I'm just a soldier. If they declare a war, I fight it. I have no power to make peace."

"Then I'll make it for you." The urge to protect him flared up in me, brighter than the luminaries kindling in the hall. "We'll make it together."

I reached out to squeeze his shoulder, in a reassuring sort of way, as a friend might. But I accidentally touched his hair, and then somehow my fingers slid up around the back of his neck, tangling in the black waves.

His eyes widened in surprise. "Amalia," he breathed.

Marcello's arms went around me, tentatively, as if I might be a creature of sea and fire that could dissolve into wrath or laughter at his touch. He didn't hold me so much as frame the idea of me between his arms.

"I don't want you to think—" he began earnestly.

"Then I won't," I promised. For now, I didn't need a future for us, no moment beyond this sliver of dusk, with the luminaries waking on the walls around us like evening stars.

I buried my face in his shoulder and just held him. He was warm and solid and real, his pulse pounding in his throat by my temple, his arms settling more comfortably around me with the inevitability of a spring rain.

It was glorious. I wanted to stand there forever, just like that, and forget about Ardence and Zaira and Vaskandar and weapons of war made by the hands of children. But every second we stayed like this was another second begging for discovery.

"Is this..." Marcello began awkwardly. "Are we..."

I laid a finger on his lips and, with the slow reluctance of the sun rising from the sea, stepped back out of his embrace.

"Don't say anything," I whispered. "If you talk about a dream, it isn't real."

Laughter echoed down a corridor, and approaching footsteps. It was a full minute before the handful of chattering Falcons and Falconers passed through the hall, but Marcello and I still stood there in silence, a few feet apart, staring at each other.

The next morning found me uncommonly distracted as I sat in the back row of the thousand-seat Assembly Hall in the Imperial Palace, ignoring an intricate and impassioned argument over proposed new restrictions on the Loreician silk trade. The afternoon recess came as a relief from the bright, sharp-edged shards of memory and worry sifting through my mind.

I joined my mother for wine and cheese on a balcony overlooking the busy main courtyard of the Imperial Palace. Members of the Assembly swarmed and bunched on the travertine flagstones below, continuing their agitated discussions or making covert deals, while a thin stream of visitors, petitioners, functionaries, and servants passed in and out through the palace gates, carefully checked by the guards. Massive marble winged horses reared at each corner of the courtyard, and statues of the Nine Graces looked benevolently down from the roof above.

My mother watched the flows of people analytically as she nibbled cheeses and crostini. I didn't expect her to say much; today was a judgment day for the Council of Nine. Her mind would be full of prisons and executions, deciding the fates of traitors and spies, none of which she was much inclined to talk about with her daughter.

But after about fifteen minutes of silence, her eyes snapped to me. "I have news that may interest you."

"Oh?" I stopped an olive halfway to my mouth. News she learned on a judgment day seemed unlikely to be of an uplifting nature.

"That smuggler with whom your Falcon had an unfortunate history. Orthys." La Contessa took a sip of wine. "I've had people investigating him."

"Lieutenant Verdi told me he was trading children to Vaskandar for dream poppies."

"Not just any children." My mother's face went hard as an executioner's ax. "Ones with magical potential."

I lowered my olive back to my plate. "So it was no accident he went after Zaira."

She nodded. "Mostly he's been targeting those with powers too weak for the mage mark. But our investigations have turned up at least one or two incidents where he got to a mage-marked child before the Falconers did, and sold them to Vaskandar."

A terrible thought struck me. "Could he have been the one who took the Ardentine children? The nobles' heirs?"

"It's not impossible. He did pass through Ardence around the right time. If he was involved, he had best start praying to the Grace of Mercy." My mother finished her wine with one neat swallow, then rose. "But it will not save him. We take kidnapping of mages very seriously. I've started a full-blown search for him. We'll have him in the palace dungeons for questioning soon."

It was almost enough to make me feel sympathy for the man. "I'll tell Zaira when I see her. I'm stopping at the Mews this afternoon."

La Contessa paused. "Ah, yes, the Mews. One more thing."

"Yes?"

She leveled a cool, appraising gaze at me. "I hear you are much in the company of Lieutenant Verdi. Is there anything between you two?"

I nearly choked on the wine I'd been sipping. "There's nothing," I managed. "We're friends, that's all, Mamma. I respect him. Nothing of a... a romantic nature."

"Good." She sank back into her chair, her voice softening to a terrifying gentleness. "Because there can't be, Amalia. Ever. You know that, don't you?"

I knew. I knew from four years of my mother telling me none of the would-be suitors who crowded me at court were good enough for the Cornaro heir. I knew from hearing the measured calculation with which the Council of Nine spoke of cementing political alliances through marriage in the drawing room downstairs. I knew it from the moment I was born to a father who had given up being a prince, the younger son of the queen of Callamorne, to come to Raverra and marry my mother so his country could become part of the Empire without losing face. But it had always been a remote thing, a sheathed dagger to protect me from foolish dandies and poor choices. Now the blade was out and up against my throat, and the edge burned.

I had to nod and say *Yes, Mamma,* like I always did. That was what came next.

But anger rose up in my chest, a great bubble of frustration at all the rules and duties that circumscribed my days. It pushed different words out of my mouth.

"Grace of Love, if I can't so much as make a friend without you dropping the ax on any thoughts of courtship, you'd best not be expecting any grandchildren."

My mother reached across the table as if she might take my hand. Her wedding ring gleamed on her finger: a sapphire for Raverra and a smaller diamond for Callamorne, bound together with delicately wrought gold. "Whom you spend time with, whom you dance with, whom you stand an inch closer to in a public square—all of these things are watched, and noted, and like as not printed in rumor sheets. Even your *perceived* interest in this man could ruin a political gambit based on the idea you are unattached and eligible. Unless you can tell me what advantage a match would bring our family or the Serene Empire, you can show no undue attention to *any* person. Do you understand?"

"So I'm not to even *think* of courting anyone?" I couldn't keep the bitterness from my voice. "You don't need to control every tiny thing I do, Mamma. You can't rule what I feel."

No flicker of anger disturbed the composure of my mother's face. People far older and cannier than I tried to rattle her every day and failed. But she stood again. The gentleness was still there, but it was swan's down over iron.

"Test me in this, Amalia," she said, "and you will see what I rule."

I was still seething all through my lesson at the Mews that afternoon, which was especially unfortunate because it was a combat lesson.

Carrying a pistol seemed unwise in my case, since gunpowder and balefire might not be the best combination, so Marcello had decided I should receive instruction in the rapier. Balos was infinitely patient with me, but all my training had been with daggers, and I didn't know what to do with two and a half extra feet of steel. It didn't help to have Zaira and Jerith watching me from a bench at the edge of the practice courtyard, slowly demolishing a tray of pastries between them as they offered up commentary on how I was doing.

Balos finally called a break in our sparring session, rubbing his smooth brown scalp and shaking his head. I kept my mouth sealed as I carefully replaced my practice sword on its rack.

"I don't know why you're bothering." Zaira lounged on her bench, nibbling almond biscuits. Scoundrel lay adoringly at her feet, snatching up any crumbs that hit the ground. "These lessons are pointless without magic. If the only useful thing Lady Precious here can do in a fight is say the release word, why don't you have her practice that?"

Balos and Jerith exchanged glances. "Because balefire is incredibly dangerous and destructive, and one tiny accident could kill us all?" Jerith suggested.

Balos nodded. "Balefire isn't something we can unleash in practice. At least, not around other people. It spreads too quickly. You should only unleash it when the situation is already deadly—when there's no other way."

Zaira grunted. "Tell that to the doge."

I spotted Marcello on the far end of the practice ground, slumped on a bench, staring at his knees. I hadn't realized he was there; he'd been out investigating a report of a rogue alchemist on the mainland when the lesson started. He must have come in quietly while I was sparring. I crossed the courtyard, propelled by frustration at both my lesson and my mother, ready to make some self-deprecating comment about my poor performance driving him to despair.

But he didn't look up as I approached. Defeat dragged at the line of his shoulders.

"What's wrong?" I asked softly, settling onto the bench next to him. "Did something happen with the alchemist?"

He lifted his face. His eyes remained dull and distant. "What? No. There was no alchemist. Just a jilted lover poisoning his rival without any help from magic."

"What is it, then? Something's bothering you."

Marcello sighed. "Istrella. I need to tell her why we're going to Ardence."

"What? Have you *still* not told her about the cannon project?" I couldn't keep the surprise from my voice.

"I know." He pushed his hair back from his forehead with

both hands. "I went up to her tower last night resolved to tell her, but I couldn't. She was so happy, working on her vanishing crown. I couldn't ruin her day."

"This isn't like you. Letting fear stop you like this."

"I promised I'd take care of her." He gave me a helpless sort of half smile. "My mother left when Istrella could barely walk, and my father wanted nothing to do with her. I was seven, but I practically raised her along with our nursemaid, until the mage mark appeared in her eyes a couple years later."

"That must have been hard."

"No, it was all right," he said. "It gave me purpose. Something worthwhile I could do, so I'd know my father and brother were wrong when they called me worthless." His mouth flirted with an ironic smile. "The colonel herself came to take Istrella to the Mews, because we were a patrician family. I told her I was coming with my sister, to be her Falconer when I was old enough."

I tried to picture Colonel Vasante ten years younger, looking down at this stubborn little boy. "So you went with her? You grew up in the Mews?"

He shook his head. "Only half the time, until I was fourteen and could become Istrella's Falconer. The colonel declared that since the rest of my family had declined the opportunity to move into the Mews, I should spend at least half my time with them. She sent Istrella home with me as often as she could, to visit, since my father and brother didn't come to the Mews to visit us there. But they were never glad to see us. We reminded them too much of our mother, and they considered the mage mark her parting curse. Istrella and I liked the Mews better."

"So you're all she has," I concluded. "And you don't want to let her down."

He nodded miserably. "I've always told myself I'm not truly

a failure so long as I haven't failed her. I can't ask her to make those cannons, Amalia. She's just a child."

I shook his shoulder. "Give Istrella more credit, silly."

Marcello blinked at me. "What?"

"She's a Falcon," I said. "She grew up in the Mews. She understands what's expected of her."

"They're talking about using her work to attack a city full of innocent civilians." The anguish in his voice wasn't for Istrella alone. I knew it too well. The same pain cut into my own heart.

"Worry about it when it's more than talk." I was too aware of the distractingly small distance between us, the angle of his body toward mine. "Everyone still wants a diplomatic solution. We have time."

One of the doors to the practice courtyard banged open. A chime sounded, to warn anyone using dangerous magic. Colonel Vasante strode out into the practice courtyard, her boots ringing on the flagstones.

"Playtime is over," she said. "We have a mission."

Marcello and Balos straightened, and Jerith stood, dusting powdered sugar off his hands. I clutched my flare locket. "Please tell me it's nothing to do with Ardence."

She barely glanced at me. "Nothing so dire. They found that smuggler. Orthys."

The pastry tray clattered to the floor as Zaira shot to her feet. Scoundrel barked, shying from the noise.

"Why does that involve us?" Marcello asked warily. "They shouldn't need magic to bring in a petty smuggler and his band."

"They got the information from a captured member of Orthys's crew." From the colonel's tone, I didn't want to know what they'd done to get the man to talk. "He also told them Orthys has some magical surprises. Artifice traps on his hideout, alchemical poisons, a crew member or two with a touch of magic. We'll need Falcons to deal with that."

Marcello checked the flintlock and rapier at his belt. "All right. I'll bring an artificer and an alchemist."

"Antelles." The colonel pointed to Jerith and Balos. "You go, too."

Jerith saluted grimly. Balos put away his practice sword and started strapping on a real one.

"Take an artificer to deal with any traps you find. I'll get a couple of squads ready to join you." She strode out the way she had come, the door chiming again as it banged shut behind her.

Zaira's knuckles showed white at her sides. "I'm going with you."

Marcello shook his head. "You can't go. We can't risk you *or* Lady Amalia."

Zaira rounded on him fiercely. "I'm not asking you, rat-sucking bootlicker. I'm telling you I'm going. You're not taking down Orthys without me."

"You're not going anywhere without Lady Amalia," Marcello snapped, "and she is staying here."

All the anger and frustration that had been boiling inside me since talking to my mother crystallized into an icy resolve. "I'll go," I said.

Marcello whirled and stared at me as if I were mad. "My lady, you can't be serious."

"You do not tell me what I can and cannot do." The voice that came out of my mouth shocked me with its hard-edged surety. I sounded like my mother.

Marcello stiffened. His posture and tone went formal and distant. "No, my lady. I do not. But I do command this military operation. I determine which forces to bring. And I'm not unleashing a fire warlock inside the city under any circumstances." He bowed. "Good day."

He left on the heels of his colonel. Jerith cast Zaira a sympathetic look, then took Balos's hand and followed. The bell chimed with mocking good cheer.

Zaira looked ready to rip a hole through the Mews wall with her teeth. "Demon of Madness split your skull, you smug, poxy—"

"Zaira." My cold, angry determination remained. I was sick of being obedient. "Let's go."

Her eyes widened, then narrowed. "You heard him. He won't have us with him. And your mamma wouldn't let you chip your highborn nails in combat, either."

"As it happens," I said, "I am rather in the mood to do something my mother wouldn't like. And as for Lieutenant Verdi, I'd never dream of interfering with his mission." I smiled. "You and I are just going for a harmless stroll in the city. Isn't that right?"

Zaira looked me up and down, as if judging how much she could get for my boots on the black market. "We'll never get close enough to get any licks in on Orthys," she said. "We don't even know where he is. But all right." She dusted sugar off her hands. "It beats sitting here waiting."

"Where are we going?" I asked Zaira. I'd had my oarsman drop us off in a respectable market district not far from the Tallows, in case he reported back to La Contessa. Three bridges later, we'd reached a mazy neighborhood of chipped plaster with brick bones showing through, and laundry hanging between windows above the narrow streets. The foot traffic seemed mostly honest laborers heading home as the shadows lengthened; we weren't near the more dubious precincts where I'd first met Zaira.

"The shipyards." Her eyes skimmed everyone we passed, searching faces as if she hoped to find Orthys in disguise. "He's not stupid. If there's a search on for him, he'll run to his ship.

There's no way he'll stick around for a platoon of uniformed soldiers to arrest him."

It made sense. My hopes we might actually find Orthys in time to help capture him lifted—and so did my trepidation. I had few skills applicable to a potentially deadly confrontation. Marcello had been right to leave us behind. This was a terrible mistake.

"Zaira..." I began.

She lifted a finger to her lips. Her stride remained smooth, but tension locked her shoulders.

"Be casual about it, but look behind you," she murmured. "Do you see the man with the black cap?"

I glanced back. "No."

"You're as subtle as a bag of bricks, did you know that? I said to be casual about it. Now he's bound to know we've noticed him."

"That *you've* noticed him," I replied, irked. "I didn't see him."

"That's because you're blind. Anyway, we're being followed."

I looked back again, instinctively.

"Grace of Mercy's tits, woman!"

I flushed. "Sorry. I couldn't help it."

"You're hopeless." Zaira shook her head.

I believed her—that someone was following us, that is; I still held some feeble hope for myself. I could think of enough reasons why various people might want to follow one or both of us that it was a wonder we didn't have a whole train of spies, guards, and assassins trailing behind us like ducklings. Still, I quickened my steps. Zaira matched my pace without objection.

A tradesman in a leather apron rounded a corner ahead; as he saw us, his craggy face lit up in recognition. He hurried toward us at once. Zaira's hand fell to her knife.

But as he approached, he pulled out not a weapon but a wax seal on fine parchment. He glanced around as if to make sure no one was watching. "Lady Amalia." He dipped his head in a truncated bow. "I have a message for you from your mother."

He flashed the seal at me. In blue wax, nine stars surrounded the winged horse of Raverra.

"Council business?" I asked. Zaira's hand stayed on her knife hilt.

He nodded, tucking the seal away. "We just captured another of Orthys's men, and there's new information. The lead the Falcons are following is a false one. It might be a trap."

"Grace of Mercy." Marcello and the others were already on their way. They could be walking into an ambush right now. "Is someone telling the Falcons?"

"Of course. But we're not certain if this new information is genuine. La Contessa hopes your Falcon can confirm whether this man truly works for Orthys, so we know whether to call off the raid."

"Wait a minute." Zaira's voice was sharp with suspicion. "How would La Contessa know we're here?"

I laughed, not without a trace of bitterness. "She always knows where I am. She knows everything that happens in this city."

The man in the leather apron bowed, with a wry smile. "As the lady says. We're holding our informant nearby. Will you come identify him?"

I exchanged glances with Zaira. Lips tight, she nodded.

"All right," I said. "Lead us to him."

The man in the leather apron led us across several bridges and through the twisting labyrinth of Tallows streets to a small, dingy theater. Paint flaked off the masks hanging over the door. It was closed for the day, but our guide unlocked the scratched wooden doors and ushered us in.

A waiting hush filled the shadowy cavern of the theater. Rows of empty seats faced the red-curtained maw of the proscenium. Our footfalls disturbed a thick silence, as if we'd entered an abandoned temple. Not much sunlight filtered in from the gaps around the door, which our guide shut softly behind us; with no windows, only two flickering lamps flanking the stage alleviated the gloom.

"Where is your informant?" I asked as our guide waved us down the aisle.

He didn't answer.

Zaira stopped suddenly, her heels digging into the carpet. "Bollocks. *This* is the trap."

"Quite correct," a voice called. "Well done, Zaira."

Chapter Fourteen

Half a dozen armed men rose from behind the seats around us, leveling knives and clubs at us. Two more appeared in the balcony seats above, with flintlocks aimed down.

They were a rough-looking lot. One sported an odd scar along his jaw, almost like a handprint. The sight sparked a flash of recognition, but the situation was too urgent for me to examine it now.

A long-haired man in a scarlet coat pushed through the curtain onto the stage and bowed.

"Welcome, Lady Amalia Cornaro."

Zaira drew her dagger. "Orthys," she hissed.

My heart battered against my ribs as if it wanted to escape this theater as badly as I did. I put a hand to my chest, fingertips brushing the catch of my flare locket. "The villain himself."

"Nothing so grand as a villain," Orthys said modestly. "In fact, all I wish is to make my exit from the scene. But La Contessa has made that difficult."

"You'll get your exit," Zaira growled. "In a hearse."

Orthys laughed. It was a cultured, sneering laugh; for that matter, his accent was pure drawing-room elite, without a trace of the docks or the Tallows. There was something familiar about his voice. "Oh, but *you*, little fire warlock, are coming with me. I've got a buyer who's been waiting for you for years."

"Release me." Zaira murmured to me, her voice raw and urgent. "I'll burn them all down."

Balos's words stuck in my memory. This situation wasn't deadly yet.

"I'd keep her hood on if I were you," Orthys called. "She isn't very discriminating about killing people close to her."

Zaira started forward. "You shut up."

"Zaira, no," I whispered. "Can't you see he's baiting you?"

Orthys raised sculpted eyebrows. "Why, how do you think I found you? I heard about the sad, sad story of the tenement fire that killed that old woman, and the miracle of the Graces that left a poor little girl unharmed."

A strangled noise tore out of Zaira's throat. The ruffians around us kept their distance, eyes wary, weapons ready. Not attacking, but blocking our escape.

"But that wasn't all," Orthys continued with relish. "I wasn't sure, you see, because you hid yourself so well. So I did some research, and I turned up *another* tragic fire, several years before that. You would have been perhaps four? And once again, everyone in the tenement died, except for one little brat, who was miraculously untouched—found crying over the ashes of her mother and father."

The Graces wept.

Zaira screamed with enough fury to shame a demon. She charged down the aisle at Orthys, knife in hand. He awaited her, unmoving, a smile curling his lips.

Before I could flip open my flare locket, or utter the release word, or do more than suck in a sharp breath of horror at what Orthys had just revealed, light flared in a circle around Zaira's feet, and she jerked to a stop.

She'd run straight into an artifice circle, painted on a mat Orthys must have thrown down on the rug. Now it rooted her feet to the floor.

"That takes care of *you*," Orthys declared cheerfully.

"Not hardly, you bloody-faced bastard!" Zaira crouched, ready to spring, straining against the circle's power. "What are you waiting for?" she snapped over her shoulder at me. "Release me, now!"

"I wouldn't." Orthys raised a cautioning finger. "She's already lost control, and she hasn't even loosed her fire. Break your seal now, and she'll take you along with us—and the whole city for good measure."

"It'll be worth it!" Zaira spat on the floor. "Do it, you simpering coward!"

He was right. He'd planned this too carefully. Even if Zaira retained control, some of his ruffians were behind me—Zaira's fire couldn't catch them without going through me first.

At this point, I doubted she'd care.

Be unafraid, Amalia. If you are without fear, they will assume there is a reason, and hesitate. And the Grace of Victory will favor you.

"You're a fool, Orthys." I let calm contempt fill my voice. "You're only making matters worse for yourself. You might have bargained your way out of this before, perhaps. But now you've acted against a Falcon and the Cornaro heir, stolen the imperial seal—"

Orthys's smile widened. "Oh, I came by that seal legitimately, from my father." He chuckled. "Or perhaps I should say *illegitimately.*"

It took me a moment, but then I realized why he sounded familiar. I'd heard that voice in my drawing room, though less often since my mother muzzled it with blackmail. "You're Baron Leodra's bastard."

"Yes." It clearly pleased him to be able to make his claim at last. "And my dear father cannot allow his rival to discover his bastard son has been selling mage-marked children to Vaskandar. Can you imagine how that would stain his reputation?" He clasped his hands piously before him, then resumed a cynical expression. "My father has such a promising career, and it's cursed difficult to get elected doge when you've been branded a traitor and stripped of your position."

He was telling me far too much. A chill certainty settled in my bones. That could only mean one thing: I wasn't leaving this theater alive.

Orthys spread his arms wide. A gray domino mask dangled from his hand: the disguise of the Shadow Gentry. "My father—out of fear for his own skin more than mine, I'm sure—has arranged to get me out of this tight spot. Even now the Falcons are finding my stand-in already dead, removing the need to hunt for me while I slip away. The evidence I'll plant here will point to Ardence." His voice sharpened to a lethal focus. The men in the balcony aimed their flintlocks at me. "With your death, my father will have his revenge for what La Contessa has done to him. And she'll be too distracted to dig any deeper, because her dear only daughter will be—"

"*Exsolvo,*" I said.

I was completely unprepared for the conflagration that followed.

Heat struck me in a painful blast. I staggered back from glaring blue radiance as a tremendous globe of pale flames erupted around Zaira, as if the jess had been holding back a new and terrible sun within her.

Yells and desperate cursing filled the theater; the two men in the balcony fired their pistols at Zaira, but the balefire swallowed the bullets before they could reach her. Within the blink of an eye, the great orb of fire swelled as high as the balcony and wide as the Mews gates, devouring theater seats as it grew.

It would reach me in another second. Cringing from the flames, I squealed, *"Revincio! Revincio! Revincio!"*

The flames winked out, vanished at the first utterance, leaving behind bright ghosts of light across my vision.

Zaira was gone. No, not gone—the balefire had consumed the artifice circle binding her. She leaped up onto the stage while Orthys still reeled from the overpowering presence of the balefire. His ruffians in the balcony scrambled to reload their flintlocks, but they were too late.

Her knife swept a vicious arc across Orthys's throat. Blood choked his scream, and he fell writhing to the stage.

Zaira whirled to face the audience, her blade trailing blood. "Who's next?" she called.

Orthys's men wavered. The man who paid them was dead, or would be in another minute. But fear and anger might push them to do anything. We weren't safe.

I closed my eyes and flipped open my flare locket.

Cries of shock and outrage accompanied the pulse of intense light, including Zaira's "Damn it, Cornaro!"

I ran for the stage while Orthys's men still staggered in blind confusion, grabbed Zaira's wrist, and dragged her out through a backstage door. The jess pressed cold and hard against my fingers.

I ran through the narrow streets, around two corners and across a bridge, holding Zaira's hand and blinking away afterimages of balefire. She tugged me to a stop in a small crossroads plaza with a statue of the Grace of Luck.

"Why are we running?" she demanded. "This is your mother's city."

"Because Baron Leodra is on the Council of Nine, too, and if he finds out what just happened before the doge does, he can order the watch, the imperial assassins, or the entire army after us." My mind raced in circles, stuttering worse than my speeding pulse. Any official I turned to for help could be loyal to Leodra.

"Then *walk,* idiot, or he'll know exactly where you are, because you'll stand out like your hair was on fire."

"Oh." I examined Zaira thoughtfully. "Speaking of fire, how come you're not falling over?" She looked a bit tired, perhaps, with less spring in her step than usual, but she was a long way from collapsing.

"Because you only unleashed me for about half a second!" Zaira threw up her hands.

"Yes. Because in another second, I would have been dead."

Zaira blinked. "Right. You were behind me." She went still and quiet. "*Oh.*"

I could tell she was thinking about what Orthys had said, about her parents dying from her balefire, too. Much as I didn't appreciate being nearly set on fire without an apparent second thought, I let the matter drop. "We have to find Marcello," I decided. He couldn't be far. "He can give us an armed escort."

"Back to the Mews?" Zaira asked.

"No. We can't give Leodra the time to prepare a countermove."

"Where, then?"

I started walking again, with an inexorable pace that was new and strange to me: a grim stride with Leodra's doom at the end of it. "To my mother," I said.

We found Marcello and the other Falcons by following the trail of street gossip about a military force in the Tallows. By the time we spotted scarlet uniforms down a crooked street and forced our way through a crowd of curious onlookers, sunset colors stained the deepening sky, and the streets and canals were in full shadow.

A soldier blocked the street, keeping passersby out of the way. Past him I could see Jerith and Balos standing in front of a tavern with a dozen more soldiers, talking to each other with expressions of grave dissatisfaction.

"You can't come down here," the soldier explained as Zaira and I approached, holding up a hand. "You can go around by Three Duels Bridge, or wait a bit longer. I think they're nearly— Oh! Lady Cornaro." He bowed, and the gathered crowd murmured and exchanged glances.

"Where is Lieutenant Verdi?" I asked.

"In the tavern, my lady. There's no more fighting, so it should be safe for you to go in." He gestured us past.

Jerith didn't look surprised to see us, though Balos shook his head as if to say, *I should have known.*

"If you're looking to kick Orthys in the privates, you're too late," Jerith said in greeting to Zaira. "By the time we showed up, one of his own men had already shot him in the face."

"Oh, I arrived in plenty of time." Zaira showed her teeth. "Though it's true I didn't kick him in the privates."

"I need to talk to Marcello." I could feel my composure slipping, minutely but inexorably, like a chip of ice sliding across a not-quite-level table. "There's a problem."

Balos took a long look at my face and nodded. "I'll bring him out."

While he stepped into the tavern, where I could hear Marcello asking questions and someone muttering answers, I glanced at Zaira. A few flecks of Orthys's blood marked her face, like freckles, and the skin around her eyes looked strained.

"Are you all right?" I murmured.

"I'm fine." She glared as if I'd insulted her, but her chin trembled. "Curse it, I told you I didn't want to know what happened to them."

"I'm so sorry." My throat went hot, thinking of that little girl crying in the ashes, long ago.

Zaira shrugged roughly. "I don't even remember them. I don't need your pity."

Jerith's eyes narrowed with recognition, but he said nothing.

Marcello emerged from the tavern, ducking under its low lintel. He strode over to us, a disapproving frown his herald. "My lady. Zaira. What are you doing here?"

The question struck me right in the unsteady teetering at my center. I pressed fingers to my temples. "Making poor decisions."

"Finishing your job," Zaira said.

"More to the point, uncovering treachery." I lifted my head and took a breath. "Marcello—"

His eyes widened with shock. I barely had time to think, *But I haven't even told him yet.*

"Amalia, look out!" he cried. And he shoved me so hard I staggered into Jerith.

A shot split the air, and the crack of a bullet hitting flagstones. A chip of flying stone scored my ankle.

Marcello clapped a hand to his side with a hiss of pain.

"Marcello!" I grabbed his hand, prying back the fingers to reveal a torn doublet and a dark stain. "Graces, you're hurt."

He wrapped his free arm tight around me, turning his back to the direction the bullet had come from, trying to shield me with his body. I twisted free, furious, in time to see Jerith whirl toward a second-floor window down the street.

"*Exsolvo,*" Balos said softly.

Jerith snapped his fingers.

A purple-white spark leaped from them, flaring into a wire-thin snake of lightning. Another *bang* slammed my ears, louder than the gun. And a figure fell from the window, slack and limp, to hit the street with a sickening thud.

A flintlock clattered from his hand. A wisp of smoke rose from his leather apron.

"*Revincio.*" Balos bowed his head.

"Amalia!" Marcello grabbed my shoulders. "Are you all right? Did he hit you?"

"No, but he hit *you!*" I brushed torn fabric back from his side, but the bloodstain hadn't spread.

"Just grazed me. Thank the Graces you're well."

He hadn't taken his hands from my shoulders. He gazed into my face, as if seeking reassuring signs there. I realized my hand was still on his side, my fingertips damp with his blood. I snatched it back. "Marcello..."

I wanted to thank him—and scold him—for protecting me. I needed to check whether the man in the leather apron was alive, and if so, to see to his capture for questioning and get us all to a safe place until the reins of power could be forcibly removed from Leodra's hands. But Marcello's name lingered in my mouth, and no other words seemed willing to take its place.

Approaching footsteps sounded on the stones. Hard, disciplined, forceful steps, of at least a dozen people. I whirled to face them, ready for another fight.

A squad of the Imperial Guard marched up to the tavern. At the center of their formation, like the flagship of an armada, sailed La Contessa, resplendent in an emerald brocade gown.

Her gaze swept the gathered soldiers, lingered on the body in the street, and landed at last on me and Marcello. I took a self-conscious step away from his side. Balos bowed, which triggered a hasty wave of bowing from everyone else. Except Ciardha, who stood alert at La Contessa's side, ready as a drawn blade.

"Report," La Contessa said crisply.

Marcello saluted. "The colonel sent us here to capture

Orthys, following information gained from a prisoner. But we found him already dead, killed in some internal squabble with his crew."

My mother's eyes narrowed. "There was no prisoner. Who gave Colonel Vasante her orders?"

Marcello stepped back from the danger radiating from her like heat. "I understood they came from the Council of Nine, Your Excellency."

"I am here," she said with icy precision, "to learn why a contingent of Falcons landed in the part of the city to which our efforts have traced Orthys, without my command, *before* we have received intelligence as to his exact location."

"Mamma." I dropped my voice so it wouldn't carry to the gawkers peering out windows or craning their necks past the soldiers blocking the ends of the street. "It was a trap."

"I am not surprised." She looked me over sharply, as if verifying I was intact. "Tell me."

I did. My mother's mask never cracked, even when I got to Leodra's involvement and when Marcello gasped in shock at my side. She stopped me once to nod to Ciardha, who performed an efficient search of the dead man in the leather apron, turning up the seal of the Council of Nine. She took that with a gentle hand, but her face went grim and full of death. I remembered it was still judgment day.

"Very well," she said when I was done. She turned to Marcello and then to the officer of the Imperial Guard at her side. "Come with me."

"To your palace?" Marcello asked tentatively.

"No. To the Imperial Palace." She tucked the seal into her sleeve. "You too, Amalia. I want you at my side until we've settled matters with Baron Leodra. We have work to do."

Chapter Fifteen

Our boats formed a veritable flotilla as we headed for the Imperial Palace. People leaned over bridge railings to gawk at the long line of small military craft in Falconer red and imperial blue. I sat with my mother in her personal boat in the center; its golden prow, carved to symbolize the winged horse of Raverra, cut the canal waters as cleanly as an assassin's knife.

"I can't believe Baron Leodra is a traitor to the Empire," I said.

La Contessa kept her eyes fixed toward the Imperial Palace, her face a grim mask. "I doubt he set out to be one."

"If Orthys sold children to Vaskandar, and his father let him use the imperial seal..."

"I know what you're thinking." My mother cast me a sidelong glance. "The abducted heirs of Ardence. The Falconer deception. Be careful about jumping to conclusions."

"It doesn't seem like much of a jump." Everything made sense now. Leodra wanted the Empire to take a stronger hand in Ardence; what better way to force the issue than to trigger a war he knew full well Ardence couldn't win?

"Leodra doesn't have any people in Ardence," La Contessa said. "He's new to the Council, and his power base is in Raverra. So far as our investigation has been able to tell, Orthys passed through Ardence regularly on his way up the River Arden to Vaskandar, but had no significant contacts there either. Neither of them would have had the connections or resources in the city to stage so precise, delicate, and ambitious an operation as the kidnapping of the Ardentine heirs." She shook her head. "It's possible Baron Leodra was involved, but if so, he didn't act alone."

That made sense. Leodra couldn't have used imperial agents to abduct the heirs, or the rest of the Council would have learned about it. If he didn't have his own hirelings in Ardence, that meant someone else had taken the children. And still held them, frightened and alone.

I stared at my own hand, white-knuckled on the slim pole that upheld a brocade canopy over our heads. The scar on the back of my wrist stood out starkly, reminding me how close I'd come to getting assassinated once again.

Scars. There was something else it reminded me of. Something I'd realized in a flash when Orthys trapped us in the theater, and forgotten in the chaos that followed.

"Graces preserve us. I think Orthys worked for Prince Ruven."

That got my mother's attention. She swiveled on her cushioned bench. "What?"

I touched my own face. "One of Orthys's men had a scar like a handprint. Half Ruven's servants have the same scars, from his Skinwitch powers. I don't know anything else that could leave a mark like that."

For a moment, La Contessa was silent. Then she drew in a long breath. "Damn Leodra to the Hell of Disaster. Cleaning up this mess may take more work than I thought."

We swept into the Imperial Palace like a winter storm, leaving courtiers shivering in our wake. My mother closeted herself in the inner council chamber with the doge and what few of the Council of Nine happened to be currently in the palace—Leodra not among them—while Ciardha, Marcello, and I stood vigil outside.

We didn't have to wait long. Perhaps a quarter of an hour passed before my mother called Marcello and me in to tell what we'd seen. The doge listened, eyes glittering, from his modest throne, while two other members of the Council stood by with tight lips and pale faces. When we finished, the doge rose. His richly embroidered robes fell about him like gull's wings.

"We will detain Baron Leodra at once," he said. "We must handle this quickly and quietly. We cannot afford a prolonged internal conflict now, with Ardence and Vaskandar watching us for weakness, and the eyes of the Empire upon us."

"It would be my pleasure to handle the matter," La Contessa offered.

The doge gave a curt nod. "You have my blessing and my full authority."

My mother swept up Ciardha on her way out the door and immediately started giving orders. "Get me a platoon of Imperial Guards. Send spies ahead to find Leodra. Set our most trusted intelligence officers to determining who is loyal to him, tracing his people and papers, finding every scheme he has his fingers in. We need to stop any contingency plans he may have in place before he sets them into motion. And especially look for any sign of what happened to the Ardentine children."

Ciardha bowed without slowing her pace. "It will be done, Contessa."

By the time we left the palace, we'd gathered a grim-faced wake. I felt very small in the center of it as we swept through the city like a cresting wave, bearing down on Leodra's palace with all the inevitability of the tide. I had set this thing in motion by escaping Leodra's trap and telling my mother. Now it had swelled far beyond me, and all I could do was bear witness as Leodra's doom came crashing down on him.

But when we arrived at the sweeping marble steps of Leodra's grand palace, Ciardha waited for us, shaking her head.

"He's fled, Contessa. Someone must have warned him. He's gone."

La Contessa closed her eyes for a second, mouthing a curse. Then they snapped back open, sharp as ever, conceding nothing. "I want his house searched."

"Of course, Contessa. It is already in progress. They've found this." She handed my mother an official-looking paper.

I peeked over my mother's shoulder. Elegant, formal script spelled out a familiar message, marred by one or two corrections. It was unquestionably a draft of the letter the parents of the missing Ardentine children had received commanding them to submit to Raverra's authority.

"Hell of Discord." The words slipped out of my mouth all in a breath. "If Ardence learns of this..."

It would justify all the worst suspicions of the Shadow Gentry. I couldn't blame them for accusing Raverra anymore. No matter what other pieces of the truth we were missing, this letter inked a clear trail.

One of the Council of Nine had been involved in the abduction.

My mother handed the paper back to Ciardha. "We must convene what is left of the Council," she said. "There is one more judgment to pass today."

A nonstop whirlwind of activity blew through my house all night and throughout the next day: spies and messengers bearing reports, Ciardha coming and going with her face grim and her eyes shadowed with lack of sleep, and the doge and half the Council calling on La Contessa—during the brief periods when she wasn't at the Imperial Palace herself.

My mother strongly advised me to stay home until she could be certain Baron Leodra hadn't left behind any assassins with orders to finish the task Orthys had failed to accomplish. Not long ago, I would have been perfectly content to spend as many days as my mother liked reading in the library or drawing up artifice-project ideas in my room, but now I found it impossible to settle to anything. I paced the library, or stared out the palace windows at the Imperial Canal, and eavesdropped relentlessly on every bit of news I could get about how the revelation of Leodra's treachery was affecting the situation with Ardence.

It seemed a thorough search of his house and papers, and even more thorough questioning of his most trusted lieutenants and advisers, turned up no further hints or evidence pertaining to the kidnapping of the Ardentine children. If he'd done more than supply the writ and seal, he'd left no trace of it. My hopes this discovery would free the children and end the threat of war faded. This wasn't so simple a matter as Leodra orchestrating the entire thing himself.

The evening after Leodra's treachery, Domenic paid a call, to my great relief. But we'd barely settled down in the parlor with a tray of rosemary-and-cheese crostini when he confessed the true purpose of his visit.

"I'm headed back to Ardence tomorrow morning." He sighed despondently. "I don't want to go. By all reports, court's more a mess of shouting and bad ideas than ever. But I have to at least try to persuade my cousin the duke to receive the Serene Envoy again. And talk my brother out of making mistakes that could destroy the future of my city."

"Are you not joining the Shadow Gentry after all, then?" I kept my voice light and teasing, but I could hear the strain under it, and I suspected Domenic could as well. "I was all ready to buy you a gray domino mask and a mysterious cloak."

"While I'm sure I'd look quite dashing in that, you'd best hold off your mask shopping for now." Domenic turned a crostini in his hands as if it were a rare artifact he was evaluating. "They do have some points, mind you, especially about the unwilling conscription of Falcons. But Gabril—well, our father was a historian, you see."

"I know. I have his *Chronicle of the Rise of Ardence*."

Domenic's face brightened momentarily. "Yes, yes! That's his best. Half the reason he abdicated the ducal throne was to write that book. Gabril loved it. All the glorious victories and clever stratagems. Those were the parts of Ardence's history he paid attention to." He took a contemplative nibble of his crostini. "But he forgets that the reason there are so many stories of great military battles in Ardence's history as an independent city-state, before Raverra defeated us and brought us into the Empire, is because we were always at war. Endless bloody conflicts with the other city-states in central Eruvia, playing out petty power struggles and helping no one." Domenic shook his head. "We may grumble about Raverra, and even rail at it sometimes, but Ardence's golden years came after it joined the Empire. We are safe, and strong, and free to focus on the trade and art and innovation that made Ardence into a city truly blessed by the Graces. I can't let them throw all that away."

I swallowed a brittle lump. "Do you think they will?"

"Unless we can convince them Raverra didn't steal their heirs, yes, they seem determined to try."

I crumbled a crostini between my fingers. I wanted to tell him about Leodra, but that was a deep state secret—and I wasn't entirely sure how he'd take it. "I hope someone finds those children soon."

Domenic nodded gravely. "I think of them every day. I hope

they're safe, at least. And if we could find them—well, that would help a great deal." He slapped his leg suddenly. "Oh! And I meant to tell you—they're not the only thing missing. Did I leave *Interactions of Magic* here by any chance?"

"You haven't *lost* it!" I gasped.

He grimaced. "I can't imagine how I could have, honestly. But I've packed to head home, and it's not where I thought I left it."

"Have you checked to make sure it didn't get mixed up with any library books? Like that time you accidentally returned Venasha's personal copy of *Ancient Ostan Artifice as Art: Tomb Wards and Temple Murals* to the university library, and I had to talk her down from shaving your head while you slept?"

Domenic winced. "I learned from that mistake. Though actually, one of my friends from the Imperial Library was visiting and asked if he could borrow *Interactions of Magic* sometime, and I said of course. Possibly he thought I meant 'now' instead of 'maybe in a few months, when I'm done reading it seven times and gazing lovingly at it and petting it occasionally,' and took it with him."

"I'll look for it. And I'll have someone check to see if it's turned up in the Imperial Library."

"And I'll ask my friend. Thanks." Domenic favored me with a brilliant smile. "I'll miss you, Amalia."

"You'll have to come back to visit soon, then," I said, with forced cheer.

"Of course. Nothing could keep me away."

But his voice held an edge. We both knew that soon travel between our cities might not be so simple.

Shortly after Domenic left, my mother returned from the Imperial Palace, her shoulders drooping with exhaustion. I was fairly certain she hadn't slept since discovering Leodra's treachery. She called for mulled wine, kicked her shoes off in the foyer like a child, and retired to the drawing room for a discussion with Ciardha.

I lurked near the half-open drawing room door, trying to overhear them. But by the time I resolved meaning from the murmur of their voices, they fell silent. I strained closer, trying to figure out what was happening. Had my mother dozed off?

"Come in, child," La Contessa called. "The door is open."

Ciardha held the door for me, amusement dancing on her lips. My cheeks warm, I entered the room. Ciardha bowed and left.

Far from dozing off in a chair, my mother stood by the fireplace, leaning against the mantel, mulled wine in hand. Deep shadows cradled her eyes.

"You no longer need to remain in our palace," she said. "It should be no more dangerous than usual out there."

"Did you catch Leodra?"

"No. He's disappeared most thoroughly, at least for now. But I'm sufficiently confident we've uncovered and neutralized any remaining resources he had." She sipped her wine, savoring it a moment on her tongue, with the lingering relish of a woman who hadn't done anything for her own comfort in some time. "We have more than enough evidence to hang Leodra for treason. It seems he sent the letters with the imperial seal and the false writs to Ardence through Orthys—we found an extra copy of the writ on Orthys's ship, which I suspect the scoundrel was keeping for his own purposes. But we still don't know who received the papers from Orthys in Ardence."

"Perhaps tracking down Leodra will uncover new leads," I said hopefully. "There has to be *some* trace of what happened to those children."

"If so, we'd best find it soon." My mother's mouth settled into a grim line. "The doge wants the Ardence situation resolved swiftly. No matter how hard we try to keep secret that there was a traitor among the Council of Nine, rumors will spread. The Serene Empire must appear more unified than ever, so that we can move past this moment with undiminished grace."

Domenic's assessment of the Ardentine side of the equation didn't seem to suggest a swift solution was likely, barring the return of the missing children. "And how does His Serenity plan to bring Ardence back under the Serene Accords so quickly?"

La Contessa set down her empty glass on the mantel. "That," she said, "is a matter currently under some debate. I expect we'll come to a decision tomorrow."

There was a certain ominous finality to her tone. "What...? Do I want to know what that means?"

"That depends on what we decide. Which reminds me. The doge requests your presence tomorrow, at the Imperial Palace."

"What for?" I could think of no reason that didn't add another handful of cold pebbles to the growing mound in my stomach.

"He wishes to tell you himself." She paused on her way to the door to lay a hand briefly on the top of my head, a touch light and quick as the stroke of a dove's wing. "But make sure you have plenty of elixir on hand, Amalia, and decline your invitations for next week. You'll need to prepare for a trip."

"Ardence. Of course you're sending me to Ardence."

I sank against the hard back of my chair, to the degree possible in a corset, not caring what the doge thought of my posture. So much for my hopes to find a way to ease the tension with Ardence. Now I'd have to help make it worse.

The spark held steady in Niro da Morante's eyes as he regarded me across a writing table. I'd known this meeting would be trouble the moment I'd heard it would be in his private study. The room had no windows, and the few lamps he'd lit failed to hold back the gloom, though they picked occasional gleams of gold from the shadows.

"You and your Falcon both." He rolled a pen between his fingers. "Can you control her?"

"Your Serenity, I doubt *anyone* can control her."

The pen stopped. "Think very carefully about that statement," he said.

A cold needle of fear slid through my heart. "Your Serenity?"

"If a fire warlock cannot be controlled, she is a danger to the Empire. It is my solemn duty to eliminate threats to the Serene City." His voice stayed relentlessly calm—a voice that had condemned people to death often enough that the words would flow familiarly over his tongue. "I ask you again. Can you control her?"

I swallowed. "I can bind her power, Your Serenity. And she can control herself. If we earn her loyalty, that comes out to the same thing, in the end."

He stared at me for a long time. I didn't look away, even when I felt like screaming at him to say something.

"Do you understand," he said at last, "why I am sending you to Ardence?"

"The paradox of force," I whispered.

"Exactly." He steepled his fingers before him. "It is my hope, Lady Amalia, we will have no need to unleash your Falcon's fire and that your presence will serve as a sufficient reminder to Duke Bergandon to behave himself. But if that hope fails, I need to be certain I can carry through on my implicit threat. Especially now, when so many other problems distract the Empire. Do you understand?"

"Yes. But, Your Serenity, someone is trying to goad Raverra and Ardence into fighting. All these other forces disturbing the serenity of the Empire—Leodra, Vaskandar—have helped create this problem." My corset stays dug into my legs as I strained at the edge of my seat. "You must see that."

"Of course I do."

"Then surely you wouldn't burn Ardence over a needless conflict sparked by deceit. We must find out the truth behind the false Falconer incident, not escalate it to war."

He raised an eyebrow. "My lady, you mistake the situation, and you mistake me."

"Oh?"

"This is not a matter of truth," he said. "This is a matter of dominion."

My shoulders went rigid. "So you don't care who took those children. You don't care who's trying to start a war. You just want Ardence to bend the knee."

"On the contrary, Lady Amalia. I *do* care. I want to see the children returned, and the ones who would dare attempt to manipulate the Serene Empire brought to justice." He spread his hands. "If you wish to seek the truth, by all means, do so, with my blessing. You are reportedly a woman of intelligence, and you have connections in Ardence; you are well suited to the task. And if the truth can prevent a war, so much the better." His voice was hard as a new-forged blade. "But that truth alone will not keep Ardence from harsh consequences. They have broken the Serene Accords twice. The only thing that can save them now is acceptance of Raverran rule."

I didn't dare speak. The words on my tongue were too bitter.

The doge leaned forward. "I have one clear priority: the unassailable strength and unity of the Serene Empire. If Ardence pushes us any further—if it rebels against the Serene City openly—then yes, Lady Amalia. It will burn. And to be clear, yours will be the word that burns it."

I stared at him, my throat tight and hot. He waited, patient as a stalking leopard.

Finally, I nodded. "Yes, Your Serenity."

Chapter Sixteen

After my meeting with the doge, my mother called on me to attend a strategy session of the Council of Nine. This did nothing to dissipate the smothering cloud of dread the doge's words had laid upon me; I had no illusions this was a simple opportunity to watch and learn. They wanted me present as the fire warlock's Falconer, not as the Cornaro heir.

Only eight members of the Council stood around the table in the Map Room. Baron Leodra had held one of the five elected positions in the Council of Nine, and the Assembly had not yet chosen his successor. Assorted generals, advisers, and the like fit in around them, including Colonel Vasante. Marcello stood uneasily at her shoulder, along with his fellow lieutenant, the ranking Falcon at the Mews. My eyes pulled straight to him, and he flashed me a small, nervous smile.

I took half a step toward him. But my mother was watching, her face cool and distant.

Fine. If she was so concerned about people seeing me next to Marcello, I wouldn't stand with her, either. I slipped into a gap near the marquise of Palova and the admiral of the navy.

The doge surveyed the assembled dignitaries a moment, then slapped his palm down on the map. Marcello jumped at the sound.

"Vaskandar first," he announced. "Their forces on the border have moved—but not through the pass. They appear to have taken up rather uncomfortable positions on and around Mount Whitecrown." The green stones had in fact shifted, forming a scattered cluster deep in the heart of the Witchwall Mountains. It didn't seem like a good vantage point from which to attack. "Can anyone explain this madness?"

The generals frowned at the map. Something tickled the back of my mind.

"Volcanic glass." The words burst out despite the fact I wasn't strictly supposed to speak at these meetings unless asked a question.

The doge frowned. "Excuse me?"

"It's a power source for artifice. Volcanoes contain an incredible amount of power, even ones like Mount Whitecrown that haven't erupted in a hundred years. Artifice can extract some of that power from volcanic glass."

I had their attention; Colonel Vasante nodded, and the Council and the generals looked thoughtful. The doge drummed his fingers on the table. "But Vaskandar has next to no artificers."

"The Witch Lords have never shown interest in obsidian before," the marquise of Palova said. "It's a good point, and we should keep it in mind. But I'm more concerned about Mount Whitecrown as a vantage point over Ardence and the central border defenses. If they're planning any kind of magical assault that requires a clear line of sight, they'll have it from there."

The doge stared at me thoughtfully for a moment, then at the marquise, then down at the map. "Mount Whitecrown is on their side of the border, just barely. If we try to take it from them, we're the ones starting a war."

"Now is not a good time for that," my mother said.

The marquise of Palova nodded. "We need to figure out what they're doing, watch them closely, and have forces in position to act. But first we need to stabilize Ardence, and quickly. We can't have rebellion threatening the heart of the Empire when Vaskandar may be getting ready to make a move."

The doge nodded. "Ah, yes. Ardence. I agree we must resolve that matter swiftly. We cannot afford to appear weak when we have faced... internal difficulties."

A tense hush fell over the room. No one looked at the spot where Baron Leodra usually stood.

La Contessa broke the silence at last. "We need to show unity as well as strength. What we do in Ardence must appear effortless. If the city can be brought back into the fold diplomatically, so much the better."

"It is difficult to employ diplomacy when Duke Astor won't speak to the Serene Envoy, save to issue unreasonable demands," the doge said dryly.

"He's receiving poor counsel from the Shadow Gentry," my mother said. "I suspect you'll see a change within the next few days, when Lady Savony returns to advise him."

"Perhaps he will be more willing to resume cordial relations with the Empire when he has a fire warlock inside his city." The doge's words rang with a steely edge. "For now, we will move in no additional troops, to preserve the serenity of the Empire."

Vasante cleared her throat. "And what exactly happens if Ardence still refuses to receive the Serene Envoy, Your Serenity? If this last attempt at diplomacy fails?"

The doge pressed his fingertips on the table, leaning forward into the lamplight. "If they refuse to abide by the Serene Accords, they are rebels against the Empire. We will stop asking nicely, and give them the choice we gave Celantis: kneel or burn."

His words sucked the air out of the Map Room.

The marquise of Palova lifted her snow-white brows. "That's rather dramatic."

"The Shadow Gentry are posting broadsides all over the city urging the duke to declare Ardentine independence, and Astor says nothing against them," the doge snapped. "He's *still* taxing Raverran merchants, and he's rejecting imperial authority. I have sympathy for the families of the missing children, but if they won't listen when we say we don't have them, that sympathy dwindles. As does my patience."

"Still, once you issue an ultimatum, any illusion of unity is destroyed," La Contessa warned. "We affirm our strength, but at the expense of tyranny. Ardence will no longer be our friend and willing subject."

The doge nodded slowly. "True. And that is why we will save such an ultimatum for a last resort. If Lady Amalia's visit to the city is a personal one on the surface, our threat can remain implicit while they contemplate the benefits of peaceful dialogue."

"She has friends in Ardence," my mother agreed. "And my cousin Ignazio was already talking about making a trip to see to some business there. She can accompany him, and pay her respects in court with all the trappings of a purely social visit."

I didn't like the talk of using my friends as a screen to hide my far more sinister purpose in Ardence. But I pressed my lips shut. I had to choose my battles carefully if my opponents were my mother and the Council.

"With all respect," Colonel Vasante objected, "if Lady Amalia is pretending to visit friends and traveling with her uncle, are you proposing she stay in the city rather than in the imperial garrison outside Ardence?"

The marquise of Palova let out a short bark of a laugh. "Staying in the garrison would rather decrease the subtlety of the message."

A thoughtful divot appeared between my mother's perfectly sculpted brows. "Putting our fire warlock in the heart of their city, smiling and attending their parties, is both friendlier and more pointed, and keeps the focus on a diplomatic rather than a military solution." She glanced at me. "However, it does raise security concerns."

"Assigning them a guard might be too obvious." Vasante chewed her lip. "I suppose Lieutenant Verdi could stick with them as much as possible, and pass himself off as a family friend rather than an official guard."

My mother's eyebrow twitched. "That's one solution."

The doge grunted. "Take what steps you see fit to ensure their safety," he told the colonel. "But frankly, I think a fire warlock is protection enough. Lady Amalia, if anyone attacks you or Zaira in Ardence, you have my permission to unleash your Falcon within the city to defend yourself."

I bobbed a stiff curtsy, too queasy to manage more than a "Yes, Your Serenity."

He turned to Marcello. "Lieutenant Verdi."

Marcello bowed, his eyes widening in panic at being addressed directly. "Yes, Your Serenity?"

"You will be the ranking officer of the Falcons in Ardence for this mission. Do you feel up to the task?"

He jerked his head in a nod. "Yes, Your Serenity."

"You will have full responsibility for assuring the safety of Lady Amalia and our fire warlock, investigating the false Falconer incident, and overseeing the artifice projects at the garrison that the colonel outlined for you."

Marcello bowed again. "Of course, Your Serenity."

The doge lifted a finger. "If Ardence initiates any violence— against the Falcons, the garrison, our diplomats, the Serene Envoy—or declares independence, or engages in any other act of open rebellion, you may consult with me via the garrison courier lamps if there is time. But if the situation is pressing, you do not need to contact the Imperial Palace. You may consider it an act of war and respond with the full force at your disposal. Do you understand?"

Marcello's throat jumped. "Yes, Your Serenity."

"You have also heard what I will require of you if, after all our best efforts, the duke of Ardence still refuses to heed the Serene Envoy, revoke the illegal taxes, and comply with the Serene Accords."

Marcello nodded, looking ill.

The doge held his eyes. "You accept the burden, if necessary, of starting a war?"

I strained against my own closed lips to speak—to support Marcello, or to stop him. This was too much to put on his shoulders. The colonel should step in and offer to take his place. But she merely watched him, assessing.

A struggle passed like racing cloud shadows over Marcello's face. Finally, he nodded again, with slow gravity, as if his head weighed more coming up than it had going down. "Yes. I do."

I touched the cold metal of my falcon's-head brooch. Now that he'd taken this madness willingly into his own hand, he couldn't set it down again; it was too late.

"That settles Ardence," the doge said with apparent satisfaction. "Colonel Vasante can give you the full military briefing, and Lady Terringer can fill you in on the diplomatic efforts. Is there anything else we need to discuss?"

The marquise of Palova glanced at my mother, then cleared her throat. "The Falcons stationed on the Witchwall will require a capable leader. Perhaps after the Ardence matter is settled, Lieutenant Verdi could proceed to the border and take command there."

Marcello blanched. I rocked back on my heels with the shock of her suggestion. There'd been no hint of this from Marcello or the colonel.

Hell of Madness. This was my mother's doing, to keep us apart.

I glared at her across the table. She met my eyes with cool interest. Watching to see what I would do.

Vasante frowned. "The border fortresses are dozens or hundreds of miles apart. I'd assumed we would coordinate command from the Mews by courier lamp."

The marquise spread her hands. "Would it not be wise to have a trusted officer on the border near Mount Whitecrown, ready to respond to unexpected situations? Clearly we have great confidence in Lieutenant Verdi, to place him in charge of such a sensitive mission as Ardence. Would he not be a fine choice?"

Her tone was questioning, not declarative. The marquise didn't meet my eyes, but my mother stared straight at me, her eyebrow raised.

Marcello's lips moved. No sound came out, but I read a name: *Istrella*. He looked ready to crumple at any moment.

Anger and fear twined in my belly like twin snakes. "Colonel Vasante is right," I said. "Sending Lieutenant Verdi to the border makes no sense. He'd have to coordinate by courier lamp anyway. And he's best able to serve the Empire at the Mews."

Around the table, cynical faces turned heavy-lidded eyes to me, too steeped in old power to think much of my interruption. This time, I hadn't offered useful new information, like I had with the volcano. I'd made the transparent plea of a young girl.

But Marcello's eyes begged me, with desperate hope: *Get me out of this*.

"Young lady." It was the supercilious drawl of one of the older members of the Council, Lord Errardi, whom I'd sometimes seen napping at meetings. "You are out of order. Your obvious desire to protect your sweetheart is very touching, but this matter is not for you to decide."

Heat flushed all the way to my ears. "He's not my sweetheart."

Wonderful. Now I sounded completely infantile. But feeling my mother watching me, I knew what I had to do.

I straightened as if in offense. "In fact, Lord Errardi, I am insulted you could make such an insinuation. I am the heir to House Cornaro. Lieutenant Verdi, though a fine man, is far beneath my station." Out of the corner of my eye, I saw Marcello stiffen. *Oh, Marcello, I'm sorry.* But I met my mother's gaze, took a breath, and drove home the knife. "I would never enter-tain the idea of courting such an unfavorable match. I'm merely considering what is best for the Falcons and the Empire, as I expect we all are."

Lord Errardi huffed, brushing imaginary dust off his doublet front. "Well, now, no need to be so touchy. It was an honest mistake. But still, this is a matter for the Council to discuss, not observers."

My mother's voice cut across the table. "I think, however, my daughter has a point. We will have more flexibility to respond to the evolving Vaskandar situation if we don't commit too many forces to specific points on the Witchwall. There is no need to move Lieutenant Verdi yet."

My shoulders slumped with relief. She'd taken my offering. For now, Marcello and Istrella were safe from exile to the border on my behalf.

But Marcello wouldn't look at me. A muscle in his cheek jumped, as if in pain.

My mother and I shared a boat on the way home. I stared out at the canal, brilliant with reflected lights, the soft evening radi-ance drawing out the beauty and mystery of the grand facades lining the water. Marcello had left the Imperial Palace without speaking to me, and I hadn't dared approach him—not with the whole Council there.

"You made the right choice," my mother said quietly.

I couldn't look at her right now. "I made the choice you wanted me to make."

"I know it isn't easy now. But it would have been harder later." I felt the faintest stirring of my hair, as if she'd barely brushed it with her fingertips, then realized now was not a good time and pulled back. "Better to never form any attachment to him, than to have to break one off when politics demand it."

"I wasn't *forming an attachment*." I faced her at last, my back stiff. "Maybe I would have. I'll never know. You didn't give me the chance."

My mother fingered the triple string of black pearls around her neck. "If you had the strength and callousness, you could form all the romantic entanglements you wished, so long as you were willing to cast them aside." She sounded strangely wistful. "But you are not so cruel."

"And I suppose that's my failing?" I asked bitterly.

"No. Not at all."

It was a rare moment. Her mask was off; only the evening shadows came between us. But even with some complex emotion naked on her face at last, I couldn't read it. Her heart spoke an intricate language I had not yet learned.

"Be careful in Ardence, Amalia." Her voice dropped low, almost to a whisper. "Someone is playing a deep and dangerous game there, one I don't yet understand, and I don't doubt they'd kill to keep it secret. I am sending you into a dark room without knowing what lies inside, and counting on you to find a way to make light."

I let out a long breath, releasing my anger into the sea air. "I expect I'll bump into everything, break things, and make a mess. But I'll do what I can, Mamma."

She nodded, her mask back on. "Then we'll see what you can do."

Unease grew in my gut as the miles opened between me and Raverra, exacerbated by the bouncing of the coach. The flat, sunny fields and tile-roofed farmhouses around us had never seen the sea. It was an open country, empty of secrets, every surface kissed with light. I yearned to be back in my shadow-hoarding maze of brick and water, perhaps bent over wire and books and crystals with Istrella, or attempting to unravel the Ardentine kidnapping mystery with Marcello from safely outside city-destroying distance.

Marcello. He'd hardly said a word to me since the Council session last night, and those few words had been stiff and formal, the necessary business of our trip. He rode alongside the coach on a blood bay mare, supervising the small detachment of soldiers sent to guard us on our journey, but he avoided my window as if looking on it would burn him.

I knew I needed to talk to him. But what could I say? *I'm sorry for the cruel things I said, but they're effectively true*?

I didn't know how to tell him we couldn't court anymore when we'd never been courting in the first place.

Istrella rode by his side, chattering and pointing at things, occasionally lowering the artifice glasses that sat on her forehead to peer at some object or bird through them. Zaira's voice drifted down from the coachman's bench, barely audible over the rumble of wheels and the clatter of hooves, chatting with the driver; she'd asked to sit up beside him, and they seemed to be entertaining each other immensely. It should have been a cheerful journey. But every time I thought about the purpose of our trip, a sickening gulf opened in my chest.

I'd always expected to return to Ardence someday, but not like this.

It occurred to me, as I glanced at the man seated opposite me in the carriage, that he might well be thinking the exact same thing.

Maybe we could distract each other. "Uncle Ignazio?"

He looked up from his lap, his brooding expression easing. "Yes, Amalia?"

"This must be difficult for you, returning to Ardence so soon. I'm sorry."

He laughed shortly. "It's more awkward for Lady Terringer than it is for me. It may look to some as if the doge is sending me to clean up her mess."

"Is she likely to be resentful?" That could be a problem, given I would need to work with her. I couldn't imagine she'd be pleased to find her predecessor watching over her shoulder.

Ignazio shrugged. "I'll stay out of her way. I'll be so quiet she'll hardly notice I'm in Ardence. And if she's bothered anyway, well, it would be foolish of her to let it affect her dealings with you. You'll be giving her orders someday, after all...in the event my cousin ever takes it into her head to retire."

"I'll die of old age first." It was my best hope.

Zaira's raucous laugh sounded above the creaks and rumble of the coach. Ignazio frowned. "She's rather exposed up in the coachman's box. I wish she'd accepted my invitation to join us in here."

"Oh, she's safe enough from assassins." I lowered my voice. "The doge wouldn't move his only fire warlock into danger without defenses. The boning of her bodice and the pins in her hair are artifice-warded runesteel. The first two or three musket balls would bounce off her like pebbles off a tile roof."

"Truly." Interest kindled in Ignazio's eyes. "What did they use for a power source? I didn't think it was possible to create a kinetic shield small enough to carry on one's person."

This was why I liked my uncle Ignazio. He spoke my language. Even if his knowledge of magical theory was weak outside of alchemy, he understood the core principles. "Warlocks are their own source of magical energy. The doge's personal artificer created it; it's linked to Zaira's power. I gather it's not uncommon for high-value Falcons working in dangerous areas to have such protections."

"Impressive. And a shame those of us without such reserves of magical power can't use them." No bitterness colored Ignazio's voice, but a frown flickered across his brow. My mother said it still stung him that his glimmer of alchemical talent wasn't enough to mark his eyes and land him in the Mews. "It would take a great deal of effort and skill to create such devices. The doge must value her highly."

"He values his plan highly." I slouched in my seat. "I'm not sure he values *people* at all."

Ignazio let out a soft breath, carrying a mist of regret. "The more power a leader wields, Amalia, the harder it becomes for him or her to value individual people over results. The doge has to consider the welfare of millions of imperial citizens, after all. How do you balance that against the happiness of one person? Or even their life?"

"I don't know," I said. "Do they always need to be in conflict? Can't you do both—take care of the Empire as a whole and have care for its individual people as well?"

"Perhaps." Ignazio shrugged. "But it's impossible to rule without getting *some* blood on your hands. When you ascend to the Council of Nine, you will see."

There was a certain ominous coloration to the pity in his voice. I hunched my shoulders.

"At this rate, if I can make it until I ascend to the Council without getting blood on my hands, I will consider myself blessed by the Grace of Luck."

In the afternoon, a light rain began to fall, and Zaira and Istrella both joined us in the coach. Zaira sat with Ignazio, and began relaying to him some of the gossip the coachman had told her.

Istrella sat next to me, hauled up a bag onto the seat between us, and pulled out a box full of artifice bits to work with in her lap.

I peered at what she was doing. "Are you making *jesses?*"

"This?" Istrella held up a thin braid of golden wire. Her own jess gleamed on her wrist. "No, no. Not yet. I'm learning the basic principles, though. The doge's Master Artificer thought I might have the potential to do it someday. It's quite an honor."

Zaira's voice faltered for a heartbeat in the midst of describing a shrinekeeper's drunken indiscretion; she flashed a sidelong frown at Istrella.

"I'm impressed," I said. "I didn't realize they let anyone but the Master Artificer work on those."

"I had to apprentice to him for a year and make about seventeen oaths of secrecy before he'd start teaching me." Istrella teased out an end of golden wire and began carefully twisting it into a tiny spiral. "I'm going to have to destroy this after I finish it, even though it's just practice; I'm not allowed to leave any intact pieces lying around."

I tried to unravel the complex weave with my eyes. "That looks like the core braid, the part that suppresses magic."

"Well, that's the idea. This one doesn't work yet. The layers that go over it are even trickier, governing all the circumstances and commands the jess has to account for." She cocked her head at the unfinished wirework. "It's so orderly and logical. I have trouble keeping myself from throwing in improvisations, or trying shortcuts, but that always ruins it. The last one I made should have stopped a person from doing magic, but instead it stopped them from seeing out of their left eye."

"Doesn't it bother you," Zaira asked abruptly, "making something like that?"

Istrella shrugged. "I grew up wearing one. It makes people feel safer around me, and Marcello leaves me released nearly always anyway. I can see why it would be more annoying for a warlock, though, having your powers sealed all the time. Especially since I hear you don't want to be a Falcon."

"Do *you* want to be a Falcon?" I asked.

Istrella's eyes crinkled into a smile, the mage mark shining gold around her pupils. "Oh, yes! I get to putter around with artifice projects all day, I have all the books I want, and I have friends who understand me and aren't afraid of me. It's lovely." She started picking through blood-red beads in a tray in her lap. The coach hit a bump, and she clucked her tongue disapprovingly.

Zaira's brows clumped in frustration. "But you can't leave the Mews without your brother, and he's gone half the time—off bringing in new Falcons, or at meetings, or arresting some poor crazy bastard with a touch of artifice who's carving explosive seals on all the village doors to keep the demons out. How can that not make you angry?"

"I do get angry at Marcello sometimes, when he's being an ass. He's my brother, after all." The twinkle in Istrella's eyes dissipated to a more contemplative shine. "But back when the colonel used to make us spend half the year with my family, he looked out for me. When Father found one of my devices and tried to ruin it, like he always did, Marcello would tell him that was property of the Empire, and destroying it was a crime. If our older brother raised his hand to me when Marcello wasn't looking, I could hold up my jess to remind him I was a Falcon now, and he'd have to leave me alone." She turned her wrist, making the red beads sparkle. "But Halmur tells me it's unnerving sometimes when he leaves the Mews, and they have to seal his vivomancer powers, and he can't sense the life around him. And I know *you* don't want to be in the Mews at all, except when you're with Terika. So I suppose it's different for everybody."

Zaira jumped a bit at Terika's name. Then she settled back

onto her bench with a sigh. "You're hopeless." She turned deliberately to Ignazio. "Where was I? Oh, right, so the shrinekeeper
arrives at the beach, *still* without trousers, and realizes there's no
bridge to Raverra, and takes it into his head he wants to *swim*
there…"

Istrella flipped her bicolored glasses down and picked up a
bead. "And now the hard part. Have you ever seen someone try
to thread a double helix in a moving carriage, Amalia?"

"I can't say that I have." I watched Istrella's nimble fingers.
It was a relief to focus on the familiar intricacies of artifice. We
chatted about the techniques she was using, our heads bowed
together over her practice jess; occasionally secrecy compelled
Istrella to remain apologetically mute on the theory behind
some cunning twist of the wire, or why she positioned the beads
where she did. Zaira cast glances our way now and then, an odd,
wistful expression sliding over her face.

But as I watched Istrella work the golden wire, I remembered
why the doge was sending her to Ardence. Those busy fingers
could unleash a destructive force nearly as great as Zaira's balefire. And we had one last chance to keep that force from being
turned on a city full of innocents.

I couldn't sleep that night. My inn room was comfortable
enough; they'd given me their finest feather bed, with lavender-
scented pillows and tall posts carved with twining vines. But
I lay awake staring at a crack in the ceiling until it became as
familiar as the curve of the Imperial Canal. My thoughts traced
the same path over and over, like the fissure I stared at: I had to
find a way to keep Ardence from burning.

With Duke Astor refusing to receive the Serene Envoy,
I didn't have much faith she could persuade him of Raverra's

innocence—no matter that her advice was supposed to be just short of imperial command. To have a chance of thwarting our unseen enemy, we needed to track down the missing children. And unless the Empire managed to capture and interrogate Baron Leodra, our best avenue of information might well be Domenic's connections to the Shadow Gentry—if I could persuade them to talk to me. And if Domenic's brother wasn't one of the guilty parties himself.

I rose, leaving the coverlet in a tangle, and shrugged on a jacket over my nightgown. If I stared at that ceiling any longer, I'd go mad. I needed sky above me.

I made my way down timeworn wooden stairs, through the deep, living silence of a house muffled in sleep. I wandered out through the inn's weedy courtyard and crossed the kitchen garden, under the bright, uncaring stars, surrounded by the scent of rosemary and basil. A chill breeze bent the grasses in a moon-soaked field beyond the low garden wall.

I sat on the wall, staring out at a distant line of cypress trees, and tried to let the diamond-edged starlight into my mind to cleanse it of troubles.

The cold, hard muzzle of a flintlock pistol pressed into my back.

"Not a sound, or I shoot," Baron Leodra whispered.

Chapter Seventeen

Every muscle in my body went rigid. My hands flicked toward my dagger, then my flare locket, but I'd left both on my bedside table in the inn.

"Don't move." Leodra stepped up to stand beside me, where I could see him. The flintlock muzzle hovered a few inches from my chest now. His once-pristine white hair had straw in it, as if he'd been sleeping in a stable, and rough stubble marred his cheeks.

"Listen," he said with hoarse urgency. "Just listen."

I held myself still as the wall I sat on, save for the rapid stutter of my pulse. "I'm listening."

"I'm not a traitor." The pistol nudged my side, trembling. "I'm loyal to the Empire."

I tried to convey the essence of respectful attention while my mind ran through various moves Ciardha had showed me for disarming an attacker of their gun. But I wasn't Ciardha, and I had little confidence I could manage any of them without getting shot.

A spasm of anger crossed Leodra's face. "Graces curse it, I should just kill you. It would serve Lissandra right. But there are things the doge must know. For Raverra's sake."

I caught his wandering gaze. "Did you kidnap the Ardentine heirs?"

"No!" Leodra grimaced in apparent anguish. "I didn't know they were going to do that. It was supposed to be a ruse to spark the Empire into action, not a real kidnapping. They pulled me into their scheme and played me for a fool, tricking me into putting my seal to those writs and letters without understanding how they'd be used. How they'd be *altered*."

"Who?" My fingers curled against the stone wall, scraping on mortar. "Whom did you give the seal to?"

Leodra's wild eyes narrowed into craftiness. "I want a guarantee of safety first."

"That's a strange thing to ask, when you're pointing a pistol at me."

"I know your mother too well." His lips twisted over bared teeth. "She'll have my head off by dawn if she catches me, *unless* I have something she needs. And she needs this. Oh, she needs this."

The pistol shook so badly now I feared he'd pull the trigger by mistake. "I can't make promises for my mother," I said. "But if you give me the information, if you tell me who's plotting against Ardence and the Empire, I'll do everything I can to save you."

"I'm not telling you everything. Not now. You can't win the game without cards in your hand." He passed a hand over his brow. "But I'll tell you enough to show I'm no traitor. As soon as I realized what they were doing, I refused to help them anymore. I'm here, warning you, because I'm loyal to Raverra. You tell your mother and the doge that."

"Yes." I wasn't going to argue with him while he was talking rather than shooting. "Tell me."

"This plot isn't what you think it is." He licked his lips. "If you go to Ardence, you're in danger, Amalia Cornaro."

My skin went tight and cold across my scalp. "Me?"

"Yes." He took a deep breath, his pistol listing off center. "They plan to—"

An earsplitting *bang* echoed through the night, and Leodra

staggered. His hand flew to his neck, trying to stop the sudden dark flow of blood. His mouth worked in silence.

I scrambled to my feet, unable to suppress a shriek. Before the crystal shards of fear stabbing through me could spin me toward the sound of the gunshot, Leodra collapsed across the wall.

"Amalia!" It was Marcello, sprinting across the courtyard in his nightshirt, smoking pistol still in hand. "Are you all right?"

Lights moved and flickered in the windows of the inn. A dog barked madly, and voices called out in alarm.

"For love of the Graces, Marcello, he was about to tell me something important!" All my nerves jangled like cracked bells. Blood soaked Leodra's neck and shoulder. He moved feebly, still sprawled facedown across the wall, but there was no sense or hope in it.

I tore my jacket off and pressed it to his neck, trying to staunch the blood, but it was no good. Grace of Mercy, he was dying in front of me.

Marcello stared, pale and wide-eyed. "He was pointing a pistol at you. I thought he was going to kill you."

Leodra's drowning eyes swallowed all my attention as I held my sodden jacket against his awful wound. "Tell me who took the children," I pleaded.

His blood soaked my hands, cooling rapidly in the night air. He reached a trembling hand up toward me, trying to pull a gasp through his shattered throat. I squeezed his fingers. "Tell me how to find them!"

But the desperate, terrified spark dulled in his eyes. His feeble, frantic movements went still.

I bowed my head. His life's blood stained my trembling arms.

"What..." Marcello swallowed. "Who was he?"

A shudder ran through me, and I forced myself to turn away. "Baron Leodra. He was dead already, Marcello. The Demon of Death just hadn't caught up to him yet."

The half-dozen soldiers escorting us flooded the courtyard,

weapons at the ready. Marcello shook himself like a wet dog and took command, ordering some to search the inn grounds to make sure Leodra hadn't had accomplices. One offered me a handkerchief, with a murmured apology that spoke to its stunning inadequacy. Others removed Leodra's body.

I didn't stay to watch. I walked out through the garden gate alone and into the soft, silvery field with its border of sentinel cypress trees and the rolling hills beyond. I wiped at my arms and hands with the handkerchief until not a speck of white remained on it, and then I cast it aside on the ground.

Tears pressed at the back of my eyes, but I refused to shed them. I couldn't feel sorry for Leodra, not after he'd tried to have me killed. But the man had been a frequent guest in our drawing room. Watching him die had shaken me to the core.

In time, the noise died down. The soldiers went back to bed, the dog stopped barking, and quiet settled over the night. The song of crickets rose to the distant moon. I shivered in the deepening cold, but I couldn't go back to bed. Leodra's blood still drenched my eyes, and the words he hadn't said hung silent between the stars.

Footsteps sounded in the grass behind me. I turned, and there was Marcello, weariness in the line of his shoulders. A glimpse of his chest showed through the plunging neckline of his nightshirt. He'd slung his belt over his shoulder, so his rapier and flintlock hung close at hand.

"Amalia. Are you…" He shook his head. Neither of us was all right, and he knew it. "Do you want to come inside?"

"He was trying to warn me of something." I rubbed my freezing arms. It was strange to feel my own living flesh through my nightgown and know Leodra had lost this vital animation, when he'd been alive and frightened an hour ago. "He wanted to tell us who kidnapped the children in return for mercy. Now he can't, and that knowledge is gone."

I didn't mean it as an accusation. But Marcello blanched. "Hells. I didn't know."

"You couldn't have."

He sank down into a crouch, cradling his face in his hands. "And I killed him. Graces forgive me."

I knelt on the cool grass, trying to catch his eyes, alarm bubbling up in my stomach. "He wasn't an innocent man, Marcello. I'm only alive because his attempt to murder me failed. You couldn't have known he wasn't about to shoot me."

"I've made a horrible mistake." He lifted his eyes to mine, and the anguish there was bottomless. "And I can't undo it. I can't put life back into him."

It was all true. I couldn't belittle him by denying it. "I know."

He closed his eyes and bowed his head, dragging in an uneven breath that bordered on a sob.

I had no words to comfort him. I had no comfort within me to offer. So I leaned slightly toward him until our foreheads barely touched. It was a solid and reassuring warmth: he was alive, too.

"I know," I whispered again.

Our coach bumped and rumbled through the long, golden countryside. The fields lifted up into rolling hills, with tall, dark cypress trees walking in lines like pilgrims. In the morning, mist lay in the folded valleys between the hills, anointing the land with grace and mystery.

Leodra's undelivered warning sunk hooked claws into my thoughts, refusing to let go. Every mile passing beneath our wheels brought us closer to Ardence, where an unknown enemy waited. I had no loose end with which to start unraveling this web, and it was far from reassuring that I couldn't see the spider.

I tried to distract myself by chatting with Istrella about artifice and about places she might like to visit in Ardence. I caught Zaira staring at us once or twice, though she quickly turned her gaze out the window. Once, I saw her smoothing the creases from a charcoal self-portrait of a smiling Terika, which her fellow Falcon must have given her before she left the Mews.

Marcello kept pace with the coach on his mare, coordinating our handful of guards, on higher alert since last night. Occasionally our eyes met through the window glass, and even across half the dusty road I could read the pain and worry in his face.

When we stopped for lunch at a roadside hostelry, I found myself momentarily alone at the table with Marcello as Zaira, Ignazio, and Istrella examined the warding charms the proprietor, a minor artificer, was selling at the bar. I gathered my courage to tell him something I should have days ago.

"I'm sorry," I said.

His eyes flicked up from the deep-scarred wood of the tabletop. "For what?"

I shrugged uncomfortably. "For what I said about you during the Council session."

An odd, sad smile passed across his face. "I can't hold the truth against you. A man like me would be a fool to think he could court the Cornaro heir."

Words backed up in my throat like flotsam. I had so much I wanted to ask, to map out the territory of might-have-been that stretched between us.

Istrella plopped down next to him, spilling a handful of rune-engraved wooden pendants on the table. "Look! Aren't these adorable?"

Marcello's brows lifted. "Only you would think artifice could be adorable, Istrella."

"Is that a challenge?" She lifted up a pendant whose crude circle scribed a ward against mosquitoes, squinting at it contemplatively. "I could build a wirework kitten around this. *Then* would it be adorable?"

"Would this wirework kitten, ah, *do* anything?" Marcello looked worried. "Remember what happened that time when you thought you were just playing with your artifice tools..."

"No one was permanently damaged." Istrella scooped the charms into her velvet bag. "Besides, I have to amuse myself somehow, since you still haven't told me about this secret project I'm supposed to make in Ardence."

Marcello flinched. I gave him my best *Really, Marcello?* look.

He glanced around at the busy room. "Not here. We'll arrive at the garrison tomorrow evening; I'll tell you then, when we have privacy."

Tomorrow. My gut tightened. I'd longed to return to Ardence since my mother called me back to Raverra from my studies at the university, but now its approach brought me nothing but dread.

On our third day of travel, we made our way safely down out of the hills toward a green valley, which the River Arden crossed in a gleaming bracelet. Ardence adorned the river like a dowager's jewel, its red roofs bright in the sun. Greater hills rose on the far side, climbing purple into the distance, until they eventually reared up into the Witchwall Mountains, visible as a faint smear of gray clouds on the far horizon.

When you cut to the heart of it, we were coming to threaten this place with destruction. To crack the red-tile roofs with the blue heat of balefire, and to scorch the verdant valley. When I made out the River Palace in the distance, its gilded domes looming over the city like a hen gathering her chicks around her, a vision flashed before me of it charred and broken, lying empty to the sky, a picked-over carcass. I shivered.

Rather than arriving in Ardence at dusk, we spent our final night of the journey at the imperial garrison, which crowned the last hill looming over Ardence. *Garrison* was a modest term for the sprawling castle, built to harbor thousands of troops. Its massive walls still bore scars from the endless petty wars that had raged between the city-states of central Eruvia before Raverra united them all under the banner of the Serene Empire. Since Ardence had been a peaceful part of the Empire for two hundred years, the soldiers were stationed there to protect Ardence, rather than menace it.

But that could change overnight. With Istrella's modifications, the fortress's cannons would easily be able to reach the city.

I tried not to think about that as I settled into my room and washed the dust of the road off in an artifice-warmed bath. But once I chased images of smoking holes in the city walls from my mind, Leodra's penultimate words filled the gap: *This plot isn't what you think.*

Trying to sleep would be pointless now. I sought out Istrella and the welcome distraction of her endless tinkering, and found Marcello visiting her.

They'd set Istrella up in her own suite of rooms, since she'd be staying in the garrison for several days. In the scant hour or two since we'd arrived, she'd already turned the sitting room into a workshop. Equipment, tools, paintbrushes, and oddments were scattered across the once-serviceable furniture. Istrella sat on the floor, bending over some project spread out on a low table. It resembled a lady's fan, if a fan were constructed from brass knives, scribed with runes, and tangled up in beaded wire. Marcello hovered over her, turning a pair of pliers in his hands.

"Come in, Amalia," Istrella called. "This design isn't coming out well, so you may as well join the party."

"Where's Zaira?" I asked.

"The kitchens." Istrella pushed her glasses up onto her forehead. "Eating dinner number two, I believe. I'm glad I'm not a warlock. I'd never have time to build anything if I had to eat that often."

I examined her work. It didn't seem to be very far along; there wasn't enough of a pattern to the curls of wire for me to guess its purpose, though the runes seemed focused on protection. "What's that?"

"Well, it was going to be a shielding fan, but I need to think some things through before I try again." She pushed it away, sighing dramatically. "If only I had some new and interesting project to begin. An assignment from the doge, perhaps."

I stared pointedly at Marcello. He grimaced and cleared his throat. "Yes, well. About that."

Istrella perked up. "Oh, are you finally going to tell me?"

Marcello nodded, misery in his eyes. But instead of telling her, he laid the schematics and instructions for the cannon down on her table.

Istrella studied them for a moment. Her brows drew down into a frown.

"This is a weapon," she said.

Marcello winced. "Yes."

Istrella traced the lines of the schematic with a fingertip. "It's a good design. So efficient. My designs always use too much energy. And look how precise these runic circles are." She sighed. "This must be the doge's Master Artificer's work. The one who does the jesses. I'll never be that good."

Marcello reached out a hand halfway to Istrella, then dropped it. "Aren't you ... Are you all right with making a weapon?"

She cocked her head. "That depends. Who will they use it on?"

"No one." I grimaced. "I hope."

Istrella lifted skeptical brows. "They don't make weapons to not use them."

"That's true." I glanced at Marcello, but the look he gave me was helpless with anguish. If I left it to him, he'd panic and tell her the cannons would shoot rainbows and everyone would be fine. "The doge wants these weapons here in case Ardence rebels. But it's more likely than not they won't. In that case, the cannons might either stay here to protect the city or get moved to the Witchwall Mountains to defend against Vaskandar."

"I see." Istrella stared at the diagrams. Her fingers moved as if twisting wire. "I suppose I'll have to trust the Empire to use them well."

"I'm sorry, Istrella," Marcello blurted.

She blinked. "What for?"

"You shouldn't have to do this." He waved a hand at the schematics. "This wasn't what I wanted for you. It isn't..." He struggled a moment, then said the words. "It isn't right."

Istrella shrugged. "It's an interesting design. It's better than making yet more courier lamps. The Empire gives me everything I ask for, Marcello. If it wants cannons in return, I can give it cannons."

The careless acceptance in Istrella's tone as she pulled tools toward her didn't make me feel any better. I could tell from the devastation on Marcello's face he wasn't reassured, either.

The gates of Ardence stood wide-open, and traffic flowed through the massive brick wall surrounding the city with the casual ease of peacetime. We passed through without any trouble, Ardence admitting the knife the Serene City held to its throat.

Our driver navigated streets wide and crowded with people, merchant lords rubbing elbows with poor wool-dyer apprentices. Raverra's secret-hoarding alleys and webwork of canals separated out space into guarded islands, a hundred tiny little provinces. Ardence, on the other hand, jumbled everything together in a heady mix of experience and ideas. Coming here to study had been like opening the door of my golden cage and flying out into the world.

We passed the Wishing Fountain; a mother, scolding her children for trying to climb in, sat on the rim where I'd once studied with Venasha. Farther down the street, I glimpsed the statue of *The Grace of Victory Defeating the Gorgon*, which Domenic had climbed when he was more than a little drunk to put a knitted hat on the gorgon's head. A while later, we approached the grand columns of the University of Ardence, and the street corner with the bronze bust of the first Bergandon duke, with its usual complement of pasted-on scraps of satirical poetry. That was another thing I loved about Ardence: the riot of art adorning every plaza and crossroads, full of life and motion, capturing a fever of the imagination that struck Ardence a century ago and thrived there in the days of the city's greatness.

But that greatness had passed. The facades of the buildings were chipped and stained, the gilding worn off, the shop signs faded. Grand palaces that once housed Ardentine river-merchant lords were now let out to visiting Raverrans, or had been broken up into shops and inns. Litter and grime besmirched the streets once walked by some of the greatest artists and thinkers of Eruvia. Perhaps it was my conversation with Lady Savony, but I seemed to notice more Closed signs and quite a few more beggars than I had two years ago.

On one corner, a handful of tradesmen gathered around a broadside posted on a hostelry wall, talking animatedly. I peered at the large blocky print and got as far as THROW OFF THE SHACKLES OF EMPIRE! FOR THE SAKE OF OUR CHILDREN before the coach rolled past. And someone had painted GO HOME RAVERRAN SHARKS across the boarded-up windows of a defunct artifice charm shop, with a crudely drawn domino mask beneath. That was new, too, and it left an unsettled feeling in my stomach.

Our coach turned from the route I expected. I almost protested, but caught the words behind my teeth. Of course we weren't heading to the Serene Envoy's Palace this time; Ignazio was no longer the envoy.

By the tightness of his jaw as he looked out the window, Ignazio was thinking the same thing.

If the brick town house Ignazio had rented for us disappointed him with its faded grandeur, the same could not possibly be true of his welcome back to Ardence. The day of our arrival found us at a fete celebrating his return to the city.

Ignazio was not a dancer. Lord Waldon, the Ardentine noble hosting the affair, seemed to know it; the soft strains of music were calculated to support pauses in conversation rather than to inspire dancing. Ignazio stood radiant, surrounded by the Ardentine elite, each of them seeking his attention with serious faces and thinly disguised anxiety. As I lingered by the wine table, looking for people I knew, I kept hearing his voice drifting across the crowd:

"Well, as you know, I'm no longer in a position to say anything official, but…"

"I can't make promises in my current situation, of course, but I'll see if I can…"

"Naturally I no longer have the intelligence access I did as envoy, but my understanding is…"

I suspected Ignazio's claims that Lady Terringer wouldn't notice he was in town were optimistic. Lady Terringer herself did not appear to be in attendance, though I glimpsed Lady Savony stalking about like a long-limbed stork, with a sour expression that suggested she'd rather be working. By the way she glared at some of the more excessively garbed nobles, with enough jewels dripping off them to ransom a king, she probably thought the party guests would be better off working on solving Ardence's problems, too. Some of them grimaced and slipped away when she approached, like children avoiding their governess.

The room hummed with a restless energy, voices rising and falling with open agitation in a way I never saw in Raverra, where everyone played their cards far closer to their chests. I heard fear in their voices, and sometimes anger. Repeated words and phrases plucked at my ears: *missing children ... an outrage ... Shadow Gentry ... Vaskandar.* And *Raverra* or *the Empire,* always with a sigh, scowl, or curse.

I instinctively searched the gathering for the familiar line of Marcello's shoulders or curl of his hair, but he was off at the garrison coordinating with the local imperial military and getting Istrella and the other Falconers set up with everything they needed for the projects the doge had set them. Zaira lingered by the buffet, eating like a starving wolf and flirting with Domenic. Much as I wanted to say hello to my old friend, I headed in the opposite direction; Zaira's presence tended to have a dominating effect on conversation.

A familiar voice called my name. "Amalia! I thought it was you!"

I whirled, delighted, to face my old study partner. "Venasha!"

I barely glimpsed her brilliant smile and bouncing curls before she swept me into a hug.

"How are you?" I asked a mouthful of her hair.

"Fine, fine!" She held me back at arm's length, grinning. "I have a new position in the Ducal Library, and I love it. Their magical-theory section is incredible. And I have students to shelve for me! I get to just do research and acquire books."

"Perfect! I'll have to visit you there." The thought of all those books was enough to distract me from my worries. "How are Foss and the baby?"

Her smile flickered. "They're well."

"I'd love to see them."

"Well, ah . . . of course."

I gripped her arm. "Venasha, don't tell me something's wrong with the baby."

"Oh, no! Though Aleki's not really a baby anymore. You won't believe how much he's grown. He's walking and talking now, and getting into everything." Her voice turned cheerful again, though worry still pinched her brows. "Foss is exhausted from running around after him while I'm at the library. He delights in pulling books off shelves and dumping them on the floor. Little barbarian!"

"I can't wait to see him." Hesitancy clouded Venasha's expression, and I quickly added, "If it's not an imposition."

"No, no." She let out a long breath. "I really want you to see him. He's gotten so big. All right." Determination gleamed in her eyes. "How about we meet in the public gardens by the River Palace tomorrow? Foss brings Aleki there most days so I can slip away from the library to see him."

"Excellent. I can't wait."

"How about you? What brings you to Ardence?"

Now it was my smile that became strained. "Well . . ."

Venasha grimaced dramatically. "Let me guess. The *Situation*."

I laughed, despite myself. "Is that what you call it?"

"That's what they call it in the River Palace. I pass through the halls on my way to the Ducal Library every day, and the nobles are always talking about it. All very serious. I mostly ignore them."

"Probably for the best."

Someone tapped my shoulder. "Amalia! There you are."

It was Domenic. The slightly panicky look in his deep-brown

eyes belied his welcoming smile. "May I speak to you privately a moment?"

Venasha gasped in pretended shock. "Already sneaking off together! Amalia has barely set foot back in Ardence, Domenic."

I blushed. There were reasons besides treason to speak to a lady alone, and Venasha no doubt remembered all too well how I'd felt about Domenic during my stay in Ardence, given how much I'd prattled on to her about him.

Domenic bowed to Venasha. "If you let me borrow her, I'll show you the new bookshop where I found that Callamornish epic you were looking for."

"Loan me your copies of Orsenne's histories while you're at it, and we have a deal," Venasha laughed.

Whispers followed us as Domenic and I stepped out into the little courtyard garden, an uninspired jumble of confused statuary and square-trimmed bushes. The lights from the party fell across the black lawn, shadows and laughter passing across the bright arches of the windows.

I shivered; my velvet cape was inside, and the night air sucked the heat right out of the low neckline of my gown. Domenic didn't notice. I couldn't help thinking Marcello would have.

He drew himself up, as if bracing for opposition. "I want to introduce you to my brother."

I looked around the empty garden. "Is your brother a shrub, then?"

Domenic laughed, but it came out a bit forced. "Oh, yes, didn't I tell you? He's a rosebush. Comes from my mother's side of the family." He made a face. "Some days, I wish he *were* a shrub. He's been at it night and day, circulating through court, telling everyone how our wonderful friends in Vaskandar will solve all our problems for us if we just stand up to Raverra."

"I take it you haven't been able to convince him this is a terrible idea?"

"No, Grace of Wisdom help me." He sighed. "I met with the Shadow Gentry last night, and I have to admit, it didn't go quite as I'd hoped."

The shadows laid across the garden seemed suddenly darker, sharp-edged with the implication of treason. I tried to keep my voice light. "Oh?"

"I should have known better, I suppose." Domenic cast his eyes up at the clouded sky, as if hoping for guidance from the Graces. No light shone through the deep black overcast. "I keep hoping Gabril is doing this for the right reasons. To help the mage-marked, and make Ardence a better place. And maybe some of the Shadow Gentry are. But mostly what I heard in that room was pride and anger."

Pride and anger could drive people to do hard things. I hoped Gabril's name wasn't one of the ones with which Baron Leodra had planned to buy his life. "I'm sorry."

"Gabril is hosting a party for his Shadow Gentry friends in a few days." Domenic's voice dropped lower. "I think it would do them good to see not everyone in Raverra is hostile to Ardence."

"Of course we aren't! Do they really think that?"

"Well, not all of them. Half the Shadow Gentry are caught up in the idea of Ardentine glory and Ardentine independence. They see Raverra as holding Ardence back from what it could become. The other half..." He shook his head. "You don't see it here, because it's a party for Ignazio, but there's a fury among many of the nobility about the children. The Shadow Gentry ride the wave of that fury. They believe Raverra has taken everything from them—first their fortunes, and now their cherished heirs—and they're willing to fight to get it all back."

"That's a terrible idea." I twisted a lock of hair in my fingers. "We have to resolve this diplomatically. There's still time."

"I hope so. Maybe you can help me convince them there's still

a peaceful solution. That it has not yet come to swords and fire."
He extended a hand. "Will you come to Gabril's party and meet
them, as my guest?"

So it was treason after all.

I could refuse his invitation, keeping my honor intact. I could
tell him I was a loyal servant of the Serene City, and would not
attend any gathering where a secret society plotted against her.

But if I did that, I would lose my only opportunity to infil-
trate the Shadow Gentry.

I reached out and took his proffered hand, with the miserable
reluctance of fishing a dropped glove out of a puddle. "If it will
help avert war, I would be happy to attend and talk to them."

Domenic squeezed my fingers and released them, the quick
pressure of a grateful friend. "Good! And you'll bring Zaira,
too, I hope?"

"I must. She's supposed to be near me at all times."

"Excellent." He hesitated, then continued with less confidence than I'd ever heard from him. "She's an amazing woman,
Amalia. I've never seen such a bold spark in a lady. She speaks the
truth without fear, and there's more fire in her eyes than magic
alone can account for. I . . . Well, I think she's . . ." He swallowed
and drew himself up into a more formal posture. "I have a great
admiration for her."

My guilt over using him to spy on his brother folded double.
"She certainly is unique."

"Do you know . . ." He grimaced. "I gather her family is of
less than noble birth."

"Rather less, yes."

"Still, that shouldn't be important. Rank is a mere footnote in
matters of the heart."

His words pricked me in a Marcello-shaped sore place. I
couldn't even manage a nod. Had the Graces sent him to this
party explicitly to make me feel like a terrible person?

Domenic took a deep breath. "Amalia, in all honesty, tell me, as a friend—what does Zaira think of me?"

I wished I could be anywhere but this vile garden. I had no stomach for more lies. Zaira was a terrible match; as his friend, I couldn't in good conscience encourage him in his affections.

But if I pushed him away from Zaira due to differences of rank and class, I'd be no better than my mother.

"She..." *She thinks you have a firm...stride.* A nervous giggle fluttered in my stomach. "She admires you, Domenic."

His eyes glowed at the words. "She does?"

"How could she not?" I lightened my tone, pushing past the stiffness in my throat. "Everyone does. You possess an exemplary assortment of fine qualities."

Domenic laughed. "You flatter me, Amalia. But thank you. And in that case, I very much look forward to seeing *her* at the party, too."

"I look forward to it as well."

I refrained from adding, *with dread.* But I thought it, rubbing my arms to warm them against the cold night air.

Late in the evening, when the older and stodgier guests had gone home and the food was running out, I pulled Zaira aside into the chilly marble foyer, currently empty.

"What do you think?" I asked her, my voice low.

Zaira leered. "The girl in the peacock-blue gown packs a fine corset, but I'd still go with Domenic. He has the nicest—"

"I mean do you have any suspects?" I interrupted.

"Oh, I'm sure they're all guilty of *something.*"

"For who might be trying to incite a war." I pushed the words out through my teeth. "I'm asking because I think you're observant and intelligent, no matter how you may try to convince me of the contrary."

"I've never tried to convince you of anything. I don't give a damn what you think." She frowned. "But no, I don't think any of them are trying to start a war. They're ready to piss themselves like little babies at the thought."

I nodded. "They seem far too eager for Ignazio to solve their problems for them. They wouldn't be turning to him for help if they were ready to fight."

"Who's ready to fight?" came a loud, slurred voice behind us.

I turned to find a broad-shouldered reveler staring at us across the echoing foyer. He listed off center like a breached ship, his beard bristling, more than a little drunk. Anger smoldered in his bleary eyes, and his hands made uneven fists.

He stared at Zaira. "I'm *plenty* ready to fight."

Chapter Eighteen

Excuse me?" I tried to turn the interrupting gentleman away with my cold tone, but he was too drunk to hear it, let alone care.

"You're the warlock." He glared at Zaira. "The bitch threatening to burn down Ardence."

Zaira snorted. "If I ever threaten you, you'll know it."

"First you sharks bankrupted me. Then you took my nephew." His voice broke on the word, threatening to slide from rage to pathos. "Now you want to set us on fire."

I recognized him, belatedly. Lord Ulmric, a member of the Council of Lords, on which Domenic also sat. "No one wants to set you on fire," I said.

"Yet," Zaira muttered.

"Seems to me if I break your neck here, we don't have a fire problem anymore." He took a menacing step toward her.

Zaira's knife flashed out. "Try it. I'll gut you like a fish. I don't even need to cook you."

"Stop it!" I stepped between them, one palm out in either direction, tensed for a blow. This wasn't some dockside ruffian. This was a lord of Ardence. If Zaira murdered him, she'd kill our last hope for peace as well.

"Please." I addressed this to the drunkard. "We're not your

enemies. Have the grace to respect your host. Don't defile his home with blood."

I suspected it would be *his* blood, not Zaira's, but I let him think what he would.

Confused emotions struggled across the lord's face, as if he couldn't decide whether to punch me or spit.

Finally, his face crumpled into despair. "Give me back my nephew."

"We don't have your nephew." I willed him to believe me, staring into his reddened eyes. "I'm trying to find the children. I swear it to you. We want nothing more than to return them to their families."

His watery glare searched my face. "If you don't have him, who does?" he demanded.

"I don't know." Graces help the boy, wherever he was.

Pain twisted his features. "Then you're no cursed good to us." He turned away, half lifting a hand that faltered and dropped before it could form a fist. "Go back to Raverra, harpies. Leave us alone."

And with that, he wove his way off into the party, muttering to himself.

Zaira sheathed her dagger. "See? Even drunk as a disgraced shrinekeeper, they don't have the will to fight."

She had a point. Despite the broadsides and graffiti we'd seen from the coach, this wasn't a city on the verge of rebellion. Whatever danger Baron Leodra had tried to warn me about, it wasn't a simple matter of angry mobs in the street howling for Raverran blood. It was a more deeply hidden threat: an unseen knife waiting in the darkness at my back, not a ruffian coming straight at me in a rage.

"You're right," I said. "They don't. But someone's trying to give it to them. We need to find out who."

As we left Lord Waldon's mansion, stepping out into the vibrant lamplit night, I spotted an unlikely and familiar figure waiting at the shadowy edge of the plaza. Prince Ruven of Vaskandar, complete with trailing servants, resplendent in a showy fur-lined coat that hung to his ankles. Bold, angular embroidery in Vaskandran designs traced paths like jagged violet lightning down his chest. A jeweled rapier rode at his hip.

"What is *he* doing here?" I murmured to Zaira.

She peered across the square. "Is that your skin-shifting suitor? Nice legs."

"Ugh. He's not *mine*." I frowned. "I should find out why he's here, though."

"Yes, let's. I'd love to meet him." Zaira's grin was less than reassuring.

More disturbing was the delight in Prince Ruven's face as we approached. He bowed extravagantly, forcing me to return a curtsy.

"Lady Amalia! What a pleasure. And this must be the Lady Zaira, I presume?"

"I'm no lady." Zaira didn't bow or curtsy. I wondered if the lack of manners was deliberate, or if it came naturally.

"What brings you here at this hour, Your Highness?" I asked.

Ruven's eyes flicked to Lord Waldon's door, where more guests still trickled out, in various stages of inebriation. "Oh, waiting for someone. But the Grace of Luck has smiled on me, to meet you instead."

"I've heard you have many friends in this city."

"The Ardentines seem eager for allies these days." His eyes traveled to Zaira. "I hope you, too, will accept my hand in friendship, my lady." He reached out toward her.

I wanted to lunge between them, but Zaira had matters under control. She curtsied now, late, both hands too full of skirts to take his. "That depends." She laughed coquettishly. "I'm a practical girl. What do you do for your friends?"

"Why, for one thing, in Vaskandar, we do not let our mage-marked be kept as prisoners or pets." He lifted an eyebrow. "You are more than welcome to join me there at any time. You would be raised up as a great lady, above the common throng."

"Tempting." Zaira held up her wrist, the jess glittering in the lamplight. "But I'm stuck with Raverra so long as I'm wearing this."

Ruven shrugged. "That could be taken care of."

A hunger came into Zaira's face. She took a half step toward him. I tensed.

"You can remove it?" Her voice strained like a taut rope.

"I have my ways. Do you wish a demonstration?"

"No," I said. "No demonstrations, thank you."

But Ruven had already lifted a lazy hand to beckon one of his servants forward. A man-at-arms, tall and fair, like all Vaskandrans, stepped forward. "Your Highness?"

"Your wrist," he commanded.

The man swallowed, going milk pale. But he pulled back his sleeve and stretched out his arm.

"No, really." I waved both hands, as if I could somehow fan Ruven away. "This isn't necessary."

He laughed. "Of course it isn't necessary. My goodness, Lady Amalia, what a tedious world it would be if we only did necessary things."

He clasped his servant's arm with one hand, then drew a long dagger with the other.

"Your Highness," the guardsman began nervously, "with all respect, what are you—"

He stopped moving. His chest rose and fell, and he stared at the knife with fear still shining in his eyes, but the prince had taken his ability to move or speak, just like that.

Ruven laid his dagger's edge against the guard's wrist.

"That's enough," Zaira said harshly. "Getting the jess off isn't worth losing my hand."

"You won't lose anything," Ruven promised. "This won't even hurt."

And he pressed the knife into his guard's skin.

I choked back a scream. There was no blood. The man's eyes strained wide against the paralysis that held him, but there was no pain in them, only terror. The dagger pushed through his wrist slowly, like a cord through butter, and the flesh knit again around it after it passed. The blade emerged clean on the far side of his arm, gleaming in the darkness. No mark scarred the guard's smooth, pale skin.

Zaira's face had gone positively green. I edged closer to her, in case she fainted or threw up. I didn't feel much better. I'd rather swallow a cup of live snails than watch that again.

Ruven released the guard, who snatched his arm back and stumbled away from his master, gasping.

"See?" Ruven spread his arms wide, still holding the knife. "Did it hurt? Tell them."

The man rubbed his wrist, trembling. "It... There was no pain, Your Highness."

Ruven sheathed his dagger with a flourish, smiling as if he'd given us a wonderful treat. "I hope you will think about my offer, Lady Zaira."

"I'll think about it," she promised. She grabbed my arm with unsteady force. "But now I have to get Lady Heiress here home. It's past her bedtime."

"And I must greet my friend. Good night, ladies." He bowed.

I dipped a curtsy and fled. Zaira all but hung onto my arm, nausea twisting her face. Our shoes tapped a rapid rhythm on the cobblestones, almost a run.

"I'll think about it, all right," Zaira muttered. "When I'm trying to sleep tonight. Grace of Mercy."

I couldn't keep my mouth shut. "So you won't be moving to Vaskandar?"

She shuddered. "Only if it's to set him on fire."

A grim weight settled on my shoulders. "Depending on how things turn out on the border," I said, "that could be arranged."

Zaira and I met Venasha and Foss the next morning in the public gardens opposite the River Palace. Marcello had promised to join us there after riding down from the garrison.

Sunshine set the gardens to glowing. The sky shone heartbreakingly blue, and the wind moved dappled patterns of shade across the winding paths Venasha and I walked, side by side, between careful arrangements of statues, flowers, and fountains. Foss ranged both ahead and behind, chasing after little Aleki wherever his stumpy two-year-old legs took him. The boy's curls bobbed up and down as he ran, with Zaira at his side half the time, laughing and trying to teach him tricks as if he were a dog.

"So what do *you* think of the Situation?" I asked Venasha. "Is everyone in Ardence truly ready to rebel against the Empire, after all these years?"

"Graces, no." Venasha waved a bug away from her face. "People grumble about it, but no worse than usual, despite all the Shadow Gentry's efforts to rile us up. It's only the Council of Lords and the nobles of the court who are so serious, because of the children." She cast a worried glance toward her son. "I can't entirely blame them. I'd be ready to chew down the River Palace if anything happened to Aleki."

It all came down to the children. "Who do you think took them?"

She cocked her head. "Well, it must have been someone who knows the city, to make them disappear without a trace despite everyone searching for them. Someone with a lot of resources and connections, to create such a convincing deception with the false Falconers. I have to admit, I assumed Raverra was playing games, first claiming to have them and then not, until you told me otherwise."

"I suppose this is what we reap from our reputation for deviousness," I sighed. "No one believes us when we're being straightforward." Not to mention that someone on the Council *had* been playing games—but I wasn't going to tell even Venasha about Leodra.

Aleki came trundling back, a fistful of bedraggled flowers held before him with great purpose. Foss followed him, a shy smile on his face as he locked eyes with Venasha, and I suspected I knew who had given Aleki the idea to bring flowers to his mother. A warm glow melted some of the worry clumped in my chest as Venasha scooped her son up into a tight hug to thank him and pulled Foss in as well, all three of them beaming.

"Be a shame to set them on fire," Zaira whispered in my ear.

I cast a despairing look at her. She stared back a flat challenge.

"Amalia!" Marcello's voice called.

He approached us along the winding garden path, striding along with fluid energy. The sun caught the clean lines of his face and set a glow in the dark waves of his hair. Grace of Love, he looked good.

"Sorry I'm late." He seemed slightly out of breath as he joined us, and I caught the scent of horse lingering from his ride to the city. He leaned in, glancing at Venasha and Foss to make sure they couldn't overhear. "We were discussing methods to trace the false

Falconers, to find out who exactly was wearing those uniforms. I had to speak with an intelligence officer over the courier lamps."

"Do you have any leads?" I asked.

"Not yet. It seems likely they must have been hired criminals, but whoever they were, they're keeping quiet." He shook off gloom like rain, turning with a smile to Venasha, Foss, and Aleki. "But enough of that. Why don't you introduce me to your friends, Amalia? I'd love to meet—" He broke off, staring at Aleki.

I followed his gaze. Venasha and Foss were talking to their son about the flowers, their backs mostly to us. Aleki's serious face showed between them as he explained something in his tiny voice, poking at the flowers his mother now held. It was the first time I'd gotten a good look at his eyes, with all the running around he'd been doing.

A faint but distinct vermilion ring surrounded his pupils.

He was mage-marked.

Chapter Nineteen

Fingers like iron bands dug into my wrist as Zaira pulled Marcello and me aside.

"Don't you dare," she hissed to Marcello.

Trouble weighed down his brows. "You saw his eyes, Zaira. You know the law."

Shock curdled any words I might have spoken. Venasha's baby, mage-marked? She hadn't said any of this, in all the silly stories she'd told me about him. But she must know. She couldn't have missed that bright circle, or not known what it meant.

"I don't care." Zaira glared at Marcello. "You can't take that brat away from his parents. Look at them. Look how happy they are."

"They could come with him." Marcello's voice hung low and uncertain. "We don't take children from their families, Zaira. We just—"

"Haul them off and lock them in a fortress on an island hundreds of miles from their homes. Yes, I know." She waved a furious hand at where Venasha had put Aleki down and was showing him how to weave his flower stems together into a bracelet, while Foss smiled at them both. "He's not hurting anyone. No one is hurting them. They have a good life here. Don't destroy it."

Marcello cast an anguished glance at Aleki, then at me. "He

has to join the Falcons, Zaira. The Serene Accords provide no exceptions."

"Pretend you didn't see him," Zaira urged.

Marcello's brows set in a stubborn line. "That would be high treason."

"And it wouldn't accomplish anything." I let out the ache in my chest as a long sigh. "His mage mark isn't subtle like yours, Zaira. It's just forming, but soon it'll be visible from across the room, with a bright color like that. He can't hide."

Zaira showed her teeth in a snarl. "He shouldn't have to."

"Um, I hate to interrupt, but I can hear you," said Foss.

The three of us whirled. He stood there, hands behind his back, hanging his head sheepishly. "I have good hearing," he apologized.

Venasha stepped up beside him, Aleki gathered once again in her arms, face solemn and worried. "You saw."

I nodded, my eyes stinging. "I'm sorry."

"Don't be." She adjusted Aleki, who'd started squirming; he grabbed a jeweled pin from her hair and seemed content to turn it in his hands, examining the way the light caught in the stones. "I wanted to ask your advice, Amalia. I don't know what to do."

The fear in her voice stabbed at my heart. I stepped closer and squeezed her shoulder. "Whatever happens, I'm here to help you. We'll keep him safe, and keep you together. I promise."

Her shoulder, rock hard under my touch, relaxed a bit. "His eyes started changing around when those children were stolen. I knew that wasn't how Falconers worked, but still . . . I didn't want to admit what it meant. Especially with the Shadow Gentry giving speeches and posting notices about fighting the Empire if it comes for our children again. But now I can't deny those flecks have formed a circle."

Foss put a protective arm around Venasha's shoulders. "He's my sunny little boy," he said softly. "I won't give him up. No matter what."

Zaira's hands formed fists. But Marcello gave Venasha and Foss a surprisingly gentle smile. "You don't have to. You're welcome to come stay in the Mews, for visits or permanently. And if you don't want to move to the Mews, he can visit you in Ardence for months at a time with his Falconer, so long as it's safe. We may even be able to get him stationed in the garrison here, once he's old enough."

Venasha's eyes widened at the talk of moving to the Mews, and her lips tightened.

Foss gave her a concerned glance. "Venasha has been, ah, working toward her position in the Ducal Library for, well... It's been a dream of hers for a while. And most of our friends and family are in Ardence."

"But you won't leave Aleki," Venasha said to him firmly. "And I won't leave either of you."

"If it's any consolation, I'm confident I can get you a position in your choice of Raverran libraries." The offer felt weak and awkward in my mouth, but it was what I had to give. "The Imperial Library, the Grand Temple of Wisdom, the Raverran University Library..."

Zaira snorted. "It must be nice to have all the friends money can buy."

Marcello ignored that. "We'll all do everything we can for your family. The Empire does well by its Falcons."

Zaira's brows raised until they seemed likely to pop off her forehead. She put her hands on her hips, but after a glance at Venasha and Foss's anxious expressions, she said nothing.

"It's still..." Venasha sucked in an unsteady breath, holding Aleki tight. "It's a lot to take in. And I can't deny it's not what we wanted."

Foss nodded his agreement. The solemn worry that had replaced the joy in his face twisted at my heart.

Aleki had thrown his mother's hairpin on the ground and was now fishing out another from her collapsing crown of braids, oblivious to the upheaval of his life. Marcello watched him thoughtfully. "Do you have any idea what kind of magic he can do?"

Venasha and Foss exchanged glances, and Foss shook his head. "None," Venasha said.

"Not a vivomancer or a warlock, then," I concluded, "since they use their powers instinctively, and they start showing up along with the mage mark."

Zaira winced, and I immediately felt like an insensitive oaf. Hers had *shown up* by burning her parents to death.

Marcello nodded. "Since he's either an alchemist or an artificer, that means there's no rush to get a jess on him. He won't be physically capable of using his powers until he's older. Though I'd be careful if he's mixing things together or doing scribble drawings, just in case."

Alarm flashed into Venasha's eyes.

"Oh," Foss sighed. "A new way for him to cause havoc. And I thought climbing was bad."

"Take a few days to think about what you want to do," Marcello told them. "Let us know right away if anything happens to make you feel unsafe—people showing unusual interest in him, or powers starting to manifest. And don't be afraid to come to the garrison for help at any hour."

"Or to me," I put in.

Foss caught my eyes. "Amalia, you've been to the Mews. Just tell me . . . Tell me, truly. Will he be happy there?"

I felt all their attention on me. Venasha and Foss, full of hope and fear, with unshed tears standing in their eyes. Zaira, daring me to lie. And Marcello, urging me with every line of his face to praise the place that was home and family to him.

"Most of the Falcons I've met seem to be happy," I said slowly. "It's a safe place. A comfortable place. The Falconers are good people."

Zaira let out a soft snort, but kept her mouth shut, thank the Graces.

Venasha tried an uncertain smile. "And I suppose if we do move to the Mews, we'll see you more often, Amalia."

This was too much for Zaira. "A little," she said with a bright, false smile. "Every now and then."

I nodded, and hugged Venasha and Aleki in one big, squirmy armful. But the knot in my throat wasn't one of joy.

Even believing everything I'd said about the Mews, I couldn't pretend this was good news. Whatever Aleki might have been, whatever future Venasha and Foss might have seen unfold for him, whatever thousand roads might have lain before him... now there was only one.

It might not be a bad road. But he was too small to know his feet were on it, let alone choose his way.

I could feel the fury radiating off Zaira like heat as the three of us left the gardens.

"I'd say I can't believe you, but I can." She glared an inferno at me and Marcello. "You're really going to take that baby from his home, put a jess on him, and raise him as a soldier."

Marcello stopped before the garden gates and faced her. "What would you have me do? I can't change the Serene Accords. All I can do is make the Mews the best place possible for the mage-marked."

"It's easy to say you can't change the world." Zaira shook a finger at him. "But people *do* change it. I don't know much history, but I know that. Don't say it can't be done if you really mean you're too lazy to try."

The memory of the mage mark boldly circling Aleki's sweet, trusting eyes cut into my heart. I curled my hands into fists.

"Maybe *you* can't alter the law," I said to Marcello, "but I can." I turned to Zaira. "It'll take years. Maybe a lifetime. And we need to find a solution that will still protect both the mage-marked and the people around them. But I'll try."

Zaira snorted. "Raverra will never give up its grip on the mage-marked. We're the source of the Empire's power."

"We can find a compromise. You're the one who just said—" I broke off.

Through the garden gates, across the Plaza of Six Fountains, the River Palace loomed in its grandiose brick splendor. The plaza teemed with all the comings and goings of the heart of Ardence's government: people arriving and departing by foot, horse, and coach; courtiers and servants alike having discussions in the open plaza, or sitting on the rims of the fountains with a book or a snack. But one figure in the livery of the Serene Envoy's household crossed the plaza toward the public gardens at a run, heading straight for us, waving urgently.

"Lieutenant Verdi!" he called. "Come quickly!"

Marcello's back stiffened. "What's wrong?"

The messenger shook his head, panting. "I don't know the details. The garrison sent the Envoy's Palace a message over the courier lamps, calling you back to deal with an emergency. A Falconer's been attacked."

The young officer's eye and nose were already swelling and darkening, and bandages wrapped his forearm and chest as he lay propped in bed in the garrison infirmary. He apologized profusely to Marcello, his eyes glazed from whatever they'd given him for the pain. Marcello sat beside him, reassuring the man it wasn't his fault. Zaira and I hovered perhaps a pace behind Marcello, toeing the awkward boundary line between a respectful distance and an audible one.

"Lemi, I need you to tell me exactly what happened." Marcello's voice stayed calm, but I could read the rigid tension in his shoulders. I knew he was remembering the same thing I was: the doge had said to consider any assault against the Falconers an act of war.

The officer nodded weakly. "A request for help came in just after you left, Lieutenant. Supposedly from a family on a farm outside the city gates, with a daughter whose vivomancy was out of control." He drew in a shaky breath. "But it was a trap."

"Who attacked you?"

Lemi gestured across his face. "They wore gray masks. And gray cloaks."

"The Shadow Gentry," I breathed. What had Domenic gotten himself into?

Marcello leaned back in his chair, meeting my eyes. "This is terrible."

Zaira crossed her arms. "That doesn't mean anything. Gray masks are easy to copy." By the paleness of her face, she understood the consequences of this attack as well as I did. "These bastards have already tried fake Falconers. This could be a trick, too."

"I'm not sure the doge will care." I pressed my fingers to my temples. "And I'm not sure it *is* a trick. If the Shadow Gentry want to start a fight with Raverra, ambushing a Falconer is an effective way to do it."

"Lieutenant...I'm sorry, sir, but it gets worse." Lemi's voice dropped to a whisper, and his face twisted into a grimace of guilt. "They took my pouch."

Zaira shrugged. "So they robbed you."

"No. I had..." Lemi closed his eyes. "Graces forgive me, but I believed them, sir. I came prepared for a new vivomancer. I had a jess in that pouch. They took it."

"Hell of Nightmare," Marcello swore. "This is bad."

My stomach plunged down to my boots. That was more than enough provocation for the doge. Jesses were a closely guarded secret of the Empire. The fact that no one else had them was one of the primary keys to Raverra's power.

"Whoever wants this war," I whispered, "I think they're going to get it."

Marcello made his report to Colonel Vasante over the courier lamps. Usually wonder filled me whenever I thought of the courier-lamp network, relaying flashes of light across hundreds of miles from one lamp crystal to another; but this time, the image of those flickering pulses traveling all the way to the Mews, and from there no doubt to the Imperial Palace, brought me nothing but dread.

A return message came back within an hour: the doge was discussing the matter with the Council of Nine. They would have instructions for us tomorrow.

Our unseen opponents—the "they" Baron Leodra had died before unmasking—had made their move. It was the doge's turn. But there were a dwindling number of spaces left on the board.

I lay awake a long time in my canopied bed in Ignazio's town house that night. When I finally fell asleep, my dreams were full of fire.

I stared at the cup of black liquid before me. Coffee again. This was precisely what I needed to make our tense breakfast with the Serene Envoy even more horrible.

It was bad enough to have Ignazio and Lady Terringer in the same room. We'd scheduled this breakfast before coming to Ardence, as an obligatory social visit; now, with the terrible implications of the stolen jess hanging over our heads, the occasion had ascended from mere awkwardness to outright torture.

Of course she'd serve us coffee. I nerved myself to take a small sip without making a repulsed face at the flavor.

"I hope you're settling in well? How's the town house you rented?" Lady Terringer's tone was stiff as her spine. She took a swig from her own cup as if fortifying herself for battle.

Ignazio forced a laugh, gesturing around the airy, gilded parlor that had been his for years. "It's not the Envoy's Palace, but it'll do."

Zaira rolled her eyes. "Listen to you. You should try sleeping on the floor of an abandoned building for a week or two. Then you'll stop fretting about whether your featherbeds are soft enough or if there's sufficient gold on your ceiling."

I glanced at Marcello and caught memory and understanding in his eyes. He was thinking of what we'd seen in the Tallows, too. My face warmed as the unspoken message passed between us; I reverted my gaze to my hostess before telltale pink could color my cheeks.

Lady Terringer snorted. "You don't mince words, do you?"

Annoyance flickered across Ignazio's brows, but he turned it to a gracious smile and shrug. "The night before last I might have slept as soundly on the floor, after how late Lord Waldon kept us up."

Now it was Lady Terringer's turn to frown. I doubted she could be pleased the Ardentine nobility were so ecstatic at her predecessor's return, especially when they refused to see *her* at all.

I couldn't stand any more veiled jabs and stilted politeness, dancing around the crisis that lay like a pile of cannonballs on the table between us. "Have you heard from the doge about the imperial response to yesterday's attack?"

"Yes." Lady Terringer took a long moment to pour herself more coffee from a silver pitcher. "He's giving Ardence until sundown the day after tomorrow."

I twisted my napkin on my lap. At least it wasn't an outright declaration of war. "What do they have to do by then?"

"Turn over the parties responsible for the attack, return the stolen jess, welcome the Serene Envoy back to court, revoke the illegal taxes, and abide by the Serene Accords."

Marcello leaned on the table as if bracing himself. "Or else what?"

Lady Terringer met his gaze unflinchingly. "Do you need to ask that question, Verdi?"

His mouth tightened.

Zaira took a noisy slurp of coffee, with apparent relish. "That's me. The unspeakable consequence. Great fun at parties."

I wrapped both hands around my coffee cup, letting the heat sting my palms. "That's a lot to accomplish in less than three days. Do we have people investigating the attack and searching for the jess?"

"We have investigators coming from Raverra, and the local intelligence agents we already had looking for the children and trying to find Baron Leodra's contacts in Ardence are working on it." Lady Terringer shook her head. "Sounds to me like it was the damned Shadow Gentry again. If we can unmask and arrest the lot of them, that should satisfy the doge—*if* we also get the jess back."

A twinge pinched my chest. Domenic could too easily get swept up in a move like that, and his brother almost certainly would. Not to mention, from what he'd said, arresting the Shadow Gentry meant hauling off a fair fraction of the Ardentine court. The doge might count himself satisfied, but Ardence would never take it quietly.

I had to find out who exactly had been behind the attack. Gabril's upcoming party might be our best hope.

I swallowed. "All right. What about the taxes, and giving due deference to you as Serene Envoy? Do you think we can get Duke Astor to return to the Serene Accords?"

"Hmph. He would have already if it weren't for the cursed kidnapping." Lady Terringer *thunked* her cup down on the table with greater force than necessary. "Everything was smooth sailing until then. I made it clear the Empire was not amused at his antics, and Duke Bergandon acted cowed enough. He was ready to drop the taxes on Raverran merchants and step back in line. Then the children disappeared, his nobles got hysterical, and everything went straight to the Hell of Discord. The timing was perfect to destroy everything I'd done."

"I know what that's like," Ignazio murmured over the rim of his cup, "when people blunder in and destroy all your careful work."

Lady Terringer's eye twitched.

I ignored his interjection. "So what will it take *now* to get the duke and his nobles to become loyal subjects of the Serene Empire again?"

"Besides finding the missing children and bringing the kidnapper to justice? I don't know." Lady Terringer's forehead bunched into grim furrows. "Several of the Council of Lords had children or grandchildren stolen, and they won't listen to anything I say— or let the duke hear me, either." She turned, with an air of reluctance, to Ignazio. "But they might listen to you. Will you help?"

Some intense emotion flickered through Ignazio's eyes, but he kept his expression schooled and blank, then carefully orchestrated it into one of dry amusement. "I thought I was removed from my position because my negotiating tactics were too subtle and slow."

"They were," Terringer said through her teeth, "when it was only the violation of the Serene Accords we were facing. Now I need the Ardentines to trust us as much as they fear us, and they haven't had time to learn to trust me." She came as close as I'd seen anyone come to visibly choking on her pride. "I need your help to make this peace, Ignazio."

Ignazio took a long sip of coffee, savoring the steam drifting off it. "I'm afraid I'm no longer the Serene Envoy," he said. "It doesn't seem there's much I can do to help you."

Terringer stared at him. Thunderheads seemed to pile up on her brow, but Ignazio smiled lazily back at her. Finally, she slapped the table, shaking the china.

"Fine. You want this city to burn to feed your pride." She jerked her head toward the door. "We're going to talk now about what happens if we need to burn it. No civilians allowed."

Ignazio stood, his voice going hard. "Well, far be it from me to intrude."

"Uncle Ignazio..." I reached out toward him. He'd pushed his needling of Lady Terringer too far, but still, it had to hurt. Not long ago, he would have been the one leading this meeting, and now he was cut out of it entirely. She was throwing him out of what had been his own parlor a month ago.

Zaira also rose to her feet, stretching. "Good. I'll go with you. I'm bored of listening to them flap their lips."

Lady Terringer's brows lifted. "These plans concern you. Don't you want to stay?"

Zaira's eyes gleamed like the reflection of a sword's edge. "And hear you talk about using me like a weapon? No, thanks. Lady Dull-As-Rocks Cornaro here can fill me in." She slid her arm through Ignazio's. "Come on. You can show me around the palace. You know it better than this old bat anyway, right?"

"Better than anyone," he agreed.

I mouthed a silent *thank you* to Zaira, glad Ignazio wouldn't have to haunt his former home alone. She winked.

"Zaira has to stay with Amalia," Marcello said. "The law—"

"Oh, unclench your arse for once." Zaira waved a hand. "I'm not going to leave the building. This place is secure, right?"

"It had better be." Lady Terringer's clipped tone left no room for doubt.

"Have fun without us, then." Zaira blew Lady Terringer a kiss as they departed.

"Just as well." Lady Terringer leaned in close over the table, dropping her voice. "Listen. We're all hoping not to have to use her balefire. But if the order comes, we have to be ready."

I nodded queasily. I didn't think I could ever be ready.

At my side, Marcello laid his hand at the edge of his seat, next to mine. An inch or so still separated our fingers, but I cupped my hand slightly, as if I were clasping his back.

"Is Duke Astor Bergandon aware of the time limit?" I asked.

Lady Terringer nodded. "I've talked to him through unofficial channels. His nobles insist he can't receive me in court, but he's sent Lady Savony over here on his behalf. I haven't explicitly told him what will happen if he can't comply with the doge's orders by the deadline, but I believe he understands the situation."

"And what is his stance?"

Lady Terringer eyed me oddly. "You tell me. He's asked to meet with you this afternoon."

"With me? Why?"

"I don't know. But he wants to speak with you alone."

"No." Marcello all but leaped to his feet. "Absolutely not. For one thing, Zaira has to be with Amalia at all times."

"She can stay in the garrison." Lady Terringer shrugged. "That's permitted for Falcons traveling or stationed abroad. Should it come to an emergency, Lady Amalia can still unleash her from there."

"It could be a trap," Marcello protested.

Lady Terringer snorted. "If they were going to lay a trap for a Raverran, it wouldn't be a Cornaro. No matter what they think of Raverra, the Ardentine court has an irrational degree of affection for your family. I'd be more worried about a trap if they *did* want you to bring your fire warlock."

"We need to hear what the duke has to say," I decided. "Especially if he's shown he wants to engage diplomatically with Raverra but doesn't feel he can do so openly. We've only got time for a few more chances at peace; we can't waste one of them."

Marcello stood, arms crossed, mouth set in an unhappy line. I knew if I were a normal Falconer, under his command, he would forbid me to go alone.

"I'll be fine," I said, more gently. "The duke has nothing to gain by threatening me, and a great deal to lose. And frankly, I don't want Zaira along on a delicate diplomatic meeting, regardless." I turned to Lady Terringer. "Please tell His Grace I accept his invitation."

Despite the confidence I tried to project, Leodra's unfinished warning echoed through my head: *If you go to Ardence, you're in danger.* But until I knew where that danger lay, I couldn't balk at every shadow, or I'd never get anything done.

"Very well," Lady Terringer said. "And now, we need to talk about balefire."

I nodded, my throat dry as week-old bread. I took a sip of coffee out of desperation, and the bitterness shriveled my tongue.

"If they run out of time on the doge's ultimatum, we want to give them every last chance." Lady Terringer's face fell into grim folds. I wondered if she'd fought in the Three Years' War; she was certainly old enough to remember it, and that hard knowledge looked out from her eyes. "First, we'll warn all Raverrans in Ardence to evacuate and withdraw to the garrison. Frankly, I doubt it will go past that point—the Ardentines will know what's coming if we pull out of the city. But if they don't back down then, they will when they see a wall of balefire creeping across the valley toward them."

It was a terrible image. "I don't..." I swallowed. "All right. I understand."

Lady Terringer's voice dropped low and rough as a river bottom. "The other possibility is that Ardence could start the war. They've already attacked a Falconer. If they decide to start a fight, most likely their first target will either be this palace or Zaira. If that happens—if Ardentine forces attack us—loose your Falcon."

I stirred uncomfortably. But Lady Terringer's flat stare denied argument. "Don't wait for an order. If they spit on peace and leap into war with a treacherous attack, they deserve no less. Let the balefire run wild through Ardence until they beg the Serene Empire for mercy."

Chapter Twenty

Zaira and Ignazio joined up with us again on the way out of the Serene Envoy's palace. The two of them walked arm in arm, Zaira smirking. I suspected they might have been saying unkind things about Lady Terringer. Their glee seemed jarring after the ominous discussion Marcello and I had just had.

When the coach pulled up and we all started for the door, I caught at Ignazio's sleeve. "Did you really mean what you said to Lady Terringer, about not helping with the diplomacy?"

The ironic edge to his expression faded and softened to something sadder. "Of course not. I'll help."

"I knew it." I squeezed him in a quick hug.

"But I'll do it in my own way." I heard some of my mother's relentless drive in his grim tone. "On my own, without Terringer. My help will be on my terms, and I'll make sure I'm the one who gets the credit."

"I suppose that's fair," I said. It would be easier if he'd work with her, but they clashed so much it might not be a good idea.

"Yes." Ignazio nodded. "It's only fair."

We walked out to the carriage together.

The River Palace, the seat of the dukes of Ardence, always disappointed me with its massive brick facade. Imposing, certainly, but its blocky wings lacked the grace of the spun-sugar arches of the Imperial Palace back home. Once the liveried servants bowed me inside, however, my surroundings became far less utilitarian. The high, arching ceilings blossomed with elaborate white-and-gold carvings and dramatic frescoes; the Bergandons had missed no opportunity to display their wealth and power.

If the duke was as impressed by appearances as his surroundings suggested, I supposed it was just as well I'd changed to a particularly ostentatious gown for the visit. One of Ignazio's servants, a maid called Beatrix with enormous brown eyes, had helped me dress. I missed Ciardha, who would have given me notes about the duke's personality and any relevant news from his court while she directed the lacing of my corset and the selection of my jewels. I'd had to decline well-meaning offers of powder and star-shaped beauty patches from Beatrix, and suffered through an extravagant curling of my hair.

I supposed I looked lovely, but I'd far rather have any idea at all what the duke might want with me. Without knowing the reason for my invitation, I had to assume my decadent surroundings were enemy territory.

Some of the courtiers I passed in the cavernous palace entry hall shot me glances full of curiosity or hope, but others scowled and turned away, fury in the set of their shoulders. One old lady in a grandly bejeweled corset and skirts wider than my bedroom doorway muttered "Raverran eel" in my general direction. A sleek young lord dressed all in dove gray—a pointed nod to the Shadow Gentry, I had little doubt—fingered his rapier hilt with a hard gleam in his eye when he first saw me. His companion, a woman who accented her gown with a gray silk sash, murmured the name *Cornaro* in his ear, and his expression softened; he swept into a bow as I went by.

A footman led me through a series of impressive chambers to the Hall of Victory. Duke Bergandon awaited me in the opulent private audience chamber, beneath frescoes depicting Ardentine military triumphs. The Grace of Victory floated over all in a painted sky, her flaming sword in hand. All things considered, it was an unfortunately warlike choice of venue.

The duke rose to greet me with vigor to match his youth. He couldn't be more than five years my senior, once I looked past the pointed beard and the profusion of gold embroidery on his doublet. We exchanged the requisite courtesies and settled into chairs flanking a low table, which bore an intimidating array of delicacies: airy little pastries, fruits and olives, fine cheeses, figs wrapped in prosciutto, tartgrass crostini. It all looked delicious, but there was no way I could take more than a few bites in this corset, even if I weren't too tense to eat.

After a suitably awkward interval of how-was-your-journey and isn't-it-fine-weather, the duke leaned his elbows on his knees. "Lady Amalia, I invited you here for a reason that may surprise you."

"Oh?" I hoped it wasn't a daggers-and-poison sort of surprise.

"Indeed." He turned a forgotten grape in his fingers. A hesitancy shadowed his eyes, which I had never seen in the doge. "It was to ask for your help."

Well. "You're right, Your Grace. That isn't what I was expecting."

"I don't want to go down in history as the last duke of Ardence." His temples flexed. "Yet on the one side, I have the Empire, demanding I turn over a jess I don't have and the perpetrators of an attack I know nothing about. On the other side, I have nobles demanding I refuse to cooperate with the Empire until it returns children it claims not to have taken. And if I cannot somehow reconcile and accomplish these impossible tasks, both sides will hold *me* responsible for the destruction that follows." He bared his teeth in a grimace. "I am trapped, Lady Amalia. I can't get out of this on my own."

"I would love to help you." I hesitated, thinking how to phrase this. "I do have, ah, a particular mission here in Ardence, however..."

"I know why you're here." His tone turned bitter. "Lady Terringer made the doge's message quite clear weeks ago. This further escalation with your fire warlock is not necessary. It may wound the pride of Ardence to bow before Raverra, but our military power is insufficient to start a war over pride alone. I assure you, I am chastened enough already."

I lifted an eyebrow. "With all respect, Your Grace, I would not characterize Ardence's behavior toward the Serene City as chastened."

His hand closed around the grape, crushing it. "Everything was going well enough with Lady Terringer. Much as I might prefer your cousin's gentler methods, we had reached an understanding, I believe. But the children! I cannot back down now, Lady Amalia. My nobles are crying out for justice."

"But Your Grace," I said carefully, "Raverra didn't take the children. Surely Lady Terringer has told you the letters claiming that the Empire was holding them were false."

"I know that." Duke Astor rose and started pacing. "But it's hard to convince my court when reports say the imperial seal was real, and no one will tell us how that came to pass. And the memory of Ardence is long. No one has forgotten Raverra did this to us before, when it conquered our city and absorbed it into the Empire. Besides, everyone knows Raverra is hardly innocent of claiming one thing publicly and doing another privately. Like when my great-great-uncle had a boating accident after he tried to stay out of the Three Years' War due to trade pacts with Vaskandar. The Empire extended its condolences to my great-grandfather, but he nonetheless understood the message and threw his full support behind Raverra in the war."

"This isn't like that," I protested. But Baron Leodra had

willingly put his seal on those documents. If the Ardentines knew that, they might not see much difference.

"Some of my nobles understand that. But some are quite willing to believe the worst of Raverra." The duke leaned on the ornately carved chair he'd vacated. "Others might see reason, if they were thinking clearly. But their children are gone. Have you ever dealt with a parent whose child is in danger, Lady Amalia?"

I remembered what had happened to my would-be kidnappers when a political rival attempted to have me abducted when I was thirteen. My mother had ruthlessly tracked down every single individual involved in the attempt, no matter how large or small their role, and had them all summarily executed.

"Yes."

"Until their children are safe, they will see no reason. They will brook no peace. They would rather watch the city burn to the ground than bow down to the ones they think stole their heirs."

"I want to avert war and find the children as much as you do," I assured him. "That's why I'm here, believe it or not."

"Then help me. I'm a proud man, Lady Amalia; it isn't easy for me to ask. Do not refuse me this." His pointed beard jumped as his jaw tightened. He'd probably grown it to look older.

I spread my hands. "What do you think I can do?"

"I can't yet receive the Serene Envoy at court again. The Council of Lords wouldn't stand for it. Ignazio Cornaro is the one Raverran my nobles trust; they see his removal as the turning point when everything went wrong. But I can't hold diplomatic talks with the old Serene Envoy while refusing the new one. That would compound the insult to the Serene Empire." The duke dropped back into his chair, leaning his elbows on his knees. "You, however, I can talk to all I want. The Cornaro name and your connections to Ardence leave you in good standing with my nobles, despite being a representative of the Empire."

"You want me to act as a go-between with the Serene Envoy?" I asked.

He shook his head. "I would not waste your time carrying messages, my lady. I can send those through other means." He spread his hands wide. "I want you to be seen in my court. Spend time here, at the River Palace, doing whatever you please—visiting me, visiting the library, speaking to the courtiers. Let all see you are welcome here: my nobles, and the doge and Council as well. Show the world that Ardence can still be a friend to Raverra, despite the dramatic gestures the Shadow Gentry insist on. Will you do this simple thing to help us make peace?"

I nodded. "I'd be glad to."

"Excellent." He ran restless fingers over his armrests. "And... one more thing. Your mother. La Contessa Lissandra Cornaro. She has the doge's ear, it's said. Could you perhaps convince her—"

I lifted a hand to stop him. This was far from the first time I'd heard *that* opening. "My mother makes her own decisions, Your Grace. If you want something from her, I recommend you use your courier lamps and ask her yourself." I sighed. "Besides, the doge is less likely to back down than your nobles are. The whole world is watching, and he can't capitulate to threats to pillars of the Empire like the Serene Accords and the Falconers."

The duke's shoulders slumped. "Then you had best hope someone finds those children, Lady Amalia. For until they're safely returned to their parents, two and a half *years* won't be enough to convince them to bow to Raverra again, let alone two and a half days."

Lady Savony stopped me on my way out. A stern glance from her banished the footman who had been conducting me to the door.

"So, Lady Amalia," she greeted me, "what did you think of our duke?"

Her tone invited candor, and she didn't strike me as a woman who valued empty politeness. "Proud," I said, "and desperate."

"Too proud." Her gaze swept the baroque excess of the palace ceiling with disapproval. "If he had listened to me and exercised more restraint, he would not have had to become so desperate. I will do anything it takes to save my city, Lady Amalia. Even if the enemy I must save it from is itself."

This seemed rather direct criticism of the duke from his supposed voice and hands. "Why are you telling me this, Lady Savony?"

She toyed with the golden chain of her spectacles. "Do you know the history of my family, my lady?"

The name Savony seemed familiar, and I was sure I'd seen it in histories of Ardence, but I couldn't recall the particulars. I shook my head.

"We ruled Ardence, once. Before it joined the Empire. But the Bergandons betrayed my ancestors, and took the ducal throne—as, to be fair, the Savony family had taken it from others. It was an unsettled time." She frowned at a painting of a battle scene, full of movement and chaos and the rolling eyes of frightened horses. "My ancestors were wise, however. Instead of seeking vengeance, they swore service to the city they could no longer rule, but could still nurture and protect. Since then we have always served Ardence, often as stewards or other positions more pragmatic than glorious. We never receive credit for what we have done, but we seek none; our sole concern is the welfare of Ardence. We have run this city, as much as any duke, and under our watch it has flourished." She took a sharp breath through her nose. "So I will not allow the current dissolute batch of nobles to ruin my city with their lack of prudence. I would rather see Ardence under direct imperial rule than see it destroyed."

"I don't want to see it destroyed, either." It occurred to me that Lady Savony probably knew Ardence better than any of my own friends, or the duke himself. "To save Ardence, we need to find the kidnapped heirs. They're either being held in the city or were smuggled out. Either way, a number of people were involved, posing as Falconers and moving the children, who knew the city well enough to disappear into it. Who would have access to that manner of person, both unscrupulous and discreet? Spymasters? Criminal lords? Someone in Ardence must have an idea who could have done it."

"You think like a Raverran." She shook her head; her dark hair, pulled back tightly to her scalp, did not so much as stir. "Ardence is less versed in such subtleties."

"You can't tell me there's no one."

Lady Savony considered me a moment. Then she flipped open her little notebook and started scribbling. "We don't have an intelligence service per se, but a few people investigate things for me from time to time. There is a gossip sheet whose editor seems remarkably well informed. One or two smugglers and proprietors of gambling dens do occasionally provide us with information. And the Shadow Gentry may have relevant connections, as well."

She tore a page out of her notebook and handed me a list of about a dozen names in an elegant, loopy script, with brief identifying notes beside each. "We are already searching for the children, naturally, but should you wish to pursue your own investigation, I would begin with these people. Some might point you in the right direction; others you should consider suspects."

"Thank you." I glanced at the page. My heart stumbled; one of the names was Gabril Bergandon. "I'll begin investigating these people immediately." I folded the paper and tucked it into my dagger sheath, for lack of anywhere else to put it.

"You will have to do more than that." Lady Savony grasped my arm, her fingers strong and thin like cabled wire. "You've met the duke. He'll never get his court in line in less than three days. You're going to have to make a choice soon, Amalia Cornaro, about how far you will go to save this city."

I stared helplessly into the dark intensity of her gaze. "I am quite aware of that, Lady Savony."

After a long moment, she released me. "When that day comes, I pray to the Grace of Wisdom you make the right choice."

She dipped the briefest bow in my direction, then snapped her book closed and stalked away, her boots echoing on the marble floor.

On the way out of the River Palace, I passed through the Hall of Beauty, the soaring central space in which all the wings of the palace came together. Sunlight poured down from windows ringing its high dome, framing an extravagant fresco of the Grace of Beauty resting on a bed of clouds, surrounded by throngs of attendants who seemed to be dressed mostly in dramatically flowing scarves.

It was the pulsing heart of the River Palace, through which all information flowed. Petitioners waiting to speak to the duke mingled with palace officials and staff. Nobles of the Council of Lords held conversations in corners. Footmen and pages hurried back and forth across the hall with messages. I scanned the courtiers lingering in the hall, wondering if I should try to overhear some conversations.

"Amalia!" It was Venasha, her arms full of books. I waved back and hurried over to her, relieved to see her smiling after yesterday.

"Venasha! Good to see you. Do you need help with those?"

"Oh, no, I'm happy to carry them. I just acquired them for the Ducal Library, and I'm quite excited. Two volumes of Ostan poetry, a Loreician dueling manual, and a new translation of an ancient Callamornish saga." She beamed with pride.

I wanted to tell her about my Muscati, but I might only have a few moments, so I stayed focused on what mattered. "How are you? How are Aleki and Foss?"

Some of the glee faded from her face. "They're fine. We're... Well, it's a lot to swallow, realizing Aleki has to become a Falcon. But we're fine, truly."

I squeezed her shoulder. "If there's any way I can help, let me know."

She shifted the books in her arms and laughed. "Maybe you could help me take these to the library after all. Mostly for the company! I'd love to show them to you."

The day after tomorrow, the doge might order me to loose Zaira's fire on this palace, and all Venasha's beloved books could be destroyed. I swallowed a hard lump.

"I'd love to see them," I said.

Most of the River Palace's more public rooms were themed after one of the Graces; the Ducal Library occupied the Hall of Wisdom. Bookshelves covered the bottom two-thirds of the high walls, with statues of noted Ardentine scholars standing on top of them, conferring with each other or examining books or instruments of science. The ceiling fresco depicted the Grace of Wisdom with her scroll, smiling benevolently down on the book-burdened library tables below.

I had barely stepped through the doors at Venasha's side, however, when I stopped as if I'd hit a wall. "What's *he* doing here?"

On the far side of the Hall of Wisdom, I'd recognized one of the library patrons reading at the tables, unmistakable even from behind due to his pale hair and high-collared coat with its jagged violet embroidery. Prince Ruven.

Venasha followed my gaze. "Ugh. He's been lurking around the library on and off for days. He spent at least two hours there yesterday, in the magic section." Venasha's nose scrunched up in distaste. "I keep my distance from him. He orders the librarians around as if he owns us."

"I can imagine." I took my lower lip between my teeth a moment, thinking. "Would you be willing to help me figure out what he's reading? I have a feeling he's up to no good."

Venasha's eyes widened. "Ooh, you want to spy on him?"

"Well, just to see what he's researching."

She gave a sort of skip. "Spying! How Raverran! I love it!"

"Ah..." I wasn't sure I wanted to know what Venasha thought we did in Raverra. "Thank you. You're a good friend."

She glanced around in an exaggerated crafty fashion. "Come with me. Let me put these books away, and we can conspire."

Venasha and I peered at Prince Ruven from behind a two-story bookshelf near the back wall, breathing in the smell of old pages and leather covers. He sat with a large book spread out on the table before him, pausing sometimes to take notes. Sunlight fell across him in a wide swath from one of the Ducal Library's high, narrow windows.

"We need to get him away from his book," I murmured. "I want to see what page he's looking at so studiously, before he has the chance to shut it."

"That's easy." Venasha bounced on her toes. "He likes a lot of light. Whenever any of us close the drapes, to protect the books from the sun, he gets up and opens them again. But you'll have only a minute or two to look."

"That's all I should need. Thanks, Venasha."

She saluted me, grinning, and hurried off. Sure enough,

within moments the bold bar of light Ruven had chosen to sit in narrowed to nothing as Venasha drew the curtains shut.

Ruven lifted his head, frowning in annoyance, and rose from his reading table.

As soon as his back was turned, I emerged from behind my shelf, trying to remind myself to walk slowly and casually so I wouldn't draw attention. But suddenly I had no idea what walking normally looked like. To make matters worse, I was still in my elaborate gown from my audience with the duke; I felt ridiculously out of place in the solemn stillness of the library.

I bent over Ruven's book, first slipping my fingers between the pages to mark his place and checking the title on the embossed leather cover: *Interactions of Magic, Volume Two*.

He'd mentioned to Domenic he was interested in volume one, so that didn't tell me much. I opened the book again and scanned the pages Ruven had been studying.

The left-hand page showed a great, impressively detailed artifice circle. Smaller circles marked the points where the inner diagram touched the outer one. I'd only seen nested circles a few times before. Whatever this design was trying to accomplish, it was complicated and ambitious.

I skimmed the accompanying text on the right-hand page. Then skimmed it again, more slowly, a weight like chunks of obsidian settling into my stomach.

The chapter outlined a theoretical way to stimulate a volcanic eruption using artificers and vivomancers in concert.

"Mount Whitecrown," I whispered. "The Vaskandran troops. Grace of Mercy."

A hand fell on my shoulder.

Full, golden light shone on the page I stared at. I hadn't noticed it brightening, in my shock over what I'd read.

"Lady Amalia Cornaro," Prince Ruven said. "Such a pleasant surprise."

Chapter Twenty-One

I turned, pulling my shoulder out from under his hand as I straightened. "Prince Ruven."

Now what? I could pretend I'd only stumbled across the book, and not known he was reading it. I could try to distract him. I could run away like a child caught stealing cakes. Grace of Wisdom, I needed an idea, and fast.

He leveled his violet-ringed eyes at me. "If you wanted to know what I was reading, my lady, you could simply have asked."

I'd had enough of pretending to be friendly to this shark in human skin. I raised an eyebrow. "Oh? Would you have told me you were researching a means to trigger an eruption in Mount Whitecrown?"

Ruven's eyes widened. "Why, no, Lady Amalia. Whatever could have made you think such a thing? I was researching the eruption of Mount Enthalus."

"Mount Enthalus. The volcano that erupted a few years ago and altered the course of the River Arden."

"Yes. That one." Ruven's mouth curved in a smile. "Do you know what caused it?"

A deep unease rose up in me, like black water behind a breaking dam. "I'm guessing you don't mean fires deep in the earth and geological forces."

"No, no. It was a Witch Lord."

My fingers curled instinctively around my flare locket. "A Witch Lord."

"Yes." Ruven nodded, as if proud of me for understanding at last. "No relation of mine. The Oak Lord, in whose domain Enthalus lay, was quarreling with his neighbor, as is not uncommon in Vaskandar. It is one of the reasons we prefer to focus our aggressions outward when we can. But this time, his opponent was the Lady of Eagles. You know her, perhaps?" His gaze sharpened until it could have cut water, as if the question were particularly important.

"The name is familiar. I fear I am not well versed in the aspects and domains of the seventeen Witch Lords." I resolved to read up on them as soon as possible.

"Hmm." Ruven sounded disappointed. "Well, suffice to say the Oak Lord found his forces outmatched. As he prepared for their final battle, near the foot of Mount Enthalus, he sought to awaken the forests on the mountain's flanks, which lay within his domain. But his power accidentally touched something else instead: the volcano's fiery heart."

Hell of Carnage. "He triggered the eruption?"

"Indeed! But the power was too great for him to control. It wiped out his own forces rather than his enemy's, and destroyed the Oak Lord himself utterly." He lifted a finger. "But not in vain! We can learn from his experience."

"That tampering with volcanoes is a terrible idea and you wind up dead if you try?" I suggested.

"No, no. That it can be done." Ruven's eyes lit, his mage mark almost glowing violet. "That it is possible to trigger a volcanic eruption. Can you imagine such power? Is it not magnificent?"

"Grace of Mercy." I could imagine it all too well. "No. That's not a power we should unlock. Volcanic eruptions bring nothing but fire and ruin."

Ruven nodded with delight. "Yes, exactly! Precisely. Like your fire warlock, no?"

I stared at him, my flare locket cold in my hand. Words abandoned me.

"So incredible, that one small human body could contain almost the same destructive force as a volcano." He crooned it, his eyes half lidded, as if savoring the idea. "I am envious, Lady Amalia. Fire warlocks are surely the pinnacle of all humankind. But you see, we do not have one in Vaskandar, so a volcano is the best we can do." He smiled. "We are the same, you see? You put the jess on Zaira because you wanted to hold the power of fiery devastation in your hands. So do we. You rule through the threat of unanswerable power; we seek to do the same. We are kindred spirits, my lady. Everything I do, I learned from the Serene Empire."

I shook my head. It wasn't the same. The servants with finger marks burned into their flesh, or Ruven's guardsman staring in frozen horror as his master pushed a knife through his arm—the Empire didn't do those things.

"I won't deny the Serene Empire seeks to gather the reins of Eruvia into its own hands," I said. "But if you can't see the difference, you've never looked into the faces of your own people."

Ruven tilted his head. "And why would I? They are common, unworthy. They are tools to be used. We who carry true power within us exist to be their masters." He extended a hand. "Come to Vaskandar, my lady. You will see."

I stared at his hand. I'd feel safer grabbing the hot end of a lit torch. Then I looked up at his face.

"Perhaps someday I will visit your country," I said. "But I hope you will understand my reluctance to do so at the invitation of a man who employed a notorious child smuggler."

Ruven blinked. Calculations passed through his violet-ringed eyes, and he dropped his hand. "Why, I have no idea what you're talking about."

"Orthys." I couldn't have been mistaken about the handprint-shaped scar on his man. "He worked for you, did he not?"

"Ah, Orthys." Ruven flipped a dismissive hand. "He wasn't mine. We had a few trade transactions, perhaps. But you see, this is one more way we are the same! As the Empire seeks to gather up the mage-marked, so do I."

A few trade transactions. A long history of trading him children for dream poppies, more like it. I couldn't keep the repugnance entirely from my voice. "I fear, Prince Ruven, I must disagree. We are nothing alike."

"Ah." He sighed. For a moment, genuine hurt might have flickered in his eyes; then it was gone. His hand dropped back to his side. "You wound me, Lady Amalia. I had hoped we could become friends, or perhaps more than friends. But by the look on your face, you think me an enemy."

"Circumstances may place us in conflict," I said carefully, "if you make yourself an enemy to the Empire."

Ruven's face brightened. "Ah, but friendship and enmity are not mutually exclusive! In Vaskandar, often the Witch Lords have close, deep, lasting friendships with their bitterest enemies. If that is what you wish, my lady, I will aspire to this fine example."

"Ah…" My hairline prickled with sweat. What in the Hells could I say to *that?*

Ruven leaned closer to me, his voice dropping to a near whisper. "Be aware, though: when a Witch Lord chooses an enemy, they use every advantage at their disposal to defeat them. They leave no weak spot unexploited, no vulnerability untargeted. Even if they are also friends." He beamed, as if this were a lovely and endearing custom, like putting flower crowns on small girls at the May festival. "I look forward to becoming your most cordial opponent, Lady Amalia."

He bowed with a flourish and departed the library. He left his book open on the table behind him, the great, complicated eye of the artifice circle staring up at me like a challenge.

"I'd bet anything Prince Ruven stole your book," I told Domenic.

Venasha and I had found Domenic attempting to escape a meeting of the Council of Lords and had pulled him into a back room of the Ducal Library to discuss Ruven's reading habits. He slouched against the wall, between a stack of bookbinding-supply crates and a shelf full of manuscripts in various stages of repair.

"That bastard."

Venasha hopped up to sit on a worktable. "I remember the volcano chapter of *Interactions of Magic*. It didn't make much sense. Kept referring back to concepts in the first volume without explaining them, and frankly, the artifice design seemed dubious to me."

"It might make more sense if you had volume one," Domenic said darkly.

I turned to Venasha. "Hide that book. Don't let him find it again."

She nodded vigorously. "I can shelve it in the wrong place. Behind something else. In the erotic-poetry section."

"Perfect."

"I never did like that man." Domenic picked at a loose splinter on the edge of a crate. "No matter how much Gabril insists he's brilliant and can save Ardence. My brother has terrible judgment sometimes."

Gabril. With a pang, I remembered his name on Lady Savony's list of suspects. "Domenic, exactly how bad *is* Gabril's judgment?"

Domenic blinked. "Well, he once wore a Loreician periwig with a Vaskandran-style robe..."

Venasha winced. "That's pretty bad."

"No, I mean, could he have been involved in the Falconer ambush yesterday? Not that I think he would do something like that," I quickly added, "but the attackers were wearing Shadow Gentry masks and cloaks."

Domenic sighed and threw his splinter on the floor. "Gabril says the Shadow Gentry didn't do it. I asked him as soon as I heard about it. But in all honesty, it could have been a few of the Shadow Gentry acting on their own. Some of them have stooped to such levels in the past, assaulting Raverran merchants and the like. Gabril doesn't know about everything they do."

Venasha hugged herself, worry pinching her face. "I heard the Falconers came to bring in a new Falcon, and the Shadow Gentry fought them off to keep them from taking the child."

"That's not what happened!" I straightened, indignant. "There was no mage-marked child. The whole thing was a trap—to steal the jess, most likely."

"There are all kinds of rumors." Venasha bit her lip. "I'm afraid someone is going to take it as an example, and start a fight over Aleki. His mage mark is showing stronger every day."

Domenic didn't look surprised; Venasha must have told him. "You might want to keep Aleki at home for a few days," he suggested, his voice uncharacteristically subdued.

"I said as much to Foss, but he says children need fresh air. He's planning to bring him to the gardens again this afternoon." Venasha turned pleading eyes to me. "He might listen to you, Amalia. Will you talk to him?"

"Of course." I hated the idea of telling him to hide Aleki, but I hated even more the idea of Aleki getting pulled into this conflict.

If we couldn't make peace between Ardence and Raverra before the doge's deadline, Venasha's family would be in far more danger from me than from the Shadow Gentry.

I plucked a pen from a nearby desk, rolling it between my fingers to keep my hands busy so I wouldn't rip out my hair. "You should tell Gabril to get out of the Shadow Gentry," I urged Domenic. "Whether they're truly involved in this plot or not, your brother could get caught up in this mess and wind up in prison, or worse. He shouldn't host that party. He needs to quit the Shadow Gentry, for his own safety."

Domenic sighed miserably. "He won't."

"He's your little brother. He must look up to you. Surely you can convince him."

"You don't understand." Domenic shook his head. "He can't leave the Shadow Gentry. He's their leader."

After my talk with Domenic and Venasha, I took advantage of my presence at the River Palace to intercept more lords of Ardence as they passed through the Hall of Beauty on their business. Though I got a few murderous glares, most of them seemed happy enough to talk to Ignazio's cousin; nearly all of those expressed a wish he were still Serene Envoy. A few proved willing or even eager to discuss a return to normal relations between Raverra and Ardence, but they all agreed on one thing: no concession was possible until the missing heirs were returned to their parents. Whether Raverra had taken them or not, the return of the children had to be the first priority, and the Empire must recognize that. All else could wait.

It was painfully clear the duke hadn't told them about the doge's deadline. They spoke of the tensions with Raverra as a serious problem, but not an immediately pressing one. In their minds, the abducted children were the emergency. It made me fit to wear my teeth down to nubs with frustration. Once, I caught Lady Savony looking at me from across the Hall of Beauty as she dispatched pages and footmen to accomplish the tasks in her little notebook; she lifted an eyebrow at me, as if to say, *You see what I must contend with?*

After several hours, I gave up and collected Venasha from the library so we could go meet Foss and Aleki. We left the River Palace together and crossed the grand Plaza of Six Fountains toward the public gardens. Gray clouds smothered the sky, threatening rain. It was just as well; I'd rather not have to navigate picnickers and dogs on the winding garden paths right now.

"I can't believe it," I muttered. "Domenic isn't an idiot. How could his brother be such a colossal one?"

"I've met him." Venasha sounded worried. "He's not stupid. He gets swept up in the passion of things, though. And he's got enough charisma to bring people along with him."

"That's not what we need right now. Grace of Mercy, Domenic is never going to forgive me if I get his brother thrown into prison." Or executed, but I didn't want to make that possibility real with speech.

"And I'll never forgive Gabril if his rash movement gets my Aleki hurt."

I stopped by the great fountain at the center of the plaza, with its ring of twenty-four stone fish spitting water at a platform on which the Nine Graces stood back to back reaching out benevolent hands to bless everyone who came to the River Palace. Under the gloomy sky, their blank eyes seemed distant and pitiless.

"I don't know what to do, Venasha," I said, my voice low.

She frowned. "About what?"

"Gabril." Savony's list of names dragged at my hip like a bag of lead. "I wish to the Graces Domenic hadn't told me he was the leader of the Shadow Gentry. That's crucial information. How can I not tell Lady Terringer? And my mother and the doge?"

Venasha whistled. "Oh, dear. Yes, that *is* difficult."

I spread my hands, catching windblown spray from the fountain. "If the Shadow Gentry are just bored nobles dressing up and spouting separatist rhetoric, it doesn't matter. But if they're involved in the plot to start a war between Ardence and Raverra, staying silent could get people killed. And turning him in could get *Gabril* killed."

Venasha frowned. "I don't much care about Gabril, but Domenic would be devastated. He has a bit of a blind spot about his little brother."

"I've noticed." I kicked at a loose paving stone.

"I suppose you could make your own assessment." Venasha tilted her head. "You're going to meet him tonight, right?"

"Yes. Domenic invited me to his brother's treason party."

"Can you wait until after the party to decide what to do?"

We had less than three days left. But it didn't make much sense to turn Gabril in before the party, given that it was the best lead I had to try to find out whether and how the Shadow Gentry might be involved in the kidnapping plot. "I suppose I could wait."

Venasha put a hand on my shoulder. "It may not make the choice any easier, but at least you'll have more information."

"Thank you." I folded her in a quick hug.

"Come on," she said with a smile. "Let's go meet my husband, and you can convince him to make better choices than Gabril."

I laughed. "When you put it that way, it sounds easy."

We finished crossing the plaza and entered the gardens. They were nearly empty due to the threatening clouds.

A stray drop hit my nose. I hoped it wasn't bringing its friends. "Will Foss even be here, with this weather?"

"When it's raining, he sometimes waits in the pavilion." Venasha gestured toward an open-sided building with white marble columns standing on a knoll, visible in glimpses through the distant trees.

But as we approached, a shout of anger and alarm sounded from the dense grove ahead, between us and the pavilion.

Venasha paled. "That's Foss. Oh, Graces. Aleki!"

She broke into a run, skirts fluttering around her. I followed.

Why did this have to happen on the one day I was laced into a corset and wearing fashionable shoes instead of boots and breeches? My chest heaved as I hurried after Venasha, lungs forced to expand upward with my waist cinched too tight for deep breathing. At least I still had my dagger at my hip, and my flare locket around my neck.

Our path rounded a tall hedge and plunged into the trees. And there was Foss, at last, but he wasn't alone.

He sprawled against a statue of the winged Grace of Victory, blood pouring down his side, his face pale with shock. A man with a long knife faced him, shaking crimson drops off his blade.

Venasha screamed and flung herself between Foss and his attacker, arms spread to shield him. I took advantage of the distraction and stabbed at the ruffian's neck.

He spun, and my blade caught him across the shoulder instead, but it was a deep gash. He swore and dropped his knife, his arm falling limp.

"Who are you?" I demanded. "Why are you attacking my friend?"

"Aleki," Foss moaned from Venasha's arms. "There was another one. He ran off with Aleki."

The attacker made a grab for his knife with his good hand. I laid a cut across it, and he pulled back, both arms bleeding now.

"Hells take you," he cursed, and sprinted away.

I turned back to Foss, my hand shaking on my dagger hilt. Venasha had dropped to her knees in a pool of skirts and held him in her lap. She had her own knife out and was slicing up a petticoat.

"Foss! Are you all right?"

"I've got him." Venasha's voice was flat as a slammed door.

"It's not deep, but I have to bandage this now. Find Aleki! Bring him back!"

"Please," Foss begged, tears in his eyes. "Hurry." He pointed off down the path.

I couldn't say no. I kicked off my high-heeled, pearl-encrusted shoes and ran in the direction he'd pointed.

I followed the path through the copse of trees, past a fountain with carved dolphins, over a rise hemmed with rosebushes, and into the massive, templelike pavilion.

There, between the rows of creamy marble columns, stood a man and a small boy, hand in hand. They stood peaceful and still, a broad smile on the man's face, and it should have been a friendly and reassuring sight.

Except that the boy was Aleki, who never stood still. His eyes shone glassy and unfocused.

And the man was Prince Ruven.

"Why, hello, Lady Amalia." Ruven's smile broadened, as if he were genuinely delighted to see me. "Look who I found. Someone seems to have lost him."

I faltered to a stop, bloody knife still out, gasping for breath. I couldn't take my eyes off Ruven's hand, clasped around Aleki's. A snake could have been swallowing the boy's arm and I would have been less afraid for him.

"It's so fortunate I happened across him." Ruven pressed his free hand to his breast. "I hate to think what could befall such a young child in the wrong hands. We were just going to find his parents. Weren't we?"

Aleki nodded, still staring blankly. Fear squeezed my heart. "What have you done to him?"

"Only helped him calm down. He was frightened, poor boy." Ruven ran the back of a knuckle down Aleki's round cheek. Aleki didn't so much as flinch. "Such a lovely boy. So exciting, to watch the mage mark manifest, isn't it? So much potential, like a bud only beginning to open before you can tell what the flower will be."

I wanted to lunge across the pavilion and knock his hand away from Aleki's face. But I didn't dare make any sudden movements. Ruven might take it into his head to hurt Aleki at any second, or tie his arm in a knot, or something worse.

"What do you want?" My voice was an unsheathed weapon, all point and edge. I couldn't play his games. Not now.

"Why, only to help you!" He spread his free hand. "I was thinking of our conversation earlier, you see. And I thought perhaps it would be useful to show you how good it is to have me on your side. How fortuitous that this boy gave me the opportunity to present you with an example!" Ruven patted Aleki's unresponsive head. "By returning him to you, of course."

"Then return him." I shoved the words through my teeth.

Ruven laughed. "My, my. Such a lovely glare you have. Here, take the child, then."

He released Aleki's hand. Immediately, the boy's face crumpled into pure terror, and he began wailing.

I ran up and snatched him into my arms, barely remembering to throw down my dagger first, anxious to get him out of Ruven's reach. Aleki planted his face in my shoulder and howled stickily into my hair. He was fine, thank the Graces.

"I'm taking him back to his parents now," I said, as much for Aleki's benefit as for Ruven's.

Ruven shrugged. He seemed about to speak when the man who'd attacked Foss came stumbling up the path, still bleeding from his shoulder and arm, his face pale and waxy. I stepped back, angling Aleki away from him, but the man merely threw himself to his knees at Ruven's feet.

"My lord," he began. "I have a report—"

Ruven reached out and laid a hand on the man's head, as if in benediction.

A spasm shook the wounded man, head to toe, and he clutched his chest with his working arm. He dropped to the path, landing on his face, and lay still as a stone.

Dead.

Ruven recoiled with a mild pretense of alarm. "Oh, dear, this man has attacked us. What a terrible fellow. I'm so glad I was here to save us."

"You killed him. You killed your own man."

"My lady, I'm sure I have no idea what you mean." Ruven raised his eyebrows. "I have never seen this man before in my life. I am quite shaken, I assure you."

I'd had enough. I clasped Aleki to me with one arm and scooped up my dagger with the other. "Prince Ruven. I am going now." I wiped the dagger clean on my own silk skirts and jammed it home in its sheath. "I suggest you stay away from my friends in the future, because if you come near this child again, I am going to do everything in my considerable power to have you arrested."

Ruven bowed, smiling. "I will bear that in mind, my lady."

"I suggest you do. Good day, Your Highness."

I turned my back on him. I prayed to the Graces my gown hid the trembling in my legs as I walked away.

Chapter Twenty-Two

I found Venasha staggering up the path, helping along a heavily bandaged Foss, both of them sporting bloodstains and stark desperation. As soon as they saw me carrying Aleki, they cried out in relief. Aleki nearly threw himself from my arms to his mother's, and the three of them huddled together, heedless of Foss's injuries, holding one another close. Their emotion was so intense I had to look away.

"We should get out of here," I said after a moment. I wanted Aleki as far from Ruven as possible.

"Yes," Venasha agreed. "Foss needs a physician."

"I'm fine," he protested weakly.

Venasha ruffled his hair and shook her head. Aleki helpfully jabbed a finger into his father's eye.

"If you don't mind," I said, "let's head for the garrison. I'll feel better with hundreds of soldiers and thick stone walls between Aleki and harm."

Foss nodded, his face grave. "Now that I've had time to consider it," he said, "so will I."

I commandeered a coach from the River Palace to take us to the garrison. Aleki fell asleep in his mother's arms on the ride, lulled by the rumbling wheels. Foss stroked his hair with a trembling hand, looking likely to pass out himself. Venasha made soothing sounds to both of them, pale as paper, her voice unnaturally calm.

The watchers on the castle ramparts must have examined our coach through a spyglass as we took the winding road up the hill to the fortress. Marcello, Zaira, Istrella, a handful of soldiers, and a physician with a box full of alchemical remedies greeted us at the gates. In a flurry of competent activity, Foss's wound was soon treated and properly dressed, and the family was settled into a suite of rooms designed for visiting nobility. I waited in their sitting room to make sure all was well while Venasha saw her husband and son tucked safely into their beds.

She emerged from the bedroom at last, shutting the door gently behind her.

"Thank you," she said. Her hands started to shake. She held them up in front of her face in wonder, as if she couldn't imagine what was happening.

"Maybe you should go to bed, too," I suggested.

"It's only afternoon...But I think I will. I wanted a bath, but I'm not going to leave them alone for one minute." The shaking traveled to her shoulders, and she flung her arms around me.

I hugged her gently. "It'll be all right. Prince Ruven has made his point. He won't bother you again."

"But someone else might. The mark is so clear in his eyes. It's only a matter of time until someone threatens him again."

"They won't." I squeezed her tighter. "Because we'll keep him safe."

She took a deep breath, let go, and straightened her bodice. "Of course you will. That's what the Falconers do, isn't it?"

I nodded, though a yawning gulf of sorrow opened under me. "Yes," I said. "It is."

Out in the corridor, between the illumination of well-kept oil lamps, I leaned my forehead against the stone wall and closed my eyes. At least they were safe in the garrison now. If Zaira burned the city, or Istrella's cannons wrecked it, Venasha and her family would survive.

Someone tapped me lightly on the shoulder.

I shrieked. Istrella shrieked too, in startled response, as I whirled to face the round lenses of her red-and-green glasses. She nearly dropped something she held in her other hand—a glass orb wrapped in beaded wire—and it flashed as she bobbled it, with shifting rainbow lights.

"Hello, Istrella," I said breathlessly, slumping against the wall. "I thought you were going to murder me."

"Oh, not at all!" Istrella clutched the rescued orb to her chest. As it stilled, the lights faded. "I wouldn't have the faintest notion how to murder someone. No, I wanted to ask you if Aleki was awake. I made him a toy!" She shook the orb proudly and it glowed again.

"What is it? A pocket luminary?"

"Sort of. More colors, and the patterns change depending on how fast you move it. And it should last longer than most pocket luminaries." She pushed back her glasses to admire it better. "Though come to think of it, do you think he's too young for something this breakable?"

I nodded solemnly. "Better add some fortification runes to it."

"You think of everything!" She bounced with enthusiasm. I forbore from pointing out she could probably remake it out of something sturdier for a lot less effort.

Zaira burst around a corner, her knife out. When she saw us, she scowled. "Were you two screaming like that over a *toy*? I thought you were being murdered."

"Amalia thought that, too." Istrella lifted her brows. "Apparently, I'm quite terrifying."

Zaira sheathed her dagger, shaking her head. "Like the Demon of Madness herself."

"Well, if Aleki's asleep, I should get back to work on my project for the doge," Istrella sighed. "I hear they want it done tomorrow now. Good night!"

She waved and left, a skip in her step, completely oblivious to the cold, queasy feeling her parting words had left me.

Zaira grunted. "If I were that cheerful about setting people on fire, they'd drown me in the lagoon."

"You're not that cheerful about anything." But that wasn't right, I realized. "Except Scoundrel. And Terika."

Zaira stared down the hall, after Istrella. "They're all right. Wish I could have brought Scoundrel here with me, but Terika's taking good care of him."

"You miss them both, don't you," I said softly.

Zaira shrugged with rough force, like she was shaking off an attack.

"They're your friends." It was an easy word to say, but it fell from my lips with more weight than a ship's anchor. I remembered the Tallows shopkeeper's words: *Zaira doesn't have any friends.*

Zaira's eyes went white-rimmed, as if I'd threatened her. Then she spun away from me, hugging herself. "Are they?"

"It's safe for you to care about them now." I chose my words carefully as if they were footsteps exploring a thin sheet of spring ice that could crack at any second. "With the jess on, you won't hurt the people close to you anymore."

"There's no one close to me," she snapped. And she strode off down the hall.

Lady Terringer herself stopped at the garrison to check on Vena-sha's family. When she found them asleep, she took me aside to tell me that given Prince Ruven's mounting history of suspicious activities, and his connections to the Shadow Gentry, she was going to have his rooms quietly searched the next day for the missing jess, just in case.

The idea of Ruven possessing a jess left a chill in my bones. He might well be the danger Leodra had warned of, and the name that had died on his lips.

After talking to Lady Terringer, I needed some fresh air. I found a no-nonsense kitchen garden in one of the garrison courtyards, where dusk gathered in shadowed corners and crept up the walls. Late tartgrass blooms cast a pungent musk across the garden. I sank onto a stone bench, my bloodstained skirts spreading around me. It had already been a long day, and I still had to get ready for Gabril's party tonight.

One of the courtyard doors opened, and Marcello stepped out into the twilight.

He paused in the doorway, staring across the garden at me, shadows pooling in his eyes. The moment stretched longer. I wished he would say something, anything, but he just stood there, as the color leached out of the sky.

I couldn't take it. "Did you come to look at me, or do you have something to say?"

My own voice sounded frail and foolish against the profundity of the evening silence.

Marcello shook his head, as if breaking a spell, and crossed the garden. Without a word, he sat on the bench beside me and took my hand in his.

His touch sent warm waves all through the core of me. My lips parted, but shock and a building, wondrous alarm choked off speech.

"Please," he said. "Don't do this."

"What?" I snatched my hand back. Was he deliberately confusing me?

Worry drew grave lines into his fine face. "This Shadow Gentry party tonight. It's too dangerous. Don't go."

I curtailed the urge to deliver a sharp retort. He had a point. One Falconer had already been attacked, and tensions between Raverra and Ardence had wound tight enough to break into violence at any moment. "I have to. It's the best lead we've got."

"Then let me come with you."

"You can't." I shook my head. "Can you imagine, an officer of the Falconers walking into a meeting of the Shadow Gentry without an invitation? You'd feel obligated to arrest them, they'd feel obligated to assault you, and it would end in an incident far worse than the ones we're trying to repair."

Marcello stared down at his lap, gripping his knees. "Everything is already going to the Hell of Discord, Amalia. I don't know how we can salvage it. I had nightmares all last night about... about tonight going wrong."

I fidgeted with my flare locket. "I'm well aware any incident at the party would be the final spark that sets Ardence ablaze, Marcello. You don't need to remind me. I'll be careful not to start a war."

"I'm not afraid you'll start a war." He looked up, and his green eyes were open, bottomless wells, clear all the way down to the bottom. "I'm afraid of losing you."

The quality of the air changed, suddenly, as if a storm were coming.

"Amalia." His voice went serious: deep as the lagoon and just as dangerous to fall into. "I'm not good at hiding or pretending."

Don't say it. I wanted to clamp my hand over his mouth. If he put that look into words, it would be too late to take it back.

"I'm a Cornaro." I tried to laugh, but it came out as a shaky breath. "Hiding and pretending is a family pastime."

He reached out a trembling hand and brushed my cheek, gentle as a moth's wing. A shiver ran down my neck.

Grace of Love help me. If I didn't kiss him now, I'd regret it.

But I'd regret it even more if I got him packed off to some distant keep in the Witchwall Mountains. I folded my hand over his, as careful as if it were a baby bird, and removed it from my cheek. I couldn't quite bring myself to let go of it.

"I'll be careful," I told him.

Marcello closed his eyes, wincing, as if the sight of me caused him pain.

I squeezed his hand. "Besides," I said, "Zaira will be with me."

"Oh, that's all right, then." His tone was light, too light, as if he didn't dare place any burden on his voice. But the corner of his mouth quirked. "When Zaira's involved, nothing can go wrong."

"It had best go *very* right." Disappointment and regret at pushing him away trickled down to join the more general flood of dread that had been rising slowly over me. "We're almost out of time."

We had less than forty-eight hours left to unravel this bitter tangle into peace. Or the Empire would write its final argument in fire.

"My, my. So these are your scholar friends? I've been missing the benefits of an education." Zaira's eyes moved appreciatively over the men and women crowding Gabril's drawing room. There wasn't enough furniture for the dozens of people, so many of them stood, holding wineglasses while they conducted impassioned arguments or serious discussions. It was the opposite of a Raverran party; everyone gathered toward the center with raised voices, rather than dispersing to little whispering clusters in corners.

It wasn't at all what I had expected. There were no masks, no cloaks, no secretive cabal plotting treason. But a certain tension lay under the laughter, softened by a liquid layer of wine. Angry voices cut sharply through the chamber music from time to time, and I glimpsed furious scowls and brooding stares on some faces. Ardentine party dress apparently didn't include a requirement to put on a false smile.

"They're not my scholar friends," I replied. The crowd was mostly young; with a few exceptions, most of the faces I recognized were the heirs of the powerful, rather than lords of the Council themselves. I looked for Domenic, to edge closer to him, but he was already across the room, greeting people.

"Oh, good. Then I'll have to make Domenic introduce me." Zaira waved a smug good-bye and sauntered off after him. Long gloves covered her telltale jess, at Domenic's suggestion. While we had no intention of lying tonight, arriving as a brazenly obvious Falcon and Falconer in this particular crowd might throw down a gauntlet we didn't want picked up.

Across the room, Zaira tapped Domenic's shoulder, grinning. He took her hand and drew her into his circle, and in a moment they were all laughing. An eddy of envious misgiving swirled in me, but I ignored it. Zaira was happy. Domenic was happy. I resolved to leave the two of them together, avoid butting in, and wish Zaira the best of luck with him.

Except that she'd dropped me like a soiled handkerchief in a roomful of potentially hostile strangers.

I'd thought of Ardence as a second home, but these weren't my friends from the university. When they spoke the name of my city, it curled their lips with spite. I didn't belong here.

I accepted a wineglass from a passing tray and took a long, sweet draft. I wasn't here to make friends. I had work to do.

"Pardon me, my lady. Are you Domenic's Raverran friend?"

Blinking my stinging eyes, I turned to find a young man with spectacles and thinning hair at my elbow. "Yes, I suppose I am."

"Name's Hollis. Very glad to meet you." He jerked his head in a forceful nod, as if I'd said something he agreed with. "It's good to have another influential Raverran backer. It gives me hope. If even *Raverrans* can be outraged at what the Empire has done to us, we have a chance to accomplish something."

"Oh, I'm not..." I swallowed. "...not the only one in Raverra with sympathy for Ardence." Admitting I didn't back Ardence against the Serene City was perhaps not the most politic choice at the moment, especially to gain more information. And I wanted to know what he meant by another Raverran backer. "Who else have you met?"

"Of Raverrans who support our cause? You're the first, actually." He pushed his spectacles up, as if to examine me better. "I've heard Gabril talking about our Raverran ally, but I've never met them. You know how he is. 'Our friend in the River Palace,' 'our patron in Raverra.' He likes his mysteries." He smiled, inviting me to share his affectionate disdain. "He even has nicknames for them. 'The Owl,' 'the Fox,' that sort of thing. The only one he'll call by name is Prince Ruven."

The *patron in Raverra* could well have been Baron Leodra, which didn't bode well for Gabril's innocence. The *friend in the River Palace* worried me; it sounded more like Duke Astor or someone in his circle than merely a member of the Council of Lords.

I forced a laugh. "How dramatic. Do you think the mystery

is genuine, or is he trying to make his connections seem more important than they are?"

"Oh, they're real. They've given us good information, and they've arranged to make sure there were no guards or soldiers in the area when we post our declarations and the like. And Prince Ruven has been quite generous financially to those of us in need of a loan." Hollis shrugged. "Besides, Gabril is the duke's cousin. Of *course* he has connections in the River Palace."

I dropped my voice. "What about the incident with the Falconers?" Hopefully that was vague enough he could take it either as the kidnapping or the attack on poor Lemi. "Did his connections help with that?"

Hollis blinked in apparent confusion a moment, then frowned. "You mean the, ah, recent altercation? That was a surprise, wasn't it?" He shook his head. "Gabril won't disavow it *or* claim credit. I've pressed him on it, but he's been rather evasive. Frankly, I'm worried some of our number may be escalating matters too far."

A thin-faced woman in mourning black nudged up next to him, wineglass in hand. "Nonsense, Hollis. There's no such thing as too far. Those imperial stingroaches have my daughter. I'll tear them all apart with my hands if I have to."

Hollis lifted his brows in alarm. "Now, my lady, don't you think that's a bit extreme?"

The lady in mourning sniffed. "No less than they deserve. Until they give my daughter back, I'd as soon stab a Raverran as look at one." She turned to me with a wolfish smile. "I don't believe we've been introduced?"

Hollis grimaced with sympathy.

I gulped a swallow of wine to buy time, but she still waited expectantly. "Ah, I'm, well..."

"Amalia." Domenic had slipped up by my side. He bowed an apology, his face tense. "I'm sorry to interrupt. But my brother wishes to speak with you."

Chapter Twenty-Three

Gabril Bergandon shared his brother's warm-brown skin, deep-set eyes, and winning smile. But he'd curled his hair into long Loreician ringlets, and his neat little beard and slight build reminded me more of his cousin, Duke Astor. He received us privately in his study, which held a single bookshelf full of Ardentine history; the Bergandon crest hung prominently above his chair.

"Gabril," Domenic introduced us, "this is Zaira, the Falcon of whom I spoke. And may I also present my friend, Lady Amalia Cornaro."

Gabril barely glanced at Zaira, but his gaze lingered on me as we all settled into leather chairs. "Indeed. It's a pleasure to meet you, Lady Amalia. Your cousin is sorely missed as Serene Envoy in Ardence. I appreciate the friendship your family has continued to show our city in this troubled time."

His voice held a compelling resonance, and he radiated an unusual confidence for such a young man. I could see why people listened to him. It remained to be seen, however, whether he had anything to say.

"I'm delighted to meet you at last," I said.

Domenic leaned forward, urgency filling his voice. "If you

appreciate the friendship of the Cornaro family, you should understand how much more valuable it is than that of Vaskandar."

Gabril's eyelids twitched with annoyance. "We've already discussed this, brother. I'm aware you dislike my friendship with Prince Ruven. I don't require your approval."

"It's not a question of my opinion of Prince Ruven." Domenic's voice heated with the flames of an old argument. "Though, since you bring it up, I should mention he's the twisted spawn of a stingroach and a cobra. But my point is that Vaskandar's friendship—even if it were genuine, which it's not—only antagonizes Raverra and makes our situation worse."

"Domenic," I murmured. Starting a fight with his brother was not going to help.

He gestured in my direction, ignoring my hint. "With allies like Amalia, we don't need to force a confrontation. It's not too late to take a different road—one that won't lead to bloodshed."

I glanced at Domenic in alarm. That sounded far more advanced than I'd hoped.

Gabril sneered his contempt. "Are you so eager to accommodate the Empire? I thought better of you."

"We are *part* of the Empire, Gabril. For better or for worse." Domenic waved an encompassing hand around the room. "You could use everything you've built here to stand up to them without putting Ardence at risk. To defend the mage-marked, and champion our city. But if you use the Shadow Gentry to make Ardence a prize for Vaskandar and Raverra to fight over, *we* are the ones who lose that battle. Change course now, before you crash this ship on the shoals of war."

Gabril glared at Domenic for a long moment. A clock on the mantel measured second after second, plucking the taut string of silence in the room.

But then he turned a brilliant smile at me, cocking his head.

"Well, Lady Amalia? What is your opinion? Is he right? Is our wisest course to avoid confrontation at all costs?"

There was a test in his voice. One I needed to pass to gain more information.

Tell them nothing, my mother said once, *and they will fill the meaninglessness of your words with exactly what they want to hear.*

"If you know my family," I said, "you know the answer to that question."

A slow smile curved Gabril's lips. "Very well," he said. "I think perhaps I do."

He turned to Domenic. "I beg your pardon, Domenic, but would you and the Falcon mind giving me a moment of Lady Amalia's time in private?"

Domenic stared at his brother, gripping the arms of his chair. A vein in his temple pulsed.

Zaira snorted and stood. "The Falcon certainly doesn't mind. I'm dying of boredom in here. At least there are drinks in the drawing room."

Domenic rose more slowly. "You're making a mistake, Gabril."

"In speaking to Lady Amalia alone?" he asked innocently. "I should think not."

"Amalia?" Domenic looked a question at me, to which I returned a minute shrug. I had no idea what Gabril wished to discuss, though I was quite curious to find out. Zaira was already heading for the door.

He nodded stiffly to Gabril. "We'll talk later, then."

"I look forward to it, brother."

The door closed behind them. Gabril eased back in his chair, smirking.

"Now we can drop the pretense, my lady."

If he could, lovely. I had no such luxury, so I tried to return a knowing smile.

"My brother is a good man." Gabril sighed. "And brilliant, of course. But he's hardly subtle. You, of course, are a Cornaro; subtlety is in your blood."

My mother might disagree in my case. But I kept my mouth shut and smiled to acknowledge the compliment.

"Poor Domenic." Gabril shook his head. "I've told him again and again I have it on the best authority Raverra will back down at the last moment if we stand fast against them. But he doesn't have the stomach for this kind of daring move, I'm afraid."

My insides turned over. I didn't know what his "best authority" was, but mine was the doge himself, and I was dead certain he wouldn't back down. I knew *exactly* what would happen if Ardence forced a confrontation.

I wasn't sure whether to try to convince him of how wrong he was, or play along for more information. It didn't help that Gabril himself might be the manipulator trying to start a war. The kidnapped children had certainly given new strength to the Shadow Gentry.

Best to hedge my bets. "To be fair, he only wants to ensure the safety of Ardence. Bold moves have their risks."

Gabril chuckled. "Oh, of a certainty. Which is why I'm glad for the chance to talk to you, Lady Amalia. This is a rare opportunity; all the court is united in its outrage over the stolen children. Once, few listened when I called for a return to the days of Ardentine glory, when we were a great power in Eruvia." His eyes sparkled. "But now, when I call for us to stand up to Raverra and remember our pride, everyone pays attention."

"Hmm," I said. He seemed to take the sound for agreement.

"We are united at last, ready to stand strong as Ardentines again. We have Vaskandar at our back, to give us the power we need to resist the Empire and its Falcons. The Council of Lords has found its courage, and they will not allow my cousin the duke to fold to the doge's demands." His excitement drove him to his feet, and he started pacing. "Our day has come. Ardence can be free and proud again, as it once was. So I have been promised. However"—he swiveled to face me—"we must rise against Raverra, but we must not push it to the breaking point while it can still destroy us. And that is where you come in, my lady."

I would, indeed, "come in" if Ardence pushed Raverra too far—by releasing Zaira's flames. But I affected puzzlement. "I do?"

"Indeed." He sat back down. "Domenic tells me you are dedicated to avoiding war. And that is desirable at the moment. Prince Ruven has warned me that while Vaskandar can provide us with some protection, it cannot yet shield us from the full might of the Empire. How much can we demand before Raverra will balk? Can we press our advantage to eliminate the Raverran trade privileges choking our own Ardentine merchants? Keep our mage-marked rather than surrendering them to the Falconers? What is the line we cannot cross?"

Gabril's perceptions were so far from reality I wasn't sure how to answer that question. "How aware are you of the current state of negotiations between Ardence and Raverra?"

"More aware than most." He leaned in toward me. "Our friend in the River Palace tells me the doge has given my cousin a time limit, which he's too afraid to tell even the Council of Lords."

I stared, nonplussed. "If you know that…"

"Why am I still seeking confrontation?" He chuckled. "Because our Raverran friend tells me it's a bluff. The Empire doesn't dare attack one of its own cities, especially with Vaskandar poking at its borders. Once we prove to everyone their threats are hollow, then we can begin the *real* negotiations."

I tried to keep my expression neutral. If his Raverran friend was still telling him things, it couldn't be Leodra. "You ask how much you can push," I said carefully. "I would suggest the more critical question is *when*."

He set his chin on his hands. "Oh?"

"If you press too hard before the time limit runs out, you risk putting the doge in a position where he *has* to enforce it." Never mind that Ardence had crossed that line long ago. I'd buy time however I could. "If you wait until afterward, you can see how he responds. That in itself should give you a clear idea of who holds what cards at this table."

If Gabril were a Raverran, he would have read a warning in my words. But he was an Ardentine. He nodded with apparent enthusiasm. "That makes sense. The Grace of Wisdom has truly blessed your family, Amalia Cornaro. I am fortunate to count you among my friends."

Guilt pinched my gut. I was still unsure what the sides were in this conflicted mess, but I was fairly certain Gabril and I were on different ones.

Domenic took me aside soon after I returned to the party from Gabril's study. Zaira lounged on a divan across the room, telling some salacious story that had all the people around her laughing.

"Amalia, can I ask what he talked to you about?"

"You can, but I don't think he said anything secret, merely expressed opinions with which he knew you would disagree. He seems bent on direct confrontation. He doesn't have a very realistic perspective, I fear."

Domenic's brow creased with concern. "I was hoping you could get through to him. He keeps insisting his secret allies know what's truly going on, and that they have a plan that can't fail. I'm dubious."

"You should be," I said bluntly. "His so-called allies are either manipulating him or are fictitious. They've told him things I know are false."

Domenic punched his own thigh. "Hell of Madness. I told that idiot not to trust Ruven, or anyone so ashamed to be his friend they won't let him speak their names. What are they using him for?"

"I wish I knew."

Whatever these mysterious allies might want with Gabril and the Shadow Gentry, they didn't seem to care about bolstering his reputation in the long-term. When it inevitably came out that his supporters were lying, and that Gabril's assurances to his followers were based on false promises, his influence at court would crumble. He'd be a laughingstock, his career over when he'd barely reached his majority. He clearly had no value to whoever was using him.

Of course, that made him expendable.

It was getting harder and harder to see an outcome where Domenic got to keep his brother, whether I betrayed Gabril or his "friends" did. And what brought down Gabril might well take Domenic with him—if it didn't swallow all of Ardence first.

It was quite late by the time Zaira and I said our good-byes to Domenic and left Gabril's town house. A chill in the air made me glad I'd worn an embroidered wool coat, but Zaira rubbed her bare arms as we hurried along. Only a few windows still glimmered with light.

"Why didn't you let Domenic escort us home?" Zaira complained. "He'd have loaned me his coat."

"Would you like to borrow mine?" I offered.

Zaira's sideways glance conveyed disbelief. "You don't understand the main reason to borrow a man's coat, do you? Grace of Mercy's tits, you're hopeless."

I was glad it was too dark for her to see the flush mounting my cheeks. "I didn't let him escort us so you could tell me what you learned."

"At the party?" Zaira snorted. "I learned Domenic has boring friends."

"Yes, but how about anything of substance?"

"I learned he's told his boring friends nice things about me. That's promising, wouldn't you say?"

"About the plot to cause a war," I said. "We were there to try to find leads, remember?"

Zaira shrugged. "*You* were there to find leads. I was there to have a good time."

"For Graces' sake, Zaira—"

She stopped and turned to face me, her gown swirling. "Do you really think I'd help you betray a group that's trying to stop the Falconers from snatching up the mage-marked?"

"I don't want to betray them! I want to find out who's manipulating them."

Zaira's eyes narrowed. "By spying on them yourself?"

"Zaira, do you understand what will happen if we can't figure out who took those children?" I slammed my fist into my palm. "Ardence will burn, and it will be our fault!"

"No, it won't." Zaira smiled. "Because for Ardence to burn, you and I both must agree to do it. And we won't. Will we?"

Despair clogged my throat. The smile faded from Zaira's face as she stared into my eyes.

"You would," she whispered. "You would do it, wouldn't you."

"I don't know," I said miserably. "Zaira, I'm a loyal daughter of the Serene City. If the doge and the Council of Nine give me an order..."

Her face twisted in anger and contempt. "You're a damned coward."

"It's not that simple!"

Zaira stripped off her glove and threw it down at my feet. She brandished a fist, the jess shining on her wrist. "I wear this, and I still make my own choices, for Graces' sake. You do, too. If you're going to burn a city, take responsibility and burn it. Don't give me that milky piss about doing what your mamma says."

"Zaira—"

"No. Don't say another word. I can't even stand to look at you anymore."

She turned on her heel and strode off, skirts swishing.

I bent to pick up her glove, taking a deep breath to hold in my anger. Who did she think she was, to speak to me like that?

It was easy for her to say she wouldn't do it, but she'd been willing enough to burn Raverra when threatened. Zaira was a survivor. She might not like it, but I suspected she'd loose her balefire on Ardence if her life depended on it. And if the doge commanded, it did.

I straightened, holding the glove, words marshaled on my tongue, but Zaira was gone. The fading echoes of her fashionably blocky heels disappeared down a side street that led in a different direction than we'd been heading.

Hell of Despair. Some Falconer I was.

I hurried after her, and at once came to a cross street. I peered down each way, but neither saw nor heard her. A whiff of garlic and wine beckoned down one street, and faint music down another; the third lay dark and silent. I hesitated, then followed my nose. Zaira was always hungry.

I passed a pair of drunken merchants heading home, singing a duet, and a rather disreputable-looking cat. I tracked the wine and garlic to a town house that still had a few candles burning, but there was no sign of Zaira. There were plenty of cross streets she could have taken, though.

I turned a corner to circle back, glancing down every alley I passed. My footsteps echoed hollowly on the flagstones, chasing ahead of me in the darkness. Another turn, and I wasn't sure I was heading in the right direction. The spire of the Temple of Bounty loomed in front of me, slashing a swath of darkness against the stars—but shouldn't it be on my right?

Panic rose up from my stomach like bile. She could be anywhere. I'd lost my Falcon in the city streets, and she might well be making a run for it. I shouldn't have let my guard down out of mere hope she might be my friend now. What was I going to tell Marcello?

I stopped. Of course. When I hunted for Zaira with Marcello, I'd been able to get a sense of where she was. I tried to quiet my mind, silencing the voice clamoring at me about how stupid I was, waiting for a fluttering pull at my attention.

There. Toward the river, if I had my bearings. Now I just had to try to navigate in the right direction. At least this time, I'd had the foresight to take my elixir before heading out for the night, and had tucked a three-hours'-grace vial into my bodice for good measure.

I'd been walking for several minutes with no sign of her when someone called out behind me, "Lady Amalia Cornaro?"

My heart jumped in an instant of hope, but it was a man's voice, and of all the names Zaira had called me, my proper title wasn't one of them. I turned and saw a figure in the street. It was too dark to make out a face. He strode unhesitatingly in my direction, a sword hanging at his side.

Suddenly every shadow seemed alive, sharp, and dangerous.

Without a word, I walked away, as quickly as I could without breaking into a run. I touched the dagger sheathed at my hip. The last thing I wanted was a fight, but if it came to that, I'd have to close at once for my knife to have a chance against his sword. Assuming a sword was all he had.

If he had a flintlock, he could be aiming it at my back right now. My heart fluttered like a trapped bird. My legs strained to break into a run, but I was afraid to trigger an attack. I had to find a busier street, or make it to somewhere safe. Even a tavern might do.

The clop of hooves rose up over my own quick footsteps. A carriage rolled into the cross street ahead of me, drawn by two black horses. Thank the Grace of Luck—a witness. And perhaps a ride away from my pursuer, if I could catch it.

Obligingly, amazingly, the driver reined in the horses right in the middle of the intersection, fifty paces ahead. The driver and another man scrambled down from the box.

I took in a breath to hail them, but stopped. There was something familiar and disquieting about the carriage.

It was a hearse.

My steps slowed. The two men slid a coffin from the back of the hearse—an empty one, by the way they carried it. Working in silence, they laid it in the street.

Then they turned to face me.

Oh, Hells.

"Take her," the man following me said.

Chapter Twenty-Four

I stepped into a recessed stone doorway and drew my dagger. All three men came at me, closing in a tightening arc.

This was the best chance I was going to get. I closed my eyes and flipped open my flare locket.

My eyelids reddened from the flash of intense light. The three men swore in surprise and pain. I opened my eyes the instant the light ceased. My attackers reeled, blinking, blinded.

It would only last a moment. I pushed between two of them, slashing at one's midsection along the way. My knife sliced his leather doublet and turned harmlessly on a rib, but I didn't care. I was past them.

As I drew in a sharp breath to scream for help, a wet rag hit the back of my neck. It reeked of peppermint.

Sleep potion. I hurled it away, but already the world swayed sickeningly. My scream died on my numb lips, and my knees buckled under me.

The strangers caught me before I hit the flagstones. I tried to fight them, but I couldn't move; my body was limp and useless. It was all I could do to keep my grip on my knife.

If I released Zaira, she'd know I must need help, assuming she noticed the return of her powers at all. But given how we'd parted, she might laugh and keep running.

"Careful," one of my captors said in a clipped Ardentine accent. "The Owl wants her unharmed."

Another grunted as they dragged me toward the hearse. "We taking this one to the same place as the brats?"

"No. This one gets special treatment."

"*Exsolvo*," I tried to say. But it came out as a soft, breathy "Ehhhhhhhhhh."

"Quickly now. We can't be seen."

They bundled me into the coffin.

Terror blazed in me like balefire at the thought of the lid closing, and it burned through the numb cloud of the potion. I managed to swing my knife arm wildly up at the men bending over me. One of them cried out and reeled away, clutching his face.

"She's not out!" Another lunged and pushed me back down into the coffin before I could more than raise my head, his face snarling with frustration around a nose crooked from previous breaks.

"Quick, the potion!"

Something warm spattered on my face. But it didn't smell like peppermint.

The broken-nosed man released me and straightened, swearing. I managed to turn my head in time to see the scoundrel who'd been standing beside him crumple, blood on his lips, eyes glassy with shock.

Behind him stood Zaira, in her party gown, a knife in her hand.

"Egghhhssssoffo," I tried again.

The man with the bleeding face slashed at Zaira with his sword. But a glowing ripple shook the air in front of her magical corset, and the blade rebounded out of his hand. Cursing louder, the broken-nosed one fumbled in a leather pouch.

"Looking for something?" Zaira held up a glass bottle.

I summoned the shreds of my strength and tried to lunge up out of the casket.

Zaira, grinning, kicked the lid shut in my face.

For one moment of sheer panic, I pushed ineffectively at the lid, still too weak to shove it open. The coffin seemed to wrap tight around me, as if I'd been encased in stone. I choked on the close air.

Then I heard glass shatter against the lid. Something bumped the casket, jarring it to the side. Faintly, the odor of peppermint seeped in. I held my breath.

Zaira flung the lid back, holding her remaining glove across her nose and mouth. She wrestled me up out of the coffin; I tried to help, but my limbs dragged like bags of sand.

Three bodies lay sprawled in the street. The nervous horses had dragged the hearse several yards off. Broken glass glittered in the moonlight.

Zaira pulled my arm over her shoulders and helped me stagger away, half hauling me. When I finally had to gasp in a breath, the fresh air cleared my head, bringing more feeling back to my body.

"You're luckier than you deserve." Zaira tossed her glove aside, now that the air was safe to breathe, but didn't slow our pace. I had to struggle to keep up. "And Grace of Victory's bloody sword, you're useless."

"Thank you." I seemed to have regained control of my tongue. I had better put it to good use before Zaira disappeared again. "I wasn't sure you were coming back."

She flicked a glare at me. "I almost didn't, Prissyface. I was trying to decide whether to go back to Ignazio's house or run for it when you traipsed past my hiding place, blind as a beggar to the footpad after you. Then I remembered that if you die, I die too, unless I get a new Falconer. So I figured I'd better make sure he didn't kill you."

"I'm sorry I snapped at you. I should give you more credit."

Zaira grunted. "I'm not sorry for anything I said to you. I meant every word of it."

"I know."

A night watchman passed on the far side of the street. He

glanced at us and shook his head in disgust. Mortified, I realized it looked as if I was drunk and Zaira was helping me home.

It was yet another reason to be ashamed. But there were other reasons I could actually do something about.

"Zaira—" I swallowed to wet my throat. "You should know. If the doge orders you to unleash your fire, and you refuse, he'll have you killed. He as much as told me so himself."

For a moment, Zaira was silent. Then she muttered, "That old bastard."

"I'm sorry," I said. "It's not fair."

Zaira glanced at me sidelong. "Please tell me you're not still expecting things to be fair. Even you can't be that stupid."

"Well, no. But I wish they could be."

"Wishes are worthless. You can't even wipe your arse on them."

There was more I needed to tell her. "Another thing, Zaira. Domenic likes you. A great deal."

"No more talking," she grumbled. "Save your strength for walking on your own cursed feet."

But as I pulled away from leaning on her, I could have sworn she squeezed my hand.

By the time we arrived at Ignazio's town house, I had recovered save for a lingering headache. The potion might be powerful, but its effects didn't seem to last.

Beatrix admitted us, fretting as she took my coat, the shadows under her eyes suggesting she would normally have gone to sleep long ago. "My ladies, there's a gentleman waiting for you. I told him the master was abed, but he refused to either wake him or depart."

Before she could finish, Marcello burst into the foyer from the front sitting room, where he'd clearly been waiting. He came straight to me, his face pale, and touched my cheek.

"Amalia! There's blood on your face! Are you all right?"

Alarmed, I raised a hand to my face. The fingertips came away smeared with dark red.

"Calm down. It's not hers." Zaira pulled us toward the sitting room. "Bring the lady something strong," she called to Beatrix. "Three glasses."

It must have been the man Zaira stabbed. I scrubbed at my face with my sleeve. I *did* need a drink.

"What happened?" Marcello demanded.

"Some men tried to kidnap me. Ardentines, by their accents."

"I found them stuffing her into a coffin." Zaira sounded admiring. "Good trick. No one asks why you're dragging a body around."

Marcello swore. "Are you all right? Did they hurt you?"

"No. They tried to knock me out with a potion." I could still faintly smell peppermint in my hair.

Marcello handed me a handkerchief from a pocket of his uniform. I rubbed fiercely at my face.

"I should have gone with you." Anguish twisted Marcello's voice. "I should have—"

"It wasn't your fault. You couldn't have been there. It turned out fine."

Zaira flashed her teeth at him. "We didn't even have to set anyone on fire, more's the pity."

"Thank the Graces you're safe." His arms folded around my shoulders in a swift, fierce hug. Surprise locked every muscle in my body, brittle as glass, but all I wanted was to melt into his chest and forget everything that had happened tonight.

Zaira cleared her throat. "I'll go get a wet cloth. All you did was smear the blood around."

She left. I became painfully, achingly aware we were alone.

Marcello started to release me. But I wrapped my arms around his waist, holding him there. With infinite care, as if I could shatter us both, I laid my head on his shoulder.

I was all but nuzzling his neck. Grace of Love, he smelled good.

His arms settled back into place, shaping themselves to me this time with gentle warmth. "You're really all right," he breathed.

I could lift my mouth to his. It was only the space of a few inches. I could take this terrible day, this miserable situation, and put something good and wonderful in it. I could let my guard down, for once, and not be alone in my jeweled box of a world.

Marcello stroked my hair, his fingers tangling in the curls Beatrix had pressed in for the party. "Why did the Graces make you a Cornaro?" he whispered.

The weight of my name settled over me like a stifling fur cloak. I stepped back, not quite out of his arms, but putting space between us. "So we could save Ardence."

Glass clinked. We moved apart as Beatrix set a tray of drinks down on a gold-inlaid table, her eyes averted. She bobbed a quick curtsy and fled the room, passing Zaira on her way in.

"Time's up, lovebirds," Zaira called. She flung a cloth at me without warning; it smacked cold and wet into my face.

Marcello muttered something into his drink about not being lovebirds. I perched at the edge of a divan and worked on wiping the blood off, glad to bury my face behind the cloth for a moment. Zaira snatched up a glass from the wine tray and dropped into a chair, snickering.

Marcello settled as well, with a deep, steadying breath. "Do you have any idea who tried to kidnap you?"

"The Owl," I remembered.

"Who?" Marcello asked blankly.

"Oh, come on, that joke's too easy," Zaira protested. Then she sat up straight as if a mouse had bitten her. "Wait! An owl! I know I saw an owl."

"An owl?" I certainly didn't recall seeing one.

From her sleeve, Zaira procured a sealed letter. "There! When

Mister Boring and Rude Host kicked us out so he could have his little secret meeting with you, I stole his mail."

I stared. "Zaira, I thought you refused to spy on them."

She shrugged. "He was rude to me. He acted like I didn't exist."

"But...you said you didn't learn anything."

"That's because you were being annoying."

I swallowed several things I might have said. "Fair enough."

Marcello's fists lay white-knuckled in his lap. "What does this have to do with an owl?"

Zaira held out the letter. "Take a look. I can't read the letter, but that much is clear."

I took it. The seal was the imprint of a coin, nothing more. But underneath, someone had crudely sketched a staring owl, its wings spread wide.

"Excellent work, Zaira." I unfolded the letter; the seal was already broken. Elegant, loopy handwriting covered half a page.

"What does it say?" Zaira asked.

"Dear Gabril," I read, "You may put aside these doubts your brother has whispered in your ears; the theft of the children was real, and the Falconers to blame. The official investigation has confirmed it, as has our Raverran Fox. Your cousin the duke still assures me he will not countenance such a crime, and the Fox speaks of dissent within the Council of Nine over the matter. Stay firm. As proof we can prevail, you should soon hear news of a Falconer stopped from taking another Ardentine child. When we combine your courage and passion with our information and resources, Raverra has no power to force Ardence to kneel. Be ready; it is almost time to act." I scanned the bottom of the page. "It's signed 'The Owl in the River Palace.'"

Zaira snorted. "Gabril is an idiot, if he believed all that."

Marcello straightened. "The Owl in the River Palace?"

"That's what it says." I passed him the letter. "Gabril seems to believe he has a well-placed contact there. Whoever it is, they knew about the doge's ultimatum, which Duke Astor hasn't even told the Council of Lords. Either the duke himself is playing a dangerous game or he has a traitor in his inner circle."

"And the men who attacked you were Ardentines." The letter trembled in his hand. "Amalia, the doge could take this as an attack on the Empire by Ardence."

I stared at him. "No. Oh, no. We have two days left."

Zaira grunted. "If that bloody-handed old ghoul is looking for an excuse, he won't care."

"We can't let that happen." I drained half my wineglass. I could use some fortification; I'd had enough shocks tonight.

"He might accept that this is a traitor acting alone, without the duke's knowledge or approval," Marcello said dubiously.

"He might. But the consequences if he doesn't are too dire." I took a deep breath. "We can't tell him about this."

Marcello shifted in his chair. "I'm a lieutenant of the Falconers. I have to report this attack to my superiors."

"You weren't there," I pointed out. "You have nothing to report."

He shook his head. "This is too important."

"Yes, it is." Zaira's eyes burned with suppressed fire. "If you make your report like a good lapdog, and your masters decide one bad apple in Ardence is a good enough reason to set the whole barrel on fire, it'll be too late for second thoughts and sorrys. Once the city is ashes, you can't unburn it."

She didn't seem as confident now as she had when we argued earlier that under no circumstances would she turn her fires on Ardence. But if I'd undermined that certainty, I could take no vindication from it—only shame and dread.

"You don't have to make your report right away," I suggested. "Take your time writing it up. Send it by post rather than over the courier lamps. Whatever will give us more time."

"Time for what?" Marcello asked. "There's nothing more we

can do. We still have an Ardentine traitor at large, trying to start a war—and coming closer to success than we are at stopping them."

"Time to catch them. We have more clues now. Think." I wound a loose coil of hair around my finger, but dropped it with revulsion when I found a speck of dried blood. But it jarred my memory. "One of my would-be kidnappers said something about brats. I think they helped steal the Ardentine nobles' children."

Marcello frowned. "So the same people arranged the taking of the children by the false Falconers, attacked Lemi, tried to kidnap you, and are manipulating these...Ardentine patriots... against Raverra. And the plotters may include someone within the duke's inner circle."

I itched to get up and pace, but my legs still felt shaky. Instead, I picked at the arm of the divan. "Taking the children and attacking Lemi make sense, if they seek to anger both sides and provoke a war. Manipulating Gabril makes sense, too; the Shadow Gentry will whip up anger against Raverra more effectively if they believe what they're saying. But why kidnap me?"

Zaira shrugged. "To stop you from releasing me. It's not much of a war if I just burn down Ardence, is it?"

"Kidnapping me doesn't keep you hooded," I said. "I can release you from miles away. Our plotter has given this scheme a lot of thought and planning. I don't think they'd make such a basic mistake."

Marcello's fists uncurled, puzzlement relaxing the rage in his face. "What *does* happen if they kidnap you, then?"

"My mother kills them." That I knew from experience.

"Well, there you have it." Zaira waved a hand. "They kidnap some Ardentine nobles' brats to bring Ardence into the war. They kidnap you to bring Raverra into the war. Everyone loses their minds and murders each other to get their children back. Our warmonger lives happily ever after. The end."

"Graces preserve us. You're right." I slumped under the

weight of realization. This must be what Baron Leodra had meant, when he said I'd be in danger if I went to Ardence: he'd known they planned to abduct me.

"And Vaskandar takes advantage of our distraction to strike our flank and seize territory while our military attention is focused on Ardence and our support from our client states is in question." Marcello shook his head. "I wish I could say it was a bad plan."

"If it were a bad plan, we'd have stopped it by now."

Marcello spread his hands. "How *do* we stop it? Aside from searching for the children and protecting you, what more can we do?"

I released a long breath. "We need to warn Duke Astor."

The next morning, I woke early, when the gray light blended with grayer shadows to paint my room with a palette of uncertainty. The knowledge that tomorrow was the doge's deadline sat in my stomach like a toad.

I went down to breakfast expecting to find no one else awake save the servants. But as I descended the stairs, I glanced through the parlor to the dining room and spotted Zaira already there, elbows on the table, cradling a cup of coffee. Opposite her an unexpected guest sprawled in his chair, picking the fluffy white center out of a roll with fierce precision: Jerith Antelles. I couldn't hear what he was saying to her, but his expression was more serious than I'd ever seen it, and his voice was low and urgent.

I hesitated at the foot of the stairs, drawing to the side a step to break my line of sight through the parlor. Whatever they were talking about on the morning before Zaira might receive an order to burn down Ardence, I suspected it was a matter between warlocks, and my presence might not be welcome.

"I hope you don't mind a visit so early."

I turned to find Balos behind me. He bent his broad shoulders in a bow of apology.

"Not at all. I'm delighted. What are you doing here?" That last may not have come out as politely as I intended it, but I couldn't fathom how or why these two had appeared in Ignazio's town house, when last I heard they'd been back at the Mews.

Balos chuckled. "We're heading north to visit Jerith's mother for her birthday. Ardence is on the way, so we stayed at the garrison last night. We thought we'd drop by before setting out this morning to say hello."

My eyes flicked toward the dining room. "Just to say hello?"

He sighed, and his voice dropped to a rumbling whisper. "We heard about the deadline tomorrow. Jerith wanted to talk to her."

"Has he ever..." I fidgeted with the lace at my collar. "Has Jerith had to, ah..."

"Not a city, no." Balos's eyes softened to somber brown pools. "But we've seen our share of battle. Probably the worst was a few years back, when a large band of pirates were harassing trade along the Ostan coast. They had their own little navy—a couple dozen ships. When the Serene Empire found the cove they were using as a base, they sent us to wipe them all out." He shook his head. "Storm warlocks get going more slowly than fire warlocks, but for a coastal camp like that, the destruction is just as complete in the end. He raised a hurricane. A lot of the pirates fled inland when they realized what was happening, but plenty of them stayed and died. There wasn't one board left nailed to another once Jerith was done."

I swallowed. "And what did *you* do?"

He caught my eyes. "My job."

"Your job." I considered that. "Being a Falconer isn't my job, Balos."

"I know, Lady Amalia." He gave me an odd, sad smile. "Do you know what yours is?"

That was a good question. I was my mother's heir; one might argue that I didn't have a job at all, yet. I might have given that answer a month ago.

But now I knew better. I was a Cornaro, and there was work to be done.

"To fix things," I said. "To fix all this mess."

Balos lifted his hand, with deliberate gravity, in salute. "You do that, then."

I nodded, my heart quickening as if it anticipated a fight. "I will."

"I'm sorry, my lady." The footman in the River Palace antechamber did seem truly distressed, his nimble fingers rubbing at each other as if friction might prove the solution to our problem. "His Grace is in meetings with his nobles until dinnertime. I've been told not to interrupt. But perhaps tomorrow morning?"

I leaned on the functionary's desk. "The news I have is urgent. It can't wait that long. It's bad enough I left it until this morning." A day and a half left. And that scant grace could vanish if the Ardentines started a fight.

Beside me, Zaira brushed back her hair, and the jess flashed on her wrist. The functionary's face went pale as he realized who she must be. He started stammering incoherently.

Before I could despair of getting any sense out of the man, Lady Savony glided into the antechamber, a bundle of papers in her arms. "Rinald, these require the duke's signature, once he's out of his meetings. Lady Amalia." Her brows arched. "Is something amiss?"

Thank the Graces. If anyone could get me in to see the duke, it was her. "We made a discovery last night that affects the safety of Ardence. For the sake of both our cities, I need to speak to Duke Bergandon."

She lifted her spectacles and regarded me through them, her eyes narrowing. Then she nodded, dropping her papers on the functionary's scriptorium. "Very well. I believe you. Come with me. I will convince His Grace to adjust his schedule."

Lady Savony brought us to the Hall of Victory to wait. This time, there was no array of pastries, which was a shame, as Zaira would certainly have done them justice.

Perhaps ten minutes later, Duke Astor Bergandon strode into the room and flung himself into the chair opposite us, his beard jutting with irritation. Lady Savony entered on his heels, then closed the door and took up a station behind him, notebook and pen in hand.

"This had better be worth it, Savony," the duke grumbled. Then he addressed me. "You have five minutes until I have to get back to Lord Ulmric. Go."

To the point, then. I threw out the careful speech I'd been mentally preparing. "Your Grace, there's a traitor in the palace. One of your own people took the children, and tried to have me kidnapped last night. They're inflaming Raverra and Ardence against each other, trying to start a war."

Lady Savony looked ready to stab someone with her pen. "Who?"

At the same time, Duke Bergandon demanded, "Do you have proof of this?"

"We have evidence enough." I had to be careful; the duke himself could still be involved, and Lady Savony was a suspect as well. I couldn't tell them how I knew until I was sure they were innocent. "I don't know who, yet, though we have clues we can trace. But it's someone within the River Palace. Look among your inner councils for a traitor, Your Grace."

His knuckles whitened on the armrests of his chair. "If this is some attempt by you Raverran eels to make me not trust my own people..."

Zaira let out a bark of a laugh. "Why would Raverra care who you trust?"

The duke's eyes fell on Zaira for the first time. A faint frown creased his brows. Then he spotted the jess.

He leaped to his feet. "You bring *her* in here? Is this a threat? How dare you!"

Zaira wiggled her fingers at him, laughing when he flinched.

"Your Grace! Calm yourself!" I kept my hands folded in my lap, fingers laced tightly together. "Zaira is with me because there was no time to make other arrangements, and I do not flout the law of the Serene Empire. Please, sit down."

He visibly mastered himself, but kept glaring at Zaira. "You have brought a weapon of war into the ducal presence."

Zaira snorted. "If you think I have to be in your presence to kill you, you're sadly mistaken."

Before the duke could explode into outrage, I raised my voice to sever that line of conversation. "Our time is short, Your Grace, and we must keep to the point. I came to warn you of this traitor, and to inform you that unknown parties in your own court are using you, and the missing children, and *all* of us, Your Grace, to start a war."

"And yet—" the duke began.

"The Lady Amalia has no reason to lie to us, Your Grace." Lady Savony's voice cut smoothly across his. "What she says makes sense. I suggest you stop looking to Raverra and Vaskandar for enemies, and search closer to home. You have your opponents in the court; this could be an attempt to overthrow you, as well."

Thank the Graces. She was backing me. "Indeed, Lady Savony. Well said."

"And if you will forgive me, Lady Amalia, your five minutes are more than up." Lady Savony bowed an apology, her spectacles swinging in a neat arc on their golden chain. "Your Grace, while I feel this is more important, Lord Ulmric will become choleric if we leave him much longer."

Duke Astor glowered at her. "Know your place, Steward. Don't answer for me like that."

Lady Savony stiffened. Her notebook snapped shut.

"Despite my steward's interruption, she's right." The duke rose to his feet. Zaira and I followed suit. "I do have to get back to Lord Ulmric. We should continue this discussion on the morrow. In the meantime, I'll think on it, and do my own investigation. I don't much like the idea of a traitor in my court, but I agree it might explain some things. I thank you for bringing this to my attention."

I curtsied. "I only wish to find the truth, Your Grace."

"I hope you do. Until tomorrow, Lady Amalia."

Lady Savony followed him out of the room, dipping a perfunctory curtsy in our direction. By the grim set to her jaw, she understood the full implications of my news, and took it seriously.

With the doge's deadline coming at sunset tomorrow, I could only hope the duke did, as well.

As we passed through the Hall of Beauty on the way out, I spotted Prince Ruven, halfway across the hall, talking to an agitated Gabril Bergandon. The prince seemed relaxed, an amused smile playing across his face; Gabril's chest swelled as if he were on the verge of erupting like Mount Enthalus.

"We should probably see what that's about," I said.

It wasn't hard to get within hearing range. Gabril was all but shouting. We weren't the only people in the Hall of Beauty who'd stopped to listen.

"This is an affront to the dignity of your noble house, and the warm relations Ardence has always claimed with Vaskandar!" Gabril spread his arms, performing for his audience. "That the Empire would *dare* search your rooms, as if you were some common criminal! If they show so little respect for royalty, how can we believe they respect their own people? We cannot tolerate this!"

Ruven patted Gabril on the shoulder as if he were a child who had said something precocious. "Very good. And I wish you luck, my friend. But it matters little to me."

"How can you stand there so calmly, when the Empire's lackeys are running their grubby fingers through your property?" Gabril demanded.

"Because they won't find anything of mine to so mishandle." A smile touched Ruven's lips, his eyes narrowing like a cat's when the cream is long since swallowed. "I meant to tell you, my dear friend—I'm departing Ardence, and for that matter the Empire. I've had a fine visit, but I fear I've outstayed my welcome." His eyes strayed to mine, across the crowd, his mage mark flashing violet. "I may not have everything I wanted, but I have what I came for."

"Surely you won't leave now," Gabril objected. "Not at this critical time, when Ardence needs you to stand strong with us against the Empire."

"I'm sure we'll meet again." Ruven swept him an elaborate bow. "Now, if you'll excuse me, my carriage is packed and on its way. Good day, Lord Gabril."

He turned and wove his way out past the murmuring crowd, leaving Gabril staring after him like an abandoned dog.

"Come on." Zaira tugged at my arm. "I don't like the sound of that."

I didn't, either. *I have what I came for,* Ruven had said.

"Quickly." I spun in the opposite direction. "We need to check the library."

"The *library?* Have you lost your *mind?*"

I didn't wait to reply, but set off running for the Hall of Wisdom. Zaira swore and followed, pushing through a crowd of courtiers still humming with Gabril's outrage and Ruven's departure.

We caught Venasha heading out the library's gilded archway, a book tucked under her arm, weariness circling her eyes.

"Amalia!" She brightened. "I was just heading back to Aleki. What are you—"

"*Interactions of Magic,*" I interrupted her. "Is it still here?"

Venasha blinked. "I assume so."

"Can you check? Quickly?" I all but danced in place. Ruven had said his carriage was on the way; we didn't have much time.

She gave a sharp nod. "Of course. Wait here."

"Why," Zaira asked, biting off each word, "are you haring off after a *book? Now?*"

"Because if Prince Ruven brings it back to Vaskandar, he might be able to use it to trigger eruptions in all the volcanoes of the Witchwall Mountains, turning the border into a wasteland of ash and fire."

"Oh." Zaira's mouth clicked shut. "Carry on, then."

Venasha soon hurried back, her face pale. My heart dropped several stories at her expression. "Venasha, please don't tell me…"

"It would seem Prince Ruven likes erotic poetry." She shook her head, face grim. "It's gone."

Chapter Twenty-Five

I swore.

"Come on." Zaira spun back toward the exit. "It hasn't been that long. We can still catch him, and break his smug jaw."

"Thank you, Venasha." I turned and started a brisk stride toward the palace gates with Zaira. "He said his carriage was on its way. If he was truly planning on leaving the city, the book could be packed in there, if he took it earlier—and volume one almost certainly is."

"You distract him, then," Zaira said. "Keep him away from the coach for as long as you can. I'll get the book."

We stepped out into the brilliant sunlight drenching the Plaza of Six Fountains. On the far side of it, a line of coaches waited to receive visitors to the palace. A black carriage, carved in smooth, asymmetric curves, stood among them, like a crow among doves, emblazoned on its side with the crowned tree of Vaskandar.

Prince Ruven was halfway across the plaza, heading for his coach, purpose in his stride and something tucked under his arm.

I didn't wait to see what Zaira would do. I hurried to intercept him, petticoats rustling. Why did I always run into Ruven when I was laced into some completely impractical gown?

"Prince Ruven!" I called.

He stopped and turned. The smile that spread across his features was taut with malice.

"Lady Amalia," he greeted me. "Such fortune, to meet you here. I was concerned I might miss my chance to bid you good-bye."

I'd caught up to him. I realized I had no plan for what to say to keep him distracted, and no idea how much time Zaira would need. "You seem ready enough to leave. Have you been planning this for a while?"

"My departure?" He spread his arms modestly. "I am no self-sacrificing hero, Lady Amalia. I can read the wind well enough to know which way the fire is blowing. I have no desire to be in Ardence when it burns to the ground."

I stared. His gesture had revealed the object he carried, without any apparent attempt to hide it: *Interactions of Magic, Volume Two*.

"You stole that book," I accused.

"This?" He glanced at it with exaggerated surprise, as if seeing it for the first time. "I'd forgotten I was holding it."

I drew myself up. "That book belongs to the Ducal Library. If you would not demean your royal blood with the shame of thievery, Prince Ruven, prove yourself a gentleman and give it back."

I held out my hand. He cocked his head, examining me as if I were some curious creature on display in a menagerie. Then he sighed, with exaggerated pathos. "It pains me that you hold me in such low esteem, Lady Amalia. Very well." To my shock, he held out the book. "If this will repair my standing in your estimation, by all means. Take it."

I reached for it. My fingers gripped the leather cover, keeping carefully away from his.

And they froze there. I could no more release the book than I could stomp a hole through the plaza flagstones.

Ruven chuckled. "Leather is also skin, my lady. It makes an effective bridge of flesh, does it not?"

The swarming tingle of his magic spread up my hand and past my wrist, numbing my arm to the elbow.

"What," I asked through my teeth, "do you think this will accomplish?"

"I had hoped we could be allies, Lady Amalia, and perhaps more. But I can see now it is not to be." He shook his head in apparent regret. "Despite my regard for you, circumstance has made us enemies. And if you are my enemy, why should I not kill you now?"

A line of ants seemed to crawl up every vein in my arm, toward my heart. I still couldn't pull away from the book.

He respected power; I must not show fear. "Because if you kill me, you start a war."

Ruven's smile broadened into pure, brilliant joy. "With this book, we will be ready for a war."

"It's the middle of the plaza, in broad daylight. There are a hundred witnesses."

Ruven shrugged. "None of whom are close enough to stop me, or even see anything amiss. I'm already leaving the Empire. It pleases me if they know I can kill."

"I could release my fire warlock." The moment the words left my mouth, I regretted them. He must not wonder where Zaira was.

But he seemed cheerfully unconcerned. "Good! Maybe she'll burn half the city, and someone will put her down. If Vaskandar cannot have a fire warlock, we certainly don't want Raverra to have one."

A heat started from within my arm, as if someone had slid shards of hot metal in through my wrist. I gritted my teeth.

"I can melt your bones, you know, and keep you standing still and quiet the entire time," Ruven said conversationally. "I can rot you from the inside out, and no one will know we aren't having a lovely discussion about this book. Or I can simply stop your heart." He patted my hand where it lay on the book's cover. "So you see, in the end, for all you bear the great and terrible name of Cornaro, you are after all only one woman. You are no match for me, who bears the mage mark and wields power over everything you are."

He was done with the conversation. I could hear it in his voice. In another moment, he would kill me.

I should have been terrified. But his words triggered something deep in my mind.

He was *wrong*. I knew it as surely as I'd known when one of my professors put an incorrect calculation on the wall slate.

"No," I said. "I am not only one woman."

Ruven checked whatever fatal word he had been about to utter. He tilted his head in mild curiosity. "Oh?"

I smiled back at him, and it was a killing smile. "I am the Empire."

I had always wondered what it was that surrounded my mother with such palpable force. What let her sweep into a room full of a hundred people and silence it without saying a word. What made her invulnerable, beyond reach as the Graces themselves, such that her enemies tried to hurt me in desperation because they knew they could not touch her.

Now I felt it rising up in me like lagoon water at high tide. *Serenity.*

"My footsteps echo with the tread of legions." I locked his eyes with mine. "My breath is the wind that fills the sails of armadas."

The prickling heat stopped spreading up my arm. The confident sneer on Ruven's face faltered.

"The whispers of a thousand spies fill my ears with all your petty plans. And my eyes bear the mage mark of hundreds of Falcons." I stepped toward him. "You stand within my dominion.

Even if you kill me, it doesn't matter. You can't outrun my courier lamps. Scores of my miles stand between you and the border, and dozens of my fortresses. I am the Empire, and I will destroy you."

Ruven took half a step back. Then he checked himself. For a long moment, he was silent, watching, assessing.

Then he laughed. "Oh, very well."

He released the book. Its full weight dropped into my hand; I barely caught it. My arm was my own again.

"I've learned enough from that thing." He waved dismissively at the book. "I don't need it anymore. And I suppose you're interesting enough to live a while longer."

He turned toward his carriage. "Look to your borders, O Lady of the Empire," he called back over his shoulder. "You may soon find your legions and armadas and Falcons are not enough."

I stared after him. The sense of power that had filled me drained out again, leaving me empty and shaken. I wondered if this was how Zaira felt, when the balefire left her.

Zaira. For all I knew, she was still in the coach. I started toward it, heart leaping halfway up my throat.

But Prince Ruven's footman had already handed him in. The door with its Vaskandran crest clunked shut. The driver flicked the reins, and the horses began to move.

There was no sign of Zaira as the coach drove away.

I crossed to where it had been, staring stupidly at the empty street. Another coach pulled up to fill the space, letting off a young courtier with her hair piled high in the Loreician style, worked with fruit and flowers.

"Over here," Zaira called.

I turned and saw her sitting on the rim of one of the six fountains. The Grace of Bounty danced with naked children in bronze behind her, water pouring from jars they carried. The skirts of Zaira's court dress spread around her. She looked ready for a picnic, not a theft.

I approached, with some anxiety. The hands she braced on the rim of the fountain at her sides were empty.

"Did you get the book?" I asked her.

Zaira shrugged. "Well, I can't read. So I don't know."

Impatience struggled in my breast like a kite trying to break free of its string. I sighed. "Did you get *any* book?"

"Not any book, no." Zaira grinned, and pulled aside her skirts, displaying a corner of the leather-bound chest they covered. "To be safe, I grabbed *all* of them."

I couldn't stop myself. I grabbed her bony shoulders in a quick hug. "You're brilliant."

"Ugh. What are you, a dog? Get off me." But she was smiling as she pushed me away. "And I know I'm brilliant. Took you long enough to realize it."

Back at Ignazio's town house, we opened the trunk. I lifted out the books one by one onto the dining room table. Marcello, who had joined us on his way back to the garrison after meeting with Lady Terringer, sorted them by apparent owner. Some had library marks on them, or bookplates from a private collection; others might have been purchased honestly. But they all had one thing in common.

"*Battle Magic of Ancient Osta . . . Advancements in Naval Artifice . . .* and here's Domenic's book." I set *Interactions of Magic, Volume One* aside from the others, to return to him. "These are all books containing war magic. Recipes for death and destruction."

Zaira whistled. "Good thing I grabbed them all, then, isn't it?"

Marcello turned a book over, peering at the title. "*Castles, Fortifications, and Defensive Wards.* Some of these might give him ideas for how to overcome the Empire's protections."

"So it's not just the volcano." Zaira poked a book as if expecting it to bite her. "Your Vaskandran friend went on a literary shopping spree to study up so he could make war on an Empire full of Falcons."

"Some of this knowledge is dangerous." Marcello picked up a copy of *Death Magic: Lethal Alchemy and Mortal Artifice.* "How much of this does he carry in his memory? Should we…" He swallowed. "Can we in good conscience let him take that memory across the border?"

"You mean assassinate him," I said flatly.

"I volunteer." Zaira raised her hand. "If there was ever a face I wanted to light on fire, it's his."

It was probably just as well I hadn't told her he'd as much as admitted to hiring Orthys. "It's not our job to assassinate people. We can report what happened to the doge and the Council, and if they want to have him killed before he reaches the border, they'll do it."

Marcello sighed and sank into a dining room chair. "I can't see him settling down and causing us no more trouble. Much as I personally dislike the idea, I think the colonel would say this is our chance to make sure he isn't a problem in the future."

"I'm not sure my mother would agree." I eyed the pile of dangerous books. "I don't doubt we'll hear more from Ruven. But killing him has consequences, too. His father wouldn't be pleased. And Ruven is at least a known quantity. I understand him now, I think. If he dies, we have no idea who or what takes his place."

"Nothing good." Marcello rubbed his temples. "And Graces forbid the attempt fails, and he escapes, with that mind full of poisonous snakes fixed on vengeance."

"So you're going to let him go." Zaira slouched into a chair, exhausted disgust in the lines of her limbs.

"Of course we are. We're not murderers," I said. "Whether the Council of Nine lets him go is another matter."

"They're *definitely* a bunch of murderers." Zaira brightened.

"Maybe they'll put his head on a pike, as a warning to others. Then I could still set his face on fire."

"You don't like him much, do you?"

"Ugh, no." She shuddered. "Besides, he was a bastard to Aleki."

"I feel better with him out of the picture, at least." Marcello started stacking the books neatly. "No more Vaskandran inter-ference. Just home-grown Ardentine treachery."

"Oh, I'm sure he's still got plenty of fingers in the Ardentine pie." I dropped into the chair next to Marcello. "A shame you didn't find the jess in his coach, Zaira."

"It wasn't there. I looked."

"If he didn't take it, we need to find out who did, and quickly. But we don't have much in the way of leads left. Except…" I straightened, remembering. "Lady Savony gave me a list of people who might have information. I still haven't talked to all of them."

I fished the folded paper out of my dagger sheath and smoothed it out on the table. Her list of names in elegant, loopy handwriting stared up at me.

There was something familiar about that writing. The curl of the *L*'s, the way she dotted her *I*'s with a slash… "Do you still have that letter, Marcello? The one from the Owl?"

Marcello blinked. "I think it might still be in my coat." He rummaged in his pocket for a moment, then pulled it out. "Sorry, it got a bit crumpled."

I spread it out on the table next to Savony's list of names. The similarity was unmistakable.

"Hells," I said. "This is Savony's handwriting."

Chapter Twenty-Six

Of course. Lady Savony had the access to the duke, the resources, and the knowledge of Ardence necessary to have executed this scheme. She had the organizational skills, the intelligence, the purpose, and the drive to be behind it. I'd even seen her talking to Baron Leodra, back at the Ardentine Embassy in Raverra. How she thought this situation would end well for Ardence, I couldn't imagine—but that just meant there was more to her plan than we knew.

This plot isn't what you think it is, Leodra had said.

Marcello leaned over the letter. "Grace of Mercy. Are you sure?"

"I can't be positive." I scanned the wrinkled pages. "But it certainly looks that way."

Zaira put her feet up on another chair and lounged with her hands behind her head. "Then tell the duke his loyal bitch is a traitor."

"Would he believe you?" Marcello asked, frowning.

"Probably not," I admitted. "Even if we show him the letter, whom will he trust: the woman who's been his voice and hands all these years or the enemies who want to burn his city? We could have a signed confession from her, and he'd still probably listen to her over us."

"We can't just ignore this." Marcello started to pace.

"Maybe if we could connect her to the missing children." I worried at a rough spot on my armrest. "Finding them is still the key, both to rescue them and to convince the Ardentine court."

Zaira shrugged. "So follow her."

"Follow Lady Savony?"

"No, the kitchen maid." Zaira rolled her eyes. "Of course I meant the gray harpy. She knows you're getting close, right? But you didn't give away you knew it was her."

"Only because I didn't realize it at the time."

"Yes, because you're so hopeless at subterfuge you have to take lessons from an illiterate fire warlock. But the point is, when someone's worried about getting caught, the first thing they do is check all their loose ends." She walked her fingers on her palm in a parody of frantic running about. "As soon as the duke lets her out of the palace, you can bet your ruddy life she'll scurry around meeting with all her people, cracking the whip at our funerary friends from last night, and checking on the little lost brats. Buttoning everything down tight."

Marcello rubbed his chin. "That's not a bad idea. I'll get some soldiers to—"

"No," Zaira interrupted. "Good Graces, not more of your pathetically obvious soldiers. They'd get caught, for sure. I'll do it."

"You can't go out in the city alone."

"I'll bring her." Zaira jerked a thumb at me. "If I have to. But no more. If we start a parade, she'll notice."

Marcello shook his head. "That would put the Lady Amalia in danger."

I straightened. "Lieutenant Verdi, you have many admirable qualities, but your overprotectiveness is not one of them."

He blinked as if I'd slapped him. "But there are kidnappers after you."

"And Zaira has proven herself capable of dealing with them."

I wished I could say the same about myself. My cheeks burned, but I pressed on. "I'm not going to stay cooped up in this town house like...like..."

"Like a bird in a mews?" Zaira's eyes gleamed with a hard light.

"Well, yes. And more to the point, Zaira is the only one with the skills to do this, and if she goes, I have to go with her."

"I don't like it." Marcello's shoulders drooped. "But you're right. It has to be done."

I took his hand and squeezed it. "I'll be careful."

He brushed my fingers with his thumb, worry shadowing his face. My hand warmed like a solar circle.

When we got back to Raverra, I'd have to keep him at a distance again. The knowledge cut at my insides as if I'd swallowed broken pottery.

I turned to Zaira, before I could do anything foolish. "So, how do we follow without her noticing?"

Zaira sighed. "Graces have mercy. I'll teach you. I'm a pickpocket, after all."

The first thing I learned about following someone was that it's dreadfully tedious when they're not going anywhere.

"There must be some better way to do this," I burst out at last, after three straight hours of finding various excuses to dawdle in the Plaza of Six Fountains in front of the River Palace with Zaira. There was still no sign of Lady Savony; but then, we could have missed her if she had departed the palace by a secondary entrance, or if the crowds of the plaza had blocked her from view.

Zaira rummaged in a large sack she'd brought along. "Absolutely. Go ask your mamma to loan us a dozen spies, and have them do it for us."

"That would take days to arrange. And we don't know whom we can trust, anyway."

"Well, then you'll survive doing a day's work for a change."

I wished we had Marcello with us, despite Zaira's objections. He'd gone to the garrison, to send a message to the doge over the courier lamps updating him on our discoveries. He'd decided to keep it to facts for now, leaving our speculations out of it until we had more information.

Finally, Zaira spotted Lady Savony striding across the Plaza of Six Fountains, heading north toward the river.

"Here, carry this." Zaira stuffed her sack into my arms. It wasn't heavy—soft and light, in fact, as if full of cloth—but it was awkward.

"Why me? What is this, anyway?" I asked as we hurried after our quarry.

"Because otherwise your movements and posture will scream *I'm being sneaky.* This way, all they can say is *I'm carrying something.*" Her sidelong glance laughed at me. "It's like sticking sweets in a brat's mouth so he can't say anything stupid."

"I see you've thought of everything," I grumbled. But she was right; I couldn't overthink acting casual, because I was too worried about how to hold the lopsided sack without dropping it.

Zaira had planned this out surprisingly well, considering she'd only had an hour to prepare. After several minutes of following a good distance behind Lady Savony, she pulled a couple of hats out of the bag and told me to sling it over my shoulder.

"To change your silhouette," she explained. "In case she's noticed us."

The first place Lady Savony stopped was Gabril's town house. I supposed I shouldn't be surprised. Fortunately, there was a small tavern across the street, and Zaira and I sat at a table in the window sipping wine and nibbling meat pies while Lady Savony paid her call.

Zaira glanced out at the street and grunted. "I was half worried Lieutenant Lover Boy would try to tail us, but it looks like we're clean."

"He wouldn't do that. He trusts us."

"He trusts *you*, you mean."

"No. Well, yes, but he doesn't trust me to stay out of trouble. He trusts *you* to protect me."

"Huh." Zaira settled back in her chair and chewed that over. "It's true he would've assumed I'd cut your throat and throw you in the Arden a few weeks ago. Maybe he finally passed that pike up his arse."

That might well be the most flattering thing she'd ever said about Marcello. I was at a loss for a response, so I watched Gabril's door out the window in silence for a moment. Still no sign of Lady Savony.

"We're lucky she didn't take a coach," I said.

"A coach?" Zaira snorted. "She's not that stupid. The driver would know everywhere she's been, and she'd stand out too much. And besides, I'd lay odds she'll visit streets too narrow for a coach before the day is done."

"I wonder what she's talking about with Gabril."

Zaira didn't swallow before replying, and I was treated to a view of masticated meat pie. "Well, what would you do if your scheme was at risk?"

"Move to the next step. Push the plan along until it's too late to stop it." I stared at the ornate carvings over Gabril's door as if they might hold answers. "She's probably making sure the Ardentines are riled up enough right now. Then she only has to do something to force Raverra over the edge into war."

That was the one part I still didn't understand: why did she want a war? Did she truly believe Vaskandar would help Ardence win its independence? Was it some power play to regain the ducal throne her ancestors had lost? Leodra's warning tumbled in my head like a spinning coin; I couldn't guess if it would come up heads or tails, and the fate of the Empire might depend on me winning the bet.

Zaira poked me with her fork, drawing my attention back to her. "We already know their plan for setting off Raverra."

"Oh?"

"Kidnapping you."

The meat pie lay heavy in my stomach. She was right.

And if I wasn't careful, I might follow Lady Savony straight into their hands.

When Lady Savony emerged from Gabril's town house, she wore a purposeful expression. When we emerged from the tavern, we wore different jackets, courtesy of Zaira's bag.

The streets we traveled became narrower and dirtier as we followed Lady Savony to less attractive quarters of the city. Soon she looked quite out of place, with her fine gray gown and golden spectacles; the people we passed eyed her with dubious calculation. Zaira and I had donned tradesmen's clothes for the occasion, and blended in well enough, at least to my unskilled eye.

"Get rid of the bag," Zaira muttered at one point, glancing around warily.

"What? But it has our disguises in it."

"They're not *disguises*. And I don't want anyone thinking we have something in there worth stealing."

She took the sack from me, and at the next opportunity tossed it into an alley that reeked of garbage. I supposed someone would find it and consider the clothes a windfall.

When Lady Savony entered a dingy alchemist's shop, Zaira hurried straight past it. I had no choice but to follow.

"She went in that shop." I stopped myself from pointing.

"I know. But we can't walk right in after her, idiot."

Zaira took us around a corner, waited a moment, and then strolled us back past the shop again. She stopped a good distance beyond it to lean against a wall, take off her boot, and inspect it most thoroughly for stones. While she poked around, I wondered whether this alchemist was the source of the peppermint potion.

"Stop staring at the shop door, for love of the Graces," Zaira grumbled.

Lady Savony didn't tarry inside for long. Shortly after she emerged, two rough-looking men left the shop in the opposite direction, toward us—including one with a familiar broken nose.

"Keep your head down," Zaira hissed. I stooped to check the sole of my boot, for lack of a better idea, my heart pounding. I didn't dare breathe until they passed us by.

"I can guess where *they're* going," Zaira muttered. "I'd watch out for dark alleyways when you head home tonight. Come on, before we lose sight of her."

Soon we were on our way to streets of less dubious character. Dinnertime was almost upon us, as my stomach reminded me; merchants and artisans crowded the streets, heading home or to their favorite hostelry. They hid us from Lady Savony, but also made it harder to keep her in sight.

The streets were in full shadow by the time Lady Savony stopped at the plain wooden door to a brick warehouse. She unlocked it and stepped inside, like a simple merchant going to inspect her goods.

Once the door closed behind her, Zaira stopped in the street. The warehouse had no windows in this wall, so we had no fear of being spotted.

"What do you suppose she's doing in there?" I asked, shifting from foot to foot. As the sky darkened, I began to doubt the wisdom of being out in the city when armed scoundrels were looking for me. Zaira was a formidable ally, if she chose to be, but they'd had time to think of ways to deal with her.

Zaira frowned at the warehouse door. "I don't know. When she leaves, we should go in and find out."

"But how will we get in? It's locked."

Zaira lifted an eyebrow. Without a single word, she gave me to understand that even though my naiveté had ceased to astonish her long ago, I still found new ways to disappoint her.

My face warmed. "Very well, so you can get us in. But what if someone's in there?"

"Then we try not to be seen. And if we're seen, you shut up and let me bluff. Come on. We don't want her to spot us when she comes out."

Zaira tucked us into an alley across the street. I hoped my friend with the broken nose wasn't similarly ensconced across from Ignazio's town house; I'd already be late taking my elixir. If we stayed out much longer, I'd have to use my three-hours'-grace vial.

"After this, I need to get back to the town house," I murmured to Zaira.

"We'll lose her when we investigate the warehouse anyway." She sighed. "I hope we don't miss something good. But at least you have your confirmation she's the Owl."

Zaira kept her eyes locked on the door across the street. They sparkled with life and excitement, and color flushed her cheeks. She looked healthier than when I'd first met her—less painfully thin, though she'd never be anything but skinny—and her hair had a rich gloss to it.

It would be easy to tell myself I'd done the right thing, putting the jess on her. But she'd never had a choice.

"Thank you, by the way," I said softly. "For helping me with this."

She shrugged. "It's more fun than sitting around some boring rich-people house all day."

"Are you happy, then?"

She turned to face me, surprise arching her brows. "Happy? What kind of a question is that?"

"Well...I want you to be happy." I hated the stiff awkwardness of my voice. But I held her eyes, willing her to see I meant it.

After a moment, a bemused laugh burst its way through her lips. "Only idiots and dogs are ever *happy*. But I'm enjoying myself."

She returned to watching the door. I wasn't sure what to say to that, so I watched with her.

When Lady Savony emerged, a frown of distaste was creasing her brow. She hurried off down the dusky street in the direction of the River Palace, shaking her head. We waited until she'd been gone for several minutes, then strolled over to the warehouse door.

Zaira eyed the lock. "Stand so you're blocking me from view in case anyone comes down the street. If you do see someone, don't jump around like an idiot. Just tell me quietly."

She reached up and pulled pins out of her hair. They weren't normal hairpins, but had hooks at the end. I positioned myself as best I could as she crouched down and got to work.

"Oh, this is easy. Ardence should have more pride." In less than half a minute, Zaira stood, slipping the pins back into her hair.

"It's unlocked?"

"No, I'm just fixing my hair. Of course it's unlocked." She dropped her voice. "Now, move as silently as you can in there, but don't tiptoe or skulk around. If someone sees you skulking, it'll be far worse than if you act like you belong."

She laid her ear to the door for a moment. Then she eased it open and stepped through.

I followed her into a dull, bare corridor. A few oil lamps burned in sconces on the lefthand wall; round mirrors on the righthand wall doubled the light. Zaira pulled the door softly shut behind us. She started forward, her feet making no sound.

Something about the mirrors bothered me. Round, like eyes...

"Wait," I hissed, snagging a handful of Zaira's hair.

She spun and glared at me, but I pointed to the mirrors. Runes circled them, carved into the wooden frames. Artifice runes.

Zaira shook her head, stepping back to my side. "I don't know anything about magical protections," she whispered. "No one was rich enough to have those in the Tallows."

I squinted at the runes. It was dim enough they were hard to make out. "We can't block the light. If we interrupt the path of the light and it fails to strike the mirror, we set off a trap."

"What happens then?"

"I don't know. Let's not find out." I bent double, keeping well below the mirrors, and made my way down the corridor. Zaira followed.

The door at the end of the corridor was new, the wood raw and unfinished save for another runic circle daubed on with black paint.

"What's this all about?" Zaira asked nervously.

I considered the runes. "The door won't open unless you press the key to the circle."

Zaira sighed. "Curse it. That's why the lock was so easy."

I bit my lip, mentally tracing the lines of the circle. I muttered the runes under my breath.

"Can you do something about it?" Zaira asked. "Is there a trick to it, like with the mirrors?"

"Maybe."

I will open only with the key, the runes said. But the spell had been slapped up in a hurry and without much thought. I suspected an untrained artificer, without enough power for the mage mark. They'd drawn the circle too large; the runes straggled loosely around it. My teachers would never have allowed slipshod work like this.

With an artifice circle, the runes dictated the rules of the magic, just as the golden wire and beads on Zaira's jess defined the laws of the spell that bound us together. But with a circle this weak and sloppy, those rules could be rewritten.

"Do you have any ink, or charcoal?" I asked Zaira.

"Why would I carry that around?"

"Because it's useful." I glanced around the corridor, but didn't see anything I could write with. "I suppose I'll have to use blood."

"What?!" Zaira drew back as if I might want hers.

I unsheathed my dagger and nicked a fingertip. Carefully, with lines more precise than the artificer's messy scrawl, I traced new runes in one of those large, sloppy gaps in the circle. I squeezed my finger a few times to force out more crimson drops as needed.

I will open only without the key.

Simple. Smiling, I pulled out my handkerchief, wiped both the dagger and my finger, and sheathed the former. "That should do it."

"What did you do?"

"Magic," I said.

I opened the door.

The room beyond was high and empty. Faint, gray light angled down from narrow windows twenty feet off the floor, illuminating a dusty space. The storeroom was big enough to use for a riding ring, but only a few crates, piled in the corner, occupied it now. Water stains on the stone floor trailed to a round drain in the center of the room, suggesting a leaky roof, or perhaps a former cloth-dyeing workshop.

"No one here," Zaira whispered. With slow, careful steps, she started toward the crates.

Something moved in the drain. Worms. White worms, lifting and wriggling. I stifled a scream.

No. Not worms. Fingers.

Small, pale fingers, reaching through the drain grating, curling around the metal grille.

Chapter Twenty-Seven

Zaira," I gasped. "Oh, Graces. Look."

She did, and swore.

"Hello?" A child's voice came from the hollow drain. "Is someone there?"

I crossed swiftly to the round grille. Two sets of little fingers pulled at the bars now. Large eyes stared up at me from pale, pinched faces. My stomach lurched.

"You're not the one who feeds us." Hope entered the clear, high voice of the little girl gripping the bars. She couldn't be more than eight. A boy with a smudged face squeezed next to her, younger still, and more crowded in, their faces in shadow. I couldn't tell how many.

"Are you here to rescue us?" the boy asked. "Is it time?"

I knelt down by the drain and reached out a trembling hand to touch the cold fingers that reached up to me.

"How can I get you out of there?" I breathed.

"There's a cellar down here." The girl waved off to the side, past the others. "It had a door, and they brought us in through it. But they bricked it up. Now they pass us food through the grating, in pieces."

"Zaira," I called softly. "Can you get this open?"

She didn't respond. I turned. She stood with both her fists over her mouth, her eyes wide with horror.

"Zaira!"

She shook herself like a wet dog and approached the drain.

"I can't get that open without tools." Her voice came out strangled. "We'll have to come back."

"She said it would be a *man* who rescued us," the little boy said, his voice quavering. "You're both girls."

"Who said that?" I asked. "The lady who was just here?"

"Yes. The one with the gray mask."

A Shadow Gentry mask. Perhaps she kept it in the crates.

A scuffling sounded in the drain.

"Quit pushing!"

"I want to see!"

"Are you going to let us out? Is it time?"

I tried to reach through the grille, but couldn't fit more than my fingers. Small hands flicked up to touch them, one after another; one little fist curled around my thumb. My eyes stung, and I had to swallow to speak.

"The lady in the mask told you a man would rescue you?"

Tiny bodies pressed in tight around the little girl now, and half a dozen pairs of eyes stared up at me, but she clung to her place in the center. "Yes. She told us that soon, when the time is right, a man will come rescue us, and return us to our parents. But we have to wait."

"What man?"

"She didn't say."

"Did she tell you anything else?"

Nods stirred the shadows below. "Yes," a boy said. "A name."

"She tells us over and over to remember the name of the one who kidnapped us," the girl confirmed.

"I'm sick of it," a thin, strong voice cried from the back. "I don't care about the name. I want to go home."

"You will," I promised. "We don't have the tools to open this now, but I swear we'll be right back. We'll get you out."

More fingers touched mine, clinging. Smiles stretched their pale faces. I couldn't stand to see the hope lighting their haunted eyes.

"What's the name she told you to remember?" I asked.

"Gabril Bergandon," they chorused, as if in school.

I stared into the drain. The shadows deepened as the last gray light faded from the sky; it was getting harder to see their faces. "Gabril?"

"She told us a hundred times," the child in the back complained. "I hate that name."

"I think she's lying," the girl said.

"You're a smart girl," I said. "She is."

So that's what Lady Savony wanted with Gabril and the Shadow Gentry. To get Ardence up in arms against Raverra, and then use them as scapegoats.

"We need to go." Zaira grabbed my arm. "Every moment we stay here is a moment we could get caught, and then no one will save these brats. We need to get the Hells out of here, grab your soldier boy and some tools, and get back here to put an end to this."

"What's your name?" I asked the little girl.

"Jaslyn."

"Mine's Padric!" the boy called.

"I'm Mirelle!" another cried. And more names, running over each other, until I couldn't hold them all. More than a dozen.

"I'm Amalia," I said. "I swear to you, on my life, we'll return as quickly as we can to get you out of here."

"Don't go!" a voice cried from the drain, like a needle through my heart.

"She has to," Jaslyn whispered. "You heard. They're going to go get tools, and come back to set us free."

"Yes. I promise, we'll be right back."

"If that masked bitch shows up, or the louse who feeds you,

don't tell them we were here," Zaira commanded. "Act like nothing strange happened, or they might hide you somewhere else so we can't find you. Got it, brats?"

In the darkness below, pale blurs of faces nodded.

"We won't forget."

"Hurry back!"

"I want to go home!"

"You will," I promised.

Pulling my hand away from those grasping fingers was worse than sticking it into a fire. I stood and turned, hating every movement that took me away from them. Hating myself for leaving them behind.

"Come on," Zaira growled. "Let's get them out of there. And then I want you to release me, so I can burn this place down."

I couldn't bring myself to disagree.

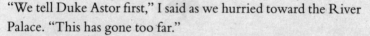

"We tell Duke Astor first," I said as we hurried toward the River Palace. "This has gone too far."

Luminaries glowed at the doors of the wealthy, coming awake with the departure of the sun; candles and lamps flickered golden in the windows of the middle class. All the lively sounds of evening lifted into the air: the talk and laughter of people at dinner, the trill of music from an open tavern. Aromas of meat cooking in herbs and wine made my stomach growl. But none of this life and light could banish the circle of darkness in my heart, from which huge eyes stared up, waiting hopefully.

"Best get to the duke before the Owl bitch does," Zaira agreed. "And I only give you even odds of making it to your uncle's house. Our minty friends are bound to be waiting for you there."

"Maybe the duke will let me use his courier lamps to send a message to the doge while we're at the palace." Though I couldn't tarry too long. I was fine for now, but my elixir couldn't wait in the back of my wardrobe all night.

"Are you sure His Pointy-Bearded Grace isn't in on this? If he is, going to the palace is a huge mistake."

"I don't think he is." We hurried across the River Arden on an old stone bridge, between rows of shops closed up for the night. "He's not subtle enough, frankly. And if it was his scheme, Lady Savony would have been able to leave the River Palace much earlier today, and we wouldn't have had to wait outside for so long."

"I suppose if the duke wanted a war, he wouldn't need to push and manipulate people into it like a matchmaking grandmother," Zaira conceded. "He could just start it himself. Still, if we have to burn our way out, I'm ready."

I raised my brows in disbelief. "Yes, a fire warlock rampaging through the River Palace is exactly what this delicate situation needs."

Zaira grinned in a manner I did not find at all reassuring.

The guards at the palace gates admitted us upon hearing the name Cornaro. We passed through the Hall of Beauty and climbed the grand staircase to the ducal apartments with an inexorable purpose no servant or functionary dared challenge, despite our tradesmen's clothes.

At the top of the staircase, we faced an antechamber full of guards and footmen. The same timid functionary from my previous visit approached us, hands fluttering, eyeing Zaira with alarm.

"I need to see the duke immediately," I told him. "Where is he?"

"Ah, His Grace has retired to his chambers, my lady."

I drew myself up, attempting to recapture the serene confidence I'd used to face down Ruven earlier. "My business is urgent. The fate of Ardence itself may depend upon the news I bear. I must speak with the duke."

I had the attention of the entire room, now. The guards, more ornamental than functional in their gold uniforms, stood at attention. The footmen whispered to each other behind their hands.

The functionary swallowed, then bowed. "Very well, my lady. One moment. I will ask whether he can see you."

He passed the doors that led into the ducal apartments, sending one last nervous glance over his shoulder. I held myself still, refraining from bouncing with nervous energy only with a great effort. The guards watched us, not with suspicion but as a cat stares at a fluttering leaf out the window.

The silence in the antechamber stretched on. I had the feeling at least a couple of the footmen had been about to head off to dinner but now felt they couldn't until we were gone. One finally straightened as if he'd remembered a vital errand and strode off with exaggerated purpose; another wistfully watched him go.

Finally, the functionary returned. He greeted us with a deep bow. "His Grace will see you in the Hall of Victory, my lady." A footman opened the door for me that led to the Hall of Bounty, the first of several audience chambers in the ducal apartments.

Luminaries glowed on the walls and in the ceiling of the Hall of Bounty, lighting the opulent carvings and frescoes and lending a soul to the faces of the dark oil paintings hanging in gilded frames on the walls. But the room itself stood quiet and empty. The footman shut the door behind us, leaving us alone. I hesitated, but Zaira strode across to the far door, her boots ringing on the marble floor. "Which one is the Hall of Victory? The next one?"

"The last one," I said.

We passed through the Hall of Bounty to the Hall of Majesty, where the glory of the Bergandons lingered in the baroque ornamentation of their gilded throne hall. Portraits of great Bergandon dukes of the past stared down at us from the shadowed walls, disapproving of upstart Raverra holding sovereignty over their city.

One last door led to the final chamber, the Hall of Victory. I pushed it open myself.

The duke waited for us there, after a fashion. But he would no longer be seeing anybody. And he was not alone.

Lady Savony stood in the center of the room, a dagger in her hand.

Duke Astor Bergandon sprawled at her feet, his golden doublet stained with fresh blood.

Chapter Twenty-Eight

Y̶ou've forced my hand, Amalia Cornaro."

Lady Savony tossed the bloody dagger at my feet. It skittered across the marble floor, coming to rest against my boot. "Murderer."

"You killed him." The words forced themselves disbelievingly out of my throat. I sounded like a simpleton, but I couldn't help myself—any more than I could look away from poor Astor Bergandon, lying twisted on the floor, staring with dead eyes at the ceiling fresco of the Grace of Victory with her flaming sword. "You were his voice and hands, and you killed him."

"Because of you. He would have denounced me as a traitor; I can't have that. Instead, he'll die a martyr, murdered by a Falconer of Raverra."

"Let's make a complete set." Zaira drew her dagger. "*You* can die murdered by a Falcon."

Before I could shake off my shock, Zaira leaped at Lady Savony, her knife flashing. She crashed into the taller woman, and the two staggered into a marble-topped table.

"Release me!" Zaira cried. "Let me burn her!"

I drew my own dagger. "No. That would only seal our guilt."

Lady Savony cried out as Zaira's knife found her arm, blood blooming on her sleeve. With surprising strength, she tossed

Zaira aside; Zaira landed in a cluster of chairs, bringing two of them down with her.

"Excellent." Lady Savony regarded her bleeding arm. "This will lend me extra credence. Thank you."

She sprang into a run, fleeing into the Hall of Majesty, calling, "Guards! Guards! Murder!"

Zaira scrambled to her feet, swearing. "Run! Before the whole palace is after us."

She dashed out the far door. I followed, panic harrying my steps. We burst through another opulent chamber, then veered right into a room filled with clerks' desks and papers. Zaira flung open the window, which looked out over sprawling gardens.

"We've got to jump." Chill night air flowed through the window as she leaned out. "It's not far. Come on."

Zaira swung her legs over the edge of the window and dropped down. A loud rustle below suggested she had landed in a bush.

A great clamor roared through the palace, coming closer like a breaking wave, full of shouts and slamming doors and cries of outrage. It couldn't be more than a few rooms away now. I took a breath and leaped after her.

I crashed down into a hedge that scratched and jabbed my arms and legs. I rolled out of it to find Zaira already sprinting away through the gardens. I ran after her; my height gave me a longer stride, but she was fast. For a moment I thought I might not be able to catch up, and would be left behind to be pulled down by angry guards like a deer fleeing hounds. But after she reached a clump of trees, Zaira veered toward the street that ran in front of the River Palace, slowing.

By the time I reached her side, my legs trembled, and my breath came high and fast, though we'd only run a short distance. "What are you doing? You're heading for the open street!"

She stripped off her jacket and tossed it under a bush. Understanding, I did the same. "The street is better protection than the gardens," she said, her voice clipped. "No one out there knows we're wanted."

She took us in a wide circle out onto the street, ignoring the cries and shouts of alarm still audible from the palace. Once we reached the road, she walked swiftly but smoothly, only the tense line of her shoulders betraying anything was wrong.

"Stop breathing like that," she muttered at me. "We're not running anymore."

I struggled to control my breathing. It wasn't easy; I had to focus on each breath, which was difficult given the fact that I was starting to feel light-headed. The edges of my vision swam and blurred.

My elixir was wearing off. I'd missed my dose.

I couldn't afford to get faint and weak-kneed now. I waited until Zaira's attention focused on an approaching party of half-drunk revelers, singing, with their arms across each other's shoulders, then fished my emergency vial out of my bodice. The tiny metal bottle lay cool against my palm.

Zaira glanced back. "No one following us. Yet."

I flicked the wax stopper off with my thumb, releasing the sweet scent of anise. I downed the elixir in one swallow, before Zaira could see.

"We have to get back to Ignazio's town house," I said. I needed my full dose of elixir before my three hours' grace was up. While it would be some time before I was in any real danger from the poison, I couldn't afford to lose tonight to recovery. Not when the doge's ultimatum ran out tomorrow.

"Are you mad?" Zaira smiled across the street at a woman with a little dog running at her heels, but there was venom in her whisper. "That's exactly where they'll look for us first!"

"I'm not a murderer, and I'm not going to act like one." I felt like one, though. Fear and horror coursed through my veins to the pounding rhythm of my blood. Lamps over doorways revealed me to enemies with their golden light; but shadows were no better, menacing with unknown dangers.

"So far as Ardence is concerned right now, we *are* murderers. They're going to send soldiers after us. And you know what the duke's orders are if they do that."

I did. My stomach twisted. "But if we unleash your balefire, Lady Savony gets her war."

"If we don't, she makes sure you die in the scuffle, and she gets her war anyway. Our only chance is not getting caught. I can handle that; I'm good at not getting caught. *You* think about what we do next."

I tried to order my thoughts. "We can't just hide. We need to contact Lady Terringer and the garrison. The Serene Empire is on our side."

"The Empire may be on our side, but our enemy controls all of Ardence. And you know she has people waiting to ambush you when you go home."

I hesitated. My mother had told me over and over again the elixir must remain a secret, so that enemies wouldn't learn of my vulnerability. But it would be rather hard to ask for help if no one knew what was wrong.

"I need something at Ignazio's town house," I said at last. "It's important."

Zaira threw up her hands. "Fine. But I'm not getting killed for you. If we get attacked, you have to release me this time."

"Can you get us into the town house unnoticed?"

She sighed. "Maybe. I'll try."

Zaira had me pay a pair of passing Loreician merchants outrageous sums for a couple of showy feathered hats and mantled capes. When we were a block away from Ignazio's town house, she stopped to scoop filthy ashes from the street and reached for my face.

"What are you doing?" I drew back.

"They're looking for a woman," she said. "Stand still and take your mustache like a man."

I stood rigid at the indignity as she smeared black on my face to approximate a mustache and little pointed beard.

"There," she said. "Now you're a right proper Loreician gentleman."

I touched the feathers trailing from my hat. "I feel like an idiot."

"You look like one, too. But it's dark, so this may work. Try to walk with a swagger, will you?"

The best swagger I could muster was closer to a drunkard's reel. But perhaps that served just as well for a disguise, because we made it to the town house door unmolested. Beatrix, opening it, gasped and started to slam the door closed again at the sight of us, but Zaira stepped forward and waved her jess in her face.

"It's me, you idiot! And this is the Lady Amalia," she hissed. "Let us in, quickly!"

With profuse apologies at not recognizing us, Beatrix bowed us in. She shut and bolted the door behind us, at Zaira's urging.

"Is Ignazio home?" I demanded.

"In his study, my lady."

"And Lieutenant Verdi? Has he arrived yet?" He was supposed to come here after he finished his business at the garrison.

"I'm here," Marcello called from the door to the front sitting room. "Are you—" he stopped, staring.

My hand went to my grime-smeared, mustached face. Heat climbed from my neck to my forehead.

"Isn't she lovely?" Zaira cackled.

"I'm glad you're all right." He stepped toward me, relief

warming his eyes. I lifted a hand between us—Beatrix was watching—and our fingers laced together for one brief moment before sliding apart.

"Drinks, perhaps, Beatrix?" I suggested.

She curtsied, but something uneasy flashed through her eyes before she left. Guilt? Good Graces, it would be like my mother to have a spy in her cousin's house. She could be reporting every glance Marcello and I exchanged. My stomach twisted. Had I just sealed his assignment to the Vaskandran border?

I didn't have time to worry about that now.

"We found the children," I told Marcello. "And Lady Savony murdered the duke."

"What?"

"She pinned it on Her Ladyship here," Zaira added helpfully. "Someone'll probably show up to arrest us soon enough, at which point I believe my orders are to set them on fire."

Marcello felt around behind him, as if for a chair, but found only the foyer wall. He leaned against it, stunned despair sinking into the lines of his face. "We've lost, then. If Ardence sends soldiers after a Falcon and the Cornaro heir, there will be war. We can't stop it now."

"That can't be true." I lifted my chin. "*Ardence* hasn't done anything of the sort. Lady Savony is a traitor and a murderer. We can't hold the entire city accountable for her actions."

Zaira snorted. "You're pretending the world is fair again. Do you think that will matter to the doge?"

Marcello pushed his hair back, cradling his forehead as if he could stuff better thoughts into it. "I have to report this. We need to retreat to the garrison, send messages via the courier lamps to the doge and the Serene Envoy—though Lady Terringer is ill, so who knows if she'll even get hers—"

"Wait." I touched his arm to stop him. "What's that about Lady Terringer?"

He lifted eyes dulled with despair to mine. "A note came while you were out. She's fallen seriously ill. I don't know the details, but apparently she couldn't even write the note herself."

I bit my lip. "No one mentioned she was sick this morning."

"It was apparently quite sudden," Marcello said.

Zaira crossed her arms. "Well, that's an obvious poisoning if I've ever heard of one."

"The timing is more than a bit suspicious," I agreed. "Maybe Ignazio can help her. But it sounds as if we'll have no aid from the Serene Envoy for a while."

Marcello straightened, with grim purpose. "The situation is a disaster, but my duty is clear. I need to get you both safely to the garrison, then contact Raverra. The doge and the Council of Nine can decide what to do next."

"Bollocks." Zaira glared at him. "You know damned well what they'll decide."

"The doge and the Council aren't bloodthirsty warmongers," I felt obliged to point out. "They might not leap to the attack. But even if they don't, that would leave Savony in control of the city, with easy outrage over the duke's murder to back her against Raverra, and all her plans and tools still in place. We'd be outside the city, holed up like fugitives, looking guilty and with no way to stop her."

Marcello spread his hands. "We can't stay here. This town house is hardly built to withstand a siege. If we don't leave for the garrison as soon as possible, she'll have you arrested or killed. Then she'll get her war for sure."

Zaira grinned, but there was no humor in her baring of teeth. "Oh, we might hold her off for a bit. If she comes here looking for a fight, I'll give the bitch exactly what she wants."

Marcello shook his head. "We have to retreat to the garrison. I don't like it, but we have no choice. I'll send a message to the doge and...and make sure Istrella has finished her cannons."

The despair in the sag of his shoulders struck me like a slap. Zaira at least looked ready to fight, but the gleam in her eyes was that of a cornered animal with nothing to lose. They were out of ideas and out of hope.

I supposed that left it to me.

I'd told Ruven I was the Empire. I'd felt, for a moment, the vast power that would some day be mine to command. But that current flowed both ways. Now we were the only eyes and hands the Empire had at this critical moment and place, this tipping point above the fiery abyss.

We couldn't walk away. Ardence needed us. Vaskandar was watching, waiting, ready. Raverra relied on us to hold together the last few threads of the Empire's serenity.

And someone else needed us, as well.

"No," I said.

Marcello frowned as if he would argue.

I lifted a hand to silence him. "No. We still have time." I turned to Zaira. "Jaslyn and Padric and the rest are waiting for us. We can't let them down."

She nodded sharply, her eyes bright.

"This is bad, but it's not the end. Savony is panicked and improvising." An odd sense of strength flooded my chest, warmer than the cold might of the Empire. If I had to pick two people to help me save Ardence, I could do far worse. "So long as we keep our heads, we have an edge. We can do this."

"How?" Marcello still looked dubious.

"First, I'll talk to Ignazio. He can head to the Envoy's Palace and use the courier lamps to inform the doge, then use his political connections in Ardence to try to spread the truth about Lady Savony and the duke's murder, and to keep things calm."

"You tell him fast, and then we free the brats from that pit." Zaira glared at me. "No making them wait while you mince around chattering with limp-brained courtiers."

"Yes," I agreed. "We head straight to the warehouse and free the children. That should give the Ardentine nobles reason to believe us, too." I took a breath. "Then we tell Domenic everything. He's the duke's cousin, and well liked, with a reputation for political neutrality. He might have the clout to have Savony arrested himself, so that Raverra doesn't have to retake the city from her by force. *Then* we can go to the garrison."

Marcello's brows lowered. "You know my orders for this kind of situation, Amalia: to pull out of the city, contact the doge, and use force if necessary."

"Your orders didn't anticipate the duke's murder."

"This isn't what the colonel would want me to do." His voice built a wall, but it was of sand, not stone. His eyes shone green with the rising tide.

"The colonel isn't here." I knew what I had to say, but the words were strange and difficult. I swallowed. "I take full responsibility, as my mother's heir. If there are to be consequences afterward for this decision, let them fall on me."

Marcello saluted, with far more energy than he'd shown a moment ago. "Of course, my lady." His old wistful smile spread across his face. "After all, you aren't under my command. If you're going to try this mad rescue against my advice, it's still my duty to protect you."

"And I have to go with her," Zaira grinned. "She may be an idiot, but she's my Falconer."

"Excellent." I beamed at them.

Beatrix appeared with a wine tray, timid and pale in the face of this nighttime uproar. She cast about fruitlessly for a place in the foyer to set it down.

"I'll head upstairs and tell Ignazio," I said. "Zaira, why don't you two repair to the sitting room with the wine and fill Marcello in on the details of our adventures following Lady Savony? I should only be a few minutes, and then we can go."

"You might want to wash your face before you talk to Ignazio," Zaira said dryly.

My ears burned so hot they threatened to pop off my head. "I'll go do that now."

Without waiting for an answer, I fled across the foyer to the stairs, covering the lower half of my face. My need to wash might be genuine, but I also had to take my elixir. Let them think it was only embarrassment that drove me to my room.

I leaped up the stairs, the marble banister flying under my hand. Halfway up, I heard Marcello cry out in outrage. Zaira must have gotten to the part about the children in the drain.

The thought of those thin faces and reaching, pale fingers tightened my chest. We had to get them out of there tonight.

I paused at the washroom to wipe off the worst of the grime with a cloth. The soft warmth of the artifice-heated water felt good on my face.

I could do this. It would be all right. First my elixir, then Ignazio, then the children. If we could free them, we could still stop Savony's war. Domenic could help us get the situation at the River Palace under control, and once Gabril knew how Savony had betrayed him, we might even gain the Shadow Gentry as allies rather than enemies. A few hours to take some key pieces away from Lady Savony, and we'd have a much better report to make to the doge. One that wouldn't point to balefire as the simplest solution.

Feeling a bit heartened, I crossed the hall and threw open the door to my own room, planning to head straight for the wardrobe where I hid my elixir bottles.

The smell of anise hit me, sickly strong.

My desk drawers, chest, and wardrobe stood open. Someone had searched my room.

A sick feeling twisted my stomach. I hurried to the wardrobe. Shining shards of glass scattered across the rug. A large fresh stain surrounded them.

Grace of Mercy.

I dropped to my knees and felt the damp carpet. Then I brought my fingers to my nose. The familiar scent of anise overpowered everything.

There was too much glass on the ground. It had to be more than one bottle. I'd only brought two.

I frantically pushed aside clothes in the wardrobe, but there was no sign of the bottles. They all too clearly lay in shards on the floor. The rug had soaked up every drop of the elixir. There was none left.

Chapter Twenty-Nine

Someone knew my secret weakness. And they were trying to kill me.

I plucked glass shards uselessly from the rug, then let them slide through my fingers. One sliced my hand, drawing a thin line of blood, but I didn't care.

I had less than three hours left before the poison resumed the deadly work Ignazio halted years ago.

Uncle Ignazio. Relief flooded me. He was home; he could make more elixir. It might take him time, and I might not have a pleasant night ahead of me; but I wasn't going to die. He'd been able to concoct the elixir in time when I'd first been poisoned ten years ago, after all.

I hurried to his study, running my hand along the wall to touch something solid in a world gone unsteady as a sinking boat. The fading light of the luminaries filled the hallway with ghosts and shadows. I tried not to think of the several emergencies riding my back like demons—the children, the murder, the elixir—and focus on the simple task of reaching Ignazio's door.

I couldn't keep my urgency out of my knock, hammering harder than I'd meant to. "Uncle Ignazio? Are you in there?"

He opened the door himself, alarm in his eyes. "Amalia! Come in. Are you well?"

His warmly lit study, lined with books and the occasional jar of herbs, enfolded me with welcome relief. I sank into a chair without invitation, my knees trembling from shock.

"Uncle Ignazio, someone broke in to my room and smashed my elixir bottles."

His face went still and serious. He closed the study door and pulled a chair up close to mine. "Did they get all of them?"

"Yes." I clenched my hands together in my lap to keep them quiet. "There wasn't a drop left, and I already took my only grace vial. I'm late with tonight's dose."

"Ah, yes, those little emergency vials. How long will it buy you?"

"Three hours from when I took it. Then the poison starts working again." Or so my mother had warned me. I'd never been more than a couple hours late with my elixir before. The memory of agonizing cramps and terrible hallucinations kept me on schedule.

"So, perhaps nine or ten hours before it kills you. Good." He stood, clasping his hands behind his back, and started to pace. "We have time, then."

"You can make more elixir?"

He stopped and turned to face me, his expression unreadable. "That, Amalia, depends entirely on you."

"...Pardon?" I couldn't have heard him right.

"I had hoped not to have this conversation with you for a while yet. But too many things have gone wrong."

I stared at him. His words made no sense. And his demeanor was all wrong: I was about to start dying, and he was giving me a look of stern regret, as if he were a professor to whom I'd turned in shoddy work.

Pieces began to come horribly together in my mind, too late.

Our Raverran friend... There was a Raverran working with Lady Savony. And Gabril had trusted me as soon as he'd heard the name Cornaro.

Ignazio. Curse him to the Hell of Corruption. I'd trusted him. I'd *loved* him. He was family.

"You broke the bottles," I whispered. "You're one of the ones trying to start a war."

"Oh, no." Ignazio looked surprised. "Why would I do that? I broke the bottles, yes, but I don't want to start a war. I want to end one."

My hands curled into fists in my lap. "There's no war to end. Unless you start one first."

"Listen to me, Amalia. We don't have a lot of time, and I honestly would prefer you didn't get hurt." He settled back into his chair, extending a hand to me as if in comfort. I jerked away from it, repulsed. "I'm sorry about the bottles. But I need your cooperation in this."

"In betraying Ardence and Raverra both? In keeping children locked up in dark cellars, and murdering dukes?" The words tore my aching throat. This was the man who had given me my first astrolabe, and taught me how to read alchemical symbols.

"All that was necessary, to put someone in command of this city who can save it from itself. Under Duke Astor Bergandon, Ardence would have fallen to ruin and like as not wound up in the service of Vaskandar. Lady Terringer couldn't save it. It had to be me."

"It won't be you." I made my voice cold and hard. "The doge and the Council will treat you with less mercy than they did Baron Leodra."

"Leodra." He sighed. "A shame about him. He understood what this city needs, and he would have been an invaluable ally if he'd been able to keep his head better in a crisis. But you're wrong about the doge and the Council."

"I think not. Do you really think my mother will have mercy on you because you're her cousin? When they hear of this treachery—"

"They won't." His voice was quiet, his face gentle. "Because you won't tell them. I know this is hard to accept, Amalia. But you must do as I say, just as Ardence must do what Raverra commands. All these years, you have survived only to serve me. You simply didn't realize it until now."

A wave of fury boiled up in me, and I slapped him in the face.

Ignazio stood, eyes flashing. "Do you think you can get your precious elixir elsewhere?" he snapped. "It is in my nature to be thorough, Amalia. Before I even acquired the Demon's Tears, ten years ago, I started hunting down every copy I could find of the formula for the cure. I have devoted more than a decade to locating every written record of the recipe, and destroying it. The elixir that keeps you alive exists only in my mind, Cousin."

So he had been the one who poisoned me in the first place.

It was too much. Angry, helpless tears stung my eyes, grieving for the Uncle Ignazio I remembered so fondly. The lie I'd believed. The man he'd never been. "I cared about you, Ignazio. For Graces' sake, you're my family."

"I care about you too, Amalia. But I have been passed over too many times." His voice twisted to bitterness. "Not quite powerful enough an alchemist for the mage mark. Not quite near enough in the succession to sit on the Council of Nine. And then not quite good enough to stay Serene Envoy to Ardence. Well, no more." He started pacing again. "I may never sit on the Council of Nine, but you will do it for me, speaking with my voice. And if I can't be Serene Envoy, I will be imperial governor. When this city devolves to the Hell of Madness and I am the only one who can solve its problems and end the war, the doge will have no other choice."

"The children said a man would rescue them," I said. "I thought maybe they meant Ruven. But that was going to be you."

"Of course. I will save the children, find the jess, and put to justice the Shadow Gentry traitors who stole them both. I will rescue my own kidnapped cousin, freeing her just in time to save the city from the balefire she loosed from afar in a panic when she was captured. I will have the backing of the Ardentine people and the late duke's own right hand. And of the Council of Nine, once Lissandra prevails upon them, for how could she not support her own cousin after he rescues her beloved daughter?"

He sighed, then, and his shoulders slumped. "That was the plan. It's going to be harder, now you've made a mess of things. But if you help me, we can still salvage this."

"I've heard enough. More than enough." I rose from my chair. "I'm not going to help you. I'm going to stop you."

And I cried out, as loudly as I could, "Marcello! Zaira!"

My voice rang out strong and clear. But only silence met it.

Ignazio smiled. "They're asleep by now."

"Asleep?"

"Every servant in this town house is mine, naturally. I sent down orders for Beatrix to serve them drinks well laced with a certain potion with which I believe you are already acquainted." He took down a bottle from a shelf and shook it teasingly. I didn't have to smell peppermint to guess what it was.

"What are you going to do with them?" I demanded.

"Zaira is still useful to me, if she's willing to cooperate—and I have worked hard to ensure she will be. Lieutenant Verdi knows too much." He frowned. "As do those children. I'd meant to rescue them, but if they talked to you about our plan... Perhaps the story might be more poignant if I merely bring their killers to justice."

"I think not."

I gulped in a breath, snatched a candlestick off Ignazio's desk, and brought it smashing down... not on Ignazio's head, tempting though that might be.

On the bottle in his hand.

He gasped in alarm as the bottle broke; that sharp intake of breath was all it took. He dropped like a stone, sleep potion splashed all over him.

Still holding my breath, I ran from the room and slammed the door behind me. I didn't know how long he'd stay unconscious. Every servant in the house was hostile, and in a few hours I'd be in no shape to save anyone. I had to act quickly to have any hope of rescuing the children and preventing war.

I tried not to think about how little chance I had of saving myself.

I made it to the sitting room without encountering any servants. Perhaps they would rather not know what was happening in the town house tonight. Zaira sprawled on the floor; Marcello slumped in his chair, a glass of wine lying on the rug below his dangling hand.

I went to him first, an instinct over which reason had no sway pulling me. I grabbed the front of his uniform and shook him, whispering urgently.

"Marcello! Marcello, wake up!"

His head rolled limply on his neck. I switched to slapping his cheeks. "Marcello!"

Nothing. I pulled back my arm and slapped harder.

His face pulled into a slow wince. "Amalia, whaa…"

"Wake up," I hissed. "We need to get out of here, or we're all dead."

That got his attention. He hauled himself upright. His eyes kept trying to drift closed, but he stayed up.

Good. The potion didn't last long. But that meant we didn't have much time before Ignazio woke up, either.

"Wha happen?" Marcello slurred.

"Ignazio's a traitor," I said. "He drugged you. I'll explain while we run."

Zaira's eyes fluttered open in response to mere shaking. The girl burned through potion as quickly as she went through food.

"That filthy rat," she spat. "Drugged! I'll kill him myself."

"We need to get out of here," I said. "We have to rescue the children. If we don't hurry, they're going to kill them."

Zaira swore. Together, we hauled Marcello to his feet, though between her slight frame and still unsteady legs, Zaira couldn't take much of his weight.

"Don't forget, we need tools to open the grate," she reminded me.

"Right. One moment." I dashed upstairs to grab my bag of artifice tools. My ears strained for any sign of Ignazio waking, but the rest of the house remained silent while I thundered back down to where Zaira struggled to hold up Marcello against his inexorable slide toward the floor. We made quite a set as we staggered into the foyer, heading for the door.

Beatrix stood before us, a dagger shaking in her hand.

"Stop," she squeaked. "You're not to leave. The master's orders."

"We don't have time for this," Zaira snapped. "Release me, and I'll burn her down."

Beatrix dropped the knife with a clatter and bolted. We limped to the door and threw it open.

Waiting for us in the street were my broken-nosed friend and an overmuscled colleague, both with swords drawn.

"Still no time!" Zaira cried in disgust. "Say it, Cornaro!"

A loud crack jolted straight through my bones, and a flash in my face nearly blinded me. Broken-nose dropped with a gurgling cry, a bloody hole in his chest. Marcello swayed, smoke rising from the muzzle of his flintlock.

The other scoundrel swore, threw down his sword, and ran.

Together, the three of us stumbled out into the chill of the deepening night.

The fresh air seemed to help Marcello and Zaira revive more quickly, and soon we could move at a brisk pace. It was an hour for lingering over the remains of a meal with cheese and wine, so the streets were free of crowds. Only occasional tradesmen heading home late, young gentry flitting from one evening engagement to another, and the carved Graces staring down blank-eyed from the frieze of a temple bore witness to our passage.

It must have been nearly two hours since I took my grace vial. That left me an hour—maybe three or four, if I could keep going through the early poison symptoms—to rescue the children, discredit Savony, and avert a war. Afterward... I couldn't think of it. I was too alive now for death to be so close, and so real.

A sharp command sounded from around the corner, along with the tramp of booted feet. Zaira swore. "They're coming to arrest us."

"They don't have the authority," Marcello objected.

"Do you think that will stop them?" Zaira pulled us into a deep, shadowed archway that led to a gated town house garden. We waited tensely as a dozen soldiers passed our hiding place, armed with flintlocks and sabers.

"Looks like we'd better move quickly," I said once they were gone. "Before those soldiers come looking for us."

Before I ran out of time.

With storehouses and workshops locked and shuttered for the night, the street lay in black shadow. I would have passed Savony's warehouse, but Zaira recognized it. She had the lock open in minutes, and we crept down the entry hallway under the round mirror eyes, in the flickering lamplight. The clink and creak of Marcello's rapier-and-pistol harness seemed loud as a shout in the pressing silence.

My bloody rune still marked the artifice circle on the far door. I pushed it open, the raw wood rough under my fingers. Ignazio couldn't possibly have beaten us here, but I was still fearful of what we might find.

The storeroom opened before us, its looming space palpable, but only the gray trace ends of starlight filtered down through the high windows. The golden rectangle cast on the stone floor from the lamplit hallway didn't reach far. Those poor children must spend every night in utter blackness. I shuddered.

"Jaslyn?" I called softly.

A rustle and faint "Hello?" rose up from below, hollow and uncertain.

"Grace of Mercy," Marcello breathed. "They really are under the floor."

I couldn't make out the drain in the grainy shadows, but we headed toward the center of the room, our footfalls startling echoes off the walls.

"It's me, Amalia. We're here to set you free."

"You came back!" Hope lit up Jaslyn's voice.

I found the drain and slid my fingers between the metal bars. Small cold hands touched mine. Jostling and whispers sounded from the cellar.

"They came back!"

"She's going to let us out of here!"

"Give me those tools," Zaira commanded, her voice hard with purpose.

I passed her my satchel. A few clinks sounded in the darkness, and then a frustrated grunt.

"I can't see a cursed thing. Do we have any light?"

"Hold on." A soft glow flared in Marcello's hand as he shook a pocket luminary awake. "This won't last long," he warned.

"Long enough." Zaira bent over the drain, blocking my view of dark staring eyes and wan faces below.

"Hurry," a boy pleaded.

"I'm working on it, brat. Stop grabbing at the bars, or I'll never get this off."

Marcello held up the luminary, giving it another shake to give the spark of light a bit more time as it faded. I sidled up to him until our shoulders and hips touched, and his free arm went around my waist. I drank in his warmth, too aware it could be my last chance.

I should tell them, Graces help me. If I was going to be dead in several hours, that was relevant information.

"Listen..." I began.

"Got it!" Zaira crowed. She cast the grille aside with a clang.

Hands strained to reach out of the hole, fingers waving like seaweed. An excited babble rose up from the cellar.

"It's open! We're free!"

"Padric, quit shoving!"

"I can't reach! Let me out!"

Marcello's arm tightened around me in a brief spasm of sympathy or pain. Then he strode to the drain without looking back. He plunged both arms into the hole and pulled up a child, quick as a conjurer's trick. The boy shrieked and wriggled; the moment his toes touched the floor, he took off and started running in circles.

"I'm going home! I'm going home!"

My eyes stung. No matter what might happen in the next hours, in this moment we were doing exactly the right thing.

"So much for stealth," Zaira grumbled.

Marcello hauled up another child, a girl not more than four. When he put her down, she threw herself headfirst into my stomach and squeezed her arms around my waist, knocking the breath out of me. I smoothed her hair as she sobbed.

"It'll be all right. You're free."

Shoulders straining, Marcello heaved another child out of the cellar, and another. When he got tired, I took a turn. Some of them burst out laughing, full of energy and joy; others clung to us, or to each other, tired and afraid. Soon a whole pack of them tore around the empty space like dogs let loose after a rainy week, shrieking and playing. I had to admire their resilience.

When we'd lifted up fourteen children, I leaned over the hole and at last saw nothing but deeper shadow below.

"Is this everyone?"

"I think so," came Jaslyn's thin voice. She counted them aloud, calling names, starting over a few times.

Marcello crouched next to me, peering down into the drain to make sure. I leaned my forehead against his. We stayed that way, for a few heartbeats. I closed my eyes, wishing I could stay in this moment, this small fragment of peace.

"We need to get this circus out of town," Zaira said.

"Where should we take them?" Marcello rose. A small boy grasped my hand, and a girl clung to my coat. "The garrison?"

"No. We need to get them back to their families."

"We don't have time to deliver these brats door to door all over the city," Zaira objected.

I bit my lip. The garrison was no good; they would look like our prisoners. The River Palace certainly wasn't safe right now.

"Domenic," I decided. "His town house isn't far from here, and we need to talk to him anyway. He's got the influence to turn the other nobles of the Council of Lords against Savony once they know the truth, and the Ardentine military will listen to him. If we get him the children, he can help us stop the war."

"Right." Zaira handed me back my satchel. "Let's get these villains rounded up and go."

It took precious time to gather all the children in the darkness and explain to them the importance of staying together, keeping quiet, and ducking under the mirrors in the hallway. Twice I had to chase down Padric, a sturdy boy of perhaps six with far more energy than anyone should have after being imprisoned in a cellar for two weeks, because he kept bolting for the door. The effort left me short of breath. Finally, we had them lined up between me and Marcello.

Zaira went first, to check if the way was clear. She paused before entering the hall, her wild curls backlit by the lamplight.

"All right, brats. Remember—heads down."

She crouched low and made her way down the mirrored corridor. The lamps glowed on, the mirrors staring blankly back at them. At the far end, she straightened, then cracked the door and peered out. The child behind me started forward, but I stuck out an arm to hold him back.

"Not yet," I murmured. My pulse surged quickly in my veins. If Savony's ruffians waited outside, we'd have to fight.

After a long moment, Zaira stepped outside the warehouse and glanced around. She beckoned to us from the open doorway, the night at her back. It was safe to go.

"Stay low," I told the children lined up behind me. Wide eyes and solemn nods came in reply.

I bent over and started down the hall. A wave of dizziness surged through me with the change of position. *Not now.* I ran my hand along the wall to steady myself.

The children followed, with Marcello at the rear to make sure no one got left behind. Zaira waited in the doorway, candlelight warming her back as she stared into the stark night outside, tense and poised as a gull ready to take flight. I stepped past the last mirror to meet her, straightening.

A whisper and a scuffle came behind me. Jaslyn called, "Padric, no!"

I spun, finger raised to my lips, but it was too late. Padric strained on tiptoe, trying to see into a mirror, while Jaslyn and a couple other children lunged at him to drag him down.

The runes circling the mirror flashed with blue light.

A squealing clamor tore the air. Something dark and massive crashed down from the ceiling.

I shrieked and leaped back. The heavy iron portcullis barely missed my nose, striking the stone floor with a dreadful *clang*. Its thick bars framed the pale, shocked faces of the children, now trapped behind it. Marcello stood beyond them, hand falling back from his rapier hilt, eyes wide.

Chapter Thirty

Zaira swore. "We were so close. *So damned close.*"

I grabbed at the metal bars, trying to heave the gate up. More blue light flared along the portcullis's iron frame. It was locked in place, by an artificer far more competent than the one who'd added the slapdash circle on the far door.

My breath came too quickly, and I couldn't pretend it was only with agitation. *No.* Everything was going to the Nine Hells again.

One of the children punched Padric's shoulder. "Stupid! Look what you did!"

I couldn't bring myself to contradict him, even when Padric burst into tears.

Marcello grimaced, in a comfortable sort of way that denied how bad our situation had become. "Now what?"

Zaira grabbed my arm. "Can you do something like you did for that circle on the door?"

I shook my head. This was a disaster. Marcello and the children were trapped, and Ignazio must be on his way, unless he'd sent hirelings ahead. Everyone looked at me expectantly, hopefully, but all I had was a satchel of artifice supplies and a complete lack of magical talent to defeat a well-crafted device.

I took a breath. "I don't know. Let me think."

The mirrors detected intruders, but their runes said nothing about dropping the trap. The portcullis itself bore no runes, nor artifice wire or beads. Something had to dictate the terms of the spell.

I hooked a hand over a rough iron bar for support and glanced upward. The top of the portcullis disappeared into the hidden slot through which it had dropped. The arm-wide gap was too full of shadows to see what was up there.

"There has to be another room above us, with a way to unlock the magical seal and reset the trap. With a mundane winch, too, for that matter." I had to pause, gathering breath. "The portcullis would drop any time one of the lamps went out, so they must need to reset it often."

"I saw another door on the side of the building," Zaira said. "Let's go."

I eased my weight back onto my own legs, which threatened to fold. For a moment, I couldn't let go of the portcullis. The children crowded against the bars, reaching through, tugging at my clothes with their tiny hands. I wanted to reassure them, but I had to focus on finding my balance again.

Marcello moved through them up to the bars, worry furrowing his brow.

"Amalia? Are you all right?"

"I'm sorry." My voice came out weak and shaky. "I know we don't have time for this. I'll go."

I straightened, fighting back another rush of dizziness. But Marcello reached through the bars and caught my elbow.

"What's wrong? You're not well."

By morning, I would be dead. But I couldn't think about that now. "I'll manage."

"Come on," Zaira urged. "If they catch us like this, I'll die of embarrassment before they can shoot me."

Marcello's grip on my arm tightened. "You're going nowhere

until you tell me what's wrong. You're sick, or hurt. Do you need a physician?"

"I need an alchemist," I admitted. "But we have to get the children to safety first."

"An alchemist! Did Ignazio poison you?"

I laughed bitterly. "Yes, as a matter of fact. Long ago. But he also kept me alive, until now." There was no more point keeping it secret. "Demon's Tears. He smashed my elixir bottles. My last dose is wearing off."

Marcello swore. He pulled me close, his arms going around me through the bars. I leaned against the portcullis for a moment, my hands seeking the warmth of his chest through the gaps. The cold iron gate pressed between us, unyielding.

"We have to get you more elixir somehow." Desperation strained his voice taut. "There's no alchemist in the garrison, but maybe we can find one in the city."

"Maybe," I agreed wearily. I didn't have the heart to tell him what Ignazio had told me. "We can talk about it after we get the children to safety and save the city from war. I should go."

His throat jumped. "Promise me you'll be all right until then."

The words stuck in my throat. My mother always told me never to give promises I wasn't sure I could keep.

Instead, I slipped a hand around the back of his neck through the bars and pulled his mouth down to mine. By all the Graces, if I might be dead by morning, I was going to kiss him first.

His lips went taut with shock. But then they melted into mine, warm and tender, between the hard metal pressing into my cheekbones. For a moment, we lingered like that, and the night was safe and beautiful, free of terror. I had to come up for air too soon, my breathing harsh and shallow.

The children laughed, squealed, and poked each other. I couldn't muster a blush.

"Take care of them," I said. "I'll get this gate open."

He squeezed my hand so tight it hurt. Then he released me, nodding. "I know you will."

I followed Zaira out into the chill night air. I stumbled twice on the way around the side of the building, my knees weak and trembling. *Not now.* I slapped my face to keep my mind focused and sharp.

The side-door lock took Zaira longer than the front door had, which gave me hope there might not be magical wards backing it up. She cursed softly once or twice. I bit my lip to keep from telling her to hurry. I glanced around constantly, but the street remained deserted.

Finally, Zaira rose, and the door swung open onto a flight of plain wooden stairs.

"And there it is." Zaira stepped aside for me to go first. "Just like you said. Maybe you're not always an idiot."

"Thanks." I stepped through the door into the gloomy stairwell. Grime darkened the interior to a hopeless, gritty charcoal. Even with the wall to lean on, by the time I got to the top, my vision swarmed with golden sparks at the edges.

A short hallway brought us to another locked door, which Zaira had open soon enough. No windows shed light within, but I could dimly make out the bulking rectangle of a desk, some shelves and crates—and, along one wall, the low bulk of a winch, and the top of the portcullis grating rising out of the floor.

I hurried over to the winch, but I could barely make out the ropes leading from it, let alone whether any runes or wirework adorned it.

"I need light," I told Zaira. "Can you go see whether Marcello has another pocket luminary? Or better yet, get one of those oil lamps?"

"All right. But don't get any idea I'll fetch and carry for you when this is over."

I didn't wait to watch her hurry out, but turned back to the portcullis in the darkness. As my eyes adjusted, I made out something round on the wall behind it—another mirror? And was that spell wire running from it to the portcullis?

My fingertips brushed it in the dark. Yes, and another wire braid ran to the winch. The mirrors below must be linked to this one. When the trap was sprung below, the upstairs mirror received the signal, dropped the portcullis, and activated the seal.

Heavy boots clomped on the stairs. That wasn't Zaira, unless she'd grown several new legs and gained a few hundred pounds. A flutter of lantern light raced up the stairs ahead of them, throwing wild shadows into the hall.

Hells take it. I hadn't figured out how to unlock the seal yet. I shoved my satchel behind a crate, hoping at least to hide what I was doing. Then I drew my dagger and faced the door, blood pounding.

Four armed men crested the stairs and approached the door. The foremost held a lantern, its ruddy light picking out gleams from swords and flintlocks. I made out the Bergandon crest pinned to their chests, but their poorly made uniforms didn't match.

There was no way someone who cared as much about appearances as Duke Bergandon would allow such an unkempt lot to serve in his guard. By the calculation in their narrowed eyes, they weren't surprised to see me. My chances of bluffing my way out of this seemed slim, but I drew myself up anyway.

"This is your last chance to avoid treason," I warned them. I tried to sound sure and unafraid, as if I had an army at my back, but my voice came out too thin and strained. "You can still save your lives and your honor if you surrender now."

The men exchanged glances. Scars marred their unshaven faces. The man carrying the lantern set it down inside the door, drawing a flintlock pistol in its place.

"Potion," one grunted to another.

I sucked in a breath and held it. A man in the rear rank meddled with his pouch, but I didn't wait. I lunged at the ruffian in front, stabbing his hand; he dropped his flintlock with a cry. The broad-shouldered brute beside him lifted his sword, but a man with a scarred chin caught his arm.

"Careful! Alive, remember?"

Oh, that made this easier. I chanced a gulp of air and pressed forward a step, slashing at their eyes. My opponents seemed unsure what to do with their weapons, jumbling back out of the doorway in an undisciplined clump.

"Enough!" Scarred Chin called. The man in the back rank hurled something at me, and glass shattered at my feet. Liquid splashed my legs. I was sure if I breathed in, I'd smell peppermint.

The false soldiers slammed the door shut between us.

The potion seeped through my stockings. I headed for the winch, struggling not to inhale, desperate to free Marcello before I blacked out. But dizziness dropped me to my knees before I'd crossed the room, and I gasped in a sharp breath of peppermint.

The world upheaved, plunging my mind into blackness before I hit the floor.

Chapter Thirty-One

When I woke again, I felt dry and empty, like a leaf from last year's autumn. Light tickled my eyelids open. I lay where I'd fallen, between the winch and the door. The lantern still burned, catching gleams from the golden spell wire binding the winch and portcullis to the mirror on the wall. A desk covered in papers stood against one wall, next to shelves bearing stacks of folded Falconer uniforms and a pile of Ardentine military badges with the Bergandon crest. More shelves bore jars of artificer's paint with ground obsidian and a pile of gray domino masks. An empty coffin stood in a corner; the sight left me queasy.

I appeared to be in a veritable storehouse of the tools of treachery.

Judging by the racing of my heart and the weakness in my limbs, some time had passed, though the poison hadn't progressed enough for the cramps to have started. Instead, it was fear for Marcello and the children that hooked into my gut and twisted.

I hauled myself into a sitting position, too quickly. Everything swam and listed. I sagged back to the floor and stared at the ceiling, panting.

The door opened.

"Hello, Amalia," Ignazio said.

I considered lunging for his throat, but the man with the

scarred chin and his brutish friends waited in the hall behind him. Better to let him underestimate me. I tried again to sit, letting him see the struggle. This time, I stayed upright.

"Hello, traitor."

He waved his hirelings back and closed the door, giving us privacy. "Is that any way to address your cousin?"

I glared. My throat was too dry to waste more words on him.

He sighed. "All right. Is that any way to address the man who can save your life?"

From his coat, he drew out a flask. My heart leaped despite myself, but when he crossed the room and proffered it to me, it didn't smell like anise.

"It's wine," he said. "You need to drink something. Take it."

"How do I know it's not drugged?"

He lifted an eyebrow. "What need do I have to poison you?"

I took the flask. It was a weak and unrefined red, but a powerful thirst compelled me to swallow some anyway. Besides, it bought me time to think. I had to find out what had become of Marcello and the children.

"The cramps haven't started yet, I take it?" he asked.

I shook my head, still drinking.

"They will soon enough." He watched my face closely. "After that, it's a painful descent into hallucinations, unconsciousness, and death."

He was out of slapping reach. I set the flask down. "Are you here only to taunt me? I can't bear to think any Cornaro could sink to that level."

"No. I'm here to give you another chance. Please, Amalia. I don't want you to die. There's still time to mix the elixir if you agree to cooperate with me."

Hope lurched in my chest. If he wanted my help, maybe Marcello and the children had gotten free somehow. "Why should I cooperate with you?"

He lifted an eyebrow. "You don't seem to have many other options, do you?" He glanced past me to the portcullis winch. "Were you hoping to free Lieutenant Verdi? You won't have much luck without these." From within his doublet, he drew out a golden chain hung with rune-marked stones, dangling it in front of me as if taunting a cat.

Before I could get a good look, the door flew open, and Lady Savony strode in. I glimpsed a brand-new artifice seal nailed to the door on a piece of canvas. *Hell of Despair.* That complicated things.

"Are you still trying to convince her?" Contempt iced Savony's voice. "We should kill her and get it over with. Do you truly think it's kinder to let her die slowly?"

Ignazio tucked the chain back into his doublet and glanced over his shoulder at her. "You agreed to follow my lead. In this, and all things."

"Because you have the vision, wealth, and influence to save Ardence. And because Astor would have destroyed it with his excesses, if he didn't hand it over to Vaskandar first. I will not let my city fall"—she shook her head—"but I have no patience for sentimentality. Don't you start dragging your feet like Leodra did over the children."

"I've admitted it was a mistake to bring him in. Have no fear—I'm made of sterner stuff." Ignazio jerked his chin toward the door, and the city beyond it. "How do things stand?"

"The River Palace is sufficiently outraged, and the lords primed. It should be trivial to place it entirely under my control. Lady Terringer is unconscious from the poison you slipped her. She may survive, but it doesn't much matter; she's out of our way for now, and my people sabotaged her courier lamps. Bedridden and without a way to contact the doge or the garrison, she's neutralized. The Shadow Gentry are set to take the blame, and the children and Lieutenant Verdi remain imprisoned below."

I stopped my eyes from drifting to the winch. So long as they were still alive, I had a chance of getting them out.

"The last pieces are our Falcon and Falconer, then," Ignazio said.

"Yes. And you promised me you'd have them under control." Savony bit off each word. "To threaten the city with balefire and then save it. Everything goes to the Nine Hells if the Empire starts *actually* destroying the city with those artifice cannons instead."

"I fear I didn't anticipate my cousin's lack of a sense of self-preservation." Ignazio flicked a disappointed glance my way. "But I have some confidence Zaira will be willing to work with us regardless. Never fear."

"Also, they're not quite the last pieces." Lady Savony fingered the spectacles dangling from her neck. "What of the children?"

Ignazio sighed and stood. "I'll have someone deal with them. I have to choose carefully. We need people who won't balk and can be absolutely discreet."

"What are you going to do?" The words burst out of me.

He didn't reply. Lady Savony glanced at me with no more interest than if I were a bug, and the two of them headed for the door.

"Ignazio! You're better than this!" I called. "If you harm those children, you will damn yourself forever. You can't come back, once you cross that line."

Lady Savony left the room without breaking stride. But Ignazio paused in the door, his hand on the frame.

"It's too late," he said softly. "I made my peace with damnation the day I poisoned you."

The door closed behind them. The lock clicked into place. A line of light flared briefly around the door as the artifice seal activated.

That bastard. My hands clenched in my lap. He didn't deserve to bear the Cornaro name. Our family might be pragmatic and manipulative at times, but even the most ruthless had never stooped to murdering children.

I sat still for a few moments more as their footsteps receded down the hall and then descended the stairs. When I was sure they were gone, I staggered to my feet, snatched up the lantern, and brought it over to the portcullis. A tremor passed through me as I examined the mirror, making the lantern light quiver, but my attention didn't waver. I had to set Marcello free, with or without Ignazio's jewelry.

One weave of beaded artifice wire carried the command from the mirror to the winch to drop the portcullis. Another ran to the portcullis itself, activating the magical seal that kept it locked in place. Five empty niches in the mirror frame awaited Ignazio's rune stones, no doubt, which presumably acted as the keys to unseal it again.

That was a problem. But Ignazio knew little about artifice. Unlike alchemy, its rules could sometimes be rewritten by nimble fingers and a skilled mind.

I held the lantern close to the golden wire that wove around an iron ring atop the portcullis, defining the seal. Five blue beads formed a pattern in the delicate traceries of wire, matching the mirror keystones. If I could line them up just right on the complex swirls, like the tumblers of a lock, it would release the energy to signal the seal to open.

I could do this.

My breath rasped more and more quickly through my lips, but it still wasn't enough air. With trembling hands, I delicately, carefully slid the beads along the wirework. I had to keep my mind sharp and focused, no matter how much my body came apart around me.

My numb, clumsy fingers kept pushing the beads too far, or rotating them on the wire. I wanted to weep with frustration. I knelt by the portcullis, the lantern oil burning lower and lower, my vision growing narrower and narrower. Those tiny beads became my entire world as I fumbled them, with agonizing slowness, into place.

Finally, finally, a jolt of energy ran through my fingertips. I had them lined up. The seal was open.

I peered down through the deep slot in the stone floor, to where I glimpsed lamplight shining on the portcullis bars beneath. My straining ears caught the high music of children's voices below. I couldn't make out words, but the dispirited tone pulled at my heart.

"Marcello," I called. "Can you hear me?"

The voices paused. A face pressed to the bars below, only a sliver of it visible through the narrow gap. I glimpsed one round, wide eye staring up at me, from a child's face. Then it vanished.

"There's someone up there!" the girl shouted. "Someone in the ceiling!"

A scuffle, and hushing sounds. Then another face leaned into the portcullis, familiar and startled.

"Amalia! Is that you?" Marcello's voice warmed me like mulled wine.

"Yes! I'm sorry I took so long. There were... complications."

"Where's Zaira? Is she up there too?"

"No." I braced my hands on the floor against the dread that settled over me. "She didn't come ask you for a light?"

"No."

The grim word sat heavily in my stomach, indigestible. But whether she'd fled or been captured, betrayed us or died, made no difference to the moment's task. One problem at a time.

"I unsealed the portcullis," I told him. "I'm going to try to winch it up. Don't let the children trigger it again."

"You're amazing." I caught a flash of white teeth through the narrow gap. "Thank you. Will you meet us outside?"

I sighed, letting a long, precious breath free to find its way down to him.

"Marcello, I'm going to tell you something hard, and you have to accept it."

A frown rearranged the sliver of brow I could see. "I'm listening."

"I'm not going with you."

"Amalia—"

"Even if I could break the artifice lock on this room, I couldn't go with you." I swallowed, but couldn't smooth out the roughness in my throat. "I'd slow you down too much. Ignazio is getting hired murderers to come kill you *right now*. You need to get those children to safety. You can't wait for me."

"I'm not leaving you here!" Anguish tore his voice.

"You're all those children have, Marcello. If you let them down, they'll die." I found the sharp tone my mother used to snap me back to sense when I was being foolish. "Go. Get them out of here."

A long pause. He straightened away from the portcullis slot, so I couldn't see his face anymore—just his hands, gripping the bars until his knuckles stood out white.

"Once they're safe, I'll come back for you."

"Fine. Now, go. Hurry."

"You're a brave and brilliant woman, Amalia Cornaro." Those strong, callused hands flexed once, then let go. "I think I might love you."

I squeezed my eyes shut. I couldn't afford to cry, couldn't sink into the bitter pain of losing my chance to be with him. It wasn't fair, for him to say that now.

"I'm going to try to raise this thing." I forced the words out through a stiff jaw. "You lift it, too." I turned to the winch, half-blind with unshed tears, and all but fell on the handle.

I was too weak from the poison to raise the portcullis far, but

Marcello and the children only needed a foot or two to slide out beneath it. Still, by the time I locked the winch in place, I was gasping and shaking. I slumped against the wall, spent.

"We're through," Marcello called up from below, after an interval of excited child noises and scrambling. "I'll get the children to safety, and I'll be back. Wait for me."

"I'm not going anywhere." The words rasped out too thin. I doubted he heard them.

Then they were gone. The last sounds of children striving fruitlessly to be stealthy faded, swallowed by stone walls and distance.

I was alone. Only death remained, close and patient, its silent wings folding around me.

"I think I might love you too, Marcello," I whispered.

Cold seeped through my back from the stone wall I sagged against. It was easier to keep my eyes closed and to focus on breathing, on stilling the tremors in my limbs. But even with the poison taking full hold, my mind kept running, mad as a dog with its tail on fire.

I had to believe Marcello would get the children safely to Domenic, and that Domenic could convince the Ardentine court of Raverra's innocence and take control of the River Palace back from Lady Savony. But that would take time—hours during which Savony still had free rein in the city. And I had no inkling of what had happened to Zaira, save only that Ignazio had seemed sure he could secure her cooperation.

There was still too much that could go wrong. Ignazio's hired murderers could catch Marcello and the children. Zaira could burn the city down, especially if she found herself suddenly released by my death. The doge could decide Ardence had gone too far, or that nothing mattered if the jess still wasn't returned, and attack the city despite all our work. Lady Savony could have Domenic killed. I couldn't die now—not with so much left to do.

In cruel mockery, pain opened like a flower in my middle, a

sharp twinge building with alarming rapidity until it doubled me over.

The cramps had begun.

It sank in, finally, that I only had a few hours left to live. It was too late even to beg Ignazio for mercy; he was gone. No one survived Demon's Tears without the neutralizing elixir, and the nearest bottle was a hundred and fifty miles away in my bedroom in Raverra.

A feeling welled up in me with slow grandeur, locked in time with the next cramp. I expected fear, but what wound through the pain was fury. At Ignazio, at Lady Savony—and at myself, for sitting on the floor waiting to die when I had work to do.

The anger gave me strength enough to stagger to my feet, clutching the wall for support. I was out of ideas and out of time, but damned if I'd stop trying.

The door banged open.

Ignazio and Lady Savony stormed in, accompanied by a handful of armed men.

With them, a smile like a pleased cat's narrowing her eyes, was Zaira.

"Where are they?" Savony demanded. She flicked her wrist at the hard-faced brutes with her. I reached for my empty dagger sheath, but I was in no condition to resist. Two of them twisted my arms behind me, and a third pressed a knife to my throat.

I laughed. Threatening me with death was meaningless now. "I have no idea."

Zaira shrugged. "I showed you which way they took the brats," she told Savony. "It's not my fault you weren't fast enough to catch up."

She didn't so much as glance at me. The ruffians weren't watching Zaira, or threatening her. She was no captive; she was with them of her own free will.

Ignazio whirled to face her. "Can you burn the entire area they're in?"

"If I'm sufficiently motivated." She cast a contemptuous glance at me. "But only if this bitch releases me first."

"Zaira..." I breathed. Another cramp struck before I could say more. I strained to fold over, but the painful grip on my arms held me up.

"*We* can release you easily enough." Savony nodded to the men holding me. They threw me down on the floor; my hip and shoulder slammed into the stone. Before I could even try to fight the surge of dizziness and nausea that overwhelmed me, one of them had a sword point tickling my side.

"Wait." Ignazio held up a hand, frowning. "She's dying of the poison anyway. It won't be long now."

"We don't have time," Lady Savony said. "If you can't stand the sight of your cousin's blood, close your eyes."

I wished I had Zaira's tongue for profanity, but another cramp robbed me of the breath to speak.

Zaira put her hands on her hips. "If she dies, I will too, unless I get a new Falconer within a few days. I don't see the profit in that."

"You want to know what's in it for you?" Ignazio asked.

"Damned right I do. I'm not helping you out of charity."

He smiled a tight, smug smile. "How about freedom?"

Zaira went still. "I'm listening."

Grace of Mercy. I'd hoped she was deceiving them, but that was the one thing she wanted above all else.

Ignazio knew it. He shrugged, relaxed and in control. "You're correct. If Amalia dies, the jess will give you a few days to get a new Falconer, then take your life if you don't. It's a simple precaution to ensure this exact situation does not arise: a rival power freeing a Falcon to work for them by killing the Falconer. But I can offer you an escape."

"Can you get this stupid jess off me?" Raw hunger colored Zaira's voice.

I lay quietly, my hand slowly creeping toward my flare locket.

I wasn't sure I could stand again, but I had to be ready to move. Somehow.

Ignazio shook his head. "Alas, no. But I can get you a new one." He reached inside his coat and pulled out a gleaming slip of gold: the stolen jess. "This will keep the old one from killing you."

Zaira snorted. "What good does a new chain do me?"

"I'll say the release word once, and let you go." He spread his hands, the jess dangling from them. "You know far too much for me to want to turn you over to the Empire, and I see no possible advantage and a great deal of risk in trying to keep my own secret fire warlock."

It made sense. By the interest kindling in Zaira's eyes, she believed him.

Ignazio saw it, too. A cynical smile tugged at his mouth. "In exchange for your cooperation tonight and your silence thereafter, I'll stay out of your life. Your power will be yours to loose or bind, so long as you keep my secrets. You'll be free."

"Free of the Falconers," I husked. "But not free of you, Ignazio."

Zaira glared down at me. "The Falconers never gave me a choice. Now I have one."

"Then make it," Lady Savony snapped. "We don't have time for indecision."

Zaira nodded curtly to Savony, but her eyes stayed fixed on mine. I couldn't read her expression.

"Do it. Release me."

Lady Savony jerked her chin at one of the guards. He raised his sword. I doubted I could roll out of the way, let alone fight back.

But Zaira's words were a double-edged dagger. The question was which hand held the hilt, and I knew the answer. I'd told the doge as much, ages ago.

No one controlled Zaira. She was her own master.

I held her eyes. "I trust you, Zaira," I whispered. "*Exsolvo.*"

Chapter Thirty-Two

Zaira laughed.

She reached exultantly toward the low ceiling. Blue flames shivered down her arms; balefire kindled in her eyes. The brutes recoiled, and Lady Savony flinched. I would have drawn back from her myself if I could have.

Ignazio reached out an uncertain hand, his face bathed in blue light. "Zaira...?"

Lady Savony's eyes narrowed.

"Finish the Falconer," she ordered the swordsman, who had paused with his blade poised above me.

He nodded and gathered his shoulders to strike.

Zaira extended her hand toward him as if blowing him a kiss. An arc of fire poured across the air between them, splashing across his chest and running fiery fingers up his neck into his hair. He screamed and fell writhing to the floor. The stench of burning flesh was terrible.

"Kill her!" Lady Savony cried. "Quick, before she burns us all!" And she leaped at Zaira with her dagger.

A wave of blue flame engulfed her before she could even get close enough for Zaira's magical corset stays to protect her. Lady Savony collapsed in an unmoving, burning heap; the balefire had gulped down her life like a starving wolf.

"That's for the children, you heartless monster." The cold, distant note in Zaira's voice sparked alarm in my mind.

One of the remaining scoundrels drew a flintlock and fired at her. With a flare and shimmer, the ball ricocheted and struck him in the leg. He dropped to one knee, howling.

The door flew open. I barely glimpsed Ignazio's embroidered sleeve flashing as he slammed the door shut again behind him. Anger flared in me like Zaira's fire. How dare he run away? But I was still too weak to rise and go after him.

Zaira had enough vengeance in her for both of us. Pale wicked flames flowed from her in waves, embracing the two remaining guards as they scrambled for the door. Their screams tore my ears until I had to cover them. Then the balefire consumed the door itself and poured out into the hallway like an incoming tide, chasing after Ignazio.

But it also spread out from Zaira's feet, licking along the floor toward me. And it chewed its hungry way out from the burning doorframe, spreading flickering blue tongues along the stony walls.

"Zaira." I levered myself up on my hands; the room wavered, and a cramp dropped me back to the floor. "Zaira," I gasped, "can you hear me?"

She made no response. Fire ran up and down her hair. She took a graceful, gliding step toward the door, like a sleepwalking ballet dancer, and then another.

Grace of Mercy. She'd lost herself to the balefire.

"Zaira! You have to stop!"

She made no sign of recognition. The blue flames swept closer to me across the stone floor.

"*Revincio*," I whispered.

The room plunged into near darkness as the fires winked out. Zaira swayed and collapsed with them.

Silence fell, broken by my weak cough as I choked on the

ashy air. It occurred to me I was breathing in the smoke from the four burned corpses scattered about the room, little gritty remnants of their lives. I gagged.

I wanted clean air and water, and to get out of this terrible place before I died. I wanted Marcello. I wanted my mother. Tears leaked from the corners of my eyes. I struggled to sit up, the room swaying around me.

Light bloomed on the stairs, and I heard the thunder of approaching boots. My heart strained toward the ruined doorway, hoping for a miracle.

But it was Ignazio, with two more henchmen. They paused uncertainly on entering the room. Then Ignazio saw Zaira's unconscious body and sighed with visible relief.

"Kill them both," he told his men.

But the one on his left crumpled, coughing, blood spattering on the floor in front of him.

The second drew a flintlock, too slowly. A slim, graceful figure withdrew her knife from his comrade's back and spun, in the same motion, to slash it across his throat.

Ignazio scurried back away from her, drawing his dagger. "You!" he cried.

Ciardha stepped over the bodies of his hirelings. Not a hair strayed out of place on her perfect head.

"La Contessa sends her regards to her dear cousin," she said.

Marcello burst into the room behind her, his flintlock aimed at Ignazio's chest. Ignazio threw down his dagger and fell to his knees, his hands raised as if in prayer.

"I surrender! Please, don't kill me! I surrender!"

"Then I will deliver you to the Council of Nine for judgment." Ciardha continued to advance on him, smooth and deadly as a tigress. "La Contessa will decide your fate."

Ignazio went white as a drowned man's ghost. He knew what my mother did to people who imperiled her daughter.

This must be a hallucination. But I could think of no more wonderful and comforting delusion to light my way to death than Marcello running to my side, calling my name, crushing me to his chest.

I closed my eyes. "I know you're not real, but kiss me anyway," I murmured.

The shadows deepened behind my eyelids as he bent his face over mine, and his breath tickled my face. But I slid away into blackness before our lips touched.

Ciardha called my name. No doubt my mother required my presence at breakfast, but all I wanted was to keep sleeping. The down-stuffed pillow cradled my head with perfect softness, and my body ached with weariness. Warm light filtered through my shut eyelids, which meant the sun had cleared the town houses on the far side of the Imperial Canal. I wished I'd thought to draw my bed-curtains the night before. Why had I been up so late, anyway? I couldn't remember.

"Lady Amalia. You must wake up. It's time for your morning elixir."

So that was why my mother had sent Ciardha to wake me. Treating me like a child again, as if I couldn't take care of myself.

But there was something wrong. Something about my elixir.

I blinked my eyes open. A strange bedroom slid into focus: pale blue instead of warm gold, no clutter of books and artifice projects, different bed. Ciardha sat at my bedside, posture perfect as always, holding a drinking glass. My world tilted, rotated, and fit into a new position, like a puzzle piece I'd been trying to insert the wrong way. I wasn't at home. I was still in Ardence. And it was morning.

"I'm not dead?" I asked incredulously.

"Of course not, Lady. La Contessa made it quite clear you must return alive."

Memory tightened its claws. I tried to sit up, but failed. "The children! Is everyone all right? Are we at war?"

"The situation is under control, for the moment, though there is work still to be done. Please take your elixir, Lady." Ciardha's tone left no room for argument as she proffered the glass.

It seemed impossible she could truly have my elixir, but the scent of anise teased my nose. I raised my head, and she slipped another pillow behind my back to support me while I drank. The familiar taste had never been so welcome.

"Ciardha, I've always thought you were good at everything, but this is a miracle."

"Not at all, Lady." Ciardha took the empty glass from me. "La Contessa heard some intelligence reports from Ardence several days ago that concerned her. She sent me to see if you needed any assistance gathering sensitive information. I brought along an additional bottle of your elixir as a precaution, per La Contessa's request."

"'Gathering sensitive . . .' Are you a spy, Ciardha?"

"I am blessed with a varied skill set, Lady."

A knock came at the door. Ciardha rose to answer it. I noticed she slipped a dagger into her hand before doing so.

"Ah, Lieutenant Verdi." Ciardha glanced a question at me.

I was still wearing my grimy shirt and breeches from the night before, but I wanted to see Marcello more than I didn't want him to see me. "Please, let him in."

She stepped aside, and Marcello entered the room. Stubble shadowed his face; his eyes were bloodshot, and his black curls uncombed. If he'd slept, it hadn't done much to refresh him.

Good. I was a terrible mess myself. If he'd bathed and shaven, I might have died of embarrassment. But if we both still shared the wear and grime of our harrowing night, I needn't feel shame.

"Amalia! You're awake!" He crossed the room to my bedside and took up my hand, pressing it to his cheek. I trailed my fingers across his stubble, fascinated by the roughness.

Ciardha cleared her throat. Marcello dropped my hand.

"I seem to be well enough," I agreed. I felt like a crab a seagull had dropped on a rock a few times to break its shell, but that was still an encouraging improvement. "Are the children safe?"

He nodded. "They're with their parents. Your friend Domenic returned them home."

I sank into my pillow. "Thank the Graces."

"It was at Viscount Bergandon's town house that I caught up to Lieutenant Verdi," Ciardha said. "When I arrived in Ardence and the Serene Envoy's staff explained you were being hunted as the duke's murderer, I guessed you might have gone to your old school friend. If I hadn't caught Lieutenant Verdi there, he would have run back to you without my assistance or the elixir, and I fear I would have had a disappointing report for La Contessa."

Marcello ducked his head. "I owe you my thanks, Lady Ciardha."

"Please, Lieutenant, I am but a humble retainer."

I repressed an unladylike snort. "What's the situation in the Ardentine court?"

Marcello grimaced. "Chaos. I don't know the details. Lady Terringer is still sick—"

"Poisoned," Ciardha murmured.

"So no one is representing the Serene Empire." Marcello rubbed a hand through his hair. "I gather there's a lot of shouting and confusion."

Ciardha bowed politely. "If I may add some details, Lady?"

My mouth twitched. Marcello didn't know Ciardha well enough to realize he'd been delivered a stinging criticism of his ability to deliver a briefing. "Please."

"Today is the doge's deadline, and I have verified with La

Contessa over the courier lamps that he has declined to move it. While the jess has been recovered, Ardence still must return to abiding by the Serene Accords by sundown, or he will order the city's destruction."

"Graces preserve us." I struggled again to sit up, and this time I succeeded. "Is there a new duke? Do they even *have* someone who could make that decision?"

Ciardha shook her head, her dark eyes grave. "No, Lady. Duke Astor Bergandon had no direct heir, and the succession is unclear. The Ardentine court is split by internal conflict. Domenic Bergandon leads the side calling for reconciliation with Raverra. His brother, Gabril, is urging an opposing faction to repudiate Raverra, relying on Vaskandar for protection from consequences; he is backed by several Lords of the Council, most notably Lord Ulmric. Much of the court still blames you for Duke Astor's death. Gabril and his allies also lay the fault for the death of Lady Savony, as well as the kidnapping of the children, at the feet of the Falcons."

"Well, that's partly true," I said. "Zaira did kill Savony. But she was a traitor to Ardence and the Empire."

Ciardha nodded. "Indeed, Lady. But the nobles of the Ardentine Council of Lords have only your word for that. All they know is that Lady Savony, whom everyone trusted, claimed to see you murder the duke; and then she was slain by your Falcon's balefire within hours."

I twisted the blankets. "I have to admit that looks terrible."

"Lady Terringer's staff are doing the best they can, Lady, but without her authority or direction they are running up against a wall of hostility in the Ardentine court. The situation is delicate, to say the least."

"Hells. There's no leadership on either side." I put my face in my hands, thinking. "Grace of Wisdom help us, this is a mess."

Marcello shook his head. "Everyone with the authority or

connections to represent Raverra and nudge Ardence into line is dead, incapacitated, or more than a day's ride away. And the Ardentines are too divided to pull it together on their own. We have to beg the doge for more time. There's no other way."

"Begging does not win you favors from Niro da Morante." I took a breath. "But you're wrong."

"Oh?" Marcello raised his brows.

"I can speak for the Serene Empire."

Worry clouded his face. "I was counting you as incapacitated."

I turned to Ciardha, ignoring him. "Get me meetings with Domenic, Lady Terringer's staff, and any influential lords of Ardence whose children were among those abducted. Also, why not, Gabril Bergandon."

Ciardha's eyes shone. "Of course, Lady. Where?"

"Here. In the Envoy's Palace. The Blue Room, where Ignazio used to conduct such business."

Ciardha bowed. "At once, Lady. And I will send La Contessa a message over the courier lamps that you are handling the situation."

My eyes stung, surprising me. "That's high praise."

"Not at all, Lady. It's merely an observation." She pierced Marcello with her dark stare. "Lieutenant Verdi, while I am making arrangements, can I trust you with Lady Amalia's life and her honor?"

"On my own life and honor, you can."

"Then I will return shortly." She bowed and left, with one last warning glance at both of us.

"Will she murder me if I hold your hand?" Marcello whispered once she was gone.

"Let's find out." I slid my hand into his. Its wonderful, solid warmth anchored me in a world that still felt fragile around me, as if it could crumble into pain and horror at any moment.

"The life is back in your face," Marcello breathed.

"I'm sorry for making you worry."

He looked at me strangely. The moment lengthened.

"What?" I asked, nervous.

"I realized something. When I almost lost you." His voice went low and rough.

"Oh?"

"I don't want to go back to acting as if I don't care for you, Amalia. I'm not sure I can."

A knot like a hot stone formed in my throat. "Grace of Love forgive me. I shouldn't have kissed you."

"No." He squeezed my hand. "I'm glad you did. Thank the Graces you finally did."

I shook my head. "It's easy to say that now, but when you're freezing in some drafty fortress in the Witchwall Mountains, you may feel differently." I pressed the heel of my free hand into an eye that threatened to become too damp. "Or even if my mother gives us some license because I was dying—even if she doesn't send you away—it doesn't change the basic truth, Marcello. I don't get to choose whom I court. Not based on my own personal preference, anyway."

"But we've come through so much together." Marcello's eyes brightened suspiciously. *Grace of Mercy, don't cry.* "Surely your mother—"

"It's not my mother's decision." I reached out and laid trembling fingers on his lips, to stop any words that might break my resolve. Their soft warmth sent a tingling up my arm more profound than Ruven's magic. "It's mine. I am a daughter of the Serene City, Marcello. I can't be selfish in this." The hurt in his eyes made my throat ache. I couldn't stop myself from whispering, "No matter how much I want to."

His lips moved against my fingers. "Are you saying we can never—"

"Never is a long time." I forced a smile, but something broke through like sunlight inside me, and suddenly it wasn't forced after all. "We're both alive. That's a good place to start. And as you say, we've overcome a lot together. Perhaps you'll turn out to be a secret prince of lost Celantis. Or perhaps my mother will disinherit me."

He returned a faint echo of my smile. "I've learned not to doubt your capabilities, my lady. I have faith you can find a less dramatic solution."

Footsteps approached, more forceful than Ciardha's noiseless tread. The door burst open. Marcello leveled his flintlock at the intruder.

"Oh, put your pistol back in your trousers," Zaira said, smirking. "If I wanted her dead, she'd be dead."

Marcello settled back into his chair with a sigh of relief.

"Thank you," I said. "For saving my life."

"Don't let it go to your head." Zaira's smile faded, and she dropped into a chair by my bed. "Too bad about Ignazio."

Something twisted in my gut. After all he'd done, he was still family. "Is he dead?"

"Not yet, that I know of. No, I meant too bad he turned out to be a conniving ass."

"That's hardly your fault."

"He's being held at the garrison for now," Marcello said. "They're going to bring him back to Raverra for trial by the Council of Nine."

I wondered if that would be hard for my mother. Or if she'd seen the flaws that drove him to betray Raverra sooner than anyone, and had removed him from his position as envoy to give him a chance to avoid the pitfalls of his own character.

"He was right," I said quietly. "It was too late for him long ago."

Marcello squeezed my shoulder.

"How about Ardence?" Zaira sprawled in her chair as if she didn't care, but the tautness of her voice betrayed her. "Is it too late for the city, too? I'm going to need a big dinner if you want me to have the energy to set everything on fire tonight."

"That appears, unfortunately, to be up to me." I gritted my teeth. "So if you two might be so kind as to help me out of bed, I should take a bath. It's going to be a long day."

I started with Domenic, because I knew he would forgive me if I made mistakes.

Ciardha helped me arrange myself in a chair in the opulent yet intimate Blue Room such that I would be able to rest without looking insultingly at ease to my guests. Still, all I wanted to do was sleep, and I had a pounding headache from the aftereffects of the poison. Ignazio probably could have mixed me something to help with the pain.

I tried not to think about how he had no motivation to mix me anything helpful ever again. Except perhaps to keep my mother from ordering his death.

Domenic arrived with the distracted air of a man who has been pulled away from struggling to put out a fire. But he listened as I told him everything I knew about Lady Savony and Ignazio's conspiracy, grimacing or exclaiming at points. At the end, he jumped up and started pacing, despite his obvious exhaustion.

"Damn them to the Hell of Corruption. They were using our pain and anger, all that time. This never had anything to do with justice. They were laughing at us."

"We need the Council of Lords and the Ardentine court to see the truth." I rubbed my temple, attempting to smooth out my headache. "So long as some of them still believe Savony's lies, making peace between Ardence and Raverra will prove difficult."

Domenic shook his head. "Lady Savony. I would never have guessed she, of all people, would betray Ardence."

"In her own mind," I said, "I don't think she did."

Domenic's brows climbed his forehead. "I don't see how it's

not a betrayal to murder your duke and push your city to the brink of a war that would destroy it utterly."

"But she never intended to let that war actually happen. And in her eyes, Duke Astor was the true threat to Ardence. He and the other decadent nobles of the court." She might even have been right that he would have plunged the city into ruin, but I wasn't going to say that to his cousin. "If he'd had a promising heir, she might simply have done away with him. But without a strong Ardentine leader to replace him, she had to create a crisis so extreme the Empire would have to step in and appoint an imperial governor. And Ignazio, the natural choice, was more than willing to assume that role."

"Hells. I know I didn't have much respect for the city's leadership either, but that's going too far." Domenic fell silent, lost in thought.

I wished I could give him time to come to terms with what had happened to his city, but I had only hours left before he would cease to have a city at all.

"Domenic." I caught his eyes. Trouble weighed down his normally lively expression. "Tell me. Do you believe Ardence's future lies with the Serene Empire?"

"I do." Domenic sighed. "How I feel about the Empire doesn't matter. It's here, and we're in it. The days when Ardence and Raverra were both independent city-states are long gone." He settled back into his chair. "It's why I never liked Gabril's talk of rebellion. It doesn't make sense. We can reform the Empire, and make it better. Sometimes we need to stand up to it. But we're a part of it, for good or ill. That's the truth we have to work with."

Good enough. "I have to ask you to do something, Domenic."

He swept his arm in a courtly flourish. "Ask, and it is yours."

"You won't like it."

He lifted a brow. "Hmm. Well then, ask, and I'll think about it."

"I need you to become the new duke of Ardence."

The stunned expression on his face was inordinately satisfying. After a long moment, he swallowed. "There are others with a claim on the ducal throne who want it more than I do."

"I know. I'm sorry." I grimaced. "I'll make it up to you. You can even have my Muscati."

His eyes lit up. "Truly?"

"Well, when I'm done with it."

Domenic leaned back in his chair, taking a long breath. "I'm not sure a Muscati is enough. I'm a scholar, Amalia. A traveler, a joker, and a dabbler. Not a duke. And you *know* how I despise politics."

"I know." I poured a full goblet of wine from the bottle Ciardha had left with me. "Believe me, I know. But a duke who hates politics may be what Ardence needs right now. I'm counting on you to make this sacrifice, for the sake of peace."

"That's a low blow." He took the goblet, and drained it by a third with a few long swallows.

"Yes." I smiled sadly. "I learned from my mother."

"If I do this," he said, "you realize I won't jump whenever Raverra snaps its fingers. If I think the Empire is doing its people harm, I'm going to speak up. And I won't be silent about the injustice of forcing children into the Falcons."

I nodded. "I know that, too."

"I can't imagine the doge will like that."

"Keep it civil and abide by the Serene Accords, and he'll manage somehow." I lifted my glass to him. "And as for me, I wouldn't have it any other way."

The parents of the abducted heirs proved a more complex series of conversations, full of changing emotions and painful subjects, but one simple fact remained: their children knew who had saved them. With each of them in turn, once we worked past the prickly fence of anger and denial, we made it through into the sunny pasture of gratitude. They were mine, forever, for bringing their sons and daughters back alive. Each promised me their support, some with greater reluctance than others.

Gabril was a more difficult matter. This was the interview I'd been dreading the most. I'd thought about asking Domenic for help with his brother, but decided in the end he was best left out of that discussion.

Gabril settled into his chair with great suspicion, and refused the wine I offered him.

"I'll take nothing from Raverra." He crossed his arms, glaring at me over them. "I thought you were a friend to Ardence. I trusted you, because of your family connections. But you murdered my cousin the duke, and Lady Savony besides. I'll hear what you have to say, but do not mistake this visit for a friendly one."

Well. That made this easier. I'd rather face an honest enemy than have an unpleasant conversation with someone who thought me a friend.

"Gabril Bergandon, it's thanks to Raverra the children your Shadow Gentry claimed to want to protect are now safely back with their families. It was Lady Savony who orchestrated their abduction and murdered the late duke. Why still hold this bitter grudge against the Serene Empire?"

Gabril huffed. "I'll believe Colanthe Savony killed the duke when his ghost tells me so. My brother may swallow your lies, but I'm not so gullible. If you're here to try to cajole me into being a good little imperial bootlicker, you're wasting your time."

I sighed. "Gabril. Let me tell you my problem."

He crossed his arms and regarded me in wary silence.

"Domenic is a good friend. I don't want to hurt him." I poured myself a glass of wine. "That means keeping you from being executed for treason if I can. But you're making it dreadfully difficult."

Gabril swallowed. "Executed for treason?"

"Consider how it looks to the doge." I held up my wineglass, examining it as if the vintage were Gabril's soul. "You're known to be close with Prince Ruven, who fled Ardence after stealing rare books and plotting to use devastating magic against the Empire."

"Ruven wouldn't do that," Gabril protested.

"Forgive me, Gabril, but you are a terrible judge of character." I sipped my wine. "To make matters far worse, the Shadow Gentry have been implicated, thanks to Lady Savony's efforts, both in abducting the Ardentine children and in the unprovoked attack on a Falconer and the theft of the jess."

Alarm grew on Gabril's face. "We didn't do any of that!"

"I know." I eased back in my chair, trying not to show my exhaustion. "But it will be much harder for me to convince the doge of your innocence if you're still acting like Ignazio and Savony's accomplice, repeating every lie they told you. Right now, on the surface, it looks very much like you conspired with them and Vaskandar to sow chaos and war in Ardence. If I were you, I would be careful—*very* careful—not to give the Council of Nine further reason to believe you're plotting against the serenity of the Empire."

Gabril's shoulders sagged, and his eyes went glassy. He reached, at last, for the wine.

I smiled. "Think on it, Gabril Bergandon, and I will see you this evening."

As the shadows lengthened toward a sunset that could prove Ardence's last, the air held an autumn chill. I was glad Ciardha didn't object to my request for a jacket and breeches, and instead helped me select a Raverran royal-blue coat with rich enough embroidery and fabric to impress the Ardentine court, but a severe enough cut to remind them I meant business. I was too drained and achy to spend the rest of the day fighting shivers in a low-cut gown.

When I set out for the River Palace, I didn't go alone. Zaira came with me, since the law required it. Marcello, as lieutenant, came to see to the safety of his Falcon and Falconer. And Ciardha fell in behind us without a word. Whatever she expected she might have to do in the palace, I was sure it would be executed with elegant precision, which both comforted and unnerved me.

Palace guards met us at the door, the Bergandon crest glittering on their doublets. Two of them escorted us, more closely than I suspected Marcello and Ciardha would have preferred, through the baroque splendor of the Hall of Beauty to the Hall of Majesty, where the nobles of the Council of Lords waited for us.

Perhaps forty men and women in jewels and brocade gathered in a space of charged, dim echoes, around a vast, shining oak table. They had the rumpled, restless look of people who had been there a long time. A thronelike chair waited vacant at the head of the table. Domenic stood at the foot, leaning on the table with his fists as if he'd been shouting someone down a moment ago. Gabril sat a few chairs away from him, arms crossed, glaring down at his lap.

As we entered, every eye in the room turned to us. Some of the nobles gave me nods of recognition; others drew back in apparent fear or disgust. A few lips curled in anger.

"Lady Amalia Cornaro," Domenic greeted me. "Please, sit. You must be exhausted." His gaze strayed to Zaira at my side before he even finished welcoming me; I had trouble suppressing a smile.

Before I could return his greeting, the scraping of a chair on the marble floor jarred the quiet of the room. Lord Ulmric, the bearded gentleman who'd accosted Zaira at Ignazio's party, rose to his feet. "If Astor Bergandon's murderer sits at this table, I will not."

A murmur ran around the table. A few more nobles rose as well.

"Then you can sit back down." I let my voice ring out calm and clear. After everything that had happened in the past couple of days, I wasn't afraid of a roomful of old people. "Lady Savony took the life of the late duke. I saw it with my own eyes."

"Colanthe Savony was the duke's right hand," a portly woman objected. "She loved Ardence more than her own life. Why should we believe some Raverran girl over the honorable lady who helped govern Ardence for so many years?"

I hadn't expected to get accused of murder quite so soon, but perhaps I should have. I supposed it was only the chaos within the Council of Lords that had prevented me from being arrested the moment I passed through the River Palace gates.

Thank the Grace of Wisdom I didn't have to return fire from an empty quiver. I nodded to a mustached lord sitting at the table, who in turn nodded to a servant behind him, who left the room.

"I understand why you don't want to trust me," I said. "Ardence has had its trust violated more than once in these difficult days. But perhaps you will believe me if I'm vouched for by someone all too familiar with Lady Savony's treachery." I looked toward the door.

Footsteps approached the Hall of Majesty, a light patter providing a counterpoint to the sedate and measured tread of an adult. A gangly, bespectacled woman entered the chamber, holding the hand of a little girl.

I almost didn't recognize her, cleaned up and wearing a yellow silk dress. But then her eyes met mine, and I did.

The girl from the drain. Jaslyn.

She must have recognized me too, because she broke out into a smile as if a shaft of sunlight pierced the painted clouds on the ceiling fresco and shone straight down in a holy beam to strike her face.

"It's you!" she cried. She dropped her mother's hand and ran to me, wrapping her skinny arms tight around my waist.

I hugged her back, my eyes stinging. "I'm so glad you're safe."

"You know this woman, Jaslyn?" the portly woman asked, surprised.

"Yes, Auntie!" Jaslyn turned excitedly to her. "This is the lady who saved us."

Most of the standing nobles sank into their seats, stunned. But Lord Ulmric's glare remained unabated. "So you set them free. You're still a liar. Colanthe Savony would never betray Ardence."

"No. She wouldn't." I gripped an empty chair in front of me for support as I stared around the table. "But for Ardence, she would betray her duke. For Ardence, she would betray you, and your children. It was the city itself she wanted to save, even at the expense of its individual people."

Agitated whispers filled the room, like the rustle of wings. They still weren't convinced, yet.

The mustached lord, Jaslyn's father, called her over to him and put a gentle hand on her shoulder. "Jaslyn." His voice was soft, but it carried. "Tell them about the woman who held you prisoner."

"She wore a gray mask," Jaslyn said.

Gabril winced.

"Do you remember anything else about her?" Jaslyn's father asked.

Jaslyn scrunched her eyes shut. "She was very thin, with long, bony arms." That ruled me out. Some of the lords exchanged glances. "She wore her hair up—it was dark, with gray in it." Jaslyn gestured vaguely around her head.

"That's good, Jaslyn," her father praised her.

Jaslyn's eyes popped open. "Oh! One more thing. She had little golden spectacles on a chain around her neck."

Murmurs ran around the table like spreading balefire.

Domenic slapped his palm on the table. "You all know who

that describes as well as I do. Colanthe Savony. We've been betrayed, ladies and gentlemen."

This time, no one contradicted him. A grim silence fell on the room. Gabril put his face in his hands.

"Lady Amalia is innocent." Domenic threw the statement on the table like a drawn knife. "Duke Astor Bergandon and his murderer are both dead. We stand with a blank page before us, Lords and ladies of Ardence, and the Serene Empire watches us write. We must choose our words carefully."

"The Serene Empire can go—" Lord Ulmric began. But Gabril, who sat next to him, grabbed his arm. He leaned up out of his chair, whispered into Ulmric's ear, and then slumped back down, not meeting anyone's eyes.

Lord Ulmric swallowed. He looked at Gabril, and licked his lips. "Can, ah, go too far. Yes. The Empire can go overly far to make a point sometimes. That's all." He sat back down, face red with anger or humiliation.

The bespectacled lord cleared his throat, putting his arm around Jaslyn's shoulders. "I owe the Lady Amalia my daughter's life. It grieves me that one of our own betrayed us, but I must accept it is true."

A rumble of assent ran around the room, and some of the tension eased out of the air. Jaslyn's mother ushered her out; she waved to her father, her aunt, and then to me. My throat tightened as I waved back.

"Now, please, Lady Amalia, take a seat." Domenic gestured me to an empty chair.

"My thanks. But the place I must take for this meeting is that of the Serene Envoy." I crossed to stand behind the seat to the left of the empty ducal throne, giving them a moment to absorb what I'd said. "I am filling in for Lady Terringer while she recovers."

More murmurs and a few grumbles were heard round the

table. I ignored them and eased into my chair at last, taking the weight off my trembling knees. No one voiced an objection, or at least nothing louder than a mumble. Zaira flopped into another chair beside me, without asking permission; Marcello stood behind me, and Ciardha kept to the shadows with the clerks.

There. Ardence had welcomed the Serene Envoy back into its inner councils. Or close enough to save it from burning tonight.

The silence held. Everyone stared at me. I realized belatedly that by sitting in this chair, at the center of power, I'd accidentally taken command of the room.

Right, then. I folded my hands on the table before me. "The first matter I suggest you decide," I said, "is the succession. An empty throne breeds dissent. The Serene Empire is eager to welcome your new duchess or duke."

Voices broke over each other immediately, like clashing waves. I leaned back in my chair to rest and let them have at it.

It hadn't been hard to convince the parents of the once-missing heirs to back Domenic in the succession. After all, he'd returned their children to them; his name was gold. With a united bloc backing him, and his general popularity, Domenic himself didn't have to do much. Within a few hours, the Council of Lords had agreed his was the best claim to the succession, despite his father's abdication.

Domenic moved, with some trepidation, to occupy the empty throne at my side. The glance he shot me was half *Help me* and half *I'll get you for this*.

I gave him my best encouraging smile and mouthed, *Muscati*. He sighed, nodded, and visibly steeled himself for the trials ahead of him.

I continued to sit quietly for a while as they discussed matters of transferring power, and coronations and protocol. Slowly, the pull of power in the whole room shifted until all eyes fixed on Domenic, and all phrases sought his approval. I could see the traces of alarm stretching his eyes, and new furrows already forming on his brow. Zaira, meanwhile, had gotten so bored she'd put her head in her arms on the table and, by the Graces, appeared to be genuinely napping.

I couldn't take it any longer. I kicked Domenic's ankle.

He jumped, caught my deliberately mild gaze, and cleared his throat. "We have some important matters that need clearing up. Ones vital for the peace of Ardence and the Serene Empire."

I strove to appear calm and attentive, and not at all as if sweat were beading on my temples. The day was nearly over. Everything depended on Domenic pushing this through so that we could send the doge good news over the courier lamps before sunset.

"My late cousin, Duke Astor Bergandon, of beloved memory, was rightfully concerned about the state of the economy in our great city of Ardence. He took steps to attempt to help alleviate the strain we feel from the changes in trade on the River Arden." Domenic sipped his wine, wetting his mouth under the weight of stares upon him. I could tell by the stiffness in his voice that he'd practiced this speech. "It is my intent also to devote great attention and energy to this problem. But to succeed and last, any solution must come from Ardence itself: from the intelligence, creativity, and spirit that have made our city great for centuries. Thus, we must turn away from any tactic that involves putting Ardence in the debt and therefore the influence of a foreign power"—he leveled his gaze at Gabril—"or that attempts to place the blame for our difficulties at the foot of the Empire of which we are a part."

Gabril sighed and gave a reluctant nod. "My brother speaks the truth. Prince Ruven offered us the friendship of Vaskandar, but then fled our city as a thief rather than standing by us in our hour of need. And Raverra has..." He swallowed, as if the words stuck in his throat. "Has helped us uncover treachery and regain our lost heirs."

There were mixed frowns and smiles around the table. Some lords whispered to each other. Domenic turned to me. "Lady Amalia, in your capacity as acting Serene Envoy, I ask you to bear witness that as of this moment I order all taxes on Raverran merchants to cease, and all Raverran trade privileges to be restored. I also formally welcome the Serene Envoy back to my court and to this Council. Now that Lady Savony's treachery has been brought to light, there is more reason than ever to renew our friendship with Raverra. Ardence stands ready to abide by the Serene Accords once more."

No outcry followed his words. I felt as if the Graces had lifted a heavy pack from my back. "Thank you. On behalf of the Empire, and on a personal level, I am very glad to hear it."

Zaira lifted her head from her arms and winked at Domenic. He barely caught himself before winking back.

"I will, however, also request aid from the Empire in addressing the difficulties we face." Domenic's face brightened. "Perhaps the artificers among the Falcons could work on correcting the River Arden's course, for instance. I might have some ideas for a series of artifice locks to ensure sufficient depth in the problematic parts of the river."

I ached to find paper and pen to sketch out concepts with him. Then I thought of Istrella and smiled. "I know an artificer who might enjoy that challenge very much. I'll pass along the request to the Empire and the Falcons, and urge them to accommodate Ardence in this matter."

A noble demanded to know what would happen with debts owed to Prince Ruven, since his welcome in the Serene Empire was now dubious at best, and the conversation shifted to a discussion of whether the Empire might, under the circumstances, offer relief from those debts. No one challenged Domenic's decree that Ardence would again abide by the Serene Accords. It was done.

Zaira nudged me in the ribs. "Guess I don't get to set anything on fire today after all."

"It doesn't sound like it," I whispered back.

She yawned. "Remind me why I'm at this boring meeting again?"

I flicked my eyes toward Domenic. "To ogle a viscount. Or a duke, rather."

"Oh, right." She grinned, leaned back with her hands behind her head, and proceeded to do just that.

So it was that two days after the Council of Lords meeting, we prepared to leave. I was well enough to travel, and our work here was done. Lady Terringer had recovered from Ignazio's poison, and had resumed the duties of Serene Envoy. The River Palace swarmed with all the activity surrounding a ducal funeral and a ducal coronation, and we were not required for any of it.

Domenic, despite being in high demand as the new duke, still found time to come say good-bye. His farewell to me was brief but warm, with promises to visit each other and to correspond about the intriguing possibility of canal locks. But he didn't seem to know what to say to Zaira. He stared at her as if he had lost all language.

Of course. Zaira had to come back to Raverra with me. Domenic had to stay here and lead his city, a fate I happened to know did not make it easy to pursue one's romantic inclinations. An awkward pity strained my chest.

I made an excuse to leave them alone together in the sitting room. But once the door closed behind me, instead of continuing on to the washroom as I'd announced, I leaned against the wall and closed my eyes.

Poor Domenic. He'd never had a chance. Even if she were free to do as she pleased and live where she wished, and even if there were any chance the doge would allow her to court an Ardentine noble, I doubted Zaira would want to be a duke's wife—no matter how delightful it would be to watch her shake up the Ardentine court. Besides, Terika waited for her back at the Mews; they might not be a couple yet, but I'd seen the way they looked at each other.

What happened behind that door was none of my business. But I knew one thing for certain: if it was truly what they wanted, neither Domenic nor Zaira were the type of person who would let differences of rank or even the laws of the Empire stop them from courting.

I thought of Marcello's clean-lined face, wistful smile, and loyal heart. I owed him nothing less. But I was not Domenic or Zaira. I was the Cornaro heir.

I opened my eyes on the palace corridor again.

I wasn't alone.

A figure in a deeply hooded velvet cloak stood between me and the next luminary. With the light behind them, I couldn't see their face.

My hand fell to my dagger. "*Exsolvo*" tickled the back of my throat.

"Good reaction, but you may want to be more subtle next time." My mother pushed back her hood, freeing the glorious fall of her auburn hair. "There are those who might be offended if you drew on them."

"Mamma?" My thoughts snarled on the impossibility of her presence. "How...why are you here?"

"Did you truly think I would sit in Raverra and wait to see what happened when word came through the courier lamps you were accused of Duke Bergandon's murder?" She crossed the space between us and smoothed an errant lock of hair from my face. "I came at once. And the most incredible reports greeted me at each stop. Near dead of poison . . . Taking over as Serene Envoy . . . You have been busy, Amalia."

I grimaced. "It wasn't my idea. Well, except for the taking over as Serene Envoy part."

"But I arrived in Ardence to discover you didn't need my help." A strange note colored my mother's voice: pride. "You'd already uncovered the traitors, cleared your name, achieved peace, and installed a new duke."

Unironic praise, from my mother. I waited for the ground to open beneath my feet, for surely this was the end of days. "I really had very little to do with the new duke. And Zaira and Marcello helped with all the rest."

She arched a brow. "Never contradict someone giving you credit, Amalia. A modest demurral is fine, but don't argue points with them."

I laughed. "Very well. Yes, I am the hero of Ardence. And Raverra, too. No doubt there shall be a parade in my honor."

"That might perhaps be too much." Her eyes sparkled even in the dim corridor. "But you did well. I used to worry what kind of heir you would prove to be, when you closed yourself in your room with your books and ignored everything happening around you. I'm not worried anymore."

"Thank you, Mamma." The words thickened in my throat. "But . . . I'm not certain I can be your heir."

"Oh?" A dangerous edge entered her voice. "Why not?"

"I only have a few bottles of elixir left." The truth I'd told no one else blurted out of me. "I don't know what you plan to do with Uncle Ignazio, but he claimed he destroyed all copies of the formula. Even if you somehow forced him to make more elixir, it's hard to imagine he could be trusted not to slip poison into it, or something worse."

"Is that all?" La Contessa threw back her head and laughed.

"I'm serious. He said the formula only existed in his mind."

"Oh, child." She smiled fondly at me. "Do you really think I would allow my daughter's life to depend entirely on one man? What if he'd fallen into a canal and drowned? I had an alchemist among the Falcons analyze and reconstruct the elixir from a sample bottle years ago. I kept it secret to avoid offending Ignazio. You'll be fine."

I slumped against the wall in relief. "Thank the Graces."

"As for Ignazio, he is a difficult matter." Her face hardened. "At the very least, he'll spend the rest of his days in prison. Whether he must pay with his life is a matter I—and the rest of the Council—have yet to decide."

"Mamma..." Despite everything, my eyes stung. "I would feel terrible if he died because of me. Even though he would have let me die for his plans. He's still family."

"If he dies, it will not be because of you. He is a traitor to the Serene City." She squeezed my shoulder. "His fate is not for you to decide. Leave that to the Council of Nine."

"About that," I said. "I'm worried. Prince Ruven made it clear Vaskandar is preparing for war. We stopped him from using Orthys to steal mages, and from crossing the border with the tools and knowledge to trigger a volcano, but I'm sure Vaskandar has other schemes in play we don't know about yet."

"No doubt. I assure you, I intend to bend our intelligence efforts in that direction."

"I want to help." I felt like a child again, saying it. Surely that was how she saw me: dozing off on the second-floor balcony, listening to the soothing rise and fall of voices below deciding the fate of Eruvia. "I've met Prince Ruven; I know him, and I want to help stop him."

La Contessa's eyes glittered. "Very well."

The acceptance in those words fell on me like a heavy cloak.

They opened a door to a room where words could kill: where a nod or a gesture could launch ships, send armies marching, dispatch assassins, or set cities aflame.

But I'd already crossed that threshold. I'd taken that mantle on my shoulders. I was done hiding in my room.

"Another thing." I took a deep breath, summoning all my courage. This couldn't be worse than dying alone on a warehouse floor. "Mamma...I think you're wrong about Lieutenant Verdi."

She didn't look surprised; but then, Ciardha must have given her a full report. She regarded me with flat skepticism. "Verdi again. Do you have an answer for me now, as to what advantage he would bring to Raverra or House Cornaro, such that I should allow you to entertain him as a possible suitor?"

This was a delicate moment. I could tell her I didn't care about bringing advantage to Raverra, and that love was more important. I could remind her that she'd wanted me to stand strong on my own, and that in this matter I would stand against her to do so.

But sentiment was the last thing that would persuade La Contessa. And besides, I wasn't sure those things were true.

"You misunderstand. I'm not asking to court Marcello. I agree with you that at least for now, I need to remain unattached, for political purposes." My chest twinged painfully at the admission, but I pressed on. "But I do think you underestimate his value as a prospect. Marcello is a talented officer of good birth, rising quickly through the Falcons. With our backing, he stands a strong chance of replacing Colonel Vasante when she retires." I lifted an eyebrow, a move I'd learned from my mother. "You wanted me to get House Cornaro a Falcon. Well, Marcello could get House Cornaro *all* the Falcons."

"He would never use them for our family's ends."

"Nor should he." I shrugged. "But that would be between us

and the doge. The other families of the Assembly wouldn't need to know that."

My mother's smile widened. "You're learning, my child. You have a long way to go still. But you're finally learning."

My mother might have relented in her threats to send Marcello off to the Witchwall Mountains, but still, I thought it prudent not to share a silk-cushioned bench with him as our boat navigated the traffic on the Imperial Canal. I had plenty of time to decide what to do about Lieutenant Verdi; in the meantime, smiling into his eyes without worrying I was dooming him to a dark fate on the Vaskandran border was very nice indeed.

Zaira shared my bench, making pointed commentary about the various deficiencies in taste of other gentry in the boats around us. Istrella sat with her brother, humming to herself and examining a symphonic shell she'd bought at our stop in Palova. Our oarsman muttered curses at a courier in a sleek little boat who dared to cut us off, and a balding old man on a town house balcony above us burst into a spontaneous ballad in a rich, beautiful tenor.

It was good to be home. The first sight of the Serene City floating dreamlike on the lagoon had pierced my heart with mingled awe and relief. For all I'd done in Ardence, I had no doubt in that moment that I was a daughter of Raverra.

Soon we passed into the open lagoon and began the short crossing to Raptor's Isle. The Mews loomed above the water, gray and forbidding. My eyes went to Zaira, who stared at the approaching fortress, her expression unreadable.

When we disembarked, I stood for a moment on the dock with Marcello while Zaira greeted Scoundrel, who danced with unbearable ecstasy to see her. Even her and Istrella's laughter, and

Scoundrel's frenzy of wagging and leaping, couldn't distract me from the warmth that charged the small space of air between us.

"I'll come to the Mews every day," I told him.

His return smile was wistful. "Will you have time, with all the new duties you're taking on?"

"I'll make time. I'm a Cornaro. Time itself must bend to my demands."

He laughed, rewarding me with a flash of dimples. "Very well, then, Amalia. Zaira and I will expect you every day, and time be damned."

"Besides, I need to work with your sister on that canal-lock design. And help Venasha and Foss settle in with Aleki, once they catch up to us."

"Perhaps I won't see you as much as I hoped, then." But the dimples stayed, so I knew he wasn't serious. Mostly.

No one was looking, so I gave his hand a quick squeeze. He returned the pressure, his fingers lingering on mine.

Zaira seemed ready to take Scoundrel into the Mews, and I had unfinished business with her. "If you don't mind," I said to Marcello, "I'd like a private word with Zaira before I go."

"Of course." He gave me a look that would keep me warm for the rest of the day, then turned to take Istrella's arm.

I caught up with Zaira before she entered the Mews. "Can I talk with you?"

She raised her brows. "Last I checked, nobody had any luck stopping you from talking." But she whistled to Scoundrel and walked with me along the dock. Soon we stood alone at the end of it, save for the restless gulls.

"Thank you," I said quietly. "For everything you did in Ardence."

She shrugged. "I didn't do it for you."

"I'm sorry you had to leave Domenic behind."

"Him?" Zaira's mouth curled into a smile. "Oh, he's pretty.

I'll miss him, until we see him again. But there are so very many other fish in the sea."

I struggled to find the words I needed. "Still. It doesn't feel right, bringing you back here. You never wanted to be a Falcon."

She stared out across the secretive waters of the lagoon. "When you brought me here, I had no choice. But in Ardence, I did. And I made my choice then."

"What, the choice Ignazio offered you?" I shook my head. "To be his Falcon, instead of Raverra's? That hardly counts."

Zaira snorted. "Do you think I'm an idiot? No, not his stupid offer."

"What, then?"

"I could have burned everyone in that room, taken the jess, and paid some random brat too small to know what it meant to put it on me and say, '*Exsolvo*.' I could have walked out of there a free woman."

I stared, aghast. "That... would have worked."

"Yes. It would have." Zaira grinned. "I make good plans, don't I?"

Good was a relative term. "But you didn't do it."

"No. And now I *am* here by choice." Zaira turned to face the Mews, a challenge in her eyes. "It's far from perfect, but it's better than most of the available alternatives, I suppose. And the company isn't terrible. I don't promise I won't change my mind, but I'll stay here for a little while."

"I'm glad. And not just because the other way, I'd have had to die." I held out my hand. "You're a good partner, and an excellent friend. I have a lot to learn from you."

She took my hand with a grin. "About time you realized it."

We walked into the Mews side by side.

Look out for

THE DEFIANT HEIR

Book 2 in the Swords and Fire trilogy

by

Melissa Caruso

CHANGE THE MAGIC, CHANGE THE GAME.

Across the border, the Witch Lords of Vaskandar are preparing
for war. But before an invasion can begin, they must call a rare
gathering of all seventeen lords to decide a course of action.
Lady Amalia Cornaro knows that this Conclave might be
her only chance to stifle the growing flames of war, and she
is ready to make any sacrifice if it means saving Raverra
from destruction.

Amalia and Zaira must go behind enemy lines, using every
ounce of wit and cunning they have, to sway Vaskandar from
war. Or else it will all come down to swords and fire.

Acknowledgments

I'd like to thank my wonderful editor, Lindsey Hall, for feedback that's always straight on the mark, and for giving my Falcon wings. I am deeply grateful to the whole Orbit team for all their hard work on this book, and to Emily Byron, my UK editor, for bringing it across the pond. Huge thanks to my amazing agent, Naomi Davis, for being my champion and co-conspirator, and for helping my dreams come true.

Thanks to my dad for buying me my first copy of *Writer's Market* in fourth grade, and for suffering through that terrible novel I wrote in middle school. And to my mom, a force to be reckoned with, for never leaving any doubt in my mind that women are powerful leaders. Celestial oceans of gratitude to my husband, Jesse King, for his unflagging support, and for the random geeky conversation on a long car drive that spawned the idea for this book. And thanks to my fabulous daughters, Maya and Kyra, for their patience, love, and understanding while I wrote it.

A big shout-out to my awesome beta readers: Silvia Park, Lauren Austrian-Parke, Constantine Haghighi, John Mangio, Beth Sanford, Paul Saldarriaga, Nicole Evans, J. P. Orminati, and Amberleigh Orminati. And extra special thanks to Deva Fagan and Natsuko Toyofuku, for sticking with me through draft after draft and book after book. Your wisdom, insight, and enthusiasm are worth more than Cornaro gold.

And finally, thank *you* for reading this book. It's not a story until someone reads it; you have made it complete.

extras

orbit

www.orbitbooks.net

about the author

Melissa Caruso graduated with honors in creative writing from Brown University and holds an MFA in Fiction from University of Massachusetts—Amherst.

Find out more about Melissa Caruso and other Orbit authors by registering online for the free monthly newsletter at www.orbitbooks.net.

author interview

When did you first start writing?

I "wrote" my first book when I was about four years old. I drew the pictures and dictated the words to my big brother. It was basically a field guide to different dragons, with descriptive text like "Gargor eats people!" (I still have it.) I haven't stopped writing since.

Who are some of your biggest influences?

There are so many fantasy authors I really admire who shaped my writing during my formative years. I particularly always envied the snappy dialogue and brilliant plotting of Steven Brust, and yearned to write something with a heroine as wonderful as Aerin from Robin McKinley's *The Hero and the Crown*. I am also a huge Hiromu Arakawa fangirl, and learned a ton from her amazing manga *Fullmetal Alchemist*. It's so good on so many levels—especially the amazing character relationships, fantastic world building, and stunning pacing in a medium where that's a particular challenge.

Where did the idea for *The Tethered Mage* come from?

I was on a long car drive with my husband, who's a video game designer, so we have all these marvelous, geeky, creative conversations together. We were talking about fantasy world building, and he said something about how if random people actually were born with powerful magic, there was no realistic way they wouldn't wind up being the ones in power. I was like, "Yeah, unless the government identified them as children and controlled their power somehow." And then I got the idea for the Falconer system, and started wondering what the relationship between a Falcon/Falconer pair might be like, and the story was off and running.

What, if any, research did you have to do in preparation for writing this book?

In early drafts, *The Tethered Mage* took place in a (very) alternate Venice. So I did a bunch of research on the Venetian Republic, and also some on the late 1600s, when it was loosely set. The world wound up diverging from history pretty thoroughly, and then became an original setting instead, but there are some remnants. For instance, Amalia's last name is in honor of Elena Cornaro Piscopia, the first woman to receive a doctorate degree from a university. Even after I moved the story to an original universe, I still looked up certain things when I wanted to get a period flavor, or would do an image search for the type of landscape, fashion, or architecture I wanted to describe, for inspiration. I got so, so hungry researching historical and regional Italian food.

Fire magic is such a cool ability. What made you chose this specific power as your hero's foremost strength/weapon?

I wanted unleashing Zaira's magic to always be kind of an "Oh shit" moment—both devastatingly effective and also really unsafe for anyone around her. Fire seemed like the perfect match for something that's instinctively alarming, yet fascinating and powerful, and can spread out of control easily.

The idea of freedom versus protection is a major theme in *The Tethered Mage*—what drew you to focus on this?

Once I came up with the idea for the Falcon/Falconer bond, it arose naturally from there. I wanted the individual characters and the world as a whole to be struggling with the issue of how to handle mages, and I didn't want there to be an easy answer that would solve all the potential problems. Freedom versus protection is a trade-off we face all the time in real life, in everything from parenting to legislation, so I think it's something we can all identify with.

Being a Strong Female Character sometimes seems to translate to being a gun-wielding, ass-kicking heroine, but *The Tethered Mage* has a wide range of female characters, all of whom are strong in their own unique ways. What were your inspirations for these characters?

I have so many strong women in my life. My mom is an unstoppable force, and I have amazing friends and family who are all different kinds of badass. But really, what it comes down to is that probably two-thirds of my characters just pop into my head as female. I used to feel kind of bad about it, like, "Oh no, I should make more of them boys, to be fair!" But then I looked around at how often you get these big teams of cool characters with just one or two token females, and I went, "You know what? Nah." When you have a lot of primary characters who are female in the same story, you naturally get more variety in the types of strengths they show.

***The Tethered Mage* has a phenomenal cast of characters. If you had to pick one, who would you say is your favorite? Which character was the most difficult to write?**

Oh, wow, it's really hard to pick a favorite. I adore both Zaira and Amalia, of course, but I might have to go with La Contessa for both my favorite and the most difficult. She's especially hard to write because she's supposed to be so smart and such a skilled political player; every line of her dialogue needs a point and an edge. For both her and Zaira, in very different ways, I had to go back in revisions and make sure nothing they said was bland—I wanted to give them their own special flavors of extra punch.

What's one thing about *The Tethered Mage*, either about the world or the characters, that you loved but couldn't fit into the story?

I keep trying to write scenes that take place in a courier lamp room, because I have this strong atmospheric sense of what they look like, and what it feels like to be in there with important messages flashing back and forth. But so far I haven't been able to keep any of those scenes, because no matter how cool the lamp chambers look in my mind, it's still basically just people sitting around texting each other, which is hard to make dynamic and exciting.

The Tethered Mage* is the first book of the Swords and Fire series. What's in store for us in future books?

It'll probably come as no surprise to anyone who's read *The Tethered Mage* that we haven't seen the last of Prince Ruven, and that Vaskandar will become more of a problem for the Serene Empire in general and Amalia and Zaira in particular. Amalia also has some hard choices in her future now that she's stepping up and taking on more responsibility as her mother's heir.

If you could spend an afternoon with one of your characters, who would it be and what would you do?

Probably Amalia, because then I could ask her to show me around Raverra, especially her favorite libraries and places to eat. I'd love to meet Zaira, too, but I suspect she'd think I was pretty boring!

Lastly, we have to ask: if you could have any superpower, what would it be?

I'd want to be able to shapechange into any animal, because that way I can get a whole bunch of powers for the price of one: flight, stealth, super senses, super climbing and jumping, you name it. Plus, I think it would be really fun to get to try out different shapes and see what they were like. If that's cheating and I have to pick only one animal to change into, well, it probably won't surprise anyone that I happen to think falcons are pretty cool.

if you enjoyed
THE TETHERED MAGE

look out for

THIEF'S MAGIC

Millennium's Rule: Book One

by

Trudi Canavan

SOMETIMES MAGIC LIES WITHIN . . .

*When the young student Tyen unearths an ancient book,
it opens the door to a realm of mystery and danger. For it
contains a clue to a disaster threatening the world.*

*Elsewhere, in a land ruled by priests, Rielle has been
taught that to use magic is to steal from the Angels.
Yet she has a talent for it, and desperate times may
force her to risk the Angels' wrath.*

CHAPTER 1

The corpse's shrivelled, unbending fingers surrendered the bundle reluctantly. Wrestling the object out of the dead man's grip seemed disrespectful so Tyen worked slowly, gently lifting a hand when a blackened fingernail snagged on the covering. He'd touched the ancient dead so often they didn't sicken or frighten him now. Their desiccated flesh had long ago stopped being a source of transferable sickness, and he did not believe in ghosts.

When the mysterious bundle came free Tyen straightened and smiled in triumph. He wasn't as ruthless at collecting ancient artefacts as his fellow students and his teacher, but bringing home nothing from these research trips would see him fail to graduate as a sorcerer-archaeologist. He willed his tiny magic-fuelled flame closer.

The object's covering, like the tomb's occupant, was dry and stiff having, by his estimate, lain undisturbed for six hundred years. Thick leather darkened with age, it had no markings - no adornment, no precious stones or metals. As he tried to open it the wrapping snapped apart and something inside began to slide out. His pulse quickened as he caught the object . . .

. . . and his heart sank a little. No treasure lay in his hands. Just a book. Not even a jewel-encrusted, gold-embellished book.

Not that a book didn't have potential historical value, but compared to the glittering treasures Professor Kilraker's other two students had unearthed for the Academy it was a disappointing find. After all the months of travel, research, digging and watching he had little to show for his own work. He had finally unearthed a tomb that hadn't already been ransacked by grave robbers and what did it contain? A plain stone coffin, an unadorned corpse and an old book.

Still, the old fossils at the Academy wouldn't regret sponsoring his journey if the book turned out to be significant. He examined it closely. Unlike the wrapping, the leather cover felt supple. The binding was in good condition. If he hadn't just broken apart the covering to get it out, he'd have guessed the book's age at no more than a hundred or so years. It had no title or text on the spine. Perhaps it had worn off. He opened it. No word marked the first page, so he turned it. The next was also blank and as he fanned through the rest of the pages he saw that they were as well.

He stared at it in disbelief. Why would anyone bury a blank book in a tomb, carefully wrapped and placed in the hands of the occupant? He looked at the corpse, but it offered no answer. Then something drew his eye back to the book, still open to one of the last pages. He looked closer.

A mark had appeared.

Next to it a dark patch formed, then dozens more. They spread and joined up.

Hello, they said. *My name is Vella.*

Tyen uttered a word his mother would have been shocked to hear if she had still been alive. Relief and wonder replaced disappointment. The book was magical. Though most sorcerous books used magic in minor and frivolous ways, they were so rare that the Academy would always take them for its collection. His trip hadn't been a waste.

So what did this book do? Why did text only appear when it was opened? Why did it have a name? More words formed on the page.

I've always had a name. I used to be a person. A living, breathing woman.

Tyen stared at the words. A chill ran down his spine, yet at the same time he felt a familiar thrill. Magic could sometimes be disturbing. It was often inexplicable. He liked that not everything about it was understood. It left room for new discoveries. Which was why he had chosen to study sorcery alongside history. In both fields there was an opportunity to make a name for himself.

He'd never heard of a person turning into a book before. *How is that possible?* he wondered.

I was made by a powerful sorcerer, replied the text. *He took my knowledge and flesh and transformed me.*

His skin tingled. The book had responded to the question he'd shaped in his mind. *Do you mean these pages are made of your flesh?* he asked.

Yes. My cover and pages are my skin. My binding is my hair, twisted together and sewn with needles fashioned from my bones and glue from tendons.

He shuddered. *And you're conscious?*

Yes.

You can hear my thoughts?

Yes, but only when you touch me. When not in contact with a living human, I am blind and deaf, trapped in the darkness with no sense of time passing. Not even sleeping. Not quite dead. The years of my life slipping past — wasted.

Tyen stared down at the book. The words remained, nearly filling a page now, dark against the creamy vellum. Which was her skin . . .

It was grotesque and yet . . . all vellum was made of skin. While these pages were human skin, they felt no different to that made of animals. They were soft and pleasant to touch.

The book was not repulsive in the way an ancient, desiccated corpse was.

And it was so much more interesting. Conversing with it was akin to talking with the dead. If the book was as old as the tomb it knew about the time before it was laid there. Tyen smiled. He may not have found gold and jewels to help pay his way on this expedition, but the book could make up for that with historical information.

More text formed.

Contrary to appearances, I am not an "it".

Perhaps it was the effect of the light on the page, but the new words seemed a little larger and darker than the previous text. Tyen felt his face warm a little.

I'm sorry, Vella. It was bad mannered of me. I assure you, I meant no offence. It is not every day that a man addresses a talking book, and I am not entirely sure of the protocol.

She was a woman, he reminded himself. He ought to follow the etiquette he'd been raised to follow. Though talking to women could be fiendishly tricky, even when following all the rules about manners. It would be rude to begin their association by interrogating her about the past. Rules of conversation decreed he should ask after her wellbeing.

So . . . is it nice being a book?

When I am being held and read by someone nice, it is, she replied.

And when you are not, it is not? I can see that might be a disadvantage in your state, though one you must have anticipated before you became a book.

I would have, if I'd had foreknowledge of my fate.

So you did not choose to become a book. Why did your maker do that to you? Was it a punishment?

No, though perhaps it was natural justice for being too ambitious and vain. I sought his attention, and received more of it than I intended.

Why did you seek his attention?

He was famous. I wanted to impress him. I thought my friends would be envious.

And for that he turned you into a book. What manner of man could be so cruel?

He was the most powerful sorcerer of his time, Roporien the Clever.

Tyen caught his breath and a chill ran down his back. *Roporien! But he died over a thousand years ago!*

Indeed.

Then you are . . .

At least as old as that. Though in my time it wasn't polite to comment on a woman's age.

He smiled. *It still isn't — and I don't think it ever will be. I apologise again.*

You are a polite young man. I will enjoy being owned by you.

You want me to own *you?* Tyen suddenly felt uncomfortable. He realised he now thought of the book as a person, and owning a person was slavery — an immoral and uncivilised practice that had been illegal for over a hundred years.

Better that than spend my existence in oblivion. Books don't last for ever, not even magical ones. Keep me. Make use of me. I can give you a wealth of knowledge. All I ask is that you hold me as often as possible so that I can spend my lifespan awake and aware.

I don't know . . . The man who created you did many terrible things — as you experienced yourself. I don't want to follow in his shadow. Then something occurred to him that made his skin creep. *Forgive me for being blunt about it, but his book, or any of his tools, could be designed for evil purposes. Are you one such tool?*

I was not designed so, but that does not mean I could not be used so. A tool is only as evil as the hand that uses it.

The familiarity of the saying was startling and unexpectedly reassuring. It was one that Professor Weldan liked. The old historian had always been suspicious of magical things.

How do I know you're not lying about not being evil?
I cannot lie.
Really? But what if you're lying about not being able to lie?
You'll have to work that one out for yourself.

Tyen frowned as he considered how he might devise a test for her, then realised something was buzzing right beside his ear. He shied away from the sensation, then breathed a sigh of relief as he saw it was Beetle, his little mechanical creation. More than a toy, yet not quite what he'd describe as a pet, it had proven to be a useful companion on the expedition.

The palm-sized insectoid swooped down to land on his shoulder, folded its iridescent blue wings, then whistled three times. Which was a warning that . . .

"Tyen!"

. . . Miko, his friend and fellow archaeology student was approaching.

The voice echoed in the short passage leading from the outside world to the tomb. Tyen muttered a curse. He glanced down at the page. *Sorry, Vella. Have to go.* Footsteps neared the door of the tomb. With no time to slip her into his bag, he stuffed her down his shirt, where she settled against the waistband of his trousers. She was warm – which was a bit disturbing now that he knew she was a conscious thing created from human flesh – but he didn't have time to dwell on it. He turned to the door in time to see Miko stumble into view.

"Didn't think to bring a lamp?" he asked.

"No time," the other student gasped. "Kilraker sent me to get you. The others have gone back to the camp to pack up. We're leaving Mailand."

"Now?"

"Yes. *Now*," Miko replied.

Tyen looked back at the small tomb. Though Professor Kilraker liked to refer to these foreign trips as treasure hunts, his peers expected the students to bring back evidence that the journeys were also educational. Copying the faint decorations on the tomb walls would have given them something to mark. He thought wistfully of the new instant etchers that some of the richer professors and self-funded adventurers used to record their work. They were far beyond his meagre allowance. Even if they weren't, Kilraker wouldn't take them on expeditions because they were heavy and fragile.

Picking up his satchel, Tyen opened the flap. "Beetle. Inside." The insectoid scuttled down his arm into the bag. Tyen slung the strap over his head and shoulder and sent his flame into the passage.

"We have to hurry," Miko said, leading the way. "The locals heard about where you're digging. Must've been one of the boys Kilraker hired to deliver food who told them. A bunch are coming up the valley and they're sounding those battle horns they carry."

"They didn't want us digging here? Nobody told me that!"

"Kilraker said not to. He said you were bound to find something impressive, after all the research you did."

He reached the hole where Tyen had broken through into the passage and squeezed out. Tyen followed, letting the flame die as he climbed out into the bright afternoon sunlight. Dry heat enveloped him. Miko scrambled up the sides of the ditch. Following, Tyen looked back and surveyed his work. Nothing remained in the tomb that robbers would want, but he couldn't stand to leave it exposed to vermin and he felt guilty about unearthing a tomb the locals didn't wanted disturbed. Reaching out with his mind, he pulled magic to himself then moved the rocks and earth on either side back into the ditch.

"What are you *doing*?" Miko sounded exasperated.

"Filling it in."

"We don't have time!" Miko grabbed his arm and yanked

him around so that they both looked down into the valley. He pointed. "See?"

The valley sides were near-vertical cliffs, and where the faces had crumbled over time piles of rubble had built up against the sides to form steep slopes. Tyen and Miko were standing atop of one of these.

At the bottom of the valley a long line of people was moving, faces tilted to search the scree above. One arm rose, pointing at Tyen and Miko. The rest stopped, then fists were raised.

A shiver went through Tyen, part fear, part guilt. Though the people inhabiting the remote valleys of Mailand were unrelated to the ancient race that had buried its dead in the tombs, they felt that such places of death should not be disturbed lest ghosts be awakened. They'd made this clear when Kilraker had arrived, and to previous archaeologists, but their protests had never been more than verbal and they'd indicated that some areas were less important than others. They must really be upset, if Kilraker had cut the expedition short.

Tyen opened his mouth to ask, when the ground beside him exploded. They both threw up their arms to shield their faces from the dust and stones.

"Can you protect us?" Miko asked.

"Yes. Give me a moment . . ." Tyen gathered more magic. This time he stilled the air around them. Most of what a sorcerer did was either moving or stilling. Heating and cooling was another form of moving or stilling, only more intense and focused. As the dust settled beyond his shield he saw the locals had gathered together behind a brightly dressed woman who served as priestess and sorcerer to the locals. He took a step towards them.

"Are you mad?" Miko asked.

"What else can we do? We're trapped up here. We should just go talk to them. Explain that I didn't—"

The ground exploded again, this time much closer.

"They don't seem in the mood for talking."

"They won't hurt two sons of the Leratian Empire," Tyen reasoned. "Mailand gains a lot of profit from being one of the safer colonies."

Miko snorted. "Do you think the villagers care? They don't get any of the profit."

"Well . . . the Governors will punish them."

"They don't look too worried about that right now." Miko turned to stare up at the face of the cliff behind them. "I'm not waiting to see if they're bluffing." He set off along the edge of the slope where it met the cliff.

Tyen followed, keeping as close as possible to Miko so that he didn't have to stretch his shield far to cover them both. Stealing glances at the people below, he saw that they were hurrying up the slope, but the loose scree was slowing them down. The sorceress walked along the bottom, following them. He hoped this meant that, after using magic, she needed to move from the area she had depleted to access more. That would mean her reach wasn't as good as his.

She stopped and the air rippled before her, a pulse that rushed towards him. Realising that Miko had drawn ahead, Tyen drew more magic and spread the shield out to protect him.

The scree exploded a short distance below their feet. Tyen ignored the stones and dust bounding off his shield and hurried to catch up with Miko. His friend reached a crack in the cliff face. Setting his feet in the rough sides of the narrow opening and grasping the edges, he began to climb. Tyen tilted his head back. Though the crack continued a long way up the cliff face it didn't reach the top. Instead, at a point about three times his height, it widened to form a narrow cave.

"This looks like a bad idea," he muttered. Even if they didn't slip and break a limb, or worse, once in the cave they'd be trapped

"It's our only option. They'll catch us if we head downhill," Miko said in a tight voice, without taking his attention from climbing. "Don't look up. Don't look down either. Just climb."

Though the crack was almost vertical, the edges were pitted and uneven, providing plenty of hand- and footholds. Swallowing hard, Tyen swung his satchel around to his back so he wouldn't crush Beetle between himself and the wall. He set his fingers and toes in the rough surface and hoisted himself upward.

At first it was easier than he'd expected, but soon his fingers, arms and legs were tiring and hurting from the strain. *I should have exercised more before coming here. I should have joined a sports club.* Then he shook his head. *No, there's no exercise I could have done that would have boosted* these *muscles except climbing cliff walls, and I've not heard of any clubs that consider* that *a recreational activity.*

The shield behind him shuddered at a sudden impact. He fed more magic to it, trying not to picture himself squashed like a bug on the cliff wall. Was Miko right about the locals? Would they dare to kill him? Or was the priestess simply gambling that he was a good enough sorcerer to ward off her attacks?

"Nearly there," Miko called.

Ignoring the fire in his fingers and calves, Tyen glanced up and saw Miko disappear into the cave. *Not far now*, he told himself. He forced his aching limbs to push and pull, carrying him upward towards the dark shadow of safety. Glancing up again and again, he saw he was a body's length away, then close enough that an outstretched arm would reach it. A vibration went through the stone beneath his hand and chips flew off the wall nearby. He found another foothold, pushed up, grabbed a handhold, pulled, felt the cool shadow of the cave on his face . . .

. . . then hands grabbed his armpits and hauled him up.

Miko didn't stop pulling until Tyen's legs were inside the cave. It was so narrow that Tyen's shoulders scraped along the walls. Looking downward, he saw that there was no floor to the fissure. The walls on either side simply drew closer together to form a crack that continued beneath him. Miko was bracing his boots on the walls on either side.

That "floor" was not level either. It sloped downward as the cave deepened, so Tyen's head was now lower than his legs. He felt the book slide up the inside of his shirt and tried to grab it, but Miko's arms got in the way. The book dropped down into the crack. He cursed and quickly created a flame. The book had come to rest far beyond his reach even if his arms had been skinny enough to fit into the gap.

Miko let go and gingerly turned around to examine the cave. Ignoring him, Tyen pushed himself up into a crouch. He drew his bag around to the front and opened it. "Beetle," he hissed. The little machine stirred, then scurried out and up onto his arm. Tyen pointed at the crack. "Fetch book."

Beetle's wings buzzed an affirmative, then its body whirred as it scurried down Tyen's arm and into the crack. It had to spread its legs wide to fit in the narrow space where the book had lodged. Tyen breathed a sigh of relief as its tiny pincers seized the spine. As it emerged Tyen grabbed Vella and Beetle together and slipped them both inside his satchel.

"Hurry up! The professor's here!"

Tyen stood up. Miko looked upwards and pressed a finger to his lips. A faint, rhythmic sound echoed in the space.

"In the aircart?" Tyen shook his head. "I hope he knows the priestess is throwing rocks at us or it's going to be a very long journey home."

"I'm sure he's prepared for a fight." Miko turned away and continued along the crack. "I think we can climb up here. Come over and bring your light."

Standing up, Tyen made his way over. Past Miko the crack narrowed again, but rubble had filled the space, providing an uneven, steep, natural staircase. Above them was a slash of blue sky. Miko started to climb, but the rubble began to dislodge under his weight.

"So close," he said, looking up. "Can you lift me up there?"

"Maybe . . ." Tyen concentrated on the magical atmosphere. Nobody had used magic in the cave for a long time. It was as smoothly dispersed and still as a pool of water on a windless day. And it was plentiful. He'd still not grown used to how much stronger and *available* magic was outside towns and cities. Unlike in the metropolis, where magic was constantly surging towards a more important use, here power pooled and lapped around him like a gentle fog. He'd only encountered Soot, the residue of magic that lingered everywhere in the city, in small, quickly dissipating smudges. "Looks possible," Tyen said. "Ready?"

Miko nodded.

Tyen drew a deep breath. He gathered magic and used it to still the air before Miko in a small, flat square.

"Step forward," he instructed.

Miko obeyed. Strengthening the square to hold the young man's weight, Tyen moved it slowly upwards. Throwing his arms out to keep his balance, Miko laughed nervously.

"Let me check there's nobody waiting up there before you lift me out," he called down to Tyen. After peering out of the opening, he grinned. "All clear."

As Miko stepped off the square a shout came from the cave entrance. Tyen twisted around to see one of the locals climbing inside. He drew magic to push the man out again, then hesitated. The drop outside could kill him. Instead he created another shield inside the entrance.

Looking around, he sensed the scarring of the magical atmosphere where it had been depleted, but more magic was already beginning to flow in to replace it. He took a little more to form another square then, hoping the locals would do nothing to spoil his concentration, stepped onto it and moved it upwards.

He'd never liked lifting himself, or anyone else, like this. If he lost focus or ran out of magic he'd never have time to recreate the square. Though it was possible to move a person rather than still the air below them, a lack of concentration or moving parts of them at different rates could cause injury or even death.

Reaching the top of the crack, Tyen emerged into sunlight. Past the edge of the cliff a large, lozenge-shaped hot-air-filled capsule hovered – the aircart. He stepped off the square onto the ground and hurried over to join Miko at the cliff edge.

The aircart was descending into the valley, the bulk of the capsule blocking the chassis hanging below it and its occupants from Tyen's view. Villagers were gathered at the base of the crack, some clinging to the cliff wall. The priestess was part way up the scree slope but her attention was now on the aircart.

"Professor!" he shouted, though he knew he was unlikely to be heard over the noise of the propellers. "Over here!"

The craft floated further from the cliff. Below, the priestess made a dramatic gesture, entirely for show since magic didn't require fancy physical movements. Tyen held his breath as a ripple of air rushed upward, then let it go as the force abruptly dispelled below the aircart with a dull thud that echoed through the valley.

The aircart began to rise. Soon Tyen could see below the capsule. The long, narrow chassis came into view, shaped rather like a canoe, with propeller arms extending to either side and a fan-like rudder at the rear. Professor Kilraker was in the driver's seat up front; his middle-aged servant, Drem, and the other student, Neel, stood clutching the rope railing and the struts that attached chassis to capsule. The trio would see him and Miko, if only they would turn around and look his way. He shouted and waved his arms, but they continued peering downward.

"Make a light or something," Miko said.

"They won't see it," Tyen said, but he took yet more magic and formed a new flame anyway, making it larger and brighter than the earlier ones in the hope it would be more visible in the bright sunlight. To his surprise, the professor looked over and saw them.

"Yes! Over here!" Miko shouted.

Kilraker turned the aircart to face the cliff edge, its propellers swivelling and buzzing. Bags and boxes had been strapped to either end of the chassis, suggesting there had not been time to pack their luggage in the hollow inside. At last the cart moved over the cliff top in a gust of familiar smells. Tyen breathed in the scent of resin-coated cloth, polished wood and pipe smoke and smiled. Miko grabbed the rope railing strung around the chassis, ducked under it and stepped on board.

"Sorry, boys," Kilraker said. "Expedition's over. No point sticking around when the locals get like this. Brace yourselves for some ear popping. We're going up."

As Tyen swung his satchel around to his back, ready to climb aboard, he thought of what lay inside. He didn't have any treasure to show off, but at least he had found something interesting. Ducking under the railing rope, he settled onto the narrow deck, legs dangling over the side. Miko sat down beside him. The aircart began to ascend rapidly, its nose slowly turning towards home.

CHAPTER 2

It was impossible to be gloomy when flying with a steady tail wind on a clear, beautiful night. The bright reds and oranges of the setting sun had ended the banter between Miko and Neel, and an appreciative silence had fallen. Leratia's capital and home of the Academy, Belton, could put on some grand sunsets, but they were always tainted by smoke and steam.

To Tyen's senses, the aircart appeared to have a bow wave. Unlike a boat in water, the ripple in the atmosphere was caused by the removal, not displacement, of something: magic. In its place the dark shadow of Soot remained, and trailed behind them like smoke. Soot was hard to describe to anyone who couldn't sense it. It was merely the absence of magic, but when fresh it had texture, as if a residue had been left in magic's place. It moved, too – shrinking as magic slowly flowed in to fill the void.

As Tyen drew in more magic to power the propellers and heat the air in the capsule he relished the opportunity to use magic without restraint. It felt good to use it, he reflected, but it wasn't a physical pleasure. *More like the buzz you feel when something you're making is all coming together exactly as you planned,* he thought. Like the satisfaction he'd felt when making Beetle, and the other little mechanical novelties he sold to help finance his education.

While it was not difficult driving the aircart, it did demand concentration. Tyen knew that his skill with sorcery had guaranteed him a place on the expedition, as it meant Professor Kilraker didn't have to do all the driving.

"Getting chilly," Drem said to nobody in particular. Kilraker's manservant had dug around in the luggage earlier, careful to avoid losing any of it overboard, and found their airmen's jackets, hoods, scarves and gloves. Tyen had been relieved to know his bag must be in the pile somewhere, not left behind in the rush to leave Mailand.

A hand touched his shoulder and he looked up to see the professor nod at him.

"Rest, Tyen. I'll take us from here to Palga."

Letting his pull on magic go, Tyen rose and, holding the tensioned rope railing for balance, stepped around Kilraker so the man could take the driver's seat. He paused, considering asking why Kilraker had let him dig where the Mailanders hadn't wanted them to, but said nothing. He knew the answer. Kilraker did not care about the Mailanders' feelings or traditions. The Academy expected him and his students to bring back treasures, and that was more important to him. In every other way, Tyen admired the man and wanted to be more like him, but he'd come to see on this journey that the professor had flaws. He supposed everyone had. He probably had a few as well. Miko was always telling him he was well behaved to the point of being boring. That didn't mean he, or Kilraker, weren't likeable. Or so he hoped.

Miko and Neel were sitting with their legs dangling over one side at the central, widest, point of the chassis, while Drem sat cross-legged on the opposite side for balance, surprisingly flexible for a man of his age. Settling on the same side as the servant, but a small distance away, Tyen took off his gloves, tucked them in his jacket pocket and drew the book out of his satchel. It was still warm. Perhaps he had imagined it earlier and now it only gave off the body heat it had gained from Tyen himself through the satchel pressed to his side. In the hours since then he'd almost convinced himself he'd imagined the conversation he'd had with it, though he hoped not.

He ought to hand her over to Kilraker now, but the man was busy and Tyen wanted to establish exactly what he'd found first.

"So, Tyen," Neel said. "Miko says you found a sarcophagus in that tomb. Was there any treasure in it?"

Tyen looked down at the book. "No treasure," he found himself saying.

"No jewellery? None of those baubles we found in the other caves?"

"Nothing like that. The occupant must have been poor when he died. The coffin lid wasn't even carved."

"Nobody buries poor men in stone coffins. Robbers must've got in there. That's gotta be annoying, after you wasted all that time working out where a tomb might be."

"Then they were very considerate robbers," Tyen retorted, letting a little of his annoyance enter his voice. "They put the lid back on the coffin."

Miko laughed. "More likely they had a sense of humour. Or feared the corpse would come after them if they didn't."

Tyen shook his head. "There were some interesting paintings on the walls. If we ever go back . . ."

"I don't know if anyone will be going back there for a while. The Mailanders tried to kill us."

Tyen shook his head. "The Academy will sort it out. Besides, if I'm only drawing the pictures on the walls, not taking anything away, the villagers might not object."

"Not take anything? Maybe when you're rich and can pay

for your own expeditions." From Neel's tone, he didn't expect rich was something Tyen would ever be.

It's all right for him. Dumb as a brick, but family so wealthy and important he'll pass no matter what his marks are or how little work he puts in. Still, Neel was genuinely interested in history and did study hard. He idolised the famous explorers and was determined that he'd be able to hold a conversation with one if the opportunity came.

Sighing, Tyen opened the book. It was too dark to see the page now, so he created a tiny flame and set it hovering above his hands. Making a flame involved moving a tiny bit of air so quickly it grew hot and began to burn the air around it. Refining it to such a small light took concentration but, like a repetitive dance step, once he got it going he could focus on something else. When he fanned through the pages he was disappointed to see that the text that had appeared before was gone. He shook his head and was about to close the book again when a line appeared, lengthening and curling across a page. He opened the book at the new text.

You lied about finding me.

He blinked, but the words remained.

You're not what they'd consider "treasure". Wait . . . how do you know that? I hadn't opened you yet.

I only need someone to touch me. When they do I can form a connection to their mind.

You can read my mind?

Yes. How else could I form words in your language?

Can you alter anything there?

No.

I hope you're not lying about being unable to lie.

I am not. I am also as open to you as you are to me. Whatever information you ask for, I must give. But, of course, you must first know that information exists, and that I contain it.

Tyen frowned. *I suppose there had to be a price to using you, as with all magical objects.*

This is how I gather knowledge quickly and truthfully.

I have the better side of the deal, then. You can hold a lot more knowledge than I do, though it will depend on what was known by the people who have held you. So what can you tell me?

You study history and magic. Obviously I can't tell you about the last six hundred years because I was in the tomb, but I existed for many centuries before then. I have been held by great sorcerers, historians, as well as philosophers, astronomers, scientists, healers and strategists.

Tyen felt his heartbeat quicken. How much easier would it be to learn and impress his tutors with a book like this at his disposal? No more searching the library and studying late into the night.

Well, not as much of it, anyway. Her knowledge was at least six hundred years old, and much had changed in that time. A great revolution in reason and scientific practice had occurred. She could be full of errors. After all, she had collected knowledge from people, and even famous, brilliant people made mistakes and had been proven wrong.

On the other hand, if the Academy was wrong about something he couldn't use her to convince them. For a start, they'd never accept one source, no matter how remarkable. They would not accept her as proof of anything until they'd established how accurate she was. And then they'd decide she had more important uses than allowing a student to satisfy his curiosity, or take short cuts with his education.

Your friends and teacher keep some discoveries for themselves. Why shouldn't you keep me?

Tyen looked over at the professor. Tall and lean, with short-cropped hair and moustache curled as was the current fashion Kilraker was admired by students and peers alike. His adventures had brought him academic respect and furnished him with many stories with which to charm and impress. Women admired him and men envied him. He was the perfect advertisement to attract students to the Academy.

Yet Tyen knew that Kilraker didn't quite live up to the legend. He was cynical about his profession and its benefits to the wider world, as if he had lost the curiosity and wonder that attracted him to archaeology in the first place. Now he only seemed to care about finding things he could sell or that would impress others.

I don't want to be like him, he told Vella. *And to keep you would mean I was depriving the Academy of a unique and possibly important discovery.*

You must do what you feel is right.

Tyen looked away from the page. The sky had darkened completely now. Stars freckled the sky, so much more brilliant and numerous away from a big city's glow and smog. Ahead and below the aircart lay lines and clusters of lights more earthly than celestial: the town of Palga. He estimated they'd arrive in an hour or so.

The book – Vella – had already connected with his mind twice. Did she already know everything about him? If so, anybody who held the book could find out anything about him. They had only to ask her. She had admitted that she must give whatever information she contained to whoever asked for it.

But what did he have to hide? Nothing important enough to make him wary of using her. Nothing that wasn't worth the risk of others finding out embarrassing things and teasing him about them. Nothing he wouldn't exchange for the knowledge gleaned from centuries of great men handling the book.

Like the "great sorcerers" she had mentioned. And Roporien himself. He looked back down at the page. He wouldn't reach the Academy for several days. Perhaps he would be forgiven for holding onto her until then. After all, Kilraker might not have time to examine her properly during the journey home. Tyen might as well learn as much from her as possible in the meantime.

Do you know everything that Roporien did?

Not everything. Roporien knew that for me to be an effective store of knowledge I must be able to access the minds of those who hold me, but he had secrets he wasn't willing to risk revealing. So he never touched me after my making. He had others ask questions of me, but he rarely needed to.

Because he already knew all that there was to know?

No. Since a stronger sorcerer can read the mind of a weaker one, and Roporien was stronger than all other sorcerers, he did not need me in order to spy on anyone's mind. Most of those he wanted information from did not attempt to withhold it. They gave it out of awe or fear.

Tyen's mind spun as he contemplated sorcerers with the ability to read minds. They must have been powerful indeed. *But why would Roporien create a book that he couldn't use?*

Ah, but he didn't have to touch me in order to use me. By having others touch me he could teach them and spread knowledge.

That is an unexpectedly noble act for a man like Roporien.

He did so for his own benefit. I was a tool for teaching his fighters the lessons of war, to show his servants how to provide the best in everything, and inspire the greatest makers and artists in all the worlds so that he could use the magic produced by their creating.

Magic produced by their creating? Wait. Are you saying . . . You're not saying . . .?

That their creativity generated magic? Yes, I am.

Tyen stared at the page in dismay. *That's superstitious nonsense.*

It is not.

It certainly is. It is a myth rejected by the greatest minds of this age.

How did they disprove it?

He felt a flash of irritation as he realised he did not know *I will have to find out. There will be records. Though . . . it could be simply that it has not been proven to be true, rather than disproved.*

So you would have to believe it, if someone proved it was true?

Of course. But I doubt anyone would succeed. Rejecting primitive beliefs and fears and embracing only what can be proven is what led us into a modern, enlightened time. Gathering and examining evidence, and applying reason led to many great discoveries and inventions that have improved the lot of men.

Like this aircart you travel in.

Yes! Aircarts and aircarriages. Railsleds and steamships. Machines that produce goods faster than ever before — like looms that make cloth quicker than twenty weavers working at once, and machines that can print copies of a book, all the same, by the thousands, in a few days.

Tyen smiled at the thought of all that had changed in the world since she had last "lived". What would she make of the progress men had made, especially in the last century? She would be impressed, he was certain. A feeling rather like pride swelled within him, and suddenly he had another reason to delay handing her over to Kilraker and the Academy.

She needed to know how the world had changed. She needed her store of knowledge updated. He would have to teach her before he handed her over. After all, if she still believed in superstitions then they might not just declare her an inaccurate source, but a dangerous one.